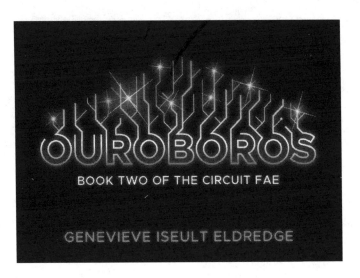

OUROBOROS

BOOK TWO OF THE CIRCUIT FAE

GENEVIEVE ISEULT ELDREDGE

Monster
House
Books

First Published by Monster House Books, LLC in 2018
Monster House Books, LLC
34 Chandler Place Newton, MA 02464
www.monsterhousebooks.com

ISBN eBook: 9781945723179
ISBN Print: 9781945723209

To my fair Fae princess

FOREWORD

Writing is a journey of growth and discovery—of your story and your characters. But it's also a journey of growth and discovery for yourself, the author. I learned a ton writing MORIBUND, and I learned a whole lot more reading all the reviews, good and bad. If you're one of those folks who posted a review, thank you! I could not continue to give you quality content without your comments, criticisms, love, and tireless support.

In implementing some of the criticism for MORIBUND, OUROBOROS grew longer and longer. The original uncut version was well over 125K.

Using what I learned writing MORIBUND, I carved 25K off the beastly draft, so what you hold in your hands right now is the streamlined version. I promise this is the longest *Circuit Fae* book, and I also promise that I've looked at every single word, mercilessly cutting repetitions and distractions to give you a solid, active story of two girls who are mortal enemies kicking butt, taking names, and falling in love against the odds.

The result is long, but for Syl and Rouen to arc in a satisfying way, for me to give tribute to their struggle, I had to make it hard. Few, if any, of us in the LGBTQ+ community have had it easy. I wanted Syl and Rouen's journey to reflect a true-to-life romantic journey.

Thank you for continuing to walk beside them—and me.
Best always,
~GIE

CHAPTER ONE
SYL

Light is always drawn
To darkness
So it is with the Fae
- Glamma's Grimm

Whoever said love is a battlefield never tried to date a dark Fae. Seriously, with all the nighttime battles Euphoria and I have fought this summer, chasing down and destroying black-magic Moribund all over the city...

It's been more like a war.

E and I haven't had one second to ourselves all summer.

But I swear, tonight's going to be different.

We're not just grabbing a couple of dogs and fries at City Dogs in between battles.

Nope. Tonight's a legit date night. No battles to fight. No responsibilities to worry about. And no Moribund trying to infest the city with its black-magic circuitry.

I hope.

With E's hand on my lower back, I step onto the rooftop restaurant, twenty stories above the streets of Richmond, and look out over a gorgeous orange and purple summer sunset, the city lights winking on one by one, like magic. "Oh…Rouen, it's perfect."

Rouen Rivoche, aka glam goth-rock star Euphoria, cracks the teeniest of smiles, and that makes everything worthwhile—all the fighting, all the chasing down rogue Moribund…

My strong, stoic Winter girl. Sometimes, she gets lost in that broody mind of hers, and I have to shine a little light on her.

It comes with the territory.

If the Faerie realm were heaven, the dark Fae'd be the rebel angels—all sinister swooping wings, vengeance, and power chords. Except the dark Fae have way less remorse and pretty much command everything Winter, right down to blizzards, lightning storms, and thundersnow.

They're your basic nightmare.

Only, Euphoria's my dream.

"You like it?" E's smile widens when she looks at me, and some of the darkness in her blue eyes vanishes, leaving a tiny ribbon of joy and light.

Yeah. I did that. Me. Syl Skye, sleeper-princess of the fair Fae.

"I love it!" Okay, full disclosure: I'm about to have a meltdown of happy because 1) it's about time we got a night to ourselves, and 2) I have something super important to ask her.

"Good." She gives me that *smexy* smirk that turns my insides to warm gooeyness.

It's okay to crush on your own girlfriend, right? Because yeah, totally guilty, even if I do have to admit, me and E are a bit…out of the ordinary.

Usually, just one dark Fae would spell death for a fair Fae, especially a sleeper-princess like yours truly.

But my girl is no ordinary dark Fae. She's the princess of the Winter Court just like I'm the princess of the Summer Court.

Winter, Summer…I know what you're thinking. We should be at each other's throats.

"Thank you." I go on tiptoes to kiss her lightly. I'm super-careful, all things considered. My power's been a little…out of control lately.

"You're most welcome, princess."

Okay, truthfully, it's been trying to kill her.

Ever since summer started, my white flame's been chomping at the bit to burn Euphoria down to her bones. The more I use my power, the worse it gets. Just another glaring example of that fair Fae/dark Fae been-at-war-for-a-million-years drama.

We're mortal enemies. So of course, we're dating.

When I break the rules, I go for broke.

"What a gorgeous view." Euphoria calls my attention back to the sunset and city lights, the James River a grey-green serpent glittering in the fading light, the muggy smell of summer on the warm breeze.

"Yeah," I say, but now I'm looking at her. She's the most gorgeous view ever. "Beautiful."

She catches me looking and blushes. Okay, can I just say that my girl is stunning, even when she blushes? Me, not so much. My curly red hair and ruddy Irish complexion pretty much guarantees that, when I blush, I turn into Rudolph the Red-Nosed Geek.

Like now.

My cheeks on fire, I look down at my Docs, but Euphoria puts a hand under my chin, tilts my face up.

"Don't hide," she says gently, meeting my gaze. Her eyes are that dark blue of a deep winter ocean, and suddenly, all the butterflies in my stomach are doing the cha-cha.

That's how the hostess finds us, starry-eyed and staring meaningfully at each other like two total dorks. "Right this way," she says, and we break off, giggling all breathless, and follow her to our table.

E pulls out my chair for me, and I sink into it. "I am so looking forward to some barbecue ribs. And more importantly…" I lean across the table to whisper, "No Moribund!"

Euphoria nods, some of the tension leaving her shoulders. "Definitely."

3

Thanks to the fallout from the Winter Formal last December—when my BFF-turned-psycho Fiann, along with Euphoria's "associate" Agravaine, tried to take over the city by infecting everyone with black-magic circuitry—we've been hunting down these super-dangerous caches of rogue Moribund that jerkface Agravaine hid all over the city.

Every single night, it's something. If it's not Moribund, it's Circuit fiends. It's enough to drive a girl batty.

So yeah, rooftop view, dinner, some quiet "us" time…

"I'm so ready for this." I blow out a sigh of relief and smooth down my cute minidress as the waitress brings us waters and menus. She takes our drink order—a cherry Coke for me and water for Euphoria.

Soda makes her all giddy. Go figure.

Speaking of giddy… I go over my plan in my head. Once we've eaten and had dessert—because, oh yeah, dessert is sooooo happening—I'm going to ask E what I've been wanting to all summer.

I touch the ring I've hidden beneath my neckline on a silver chain.

I can barely think of it without squeeing. To distract myself, I pop open the menu. "What are you getting?"

"Hmm…" E's super-serious as she looks over the options. She pushes a few strands of jet-black hair from her face, but they fall back anyway.

Her casual beauty makes my heart leap.

And yeah, I totally get why I should stay away from her. I may be new to Faedom, but it doesn't take a genius to understand that her Winter Court and my Summer Court hate each other.

And if either of our people wake up from their self-imposed sleepy-time in Faerie, missing out on date night'll be the least of our problems.

I finger the ring again. It was Glamma's way back when, and it's been in my family for years and years.

I want tonight to be perfect, the perfect moment when I give it to Euphoria.

"Syl?"

Crap. I'm spacing out. I snap out of it. "Sorry! I was just…
thinking."

"About the Ouroboros?"

Ugh…the Ouroboros is a total mood killer.

I smile gently at her. "Look…don't get me wrong. Destroying
evil-dark Circuit Fae magic is always on my Top Ten list of fave
things to do and all, but tonight is the last night of summer."

Tomorrow, I go back to school as a junior at Richmond Elite
High. Euphoria, too.

And I swear, if I have to spend tonight killing Moribund—

Ouroboros, I correct myself. *When they're a zillion times more
deadly and just one teeny circuit can evolve and destroy/devour an
entire city, they're called Ouroboros.*

Euphoria glances at me over her menu, and her shoulders sag.
"Sorry. I shouldn't mention it. We want to relax and have a good
time."

I can't help but giggle at her super-serious tone. My Winter girl
tackles having fun the same way she tackles fighting Ouroboros—
with all the grim graveness of a dark Fae. "It's okay." I reach across
the table and touch her hand.

Her bronze skin is soft and cool, and I want to tangle our fingers together, hold her hand, but…touching for more than a few
seconds at a time is a serious no-no. Already, I feel my white flame
firing from slow burn to bonfire.

"Is it okay?" she asks, arching an eyebrow at me.

With a final squeeze, I pull away reluctantly. "Yeah."

And it is. When you can kill your girlfriend with a simple touch
like I can, you appreciate the little things.

I mean, that's what date night's all about. Us finding our place in
this world, a place where we can just…be.

No Agravaine, no Fiann, no dark or fair Fae, no Moribund or
Ouroboros.

The waitress comes to take our orders. I know what I want, but
I also know that E hasn't really looked yet. "Could we have a few
more minutes?"

"Sure thing." The waitress smiles and heads off.

When I turn back to E, my vision goes a little blurry and I see the urgency rising off her with my Fae-sight—her aura cloaking her in a deep purple. Like all dark Fae, she's duty-bound and über-traditional. She's laser-focused on taking out the Moribund.

Ugh. Thanks, Fae-sight. I've had it ever since the train crash that started all this, and while it does show me the surface mood—the aura—of whoever I look at, sometimes it's really TMI.

"Look." I reach out and barely brush her fingers with mine. "We can put this night on hold." *Let's face it, Syl, saving the world from dark Circuit Fae magic is waaaaaay more important than date night.*

But Euphoria shakes her head, her dark hair haloing her beautiful face. "No way," she says emphatically. She shifts in her seat and fidgets a bit, and my inner worrywart sits up and takes notice.

Euphoria is serious and broody, but she's not one to fidget.

What's wrong? And why does she keep touching her right front pocket? "Are you okay, E?"

The nod she gives me is a little too eager, her smile strained. "I…I'll be right back." She shoves her chair back and heads into the restaurant toward the restrooms, leaving me staring after her.

What just happened?

Whatever it was, it's not looking good for date night.

CHAPTER TWO
ROUEN

Do I dare love you
Sweet Summer princess?
My darkness yearns
To take you, possess you
"Possess You," Euphoria

Breathe, Roue. Breathe. I finally can once the door whumps shut, the antiseptic stink of bathroom blotting out all other smells—the savory tang of cooking food, the humidity of summer, the gas-and-river-and-steel smells of the city…

And Syl.

I stagger to the sinks, my heart hammering like a kick-drum. Despite my cool appearance—flowy burgundy shirt, leather pants, smoky eyeliner and shadow, my black hair falling in loose waves to my shoulders—I'm so not. My senses are drowned in the scent of Syl, sweet vanilla and skin musk driving me wild.

I can't get enough of her, and at the same time, it's all too much.

Viciously, I twist the tap on. Water rushes out, and I put my hands under, needing to feel the cold, needing it to remind me that Winter flows through my veins, that I shouldn't be so...hot and bothered.

But can you blame me? I've been running around all summer, battling Ouroboros and Circuit fiends with Syl, who looks completely kissable and adorkably yummy when she fights.

We've fought some tough battles.

But I've been battling myself even harder.

Even now, my dark heart races, urging me to go back to her, to take her and possess her, body and soul.

I turn the water off, dry my hands, and press them to my cheeks. They're burning up, like the rest of me. Burning up to be close to Syl.

It's probably good that her power's been trying to kill me.

If her white flame didn't keep me away from her, there's no telling what I might do. After all, it's a dark Fae's nature to possess the things, and the people, we want.

It won't be like that with Syl. I swear it.

Reaching into my pocket, I take out the ring. A winter topaz in a wintersteel setting. A ring befitting a princess.

My princess.

Flooosh! One of the toilets flushes, and the stall door pops open. Silly me, didn't think to look.

My mind whirls. *Hells and Harrowing, I didn't say any of that out loud, did I?* Because that'd be awkward. I turn toward the mirror, letting my raven-dark hair hide my face like a curtain. Maybe I can just act chill until whoever it is leaves.

"Euphoria?"

Damn it. Please don't be a fan, please don't be a fan, please don't—

"Hi." I turn, and there's Lennon, dressed up and smiling at me. She looks different away from school—no cat-ear headphones or anime backpack—but she's wearing a cute black A-line dress and her stylish Pusheen Mary Jane's, her long straight black hair tied back with a simple ribbon.

"Hi, Lennon. What are you doing here?"

"Came with my folks." She moves to the sink. "You?"

"Here with Syl." A pang of guilt hooks me. We haven't hung out with Lennon even once this summer. She helped us a ton when Syl and I were undercover last year trying to figure out Agravaine and Fiann's master plan, and I know Syl misses her.

"Are you okay?" Lennon washes and dries her hands, looking at me in the mirror.

"I'm good." I put on my game face as Syl calls it, but I'm forgetting one small detail.

"Oh, wow, is that a ring?" Lennon forgets all pretense and leans into me, her hand hovering over mind where—yup, the ring is sitting there, making me look guilty as sin. "Are you..." Lennon's eyes meet mine in the mirror. "Are you asking Syl out? Like, for real?"

Sweat breaks down my spine. *Am I?* I'm not one hundred percent familiar with mortal customs. I just know I want to bind myself to Syl. Forever. "Y-yeah... Well, I want to."

I sigh inwardly. *What's your problem, Roue?*

Well, let's see: I can't touch her because of her power. And if I could touch her, my darkness might hurt her.

You know, ordinary couple stuff.

"I just don't know when," I finish, feeling like a complete fool.

But Lennon's got this goo-goo-eyed face on, like this is the most romantic thing she's ever heard. I don't get it. I'm completely messing this up. If this were a movie or TV show, I'd look at the camera, and some narrator would help me out.

But here, in the bathroom of the rooftop restaurant where I'm supposed to be on a date night with my girl? No such luck.

Lennon's waiting, a *Well?* look on her face.

I clench the ring and stuff it back into my pocket. "I just want the moment to be perfect."

"I totally get it!" Lennon lets out a girly little sigh-squeal, clasping her hands together. "This is so romantic."

If she only knew.

It might be romantic, but it's torture. I want so much to get close to Syl, but our powers are warning us away from each other.

If there's one thing I've trusted through all this, it's my powers.

"Yeah." I slump against the sinks, trying not to let "my broodiness" as Syl calls it, run away with me. I have a tendency to be gloomy-doomy. I want this to be a happy moment.

But…our powers, the Ouroboros, school tomorrow—there's so much in our way.

"Maybe I should wait."

Lennon nods excitedly, her dark brown eyes on me. "I understand. You want the moment to be perfect. I don't blame you. It's like a fairy tale, you and Syl."

"I'm really lucky to have her."

"Don't forget it." Lennon gives me a little warning look, which is funny because she's about as intimidating as Luna Lovegood. "Well, good luck. I've gotta get back to my folks. See ya!"

With a smile and a wave, she leaves.

I wave, and the door whumps shut again.

Okay, what am I waiting for? I splash some water on my face, dry off, and take a deep breath. I'm in it with Syl. No matter what happens. I want to be with her.

I'll give her the perfect moment she deserves.

Steeling myself, I push open the door and stride out of the ladies' room.

Syl's waiting at the table, halfway through her cherry Coke. She's waited for me to order. I can tell. When she sees me, she looks up, the concern and worry in those summer-storm-grey eyes hitting me like a punch to the gut.

I made her feel that way.

Well, I'm going to fix that. Right now. I stuff my hand in my pocket and feel the ring. *Do it now, Roue. Before you lose your nerve. Before something else happens.*

My hand edges to my pocket. "Syl, I—"

A stabbing pain lances my chest. I double over, my fangs gritted over a cry. In a flash, Syl's out of her chair and right there next to me.

"Rouen!" she cries, and I'm pretty sure I'm dying. Syl never calls me by my real name unless it's serious. I clutch at my heart, half expecting to see blood gushing from a wound, but no.

10

It's just the Ouroboros.

It does this every time one of them awakens and spawns somewhere in the city. Except, right now is literally the worst timing in the history of ever.

Everyone's looking, all the other people in the restaurant, Lennon and her parents, the staff, Syl…

Embarrassed, I get to my feet. My breath comes hard, sweat slicking my brow and not just from the hot summer night. "I'm okay." But I'm not.

I know what comes next.

A terrible pulse begins to beat inside me like a second heartbeat trying to strangle my own. The Ouroboros! Syl helps me into my chair and slides my water closer to me.

I grab it, take a sip. The coolness clears my mind a bit.

An Ouroboros is spawning somewhere in the city. If we don't hunt it down and destroy it, it will infect everything it touches—living and dead—with Moribund circuitry, turning it into black magic machinery hell-bent on killing everything in sight.

"We don't have much time."

Not to mention, a spawning Ouroboros leaves behind harrow-stitches—tiny snags and pulls in the Shroud between realms.

And that can't be good.

"Rouen…" Syl's face falls.

I try not to see the worry, the hurt in her eyes.

The pulsing in my chest grows stronger, pounding in my ears. I stand up through the pain, and look at her. My beautiful sleeper-princess.

Tonight was supposed to be the night. The night everything changed between us.

But no.

"I'm sorry, Syl. The Ouroboros…"

"Come on." My girl wastes no time. She throws down a ten for our drinks and takes my free hand. "We'll just go take care of this super-fast and be back in no time."

She smiles so brightly, my heart hurts.

She loves you, Rouen.

That thought exhilarates and terrifies me.

I am supposed to be her enemy, and I am leading her right into danger.

Again.

My hand, still stuffed in my pocket, lets go of the ring.

Will we ever get our perfect moment?

One thing's for sure: I'm going to make the Ouroboros pay for messing up this one.

CHAPTER THREE
SYL

Once spawned, the Ouroboros infects
Everything it touches
Living or dead—
People, cars, buildings, cities, the entire world…
- Glamma's Grimm

Never challenge a dark Fae to a race. You know why?

They cheat.

"Ready…" I call, standing atop the railing of the rooftop restaurant. I'm always stressed when we're hunting down Ouroboros, so Euphoria and I make a game of racing to wherever one pops up. It sounds silly, but it keeps my mind off the fact that the entire city's at stake.

No pressure or anything.

"Steady…"

Euphoria and I both have our don't-see-me Glamouries on, so we're practically invisible. I throw one last look over my shoulder. *Goodbye, barbecue ribs and chocolate cake.*

Goodbye, date night and "us" time.

I touch the chain around my neck. *Goodbye, giving Euphoria Glamma's ring.*

"Set…"

Whoosh! In a rush of wintry fairy wind, Euphoria leaps off the railing into the night.

"Hey!" I get my butt in gear and go after her, the little cheaterface.

At least she cheats for a good cause.

I chase E through the night, over the rooftops in Richmond's center, over banks and office buildings, over the newly built Dominion tower—thirty-three stories of metal and glass. And me? I leap it in a single bound.

It's a bird, it's a plane… It's Syl Skye, Awakened sleeper-princess! I'm pretty badass. Well, kind of. Sort of.

Euphoria's way ahead of me—all black leather, gothy-dark eye-liner, and bad-girl attitude. She's the true badass here, not me.

She flashes me that smirky-smirk and teases, "Are you even in this race?"

"Am I—Oh!" *That little…* But it's mock-indignation. Her flirty teasing just revs my heart up faster. "We'll see who's in the race."

I kick it into high gear.

In three strides, she crosses the next building and leaps—all grace and power and sexy dark Faeness—across the crazy-wide gap of Main Street. One hundred and fifty feet, she hurtles out into the night, her hair streaming like black flames. She lands on the other side, easy-peasy, tossing that teasing grin over her shoulder.

"Come on, princess!"

I screech to a clumsy stop at the edge of a hotel rooftop. Main Street is a million feet down, the cars like tiny ants meandering across a damp black ribbon.

Maybe it's a good thing there weren't any barbecue ribs, because my guts are doing more barrel rolls than an X-Wing trying to dodge the Death Star.

So far to fall. *Blurggg…*

Euphoria stands waaaaaaay on the other side atop the SunTrust skyscraper, blue eyes all intense and glowy. She glances at her wrist like she's reading an invisible watch. "I'm waiting."

"Yeah, yeah." *Darn dark Fae princess.*

Even if I couldn't make it, I'd totally jump for her.

You got it bad, Syl.

The irony's not lost on me. We're deadly enemies—a dark Fae princess born to royalty and a newly Awakened fair Fae sleeper-princess.

So of course we're dating. Our status is officially "It's complicated."

"Get ready!" I flash her a flirty smile and jog back from the ledge. My enhanced strength will only get me so far. I'll need to summon my own fairy wind to get across.

This is where it gets hairy.

Because ever since summer came—the summer solstice, to be exact—my power's been ramping up, getting stronger and stronger as the weather gets hotter and hotter. It's like I just leveled up like twenty times in D&D. Which would be awesome, except for two things:

One, there's no rulebook for being a sleeper-princess. I'm the last one.

And two, my power seriously wants to murderface my girlfriend.

It's okay, Syl. You can do this.

I pelt for the edge. My heartbeat pounds like crazy as I sail out into the darkness. The city lights flash by beneath me, the wind in my red curls probably turning it into more of a rat's nest, but hey. Date night went kablooey, and it's not like I need perfect hair or the perfect outfit to fight Ouroboros.

I mean, yeah, my cute Alice in Wonderland minidress, fishnets, oxblood Docs, just the right nude-tone lipgloss, my eye shadow a subtle, glimmery gold to bring out my grey eyes…

Ugh. It was perfect.

Quit being a Miss Whiny-Pants, Syl. E needs you. I get my head in the game. *All right, Ouroboros, it's on!*

But first, we have to find it.

The skyscraper's rooftop comes into view. At the height of my leap, I reach for my personal magic, my *gramarye*, tapping into the fair Fae magic in my blood, calling all things Summer to me.

In a *whoosh*, my fairy wind comes, all hot breezes and the stifling humidity of Summer wrapping me up, catapulting me across the gap.

My oxblood Docs slam down, roof-side. *Whew!* I stumble a little on the landing. *Misjudged a bit.* I look up at E, grinning. "How was that?"

And then my power surges, ripping out of me.

Crap! White flames burst from my hands, flaring out at Euphoria.

But my girl's ready for it. She dodges the first blast, ducking behind a rooftop HVAC, and then, I'm struggling, wrestling with my power. Only, wrestling my sunfire is like trying to hold with a burning white tiger by the tail.

"Syl?" E's voice is worried, her aura flashing from light blue concern all the way to red-orange fear.

Because yeah, at the Winter Formal, my very same sleeper-princess sunfire burned Agravaine to ashes. To be fair, dude was an evil Circuit Fae who spliced black-magic Moribund circuitry into innocent people to enslave them and feed on their life-forces. All to give the entire city of Richmond a dark Fae makeover...

Euphoria was on his side for a hot second.

And it's like my power remembers.

I pull back on the reins, hard, willing my gramarye to chill out. "Whoa!"

E's nothing like Agravaine. She teamed up with me to defeat him. "Almost..." I struggle with my sunfire flames as they twist and leap.

"Relax," Euphoria calls. "Breathe out."

"Okay!" *Deep breaths, deep breaths, deep...* "Got it!" The flames flare down, and I breathe a sigh of relief. "That was too close." Closer than ever before. *You're getting worse, Syl.*

Slowly, Euphoria comes out of hiding, sweeping her black hair from her face. I'm half-expecting her to be mad, but there's only worry and those electric-blue eyes of hers smoldering on mine.

Suddenly, all the butterflies in my stomach are Riverdancing.

"It's okay, princess. See?" She twirls, somehow looking ridiculous and badass all at once. "Not even singed."

"I'm so glad!" I move to hug her, but my mind flashes, *Warning! Warning! No touchy.* I back off, sudden tears stinging my eyes.

Not being able to touch her sucks worse than a million wrecked date nights.

"Hey…" Her voice is gentle as she brushes a few stray red curls from my face. "It'll be okay."

She barely touches me, and my power leaps up from inside, super-eager to burn her face off. "No!" I jerk away. My chest tightens, and it's hard to breathe. A tear escapes down my cheek. *Darn it!* I'm a raging ball of teenage hormones.

And I want so much more than just fighting Moribund and Ouroboros.

I want everything with her.

But with my power going all murder-death-kill, even my positivity's taken a hit.

"Syl…" Euphoria's gentle. She senses I'm upset about tonight—about all the nights this summer. "We have to go. The Ouroboros…"

"I know." A heavy sigh escapes me. *Stupid Agravaine.* This is all his fault—hiding Ouroboros throughout the whole city, setting them to spawn at random. Euphoria won't rest until they're all destroyed.

We have no idea how many there are, even.

"We're running out of time." Her irises weirdly bleed from deep blue to ghastly green, and she gasps in pain.

My heart jackrabbits, but I keep my cool. This is the new normal for us—Euphoria feeling the Ouroboros like a second heartbeat, where she used to feel the hearthstone.

Like feeling something rotting inside where healthy tissue should be.

Her eyes are creepy green, and she's gripping her heart so hard her leather jacket creaks.

I shouldn't get close, but I want to comfort her. "E?"

"This way!" *Whoosh!* In a rush of her chilly fairy wind, she's gone.

I make sure Glamma's ring is tucked away as we race down East Main and over the interstate at breakneck speed. I'm glad my mom's not here to see me dodging cars.

And just like that, my crappy track phone buzzes from my boot.

No choice. If I don't pick up, she'll come looking, and my mom? She walks softly and carries a really big gun.

I snag the phone out of my boot and hit Accept. "Hi, Mom!"

"Syl?" Her voice crackles down the line. "Where are you?"

Ugh. Of course she picks up the sounds of people, traffic, sirens—city noises. "At the restaurant." I wince. I hate to lie, but Mom barely tolerates Euphoria living with us, never mind Euphoria leading me to fight Ouroboros, Circuit fiends, and who knows what other horrors. "I'm coming back from the restroom. There's some accident on Main."

"You sound out of breath."

Seriously, the woman notices *everything*. "It's…uh…a big restaurant."

Silence.

She knows! I wait, my heart pounding as I race after Euphoria, trying super-hard not to breathe heavy into the phone.

Finally, "You ready for school tomorrow?"

"Oh, yeah. Sure." Tomorrow is the first day of my junior year at Richmond Elite High School, but right now it's the last thing on my mind.

"Okay. Just be home before eleven."

"You got it. Bye!"

I sigh as I jam the phone back into my boot. I'll explain everything to Mom later. Right now…

Hollywood Cemetery looms up out of the night, the silhouettes of mausoleums and statues sending chills shooting down my spine. Place is huge, and yeah, totally haunted.

"Holy… A graveyard?" I cock an eyebrow at E. "That's pretty darn cliché, even for Agravaine."

I mean, the guy did have a penchant for crappy 80s-style villain monologues. *"You'll rue the day"* and *"You can never defeat me."*

What a dope.

"Syl." Euphoria turns to me, all serious. "You don't have to come."

Every line of her is intense and gorgeous, and I see through her Glamoury to the real her—pointed ears and fangs, her skin dark and glowing with an inner light, sapphire-blue eyes ringed in gold piercing my soul, and full lips that I want so badly to kiss. Love washes over me, slamming into me like whoa.

"Rouen…I could never leave you."

It feels like an age ago when she came to kill me, but now she's my best friend, my girlfriend. I blush at that thought, and her lips curve in a soft smile.

"I could never leave you, either."

A breeze blows her scent wild about me—crisp autumn leaves, amber, and bourbon-vanilla. The scent of darkness. Alluring, intoxicating. I step closer to her, basking in her scent. Her heat. *Her.*

Instantly, my power flares up, and I shove my hands into my minidress pockets. "Right. Ouroboros. We should…yeahhhh…" Suddenly, I find the iron fence surrounding Hollywood Cemetery super-interesting.

Euphoria wouldn't go near cold-wrought iron unless it was one hundred percent necessary. "It's here," she says simply.

"All righty." I leap the fence. No sense in lollygagging, Glamma would say.

Hollywood Cemetery is dark and deserted at this time of night, all creepy silence and jagged, stretched shadows in the thin moonlight. Euphoria leaps the fence, wincing as she lands. As a *sluagh*, which is a kind of dark Fae pariah, she has trouble being on holy ground, and the wrought iron doesn't help any Fae. She'll be weakened here.

Me, on the other hand? It's been ages since a sleeper-princess Awakened, so no one has any idea the limits of what-all I can do.

Lucky me, iron doesn't seem to affect me.

She glances at me. "Ready?"

"Bring on the Circuit fiends."

Together we head deeper into the sprawling graveyard, dodging headstones, stepping over tree roots. Our guard is up, but we don't come across any Circuit fiends.

No, the cemetery is deathly quiet. Weird.

"This way." Euphoria beelines toward the older section, and we're surrounded by towering pillars and grim mausoleums punching up from the ground like the teeth of some monster trying to devour us.

Quit it, Syl.

Euphoria stops at an old, crumbling mausoleum. A gnarled tree hangs over it in a tangle, the roots draped over the front door all creepy, like Spanish moss. I can't even read the name on the stone, it's so ancient and covered with tree gunk. The whole thing looks like one of those dark fairy mounds in a Brian Froud book.

Points for finally getting on-theme, Agravaine.

And the door is already open.

Not much, just a crack. Enough to let in someone small.

Someone like…Fiann?

My Spidey sense is tingling, and I see it like smoke hanging in the air—smears of a green and purple aura. The aura of Fiann's special brand of crazy.

But no… Fiann's supposedly in "rehab" (i.e., the hospital, recovering from her botched attempt to steal Euphoria's gramarye), and Agravaine's dead.

No one else knows.

Euphoria meets my eyes. She's thinking the same thing: no Circuit fiends…the door already open. "Let's be extra careful."

"Oh, yeah."

She grabs the door and heaves, her dark Fae strength working, all her muscles bunching in a way that makes my hormones sit up and take notice. With a *crunch-crack* like pulling out a giant rotted tooth, she yanks it out of the earth, taking a tangle of black roots and dirt with it.

The pitch-black tomb yawns ahead of us, and even with the moonlight and my enhanced sight, I see only darkness. Pulling out my phone, I activate its backlight.

Euphoria and I head inside.

The stench of old earth and decay envelops us, and my heartbeat ramps up to DEFCON 1. I hate small spaces. Suddenly, I'm panting and sweating like crazy.

Yup. Syl Skye, super-cool sleeper-princess, and I'm about to freak.

"Come on, princess. You're not going to wimp out, are you?" Euphoria's teasing is good-natured, meant to snap me out of it.

Flirty banter is kind of our thing.

I scoff. "You'll wimp out before I do."

"We'll see about that."

"Yeah, we will, Miss Smarty-Pants dark Fae."

She chuckles, the sound warped by all the earth around us.

We head deeper in, and I try my hardest not to look at coffins or crypts or anything that might possibly resemble a dead body. As soon as we step foot inside the main vault, the pressure changes, the air thickening.

A hollow moaning echoes in the darkness with the sinister creaking of tree limbs. Shivers spike my spine at a gooey, sucking sound like sticky tentacles sliding against one another. My burner phone can't pierce the darkness.

"Hold up." Euphoria stops and hums softly. A lick of purple lightning coils in her palm.

The area lights up in violet.

Hissing like a steaming kettle, the darkness *recoils* all around us. A gajillion tiny black circuits jigger and teem, crawling over one another, consuming the dead tree roots and *rebuilding* them into dark, soulless machinery. Circuitry glows green, threading through rocks, soil, leeching their way up toward the surface.

Crap! This Ouroboros has already hatched from its egglike *ovo*. It's spawning.

"Syl, target its master-key circuit!" Euphoria's voice is weirdly muffled by all the shifting earth.

"Got it!"

And then it's on like Donkey Kong.

Before I can find the master-key circuit—much less target it—the entire mausoleum rumbles and quakes. The ground shudders, heaves, then slams sideways in a shower of flying dirt.

"Look out!" Euphoria shoves me one way, leaping the other.

Gnarled roots rip through the main vault, spearing in at us. Tree boughs tear through the ceiling, raining stone and soil.

Euphoria zigs, and I zag, but the tree bars our way with a tangle of roots and tendrils. They're being rewritten into machinery-tentacles as they come, a darkling current racing over their circuits.

Crap, crap, crap...

The roots slam into the floor, rip toward us, hem us in, and then the tree grabs us up, squeezing the life from us while the branches plow the soil back in.

We're being buried alive. Oh, happy day.

All around us, the infection of the tree continues, Moribund circuits eating up its bark, its branches, the creepy-green current from the key circuit racing along its boughs...

Rouen sings a note, blasting the branches with violet lightning, but they only grow back, splitting into two, three, four more branches, blocking her from me.

"Rouen!" I can't see her, and I'm freaking. I don't dare use my powers in such close quarters.

"Syl..." Her voice is strained in the darkness. "You have to find the key circuit...burn it down."

If I do that, if I kill the key, the Ouroboros will stop spawning. It'll turn on itself, devour itself.

I twist, fighting for leverage against the massive branches. E's weakened by cold iron, unable to break free. Sure, I could light the tree on fire, but what if I lose control?

If she can't break free...I could kill her, too.

But if I don't, we'll die here anyway. We are well and truly screwed.

All around us, the Ouroboros circuits knit and twitch, transforming the tree, the rocks, the earth into black-magic machinery.

It's only a matter of item before it gets us, too.

We'll both become soulless Moribund constructs.

Even now, the hungry rumble from the tree sends terror clawing down my spine. I can't find the key circuit, can't trace it back, a green glint flittering about in the darkness, fast as a firefly.

Euphoria's struggling with a huge root. "Any time now, sleeper-princess."

"All right, all right, hold your horses!" I switch to my Fae-sight, and whoa… The darkness warps and wefts, sending nausea rolling through my guts.

I strain to see…

There! The racing current and its source, the glint of a tiny intricate circuit.

The master-key circuit!

"Got it! But…" My sunfire barely touched Agravaine, and he went up like the Fourth of July.

"Do it already!" The roots wrap her tight, squeezing. I hear a sharp *pop*—ribs breaking—and her face goes white. "Syl! Do it now!"

There's no hope for it. The roots lash at us, wrapping us tight. A branch slashes my cheek. The scent of blood and the bright-red fear of E's aura shoot panic through me, making my heart rabbit-kick my ribs.

The tree squeezes, rumbling. Pain erupts through my body.

I can't breathe. I can't focus…

I can only hope my control doesn't fail me now. All fingers crossed, I summon my white flame. "Burn, baby, burn."

The power I've suppressed for so long leaps from my fingers. Joy fills me up to the tips of my fingers and toes, lifting me up. This is the only time I feel like my true self—the only time I feel at home in my own skin.

This is who I am. Brightness and fire and light.

I set the tree on white flame.

And hope Euphoria will be okay…

CHAPTER FOUR
ROUEN

My heroine, my downfall
Find me in my darkest place
Bring me into the light
- "Heroine," Euphoria

Brilliant white sunfire lights up the depths of the mausoleum, bringing scorching heat and blotting out the darkness, washing over the Ouroboros tree, blinding me, making every dark Fae nerve in my body flash into panic mode.

This is Summer, pure and fiery, the enemy of Winter.

The enemy of me.

The first of the flames licks closer to me, the wicked tree pitching wildly, black circuitry shrieking as it's scorched to cinders. I jerk away, and now I understand why the arch-Eld, wisest of the dark Fae, sided with Agravaine over me.

Because instead of murdering the sleeper-princesses, I wanted to stop the fair Fae/dark Fae war and use their power to heal the hearthstone.

I wanted to team up with them.

But you can't team up with someone whose very existence means your death.

Crack! Pain brings me back to reality, the Ouroboros tree squeezing hard. *Not the best time to take a trip down bad-memory lane, Roue.* My broken ribs stab into me, stealing my breath. I clench my fangs and fight. The stench of ozone and copper—the master-key circuit rewriting the tree into dark machinery—blasts all around me. I nearly break free, but the combination of holy ground and cold-wrought iron saps my strength, makes me heavy, sluggish, unfocused.

I can't access my gramarye.

I'm not one-tenth my true self. *Would it be too damsel-in-distress of me to scream?*

And then Syl lights up the darkness like a supernova.

My beautiful Summer girl. I know she's scared for me, but she throws herself into the fight with all the passion and fire she possesses—the passion and fire that utterly compelled me that night on the train tracks. That night she unleashed her white flame for the first time.

She nearly burned me to my bones.

Here's to second chances, my inner grump jokes unhappily as the white flames lick closer. I brace my feet against the tree's trunk and push. I have to get free before Syl's power touches me.

It won't be like that night at the Winter Formal, when I was immune for a hot second. That night, I thought we were on our way to being soul-bound—unconditionally in love and immune to each other's most destructive powers.

But no.

"E, get out of there!" Syl's voice is panicked. She's losing control. White flame flares over the Ouroboros tree, lighting up every circuit, bright as daylight. The flames lick closer, closer. My heart revs up like my Harley taking a steep hill. *Oh no, no, no, no, no...*

All my self-preservation instincts kick in, and I thrash, fighting harder. I am of the Winter Court. Ice and snow flows through my veins. This is the power of Summer unleashed.

It can kill me on contact.

And no matter what I want, Syl and I can't be soul-bound. One, I'm not royalty anymore. Two, there's never been a girl/girl soul-bound pair. Not in all dark Fae history or legend.

Not even in myth.

Save it for your lyrics, Roue. I steel myself. *Less broody-face, more rescuing action.*

"Rouen!" Syl's white flame eats up the darkness, tendrils of fire racing along every root and bramble, racing toward me.

It's now or never.

I heave all my strength at the tree, and it gives an inch. Just enough! Slipping free, I sing my violet lightning into being. And as the white flame scorches in, I blast it full-power.

Zorch! White fire and violet lightning zap and carom around each other, forming a massive snarl of energy, and then…the whole thing backlashes. It hits me like a wrecking ball, throwing me out of the main vault, down the hall. I land at the entrance in a heap of arms and legs.

"Urggg…" This is not my best moment.

In the blink of an eye, I'm on my feet. My impromptu flight's put me on the other side of the roots and brambles, the tree thrashing, throwing up dirt. I duck a clod of flying earth. "Syl!"

I catch sight of her trapped in the main vault, a massive tangle of roots between us.

I sing my power to my hands and lash the tree with lightning.

"Keep it up, E!" My girl sees the key circuit now, chasing it with her flames. Desperate, the tree throws branch after bramble as a shield, but she burns it all away. The heat in here blasts up to sweltering. Sweat pours down my face.

Violet lightning wreathing my hands, I snap roots in half and pull them from the earth. On the other side, Syl burns and blasts.

But the master-key is too fast. It zips and zigs around, a green glint barely visible in the dark and flashing fire and lightning.

I shout encouragement to my girl. "Keep trying, princess!"

We fight our way back to each other, tearing into the tree, gutting the mausoleum with flame and lightning and brute strength. I'm careful to dodge and play keep-away with Syl's white flames.

I do not want a repeat of being a dark Fae cannonball.

I raise my voice, sing a single pure note, and bolts of violet lightning blaze through the air, shearing branches and brambles apart, clearing our path.

That's when I see it, the master-key zipping over a black bough. Just a tiny green glint in the gloom. "Behind you!"

Instantly, Syl turns, flames arcing in white sheets from her hands—

But the Ouroboros tree retreats into itself, pulling back every root, every tendril and bramble. *I have a bad feeling about this.* The earth shudders.

"Brace!" I yell.

The tree slams into the earth. Rock and stone and clods of dirt rain down, smothering my lightning and her fire. The tree shovels it all toward us in great, heaving waves, threatening to bury us alive. We dodge the main force of the attack, but Syl gets clipped. She staggers to a knee, spitting dirt.

"Syl!" I protect her with my body, not caring that I'm in the line of fire.

She spins, sees something over my shoulder. "Rouen!" Her hand flashes up, trailing bright fire. *Bloody bones!* White flame shoots toward me, and I barely bite back a scream.

Tell no one.

Searing heat blasts past my cheek, and she burns down a tangle of black-circuitry roots about to pierce me through. *Nope. I'm so not freaking out. I'm cool.*

"Thanks." I give her a wry smile. "Next time, warn me, princess."

"Where would be the fun in that?" she teases.

Instantly, my sweaty-hot panic turns to excitement. I am suddenly burning for her. Our gazes meet.

Did I mention it's super-hot in here?

I'm grinning like a loon, loving that burning connection between us. Me, the princess of the Winter Court, lured to the Summer within her. "Ready?"

She nods, so wild and beautiful, bathed in white. "You'd better stand back."

I do, ducking behind a fallen section of dirt just in case. From there, I sing and blast the tree again, and as it shifts, Syl targets the key circuit. A *whoosh* of flames washes it white, and it burns, curdling like black, spoiled milk.

Instantly, the Ouroboros tree writhes, lashing out in desperation, trying to maim or kill.

"Come on, princess!" Throwing caution to the wind, I grab Syl's non-flamey hand and drag her to the opening, blasting the tree for good measure. The tree is thrashing, screeching a high-pitched wail that only Fae can hear—like squeaky nails squabbling on a chalkboard. Outside, I let go of her, her white flame lashing at me like a spitting cat. I jerk back and see the entire cemetery glowing a ghoulish green. The ground, the gravestones, grass, trees—everything is infected with Ouroboros circuitry, the green glow bleeding out in waves from the tree's nexus point.

Syl will have to burn it all. "Do your thing, princess."

She does, flames leaping from her hands, purifying the dark circuitry, scorched-earth style. Ashes rain around us, foul and bitter-smelling snow. The Ouroboros shudders, black circuitry shredded and scorched by fire, recoiling into a tighter and tighter ball in the center of the trunk. Its master-key sparks and sputters, trying to respawn the circuits around it.

Already, the Ouroboros has devoured smaller gravestones, leaving behind machinery constructs like rotted teeth stuck in the ground. All around us, harrow-stitches are forming, brackish-green vortexes warping the air, pulling on the Shroud.

Left alone, the master-key would heal, rebuild itself, infect more hosts…

Thing is, nothing dark can escape the white flame of a sleeper-princess.

Syl hits it again dead center, a fierce joy on her face as she burns and burns, the Ouroboros shrieking, writhing like it's one of those crazy wind-sock puppets advertising a gas station. She washes the tree, the soil, the stones—all of it—in white flame.

Across the cemetery, Ouroboros constructions shatter and pop, crumbling to ashes.

I throw up a don't-see-us Glamoury against any prying mortals' eyes and ears. What with Syl firing her white flame power up in here and the tree doing its bizarro St. Vitus's dance, people would seriously notice.

Syl nods her thanks, sweeping the fire back and forth across the tree. With nowhere to flee, the spawning Ouroboros blackens and burns, wailing, hissing as it dies.

"Make sure you get it all." I eye the mausoleum with suspicion. Someone else was here, they forced the door, and I have a pretty darn good idea of who. "And burn that key circuit to ash."

The Moribund is bad enough, but at least one Moribund creature couldn't infect another. But the Ouroboros? It's a black hole of destruction. It'll consume and consume and consume…until everything it touches becomes a dark and soulless machine.

Not to mention the harrow-stitches straining the Shroud.

If the barrier betwixt and between all realms—Fair Faerie, Dark Faerie, the mortal realm, et cetera, et cetera—ever tore, if Faerie ever bled through to the mortal realm, it'd be like *Labyrinth* and *The Dark Crystal* meets grim-dark *Pan's Labyrinth* up in here.

Does Fiann know she's the one playing with fire?

I know Syl thinks her old BFF is stuck in rehab, but I know firsthand the addictive power of Faerie. Fiann tasted dark Fae power in that gym last year.

There's no way she's going to just give that up.

I inhale deeply, calling on my dark Fae senses. When I hunted sleeper-princesses, I did it mostly by scent, and now, beneath the scorching of tree and circuitry, I smell…

Burning rubber and asphalt. Agravaine's scent.

It makes no sense. Agravaine is dead, and if Fiann smells like him, that can only mean one thing. Jealousy coils sickly inside me.

Those two villains were soul-bound. But how?

My gaze goes to Syl burning away, her fire, her passion, her life-force so vibrant in the night. I can smell her sweet vanilla and skin musk, and beneath it, the sweeter blood of a fair Fae princess.

Sweet, magical, able to sustain the hearthstone—and wash the sluagh taint from a dark Fae.

That's how he did it. The blood of the sleeper-princesses.

You could do it, too, Rouen, the dark part of me whispers. *She's right there.*

No. I crush down my dark self. *I'll never hurt Syl.* Not even if it means I'd be royalty again, my outcast sluagh taint washed away. Anger surges inside me, and for one wild second, I wish the Ouroboros would put up more of a fight. I want to smash something. Anything.

But the Ouroboros only dies in the wake of Syl's fire.

My girl. My fair Fae sleeper-princess. So bright it hurts to look at her. So beautiful, with her red hair and grey eyes, those freckles on her button nose, her small chin and bowlike lips that I can't stop kissing.

She's my binary opposite in every way. We don't belong together and yet we do.

But soul-bound?

There are only two ways. One, put my fangs into her, drain her blood, and become royalty again. Or two, become the ruler of the dark Fae, able to soul-bond with whomever I wish.

But for that, I'd have to duel my father to the death.

"E, I need you!"

Syl's cry tears me from my morbid thoughts. She burns and blazes, the Moribund shuddering in its death throes. Stepping up next to her, I carve through the branches with my violet lightning, keeping them from striking out at her.

Syl and I work as a team, but I'm careful not to get to close.

Soul-bound, Rouen. If you were soul-bound, you wouldn't have to worry.

But at what cost? I won't hurt her, and I can't fight my father. Even if he wasn't caught in the stasis of Winter's Sleep with the rest of my people, it's against our every dark Fae tradition.

Blood does not fight blood.

"Whew!" Syl finally drops her hands and calls off her white flames. The last tendrils eddy around and wisp out in puffs of smoke. All around us, the cemetery is smoldering, coils of black smoke reaching up to the sky. The stench of ozone, burned circuitry, and scorched metal makes me feel ill.

The Ouroboros crumbles, collapsing, the entire mausoleum caving in, the grating, grinding of stones and earth sucking into a swirling sinkhole.

It's a little more than my Glamoury can cover. "Hold that pose," I tell Syl and then head to the nearest streetlight.

I'm no longer a Circuit Fae, but some of that power still resides within me. I hate using it, but I've no choice. I touch the lamppost, feeling all its electrical workings, the cables and wires, the flow of power within and between them. I croon to the cables, coaxing.

Violet tendrils of power light the surface like circuitry, then they flash, racing up to the bulbs. *Pop-pop!* Glass rains down on me as I'm cloaked in darkness. A coppery taste floods my mouth, the scent of ozone stinging my nostrils.

I push more power into the lamppost.

Pop! Pop, pop, pop! The rest of the streetlights blow out, one by one by one, all down the street. In no time, the entire area is blanketed in darkness. Good. I can cover the rest with my Glamoury.

I take my hand away, shaking off the Circuit Fae power in a shower of violet sparks, and return to Syl.

The fight is over. Another Ouroboros destroyed.

The city is safe for another night.

"We did it!" Syl high-fives me, our brief contact causing a spark of white. She's breathing hard and grinning. "Euphoria…" I see it in her eyes; she wants to leap into my arms.

I so want her to.

But right now, being close isn't possible for us.

Hating myself, I shake my head and step back. The disappointment in her summer-storm-grey eyes kills me. I swallow a lump of dust. "Come on. Let's go home."

"Okay." Even downtrodden, she smiles, the light in those eyes so hopeful.

But all I can see is darkness.

The wintersteel ring in my pocket weighs me down. Syl and I can't be soul-bound. I can't harm her. And I can't fight my father to the death.

Besides, she belongs with her own people. And I belong with mine.

I touch the ring once and then let it go.

CHAPTER FIVE
SYL

A sleeper-princess
Is vulnerable only to one thing:
The power of OverHill
And its royalty
- Glamma's Grimm

I'm having the best dream in the history of ever. It's the height of summer, and I'm standing in a gorgeous emerald-green meadow splashed with a riot of wildflowers. All their scents tingle my nose, making me giddy. I spread my arms wide and spin around like when you're a kid trying to get dizzy.

The grass is whispery against my bare feet, the perfect combo of cool and dewy and spiky. Summer's heat wraps around me, sunlight flashing on my closed eyelids as I spin and spin and spin...

And finally fall down laughing into the soft grass. It tickles me like butterfly kisses, the wildflowers perfuming my skin. Fat yellow-and-black bumblebees drone in the air, all tipsy from pollen, and colorful hummingbirds zip around, sipping from beautiful, flutelike flowers glistening with sticky-sweet nectar.

It's perfect. Well, almost.

If only Euphoria were here.

Because here is where I belong. The realm of Fair Faerie.

Its purity is blinding, and everything is Technicolor-hyper-real—greener-than-green meadows covered in carpets of wild-flowers and ringed with golden oaks and white birch, musical birdsong filling the air, the sky above an impossible cloudless blue stretching on and on, the sun warm, welcoming…

I feel complete, at home in my skin, with my powers and who I am.

So clearly it's a dream because real life is no way this perfect.

Must've been that late-night pizza. I roll over in the grass and pluck a strand.

After fighting the Ouroboros, I was starving. Fighting always makes me hungry. Euphoria humored me by ordering up my fave: Hawaiian pizza with extra pineapple, and now?

Weird pizza dreams.

As if being the sleeper-princess isn't weird enough.

I put the blade of grass between my thumbs and blow on it. The perfect whistle echoes.

At least it's a pretty dream. I turn to the east, where soaring pillars and curved archways sweep up from a castle so bright it hurts my eyes. Its golden towers and turrets look like solidified sunlight, and all around it runs a ginormous garden of white rose hedges, calla lilies, and groves of white birch with silver leaves.

It's like *The Lord of the Rings* on overdrive.

And over the castle towers comes a song of heart-rending silver pipes.

It's so beautiful I want to cry. I want to laugh. I want to dance and sing until I fall down breathless. My heart aches as the haunting pipes swell even louder, make me even dizzier. My head's as heavy as a lead balloon, foggy at the white blare of this place, its silvery pipe-song making me woozy.

Ugh, I'm getting all faestruck. Get it together, Syl. I push myself up and start toward the gleaming white and gold castle. I wonder what the people here look like.

My people.

No one's seen a fair Fae in hundreds of years. Not since they sent a sleeper-princess to poison the hearthstone in UnderHollow, the center of Dark Faerie. When that didn't kill the dark Fae outright, the fair Fae went into hiding.

When they wake—and the dark Fae, too—me and Euphoria will be caught smack-dab in the middle.

It'll be war again.

Unless we can figure out a way to stop it.

Stop an ancient war? my inner killjoy nags. *That's rich. You couldn't even handle a simple date night, Syl.*

Whoa... I pull back hard on the negativity. I won't think like that. I pick up the pace, leaving those dark thoughts behind. Dew tickles my skin, my bare feet loving the feel of the soft grass. As I pass, wildflowers bend and sway around my legs, making musical notes.

But I'm drawn to the silvery pipes.

I half-expect to run into Elrond or Galadriel or at least some giant eagles on my way through the meadow. I'm just warming to the idea of first *and* second breakfast when the silver pipes get louder, like they're trying to warn me.

Louder, louder...

Wahhh-wahhh-wahhh!

I jolt upright to the ungodly wail of my alarm.

Nooooo. I roll over, shoving away my e-reader and an empty pizza box, and stuff my pillow over my head. With my other hand, I flail like a baby seal, finally whacking the crappy old alarm to the floor where it—of course—keeps right on blaring.

Waaahhh! Waaaahhh! Waaaahhh!

Yup. That's me. Syl Skye, sleeper-princess by night; normal, sleep-deprived girl by day. I swear, could I have, like, a second here? Agravaine's dead, another Ouroboros has been destroyed...

But how many are left, Syl?

Waaaahhh! Waaaaahhh! Waaaaahhh!

I tuck my pillow tighter, trying not to remember the smear of green and purple aura, the smell of burning rubber. Fiann's aura. Agravaine's smell. Did she somehow take on his power?

Ugh, Agravaine. I'd hoped we'd heard the last of him when we donkey-stomped him and wrecked his Grimmacle that was supposed to infect the entire city with Moribund, turning everyone into Circuit slaves.

Waaaahhh! Waaaaahhh! Waaaaahhh!

Darn it! I sneak a foot out from under my Gryffindor comforter and flail around, trying to turn the stupid alarm off. Mom always says I have prehensile monkey toes. I can even pick up pencils and write my name. So, yeah, with those babies, I manage to flick the switch.

Waaa! Wa—Click!

Ahhhhh, blessed silence.

And then, "Syl?"

Urgggg…

Our apartment is tiny, and I can hear Mom clear as day, even though she's calling from the kitchen. The *clink* and *clank* of pots and pans totally smashes the last hope I have of getting five more minutes of shut-eye. Mom's fixing me breakfast, which is super-sweet of her since: one, she probably worked all night, and two, I've been able to cook since I was ten. Glamma insisted on it. She was a tough cookie, a spitfire Irish lass off the boat, and she didn't put up with anyone being a Miss Whiny-Pants. I miss her every day.

"Syl, are you up?"

Seriously, Mom, it's 6:30 a.m. I'm not up for anything. Why is the first day of school so early anyway? Can't we ease into it, say, around 9-ish?

Okay, okay. That's enough, Miss Whiny-Pants. I give myself like two minutes a day for whining. The rest is for getting stuff done and kicking butt.

I roll over onto my back, stare at my ceiling, and mentally prepare myself for today. Junior year. All I want is for it to be the complete opposite of last year. Quiet and filled with regular school stuff, not evil Circuit Fae trying to take over my school, my world, my entire life.

Between surviving the train crash, being the weird "girl who lived," finding out I'm the last sleeper-princess of the fair Fae, then Awakening, fighting Agravaine and his Wild Hunt—not to mention Fiann going from my BFF to my high school rival to crazy Harley Quinn henchwench…

Please tell me that wasn't her aura last night.

Hey, a girl can hope, right?

The alarm's snooze activates, and the dark synthwave of Euphoria's vocals and violin fills my room.

Oh my God. Euphoria… Let's not forget that.

We went from me fan-girling at her at a club in DC to her chasing me to Richmond and trying to kill me, to us teaming up, defeating Agravaine, and exchanging I love you's.

Yeah, it's been a roller coaster, for sure.

My dark Fae princess, she's been quiet and broody all summer. I know she's dying to help her people. But since our fight with Agravaine collapsed the pathways to UnderHollow, we don't have any way to do that.

I'm determined to find a way, though. Just you wait.

"Syl!" Mom's voice has that Mom edge to it, and I remind myself that the lady carries a giant hand cannon of a gun. I've seen her take out a dark Fae at twenty paces.

Yup. I'm up. "Be right there."

I drag my butt out of bed and slouch over to the mirror. A huge yawn splits my face, showing all my super-straight, post-dental-surgery-in-the-eight-grade teeth. I ruffle my hair. My teeth might be perfect, but the rest of me looks like Anna from *Frozen* waking up on coronation day. My curly red hair sticks up, and my eyeliner is smeared. And of course, the freckles.

"Syl, you're going to be late!"

"Shower first!" I call, grabbing up a fresh pair of undies and my school uniform. I high-tail it to the bathroom, only to find the door closed, the shower running.

Euphoria must be... Ohhhhhh. A blush crawls up my face.

I slump against the door since my knees literally feel weak, and try super-hard not to think of her in there. Doing whatever hot dark Fae girls do in the shower. With all that water and soap and—

Not helping, Syl! I push away from the door, suddenly sweaty-hot in a way that has zero to do with my white flames going all wonky.

Euphoria's super-cool, smart, dangerous... I'm drawn to her, like a moth to a dark flame. Or would that be a moth to a dark winter's night?

And then I hear it. Her voice. She's singing.

The heat in my face travels south. *Soooo not helping.*

"Syl...breakfast!" Mom calls.

I want to crawl back into bed, all warm with my thoughts of Euphoria, but Mom's onto me now. She knows I'm up and about and...standing by the bathroom door like a creepy stalker. I mean, Euphoria's my girlfriend, but still.

With a supreme effort of will, I head to the kitchen, holding my stuff.

Mom's there, bustling around, making—*Mmmmm...* The sweet, syrupy scent hits me like a dream. Heightened Fae senses for the win! "Are those banana pancakes?" I'm practically drooling.

"Yes." Mom is clearly the queen of understatement because those are *banana freaking pancakes* in that pan. I can't remember the last time we had those. Well, I can, but I don't like to think about the past much.

I sneak past her and try to nab a bite from the pan.

She swats me playfully with the spatula. "I don't think so, buga-boo." That's what she calls me when I'm being particularly sassy.

"Where did you get all the bananas?" We don't usually have fresh fruit in the house.

"The cafeteria at West End High was throwing out a batch of brown ones, and the manager said I could take them." She smiles, but it's tight around her eyes. I know the hit it must've been to her pride to take those bananas.

Mom sacrifices for me every day, even with stuff that seems little, like banana pancakes. It seems little, but actually? It's huge.

I kiss her cheek. "They look super-yummy."

She smiles for real now. I know she blames herself for Dad leaving when I was thirteen, for the checks that stopped coming, for us having to move from the swanky suburbs of the Fan to the tenements in Jackson Ward last year.

I lost a lot of friends, but you know what? They weren't friends to begin with.

I pull out the beat-up barstool and look around the small kitchen nook. Our tenement isn't exactly cozy, but we've made it homey, Mom and me. And I'd rather have Mom than any big house or anything.

Mom and…Euphoria.

She walks out of the bathroom, tall and über-glam, wearing only a towel. Her jet-black hair glistens all wet down her bare back, water clinging to her bronze skin.

Holy— My heart's beating so hard it feels like I'm going to have an anime-style nosebleed.

Euphoria doesn't bother with a Glamoury here in the house, so I don't need my Fae-sight to see her as she really is. A dark Fae, all pointed ears, sapphire-blue eyes, glowing bronze skin, and fangs. *So super-sexy. Sigh.* I watch a water droplet run down her shoulder. I want to kiss it away, and that thought heats my face like a furnace.

Way to act cool, Syl. With my pale Irish complexion, I'll be wearing this blush all the way to school.

And of course my mom notices. She notices, like, everything. Must be something they teach you in mom school: How to Notice Your Daughter's Embarrassing Crush 101.

Like clockwork, Mom puts the kibosh on my hormonal drooling. "Why don't you plate the food, Syl?"

"Right!" I turn to grab some plates from the cabinet, but I can't help sneaking another peek at my girl.

Euphoria totally catches me staring through the curtain that separates her little alcove from the rest of our tiny living room. All it takes is a flash of sapphire-blue eyes ringed in gold, and the butterflies in my stomach are doing burpees.

My hand goes to Glamma's ring on its chain beneath my top.

"Are you ready for today?" Mom's question shatters my thoughts. Part of me wants to tell her she already asked me that last night, but I don't want to bring up the phone call.

Or the fact that I lied pretty hard.

Guilt hits me low in the gut, and I can see it in her eyes—she totally knows. I haven't exactly been honest about our Moribund-fighting vigilantism.

"Yeah, I guess." I slide pancakes onto plates.

Mom shakes her head no when I offer her one. "What about Fiann?"

Ugh, I knew that was going to come up. "What about her?"

Fiann's still in "rehab" for drugs, which is a dirty lie—at least the drugs part. Spending twenty-four hours faestruck really messed with her, and when Agravaine died, Fiann nearly died, too, infected with all the dark magic she'd stolen from Euphoria. It tore through her system, starving her, dehydrating her, making her mad as a hatter.

"Will she be back?" Mom keeps her voice mild.

Euphoria comes to the bar, and I slide our plates over. "Doubt it," I tell Mom as I take my seat. My old school rival has better things to do than boil my bunny. I feel sorry for her. Then again... she did try to kill me. And Euphoria. And she helped Agravaine nearly kill my mom.

Yeahhhhh, I think I'll put my sympathy on hold for banana pancakes.

I dig in to all the glorious, gooey deliciousness, E beside me, and Mom at the counter, watching me like a hawk. She sips her coffee. Over the rim, her eyes flick to Euphoria.

They were enemies once, and they still bicker like a couple of ravens trying to occupy the same perch. Mostly, I think they're done trying to kill each other, though.

Mostly.

Euphoria and I eat in friendly silence, stuffing our faces with delicious gooey bananas and instant pancakes. We reach for the syrup at the same time and bump hands.

She jerks away, "Sorry," and Mom definitely catches that. Her eyebrow arches, but she doesn't say anything. Mom's one of those quiet, calculating types.

It's equal parts cool and terrible, and it means I'm off the hook for now. But once she puts my late night, Fiann's rehab, and me not touching Euphoria together?

I'll have some heavy answering to do.

"Here you go." I push the syrup E's way.

She waves a hand. "No, you. You're a growing sleeper-princess, after all."

"True," I say all braggy because last night who saved who again? That's right. Me. Her. I swipe the syrup for emphasis.

She chuckles a bit, teasing. "So modest."

I stuff a heaping forkful of pancake in my face. "Hey, I kept up with you last night." I wave my fork in the air.

Mom's shrewd look pins me to my stool.

Ruh-roh.

"At the restaurant, I mean." I swallow hard and cover by taking a sip of my tea. *Real smooth, Syl.* I'm already thinking up ways to avoid Mom's questions. I don't want her to worry. I mean, there's no real way to say, *Oh yeah, Euphoria and I fight Circuit fiends and evil-dark Ouroboros every night* and make it sound like it's no biggie.

Euphoria smirks, all sexy and cool. "Maybe I let you."

"Don't be a sore loser, E," I tease, warming to our flirty flirting. "Pretty soon you won't be able to keep up with me."

"Ha!" She shovels in more pancakes.

Seriously, I love watching my girl eat.

Mom taps her wrist where a watch should be, and I look at my beat-up phone.

Ugh, good thing I showered last night before bed.

"Gotta run." I get up, throwing my clothes on while shoving more food in my face and chewing for all I'm worth. I slip my feet into my Docs, hoping against hope we can make it out the door before Mom makes a fuss.

"When you're ready, Syl, I want the truth." Mom's green eyes are sharp, though her voice is casual.

Too late.

"Um, okay." I stuff in more pancakes, glancing at Euphoria, but my Winter girl is statuesque and silent.

"Made you these." Mom slides two bentos across the tabletop, and I nearly squee with delight. She gives Euphoria the stink-eye before E can say anything snarky about Mom being all...well, Momlike to her.

I swipe the bentos. "Thanks, Mom." I kiss her temple. "See you tonight. We'll make dinner."

Euphoria starts to choke, and I elbow her.

"Fine, fine. Dinner," she grumbles, and then we're out the door.

"Bye, Mom!" We rush down the stairs, passing Miss Jardin's door with the *J.J.* on it. I get a whiff of habaneros, and I'm reminded of the way Miss J saved my bacon last year. I still don't know what-all she is, but at least she's on our side.

At least...I think she is.

Miss Hillary, her petite tuxedo kitty, zooms up the stairs. She lets out a yowl when she sees Euphoria and darts past us.

"Put your Glamoury up," I remind E.

"Not like that cat doesn't see through it anyway." Her eyes glaze for a split-second as she throws on a Glamoury to hide her true nature from the world. In a shimmer, her glowing-bronze skin, fangs, pointed ears, and sapphire-blue eyes dim down from ethereal Fae beauty to normal, human-level attractiveness. The glow fades from her dark skin, her fangs and pointed ears vanish, the gold rings vanish from her eyes and they turn a bright electric-blue.

Me? I don't have to worry about that.

Maybe sleeper-princesses look totally normal?

We go outside to E's motorcycle and get on. Through a lot of trial and error, we've learned that as long as I'm not trying to touch her with my hands, or touch her skin-to-skin, we're good. My power stays put.

Thank goodness for small favors and all that.

She hands me the helmet. We share a smile, the world narrowing down to just the two of us, and for a minute, I forget that she's the dark Fae princess and I'm the fair Fae princess.

Then the minute passes, and we're off to the first day of junior year.

CHAPTER SIX
ROUEN

What's another year, my love?
When I choose forever
With you
- "Forever," Euphoria

I gun my Harley and signal into the turn, fate and inertia pulling me and Syl down the long drive of Richmond Elite High. I've been dreading this for weeks, the inevitable return to high school hell.

I'm no fan of summer, what with its sweltering heat and blistering asphalt, air so hot you can barely breathe. No dark Fae in her right mind would miss it. Our power comes from winter—chill winds and icy squalls, sleet and storm and snowfall. Summer weakens us, the heat a constant drain.

Still, the vacation part wasn't entirely bad.

I slow the bike as we come up on the school, the tall buildings peeking out above the tops of the trees that line the drive. Students are already gathering in groups on the walkways. *Gah! Dread, dread, dread...*

A part of me misses our summer shenanigans—me and Syl abandoning the stifling tenements for the condos down in Shockoe Bottom, where careless hipsters left the gate to the community pool open. We'd spend the day goofing around, swimming and cooking dollar-store hot dogs on the grill.

The nights were a sweltering blur of playing shows at the Nanci Raygun, dowsing and then racing across the city, cloaked in our Glamouries, hunting down Ouroboros and Circuit fiends.

I know it wasn't Syl's ideal. She wanted to go on a real date. She wanted making out at the movies, late-night trolley rides, and sneaking into clubs like Mars Bar to dance to retro-80s tunes.

It seemed like such a small thing, yet we could never quite get it together. There was always another Ouroboros, another Circuit fiend…always another interruption. If we can't find a place for us in this world, how will we find it in Faerie?

Especially with her power all geared up to kill me.

I put my foot down as we bank into the parking lot. Behind me, Syl shifts, barely daring to touch my shoulder. A wistful ache stabs my heart like a blade.

I miss being close, touching her, kissing her.

I reach back and lay my gloved hand on her knee. "I swear, Syl, once the last Ouroboros is burned to ash and the city is safe from Moribund, I'll spend every waking moment making you happy."

"I know," she says gently, her voice muffled by the helmet, but I don't have to see her face to hear the unspoken *When?*

That question is an arrow in my heart. Even now, I feel the wintersteel ring, cold and heavy in my pocket. *Make her happy right now, Rouen.*

But I can't. I'm a sluagh, an outcast to my people, an enemy to hers.

Besides, a binding with rings is serious. Dark Fae are creatures of winter and steel, fickle as a chill breeze, tempestuous as a snow squall. To bind ourself to another is serious magic, ancient magic.

I want the moment I ask Syl to be perfect, not sandwiched in between school and work and saving the world.

For it to be perfect, you'd have to restore your nobility, Roue.

But to do that requires—*No.* I touch the arm Syl has wrapped around my waist. I could never... I won't consider, won't even think about it.

I'm not a huntress controlled to seek out sleeper-princesses for their blood anymore.

No, you're a sluagh.

And purging the sluagh taint from my blood comes with a heavy price.

"Soon," I promise her. I'll hate myself if I can't keep that promise.

I pull into a parking spot and throw the kickstand down. In a flash, I'm off the bike and giving Syl my hand, my gloves protecting me from her power flare-up. She pulls off the helmet and grins her thousand-watt smile.

"It's okay, E. Really." She touches my gloved hand briefly.

I find myself smiling with her. Even though grinning makes me feel like a goof, Syl looking at me like I hung the moon and stars makes it worthwhile.

"What do you think this year will bring?" Syl asks, holding my helmet. A group of sophomore girls passes by, already snickering and whispering, tied up in whatever high-school gossip is the new hotness.

"I'd like...less drama," I say, trying to keep it light. But just looking up at the school, with its heavy brick buildings, the gym, the parking lot filled with students, sends shudders down my spine. All summer, I've felt it in the hot breezes, in the scent of dandelions and shimmering humidity...

The clock is ticking on the safe little bubble we've built.

The fair Fae are coming for her.

"Less drama sounds great." Syl grabs her backpack and hands me mine.

"Sure does."

We head toward the main building, dodging other students and the occasional car. My focus is entirely on Syl, but I always watch for potential threats.

We fall in step. A single glance at her has all my instincts kicking into overdrive. I'll do anything to protect her. *To possess her,* the dark part of me whispers.

It's true.

The part of me that is your typical dark Fae wants to sweep her up and spirit her away somewhere, to keep her locked up, to keep her safe and only for me.

Mine.

I could do it, too. Samhain—what the mortals call Halloween—is coming, and not far behind, the winter solstice, the peak of dark Fae power. I'll be at full strength.

And then what? Will you fight all the fair Fae just to keep her prisoner?

No! With effort, I shove that thought away. *I won't take away her choices.*

Syl is the last sleeper-princess. I've fought hard, been punished and exiled by my own people so she can remain alive and free.

"Hey, guys!" She's waving at Nazira and Octavia, my bandmates, and they turn and come our way. I force a smile, trying to stomp on my black-hearted thoughts.

"Euphoria!" Octavia scolds me the second she's in earshot. "We didn't see you once this summer. Not even for practice."

Naz comes huffing up, lugging her cello case and backpack, her warm chestnut-toned complexion ruddy beneath her hijab.

I look them both in the eyes. "I'm sorry." And I mean it, too. I like Naz, Octavia, Marcus, Chuck—all my bandmates. We're all kinds of geeky nerdiness. Playing music with them, mentoring them, it's the best part of high school except for Syl. "It's been a duty-first kind of summer."

"Sure it has." Octavia looks pointedly at Syl and elbows Nazira, who edges away, annoyed at the casual touch.

Syl blushes a pretty shade of pink. "Guys…"

"Come on." Nazira is all business, as usual. "We'll get you up to speed on all the band things."

"Yeah," Octavia breaks in, sweeping dyed-black hair from her tanned face. "There's going to be a Battle of the Bands."

"Really?" That piques my interest, and as we head into the school, I listen to Naz laying out our perfect plan of attack. In a nutshell, it's practice, practice, and more practice.

"Every night?" Octavia groans, and I have to agree. School, homework, me and Syl running around fighting Ouroboros and Circuit fiends, not to mention my regular gigs at the Nanci—that's all going to put a crimp in my practice schedule.

Still, I try to channel some of Syl's positivity. "We can try."

"You'd better practice, nerds!"

The catcall comes from, you guessed it, Fiann's mean-girl posse—minus Fiann herself, of course. They're gathered around a silver Lamborghini, and a pretty brunette's heading them up, her school uniform pressed to within an inch of its life, a silver softball charm hanging from a thin chain around her neck. She high-fives the usual crowd of Danette Silver, Maggie Xiao, and Jazz Martinez, and they all laugh.

At us.

Syl just rolls her eyes and heads toward Yellow Hall, where the lockers are.

I lower my voice. "Who…?"

"Becca Buchanan, captain of the softball team."

"Ugh, she's even worse than Fiann," Octavia says, eying them as they stand near Becca's Lamborghini, giggling and teasing everyone that passes.

"No one's worse than Fiann." Syl's voice is matter-of-fact, and I don't blame her.

Fiann was a complete nightmare.

"Well, at least she's not here." Octavia hitches her backpack higher and helps Naz get her cello through the huge front doors of the school. We spend a second navigating cello, backpacks, and ourselves through the door and the crush of other students. Becca shouts something else after us—typical high school drek—but we ignore it.

Syl doesn't seem too miffed about the catcalls, but me?

The idea of another year fighting the mean-girl posse annoys me to no end. But with all the passages to Dark Faerie destroyed by Agravaine, I'm trapped here in the mortal realm. If I want to live in Syl's world, then being Rouen Rivoche, high school junior, is the price I pay.

She shoots me a bright smile.

All right. It's not so bad. Sure, I've lived a way *less* sheltered life than most students. I could probably teach these classes—if they were about cool stuff like battling redcaps, tracking an elusive Faerie Raide, or breaking a will-o'-wisp's charm.

But all the reason I need for going to high school is standing right next to me.

Technically, I should be with my people, waking them from Winter's Sleep, but to what end?

To war? So Syl and I can be torn apart?

We turn down the locker hallway, the bright yellow nearly burning out my retinas. Naz and Octavia stop at their lockers, and we wave. I hand Syl her backpack and sling mine over my shoulder. "Ready?"

She smiles. "Yup. You?"

"Born ready." Brave words, but am I ready? So much lies before us—saving my people, keeping us from war, carving out a place for me and Syl.

I raise my chin. Sluagh or not, I was born princess of the dark Fae.

I will find a way.

CHAPTER SEVEN
SYL

Bad magic is like
A bad penny
It just keeps turning up
- Glamma's Grimm

We walk into the school like we own the place because, really, we should after all that went down last year. These kids don't know it, but it's because of me and Euphoria that they're not all copper-top batteries powering Agravaine's dark Fae heaven on earth, like in *The Matrix*.

I totally feel like Neo from *The Matrix* as I walk down the hall, Euphoria next to me. Except, instead of dodging bullets, I'm dodging stink-eyes. Good to know my status as a weirdo is still intact.

Everyone knows I survived a train crash that no one else did except Fiann—and she went completely bananapants crazy. They know I'm one of the only ones who didn't need to be hospitalized after the Winter Formal. They know I'm dating Euphoria, and only a handful of kids in my school are out.

So, yeah, I'm still a registered oddball in these parts.

A group of football jocks snigger as we walk past their lockers. One of them, a tall guy in a Yankees baseball cap, calls out all snide, "Hey, Syl. Lez be friends."

Seriously? Some people need to grow up. But Glamma always said the best way to defeat a troll is to ignore him. That, or hit him with fire and acid, but since I don't have either, I clap back with, "Love is love. Jerk."

A few bystanders laugh, but not at me.

I hold my head high. Let the world think I'm weird. How many of these other kids can say their girl took on a dark Fae menace and nearly sacrificed her life for them?

Spoiler alert: zero.

And speaking of my Winter girl… You can almost hear the needle drag across the record old-school style as she stops in front of the jocks. "Something else to say?" She's all dark glamor and grace, strength and broody power. The jocks can't even meet her eyes.

"Forget it," Baseball Cap mumbles.

For real, most of these guys would've wet themselves if they'd faced Agravaine at his dark Circuit Fae worst. My girl went toe-to-toe with him.

She keeps Baseball Cap in her sights for a looooong moment, the dude squirming like a toddler in a high chair. "Easy enough," she tells him. "You're entirely forgettable." Then she takes my hand, and we head to our lockers while the football jocks hunker by theirs, licking their wounds.

"Wow. How to Win Friends and Influence People by Rouen Rivoche," I tease her.

Euphoria snorts. I miss her touch when she takes her hand away.

It's probably for the best, though. Lighting the school on fire on day one is so not on my list.

We make our way down Yellow Hall. Admin calls it "Gold Hallway," but really? It's a super-bright canary yellow. Who are they kidding? Worse, Richmond E's colors are green and gold, so the lockers on both sides of us are painted ridiculous kelly green.

Ugh. I'm Irish, and even I don't like kelly green. It's like the Lucky Charms leprechaun threw up in here.

We get to our lockers, right next to each other as luck would have it.

"Hmmm..." E's looking at hers like she's going to carve it open with her lightning. My girl's a brilliant warrior and violinist, but her memory for any numbers not directly related to music is terribad.

As for me... "It's eleven right, twenty-seven left, back to thirteen." I've been a mathlete for five years running now. Math and science are totally my jam. So is memorizing mostly useless facts.

"Thanks, princess." Euphoria gives me that sexy side-smirk, the one that makes my stomach do barrel rolls like an X-Wing trying to evade a TIE fighter.

You're so hot for her, Syl.

A blush scalds my face. I am.

Our official status is definitely *It's complicated because I'm a fair Fae sleeper-princess and she's princess of the dark Fae.* Not to mention the no-touch rule.

But hey, I'm working on it.

A few of new students gawk at Euphoria. She's kind of infamous around here—glam goth-rock star—and though she tries to keep it on the down-low, she's high school royalty.

At least, among the freaks and geeks.

"Move aside, losers!"

The crowd parts as Becca Buchanan and the mean-girl posse waltz down the hallway, calling attention to their trendy, balayage hair, their high-end makeup, Louis Vuitton backpacks, and Gucci heels. Dani, Jazz, and Maggie flounce by, giving me and E some nasty side-eye.

Becca stops and gives us the once-over. "You're on notice."

"On..." I exchange a glance with Euphoria. "What?"

"We know what you did to Fiann." Becca's big brown eyes narrow on us.

Stopped her from killing all of you so she could steal E's power and become some kind of self-styled dark Fae queen? But all I say is, "Oooookay."

She keeps glaring, but I turn my back and unload my backpack into my locker.

"You should move along now." Euphoria steps in, looming, and finally, Becca and company flounce away, high ponytails swishing.

"Wow. That was tense." I heft my bag—so much lighter now. "Ready?"

E nods. It's a few minutes till homeroom, but it never hurts to get there early. We head into the atrium, where all the halls dump out. The place is packed wall-to-wall. Jocks slapping each other on the butt and yelling "no homo," geeks huddled over the newest handheld consoles, the stoners staking out the alcoves where teachers can't really see. The noise in here reaches epic levels of loud. Not to mention, all the different auras—nervous greenish-yellows, cheerful pinks, tired greys—swirl and dance until nausea rolls through my guts.

Urrrrgggg…

"Syl!" I hear a high-pitched, girly squeal and turn to see Lennon hurrying my way with her books clutched to her chest.

She's adorable as ever, wearing a cute white sweater with three pink skulls on the shoulder. Her long black hair is pin-straight and shiny, and she's smiling, her dark eyes sparkling. She's pulled off her hot-pink cat-ear headphones, and the sound of K-pop blares out. How the girl hasn't already gone deaf I'll never know.

It's nice to see her. I've missed her.

"Lennon!"

She hugs me tight, all flushed and filled with first-day excitement, her aura as bubbly bright pink as her headphones. "Hi!" She's breathless as she steps back, and there's this awkward moment where she looks at Euphoria like, *Do we hug?*

Euphoria shakes her head slightly. I'm the only one who can hug her. My Winter girl is tough on the outside, but for me, she's a big softie.

Well, normally. You know…when we can touch.

"Did you have a good summer?" Lennon's back to being shy, clutching her books.

I haven't really seen her much. She used to hang with Fiann, but she got tired of Fiann's catty attitude. Since then, we've sorta patched things up. Sometimes it's hard to believe that me, Lennon, and Fiann were besties.

After the train crash, Fiann just got meaner and meaner. Until she met Agravaine.

Then she went all prom-queen, dark-Fae crazy.

Earth to Syl. She asked about your summer, dummy.

"It was good," I say, but there are practically storm clouds forming over my head. I miss my old life, my normal life, even though I wouldn't trade Euphoria and me for anything. Still, there are nights when I wake up in a sweat, the image of Fiann sawing away at E's violin, her fingers bleeding and raw haunting me.

And there was that crazy *Lord of the Rings* dream I had this morning.

I can still feel my heart tugging me toward those shining towers...

"So what classes do we all have?" Euphoria seems friendly enough, but I hear the strain in her voice. She'd rather be on fire than be here.

Can't say as I blame her. A dark Fae going to high school is like a tiger joining a kitten parade.

"Lemme check." Lennon pops out her smartphone. Euphoria looks over her shoulder.

My girl's trying so hard. For me.

I nudge her arm as I dig out my own schedule. Wiping away the satay sauce from my break at Elephant Thai, I compare it to Lenn's. "Looks like first period's Astronomy with Miss Mack." Miss Mack's a drill sergeant. "Advanced Art with Ms. VB." Miss VB is a total cinnamon roll. "And... Wait, I didn't sign up for library studies with..." The name jumps out at me from the paper.

Miss Jessamine Jardin.

My Spidey sense tingles. Miss Jardin saved my butt last year. Big-time. Fiann stabbed me with a Moribund blade, and Miss J cast a powerful Glamoury to hold back the infection so I could get to the Winter Formal and throw down with Agravaine. I'm one thousand percent sure Miss J's *something* Fae, but she's not exactly chatty about it.

And…the world was pretty much ending, so let's just say, I was a wee bit busy.

She's up to something.

But is Miss Jardin with us or against us?

Euphoria gives me her patented suspicious side-eye. I mouth, *Later*, over Lennon's head.

"Syl!" In a flash of olive skin and mermaid blue-green hair, I'm enveloped in a crushing hug from behind.

"Pru!"

Prudence crushes me a little more before letting go. "Hey there." She hip-checks me, probably to remind me of that time Fiann called her "troll hips." I smirk, because Pru totally got the better of Fiann by unplugging her mic during a pep rally.

Let's just say that Fiann's freak-out was epic.

"What's new and amazing?" Pru sweeps her mermaid hair out of her face, looking Euphoria and me up and down. I totally see the *ohhhhhh* come over her face. "It's about time," she deadpans, and I swat at her. "Hey, it's true. You had it bad. Soooo bad."

"Pru, shut up!" But I'm laughing because Euphoria, my super-cool girl, is going pink to the tips of her ears. Lennon and Pru break into laughter, too, and I nudge Euphoria, letting her know it's all in good fun and teasing.

After all, E's boss at tease-flirting.

We're just coming down from our laugh-fest when a group of guys our age blow in from the side door.

"Look out!" someone calls, but it's too late. One of the bigger guys slams right into me and Euphoria, knocking us apart. She catches herself. Me? I'm not so lucky.

Euphoria reaches for me as fast as she can—she has to hide her dark Fae strength and speed—but the lead guy, a tall blond with pale golden eyes, catches me. His hand is warm, calloused but still soft. And when he touches me, I get a flash of this morning's dream—white towers, birch groves, wildflowers, the sound of haunting silver pipes.

For a second, I'm dumbstruck, almost *faestruck*, and then I shake it off.

He's looking into my eyes. "Well, hello there, beautiful."

The words are super-lame, but somehow, he's like...suave, so he makes it work. He's also casually handsome in that way some guys are—all messy hair and easy grin, tall and athletic.

"Hi?" I try, stepping back. I don't want him getting the wrong idea, and I hate having to out myself to reject a guy.

Been there, done that. No, thanks.

"I'm sorry about that." His eyes sparkle, and when he smiles, he has one dimple in his cheek, because of course he does. There's a brightness around him so painfully blaring it's like looking at the sun—all you come away with is a headache and black spots on your vision.

Even my Fae-sight is blinded.

He steps back into my personal space, and haunting, silvery pipes echo in my mind. Warmth washes over me like a sudden flood of sunlight.

What is happening?

"Are you all right, Miss..." He fishes for my name and my hand.

Euphoria's watching us, all storm and broody fury for this guy. I want to tell her to relax. Dude's handsome, but...nope. So not into guys.

Plus, no one compares to her. Not even close.

But by the way Golden Guy is rubbing the back of my hand, one thing's crystal clear: he is not getting the message.

I jerk my hand away. "That chafes, you know."

His smile hitches a bit like that was not what he was expecting, but then he pours on the charm. "I'm very sorry." He presses for my name again. "Miss..."

"You should watch where you're going." Euphoria steps in as he tries to take my hand again. "And no means no, buddy-boy."

Uh-oh. When Euphoria calls a guy "buddy-boy," I know crap's about to go down. Like him. Onto the floor. Crying like a toddler.

He straightens, that bright smile going dark like thunderclouds rolling in over a summer's day. His eyes flash from a warm to fiery gold.

Whoa… Suddenly, I feel the power radiating off him.

Holy crow, he's Fae.

And judging from the sunny brightness around him…? It hits me like a punch to the guts.

He's fair Fae.

Panic and excitement, dread and angst swirl in my stomach, making me feel like I'm going to hurl. Sweat breaks over my skin, clammy and gross. My heart is pounding, my mouth is dry. I've been waiting so long to meet one of my people, and one just *shows up*? At my school?

Chill out, Syl. You're jumping to conclusions. Maybe he's not fair Fae.

Next to me, Euphoria clenches her fists so tight her knuckles crack. Beneath her Glamoury, her sapphire-blue eyes glow, the golden rings around her irises molten and super intense.

Oh, he's fair Fae, all right.

But how? All the fair Fae went into hiding after they poisoned the dark Fae hearthstone.

Euphoria takes a step toward him, shattering my internal Q & A. *Okay, Syl, less wondering, more making sure your girlfriend doesn't kill this guy.*

But Golden Guy's just standing there, completely unafraid and super-smug, like he's taunting Euphoria without even saying a word.

I feel the tension rolling off her in waves.

They're darkness and sunlight, warring it out in the middle of a high school hallway. I try my Fae-sight again. My vision goes double for a sec, but I still can't read his aura. It's too bright, too painful, like sun stabbing into my head, leaving me with dark spots on my vision.

I stagger back a bit, putting my hand to my temples.

Euphoria steadies me, her gaze never leaving him. Wow, she is having a serious glare-fest with Golden Guy. She straightens to her full height and bares her fangs at him in a silent threat.

Finally, he steps back. That easy smile returns, and he's all warm and golden again. "Perhaps I'll ask your name later," he says like we're at a fancy ball or something, and then he moves off to join his dude friends.

Of course he hangs out with the jerky jocks. They slap him on the back, looking my way with sly gazes. It takes about two seconds before a few of the popular girls drift over to his group, playing coy and hard-to-get.

The haunting silver pipes get even louder, and I watch as the girls' auras turn from pale-pink coy to a sicky-sweet pinkish purple. *What in the—?* In two seconds, they drop the too-cool-for-school act and laugh and fawn over him while the other guys look on jealously.

Whoa, they're faestruck!

Who is this guy? He can't be your garden-variety fair Fae, that's for sure. Mass-Glamouring a bunch of people is definitely a pulling-out-the-big-guns power.

And yeah, dude is not shy about using his gramarye. But what is it? Emotion control? Love? Super-flirtation powers? All of the above?

I pull E off to the side. "I think he's..." My voice cracks on a whisper. "Fair Fae."

She meets my gaze, and what I see there rocks me a little. My girl looks like she's in pain. Almost the same way she looks when she feels the Ouroboros spawning.

"E?" Now *I* want to crack some heads. No one hurts my girl.

I glance at Golden Guy, but he's just watching me. I turn my back to him and concentrate on Euphoria. "Did he do something? Glamoury you? He's got some woojy-woo going on. I can't see it, but I can feel it."

She opens her mouth like she's going to answer, but Lennon gasps loudly. "You might want to... Um, Syl."

"Holy cow on a cracker," Prudence deadpans, and it's now I realize that the crazy loudness of the atrium's fading down to a rumble, then a whisper, then nothing.

Dead silence.

I turn like everyone else and look.

My heart drops out of my chest.

Blonde hair, pretty, a cold smile on her lips, that crazed light in her green eyes.

Fiann.

She's back.

CHAPTER EIGHT
ROUEN

Darling, I will fight for you
I will stand by your side
Your one and only
- "One and Only," Euphoria

Fiann.

The most popular girl in school, the teen Queen of Mean who made my girl's life a living hell last year. Fiann lied about saving Syl after the train crash (it was my girl who saved *her*) and tried to pretend *she* was the sleeper-princess. She bullied Syl all last year. She even wanted to take my place as the dark Fae princess.

Worse, she wanted to be queen.

In a lot of ways, Fiann was even more of a villain than Agravaine.

And now here she is, standing in the atrium of Richmond E, sucking up all the attention as the popular girls swoon and simper. They flock like ducklings around her, telling her how brave she is and how they're just so, so happy to have her back.

Gross.

Fiann laughs, flips her perfect blonde ponytail. She catches my eye and looks me up and down in a way that makes my skin feel too tight. Then she winks.

Tearing her head off right here would probably be bad, so I give her my patented dark Fae glare, flashing a bit of fang so she gets my meaning. *Bring it, Fiann Fee.*

I'm not afraid of her. That high school mean-girling might make my sweet Summer girl feel bad, but me? I'm a dark Fae princess.

We don't feel bad. We *are* bad.

And if Fiann thinks for one second she's going to make Syl's life a living hell again this year, she'll find out just how bad.

Syl edges closer to me as Fiann's friends rally around her, hugging her, making a spectacle of her. Because that's what Fiann always wants—to be a spectacle. The center of attention, no matter what it takes to get there. Her mean-girl posse *oohs* and *ahhs* over her. No one asks where she's been, although everyone knows.

At least, they know the lie. Rehab.

I snort. I guess it fits her image—Fiann Fee, rich, entitled girl who got in too deep with drugs. *Oh, poor her* and all that. The truth is, she was so ravaged by the Moribund her body practically shut down, dehydrated and malnourished. Her mind came unhinged. A screen door banging around in a windstorm.

That's what happens when mortals truck with the Fae.

"Hi-hi!" Fiann waves at us over the heads of her posse.

Lennon halfheartedly waves back, but Syl just sighs, and me? I keep right on glaring. *Make your move, Queen of Mean.*

But Fiann only goes back to being the center of attention. She still looks crazy around the edges, but she's always been super-good at smearing sugary civility over her nastiness. Her own personal Glamoury, if mortals could use Glamouries.

Just to be sure, I take a deep whiff, dowsing for dark Fae power.

Lime and bergamot assault my nose from her designer perfume, and beneath that, sandalwood from her bodywash and lotion.

Beneath *that*, a hint of asphalt and burning rubber.

Agravaine.

My body tenses up. I'm starting to rethink the whole soul-bound theory. Soul-bound rarely survive the deaths of their partners. Fiann looks healthy as a horse, except for that crazed light in her green eyes. Not to mention, she never loved Agravaine.

But that didn't keep him from leaving a smidgen of his power within her.

A dark circuit glinting.

I glance at Syl, standing there, watching her Fiann-free year go up in smoke. She sees it too, as if Fiann's lit up inside with sinister electricity.

Here we go again...

"Come on." Gently, I steer Syl away.

Fiann's giggle is claws on a chalkboard. "Awww, Syl, leaving so soon?"

"Yup," Syl responds easily. "Something smells rotten in here." She turns on her heel, and I fall in behind her like a sworn shield in medieval times.

Fiann calls after us, her threat obvious. "See you later, Syl."

Oh hells no. My girl is not going through another year of Fiann's bullying. I pin Fiann with a warning glare. "Don't even think it."

She put on a wide-eyed, innocent look. Translation: *Oh, Rouen, whatever do you mean?*

I dial my glare up to a thousand. Translation: *I will cut you.*

Fiann drops her gaze, and I follow Syl down the hall. Lennon and I flank her like we're Secret Service agents. Which is hilarious because Lennon's a good foot shorter than me and about as menacing as Hello Kitty.

I'm on high alert, all my senses hyperaware.

Instantly, I feel a glare boring its way between my shoulder blades.

"Syl!" Golden Guy comes running up from behind us. The stink of dandelions and elderflowers follows him in a cloud, like when one of the jocks goes too heavy on the Axe body spray.

My girl turns. "Uh...hi?" She shifts from one foot to the other.

"May I walk you to your class?" He offers his arm, his eyes glowing that molten gold. He's handsome and athletic, every girl's dream.

Every girl, that is, except Syl, apparently.

She steps back, shaking her head. "No, thanks." She's trying to be polite, but he's having none of it.

"Aw, come on…"

"Look, pal." I step in, my finger finding the center of his chest. "I get that chivalry's not dead, but it's going to take a serious beating if you don't stop."

"Really?" He squares up to me. His eyes go stony, and I feel the power radiating off him in waves of Summer heat. He's a fair Fae, all right. A summer-loving, dandelion-wine guzzling, Glamoury-ridden fair Fae. Maybe even a prince.

I'd be crazy to think he isn't dangerous.

Still, I don't back down. "Yes, really."

He stares a moment longer, then eases back, lounging against a locker. "Okay, then. See you later, Syl."

The threat is every bit as real as Fiann's, even though it comes with Legolas good looks. Everyone knows the dark Fae are terrifying, cold and austere as ice statues, merciless. But the fair Fae are just as terrible, with their Summer blood given to fits of passion and extreme temper.

And…he's the first fair Fae Syl's ever seen.

All my fears of her people coming to take her away rear up, torrid and angsty, in my mind. I want to sweep her up and carry her off, to protect her from the inevitable war between our peoples.

Do it. Do it now, my dark self urges.

But I can't. I won't.

I love her, and love means trusting her. Maybe even letting her go.

My heart aches. It takes all my willpower, but I nudge her toward Golden Guy. "You can go talk to him. If you want."

Syl studies him with her storm-grey eyes then shakes her head so her red curls bob. "Not now. Not here." She turns away, and her bright smile is for me once more. "Besides, Astronomy's right after homeroom, and I don't want to be late. We're studying sun flares this year."

"Fine by me." And speaking of studying…

I study Mr Flirty again, surrounded by girls, his golden gaze fixed on *my* girl. Something cold and dark slithers beneath all that sunlight and brightness. It's subtle, but it's there. He notices me noticing, but I don't care.

I see you, buddy-boy.

And I feel the gauntlet thrown down between us. Good. I hate long waits.

Syl pulls me around the corner to her classroom. "Looks like this is where we part ways. Have fun in baaaaand." She rolls her eyes, teasing me in that tone that sends heat racing through my cold heart. "Like that's even a real class."

Looking at her, I remember last year when we couldn't be apart longer than an hour without risking the Grimmacle breaking. It was those crazy times that brought us together, that had us falling in love. It wasn't the easiest or best of times, but what came of it—me and her—is magic.

I chuckle and tease her right back. "Okay, Spock. Try not to release any Tribbles in astronomy class."

She straightens, gets Vulcan-serious. "Live long and prosper."

"Oh, I intend to." I lean down to kiss her cheek, ignoring the *woo-woos* from the other kids already in the classroom. I mean, seriously? Jealous much?

I linger to watch her and then head to the band room. With every step, I feel my mother's ring in my pocket like a lodestone wanting to drag me back to Syl.

Now is seriously not the right moment. A fair Fae wearing a dark Fae's ring... It would only brand Syl a traitor to her people.

And Golden Guy's appearance isn't just coincidence. He's got some kind of secret agenda.

Another mystery we'll have to solve.

I head into the band room. No one's here. Damn weird, because I swear I passed at least two dozen kids carrying instrument cases in the halls. Seems our YouTube vid from last year's Homecoming went viral. Now everyone wants in band.

Not to mention the Battle of the Bands this year.

So, where is everyone? I was at least expecting Nazira to be here, frowning beneath her hijab as she makes her cello sing, her bow-work precise as clockwork.

But nope. No one. It's all crickets up in here.

I sit down at the bench and unzip my violin case. The shiny, glasslike surface of my instrument gleams up at me. I love my violin. I'm glad to have it back. Taking it out, I run the sleeve of my hoodie over it. Fiann used it. Who knows where she's been?

A soft footstep echoes in the doorway, and a shadow falls on me.

A wave of amber and asphalt hits me. *Speak of the she-devil.*

Designer heels *clack-clack* on the floor as she walks right up and stands in front of me. Like I'm going to drop everything and attend Her Majesty. Ha! She's hilarious. Her six-hundred-dollar Louboutins tap the ground, showcasing her impatience.

Now I know why there's no one else in here. *She wanted to get me alone.* She's been creepily after me since last year. Gah! Girl cannot take no for an answer.

I have to count to three in my head to avoid strangling the crap out of her. "What do you want, Fiann?"

"Just to talk."

She's trying to be sincere, but everything she says is tainted by the past—the fact that she tried to kill Syl, that she helped Agravaine, attacked Syl's mom, that she stole my gramarye and used it against me, against the entire student body. Fiann did a million terrible things. And now she wants to...*talk*?

Yeah, right. I give her what Syl calls the stink-eye.

Fiann doesn't back down, though, because girls like her never do.

"My parents made me take lessons as a kid," she says, toying with my bow. I resist the urge to slap her hand away. "I hated it. But I was pretty good."

"I'm sure." I busy myself adjusting pegs. Fiann's very presence makes my violin go out of tune the way milk curdles when there's a bad spirit nearby.

I look at her, all perfect on the outside and rotten on the inside. She's a bad spirit, all right.

"Your hand." She gestures with my bow. "It looks…better."

I flex it. Skin, muscle, bone—it's still sensitive from where Syl purified the Moribund. I remember being seized, strapped down, watching those black circuits crawling up my arm like mechanical spiders. Agravaine made it infect only my hand. He wanted me to feel the rest of my body—so I knew what else I stood to lose.

If not for Syl, the Moribund would have eventually taken me over, turned me into dark, soulless machinery.

"But you're not really healed." Fiann sits down, her perfect high pony bouncing. "You're still a sluagh."

Sluagh. Outcast from my people, dead to them. The word hits me with the force of a troll's hammer. "How did you—?"

"Aggy told me."

Aggy? By the Harrowing, Agravaine would be rolling over in his grave. If he had one.

"He told me a lot about you." She waves my bow like a wand, and I wish any of the band kids would come along, or better yet, a teacher. But Fiann's the principal's daughter. She's clearly pulled strings to get me alone.

"Good for him." I give her my patented dark Fae glare. "My bow." I hold out my hand.

She yanks it out of reach like a ten-year-old playing keep-away at recess.

Fine. I'm not letting her hold me hostage. "We're done talking." I stand up, but she grabs my arm.

I look down at that hand and then back at her. I bare my fangs.

Fiann's one of the Wakeful, those rare humans who can see through a Glamoury. She sees my fangs, all right, and jerks her hand away. "He also told me that you could go back to being a noble dark Fae, a princess. For real." She looks at her nails. "Not for show."

My lips twist wryly. "What's your game, Fiann?"

She smiles that smile that entitled people often get when they think they've got the upper hand. She even knows I could tear her head off and use it as a piñata.

The stupid. It burns.

"You need the blood of a fair Fae to return to your true self." She gets up and paces like a teacher making an important point. "But not the blood of just any old fair Fae." She pins me with those cruel green eyes. "A princess. Like you."

She's right. Blood calls to blood.

I've known it since the moment I laid eyes on Syl and never once allowed myself to think it. Until now. My dark self knows… Fiann is right.

Even if I do save my people, nothing can change the fact that I'm sluagh. I can never be a true princess again.

Not without Syl's blood. The thought sickens me.

"Screw you." But whether I say that to Fiann or to the darkness inside me, I don't really know. I yank my bow from her grip.

"There's another way."

That stops me cold. I don't want to ask, but… "What other way?"

"You could rule with me." Her green eyes light up with malicious glee.

"What?"

"You heard me." She sidles closer, runs her fingertips down my arm. "I'll be Queen of the dark Fae, and you can be my queen-consort."

What the what? "You really are crazy, you know that?" I jerk away from her and start gathering up my things.

She pouts, looking like a spoiled child about to stomp her foot. "Agravaine promised me I'd be queen."

"Yeah, well, Agravaine lied. There's never been a dark Fae queen." It's against the fádo, our most ancient and revered traditions. *Only a king can rule.*

But what if…what if I could change that? Become more than a princess?

What if I could become queen?

Fiann leans in. I feel the heat of her body. "Are you sure? As queen, you could show your people another way, a way that doesn't mean war between dark Fae and the fair Fae."

An end to the killing and hatred? I'd do anything for to make that a reality. And she knows it. Damn her.

I straighten to my full height like a bridge between the earth and sky. Time to go on the offensive. "You were at Hollywood Cemetery last night."

That shocks her. I see the truth flash on her face before she schools her expression. Her chest rises and falls with the deep breaths she's taking. Gotta give it to her. She's really mastered Anger Management 101. "You're changing the subject."

"What were you doing there?" I already have a good idea. She was looking for the Ouroboros, too. But not to destroy it. Oh, no.

She wanted to use it. She's gathering power.

Simpering, Fiann smooths her skirt. "You should rethink my offer, Rouen. After all…" She smirks. "Where has playing by their rules gotten you, hm? You're a sluagh, outcast and alone. Maybe you should start making up your own rules."

I stare at her. It's like seeing a spider in your shower. Nothing good can come of it. I should squash her right here. But I'm not a killer.

Not anymore. And I don't believe in violence for the sake of violence.

But I do believe the best defense is a good offense. "Agravaine left them for you, didn't he? The Ouroboros."

Again, Fiann's face registers shock.

That would be a yes, then.

"Rouen…" Her green eyes are deadly bright. Ugh, here comes the wheedling. "The Ouroboros will make us powerful, and then you and I can rule as queens. Together."

"And you think that's what Agravaine wanted?"

"He promised me!" She tilts her head, her look calculating. "And dark Fae keep their promises, don't they?"

I sigh heavily. With all her lies, does she not understand how easy it is to twist words, to keep a promise while simultaneously screwing someone over? "Agravaine was a dark Circuit Fae. He cared only about power. And power always comes with a price." I walk to the door. "Stay away from me."

Her parting shot chases me. "You'll regret it, Rouen Rivoche! Agravaine promised me I'll be queen, and I will. And you—you'll serve me, on your feet or on your knees. I will be Queen of the dark Fae!"

I ignore her and walk away.

Because if anyone's going to be queen, it's going to be me.

CHAPTER NINE
SYL

Just because one is fair
Does not mean one is good
- Glamma's Grimm

Day one of my junior year, and already Fiann's throwing a monkey wrench into the works. After her bid to give the world a dark Fae makeover, I was so looking forward to a Fiann-less year. I mean, I sympathize with how hard it must've been to be in the hospital, locked in and kept from the rest of the world.

But she's out now. With a vengeance.

Aaaaand she's got a sliver of Agravaine's power, a dark current rushing around her, buzzing in the air like a hive of angry bees.

But what does it all mean? Is Fiann infected with Moribund? Or does she somehow have power of her own?

By the end of third period gym, I've got my answer.

First off, I hate gym. Team sports are so not my thing, and I've never been any good at them anyway. When was the last time you saw a shy, introverted geek girl dive for a loose ball? Second, I hate being *in* the gym—it's a huge, cold, echoey reminder of last year's Winter Formal, when everything went arseways and beyont, as Glamma would say.

At least Euphoria's in my class.

She's all kinds of athletic, though she stays on the sidelines with me for geek solidarity. We slouch against a stack of blue mats, waiting for class to start. The gym echoes with the shouts of the other girls warming up. I'm one thousand percent aware of my too-big uniform polo and my too-short shorts. Fiann, though? She's prancing around the basketball court in her tiny shorts and Richmond Elite Spiders tank top like she's Queen of PE.

The mean-girl posse surrounds her—Maggie and Jazz, Becca, Dani dribbling a basketball because, ugh, of course today is basketball.

I swear, this is a slice of my own private hell.

I look up toward the track on the second floor. It sits above the court in a ring around the entire gym. I wish we could just be up there, running laps or stretching at the different stations.

But nooooo... Mr Ludwick is the PE teacher. He's also coach of the girls' varsity basketball team, and he's all about Dani since she's the captain. Ick.

"Looks like today's gonna be a banner day." Pru walks up and leans against the mats.

"Yup." I cross my arms and hop up and down to keep warm. How is it like fifty degrees in here when it's still eighty outside?

Euphoria's eyes never leave Fiann. My girl's working out something in that smarty brain of hers, but what? Note to self: ask her when this torture session is over.

The three of us watch as the whole class surrounds Fiann and her friends. Dani's running layups and taking fade-away shots. Showoff.

I pull at my shorts. Gah! I hate these stupid things. My legs are so white they're practically Day-Glo. Even if I tried to tan, I couldn't. Irish girls just burn and peel.

Euphoria, on the other hand, is hotness incarnate, the gym uniform fitting her snug in all the right places. Whoa... Okay, maybe gym's not *all* bad.

She catches me drooling over her curves, and that sexy smirk curls her lips. My cheeks burn.

At least I'm not cold anymore.

Pru nudges me teasingly. She doesn't look uncomfortable, though. Nope. She just owns her Spiders polo and shorty-shorts. "This blows."

"Yup."

Fiann waves at us, all saccharine sweet. "Hey, freaks and geeks!"

Euphoria only glares.

"I hate her," Pru deadpans.

"Yup." Apparently, I've become capable of only one-word answers.

Third period, and Fiann's already back to her old self—ruling the mean-girl princess posse with an iron pom-pom, snarking at the "freaks and geeks" who don't fit into whatever worldview comes with rich entitlement, Daddy-bought cars, and Spring Breaks in Paris.

"All right, ladies!" Mr Ludwick starts dividing up the teams. He does it mostly fairly, splitting up Fiann and her posse even though they totally try to run the show. He gives in a little, making Dani one captain and Fiann the other.

Ugh. I so hate gym class and all the mean-girl hazing that comes with it. I'm short and kind of a zero in the athletic department. Plus, I'm not popular. Pru, E, and me'll get picked last, for sure.

"Solidarity." Pru fist-bumps me. She's thinking the exact same thing. Euphoria nods. At least we've got each other's backs.

Fiann starts by picking Jazz, and Dani picks Sofie, a tall Asian girl who, rumor has it, can totally dunk.

With a smug smirk, Fiann calls out, "Rouen."

Don't think I miss the way she eyes my girl like E's a slab of fresh meat.

Pru rolls her eyes. "She's the worst."

"Yup." Gah! Another one-word answer. I may as well be a grunting Neanderthal. *Basketball bad. Fiann bad. Ook-ook, tookie-tookie.*

Dani picks Maggie, and then it's Fiann's turn again.

"Oh, Syyyyy!" Fiann calls out sweetly.

I try to pretend I don't hear.

"Skye!" Mr Ludwick barks, gesturing.

At least I get to be on Euphoria's team. I drag my butt over.

"Try not to suck," Fiann hisses, keeping that sweet smile on her face, and then she whispers to Dani, "Pick that Prudence chick last."

Dani laughs. "Yeah, no kidding. It's not a pie-eating contest."

My face heats with anger. Pru's no petite flower, but seriously? Who. Cares? *Fiann, apparently.* Yeah, she's back, and she hasn't changed one bit. Still the same old Queen of Mean.

Worse, she's up to something.

Picking me and Euphoria for her team? She's definitely scheming. An all-too-familiar sick feeling rolls around in my guts. Being bullied by her all last year, waiting for her and Agravaine to spring their rotten plan—that was hard enough.

Now it's happening again, and of course it has to do with the Ouroboros. Between classes, Euphoria filled me in on her little "talk" with Fiann in the band room. At first, I thought Fiann was trying to infect herself, but she's not that dumb. Not after last year when Agravaine infected the jocks with Moribund—and landed them all in the hospital. Not to mention her own experience with Euphoria's gramarye. Fiann's gotta know that all a Moribund infection gets you is drained.

Or worse where the Ouroboros is concerned—dead.

"All right. Prentiss, I guess." Fiann rolls her eyes.

Pru narrows her eyes—either at being picked last or being called by her last name, I'm not sure—but at least she's on our team. She comes over, cracking her knuckles, glaring at Dani like she's dead meat. Suddenly, I'm very glad I'm not Danette Silver.

Mr Ludwick tosses the ball for the tipoff.

Dani wins it, of course, and the other team takes off down the court. It's mildly terrifying how the mean-girl posse turns into a pack of girl-eating piranhas as soon as that ball is in play. Pru and I just shrug. E hangs back too, but Mr Ludwick starts yelling at us.

"Get in there, ladies!"

Okay, did I mention that my mom will officially kill me if I fail a class, even gym? Yeah, she will. So, I crank it up into a halfhearted jog. As I'm awkward-running down the court, I catch a flash of gold.

I turn, and I swear to all that's holy, I see Golden Guy standing there on the bleachers. They're all folded up, so the top is super high. It's only by chance that I see him, walking across that narrow ledge like Legolas walking on snow in LOTR.

What in the heck is he—"Oof!" I plow right into someone, and we do that dizzy two-step thing where we grab each other to avoid falling.

"Watch it, Skye!" Becca shoves me off. "Mr Ludwick, that's an offensive foul!"

Mr Ludwick looks at her. "It was an accident, Miss Buchanan. Let it go."

Becca gives me the stink-eye, but whatever. Her team's already scored. Ugh. I look back, and sure enough, Golden Guy is still there. No one else seems to notice that he seems to be watching yours truly.

Okay, so one of my people finally comes to the mortal realm and...the dude stalks me? Seriously, what is going on?

"Do you see that guy?" I ask Pru as we jog down to the other end. She looks around. "What guy?"

Crap. He's got a Glamoury up. Now I'm totally off my game because Golden Guy is clearly a powerful Fae and a stalker, and *he just keeps on staring.*

Dani scores a three-point shot as Pru and I are totally lollygagging down the court.

Fiann looks none too happy. She whips her high pony around and scolds us. "Come on! You guys are like a bunch of grandmas!"

Except, my Glamma could probably kick Fiann's sorry butt from here to Faerie and back.

I sidle up to Euphoria, whispering, "The Fae guy's back."

"On the bleachers. I know." She looks at me, not give anything away.

"What's he doing here?"

Her voice is tight. "Staring at you."

I meant *here*, as in the mortal realm, but clearly Euphoria's fixated on more immediate concerns, like some fair Fae dude creeping on her girl. It doesn't take a genius to know she's thinking of smacking his face off his face.

Fiann runs past, a sour look on her face. "Get your heads in the game, losers."

I snort, but she keeps right on fussy-facing.

"God, Rouen. I picked you because you're supposed to be this goth badass."

Euphoria just raises an eyebrow. "Goth badass?"

Our team gets the ball. I tip E a wink. "Come on, Your Gothiness."

She gives me a look that sets my blood on fire. I love flirty flirting with her. Forget Stalker Boy.

Even with all his sunshiny brightness, he doesn't hold a candle to my girl.

I'll talk to him eventually, when he stops acting like a creepy stalker. But for now...

Fiann passes the ball, but Maggie steals it, and the other team scores again. Fiann's freaking out, yelling at us. Our teammates all look super-glum. There's not much we can do, though. Dani's got the majority of basketball girls on her team.

In, like, two seconds, we're getting crushed. The score is 11-2, Euphoria's made our only basket, and there's only a few minutes left. Pru and I plod along. She makes a halfhearted attempt at stealing the ball and misses.

Fiann practically shrieks. "You stupid troll-hips!"

Pru gives her the stink-eye. "Careful, Fee. Remember the last time you called me that?"

I giggle 'cause, yeah, last time, Pru totally ruined Fiann's day. I can tell Fiann remembers too, because she makes that puckered-up, angry-girl face. When the ball comes to her, she hauls butt down the court.

Dani goes at her. *Here we go.* Fiann'll get the ball stripped from her in a second. Maybe then she'll stop telling us we're the losers. Dani lunges for her, and Fiann dodges.

Holy—She *dodges*. Euphoria and I are like, *Whoa*...as Fiann dribbles down the court, faking out every single girl from the b-ball team, and makes a crazy three-pointer. The ball swishes, nothing but net.

That is all sorts of wrong.

Fiann's a smirky cat that got the cream. "See, losers? That's how you do it."

Yeahhhh...that's how. With supernatural speed and agility. That sick feeling in my stomach gets a whole lot sicker. My mind immediately flashes to that last Ouroboros, the door to the mausoleum open...

She must've found a way to harness the Ouroboros. To use it.

Crappity, crap, crap, crap.

Euphoria nods at me. She's thinking the same thing. My Faesight confirms it—underneath Fiann's red anger and pink excitement, not to mention green envy and muddy purple dissatisfaction, runs that black current.

But what is it, exactly? An Ouroboros circuit?

I turn to E. "What just happened here?"

Euphoria studies Fiann. "She went all Teen Wolf."

"Seriously, you gotta stop watching cheesy 80's flicks."

She chuckles, deep and sexy. "What about your aura sight?"

I shake my head, red curls bobbing. "I can't tell exactly. She must have some kind of Glamoury going on."

"It'd have to be ridiculously powerful."

"Well, Fiann's got the ridiculous part down."

For some reason, I look to the bleachers. Golden Guy's sitting there, watching us intently. A lot of girls would be flattered at the attention. After all, being a stalker boy is totally cool as long as you're a vampire or werewolf...or a fair Fae.

"Come on, Skye, Rivoche!" Ludwick gets in our faces, cutting off our impromptu strategy session. "Hustle, hustle, hustle!"

Darn it all. Yeah, we hustle. Sort of.

The next play, Fiann passes to me. I'm all like, *No way will I show my powers*, until Dani checks Pru as she goes for my pass. Pru goes down hard. The ball bounces out of bounds. Everything stops dead, all the girls' auras tinged with yellow-orange panic and *it wasn't me.*

"Is she okay?" someone stage-whispers.

E and I rush over and help Pru up. Wincing, she gets to her feet, court rash bleeding down the side of her leg. She takes in a hissing breath that tells me she's hurt. Mr Ludwick is one of those "rub some dirt in it" coaches, though, and he tells us to play on.

"You should sit this one out," I tell her.

"Naw." Pru grits her teeth, her face pale beneath her olive complexion, and mutters something I'm sure is a curse word in Portuguese. "It's on now."

And it is.

Dani's team gets the ball, and she tosses it in bounds.

I put on a tiny burst of speed and steal it. Pru goes racing down the court like a house on fire. She checks Jazz, who tries to illegally grab her, and I chuck a pass down the way. Pru makes a textbook layup.

"In your face," I say to Dani.

She gets in my face, all right.

"You little dweeb." She towers over me.

Maybe it's the sleeper-princess in me, but really? Glamma said never back down to a bully, and so I don't.

"Something to say?" I ask her, deadly quiet. I square myself up to her, all five-foot-two of me to her five-eight.

She takes a step back, clearly freaked out by how calm I am. I stand like I've seen Euphoria do, straightening myself up like a bridge between the earth and sky.

Dani takes another half-step back. "I'm warning you, Skye…"

Mr Ludwick gets between us. "Break it up, ladies."

And then the bell rings.

Ludwick doesn't move. "Hit the showers."

"Whatever. My team still won. Losers." Dani looks like she's going to throw caution to the wind and push me, but then she spots Euphoria.

"Go ahead." E's voice drops an octave, her smile so cold it could freeze the sun.

Dani just *humphs* and stalks away.

All the girls start to file out. Out of the corner of my eye, I see Golden Guy jump down from the bleachers, silent as a cat. He slips through the door, giving me a wink before he goes.

I don't get it. Why is he creeping on me when he should be—I don't know—filling me in, announcing the return of my people, doing anything at all important?

Color me officially confused.

Fiann walks past me. She flips her high pony. "Aren't you glad we're on the same team?" She gears her comment toward Euphoria with more than a hint of a threat.

"Game's over," I tell her.

"Wrong," she says, those green eyes of hers glinting like knives. "The game's just starting." She fixes me with an evil glare, and then she laughs and flounces away.

I exchange a glance with E. I can tell we're on the same wavelength. Fiann's back, and she's got powers. And she won't be satisfied until she gets all the Ouroboros, no matter how many there are. But setting the Ouroboros free would only kill her, create harrow-stitches, destroy the city, and turn everything into total death and chaos.

She's smarter than that. I know she's got a grand scheme brewing in that blonde head of hers.

One thing's for sure: we have to figure out what scheme is, but really?

I know I'm not going to like the answer.

CHAPTER TEN
ROUEN

The Winter in my blood
Makes me stubborn
Makes me secretive
Old habits die hard
And mine are the oldest
- "Tradition," Euphoria

After the bell rings, I linger behind in the gym, drawn to the stage where Agravaine nearly killed me last year, where the ley lines converged in a circle to drain me of my life-force. When Syl and I broke his Grimmacle, the power backlashed, ripping through UnderHollow and shattering the hearthstone. I felt it like my own heart splitting open. The ley lines collapsed, taking the gateways and all the Snickleways to Dark Faerie with them, trapping my people.

If I don't get to them soon, Winter's Sleep will become permanent.

They'll slumber forever in the darkness.

Now I must find a way to heal the ley lines, open the Snickleways once more, and wake my people.

And then what?

They'll come for her, Rouen. It's inevitable.

"You coming, E?" Syl calls. She and Pru are by the door. Pru
looks pretty bad, angry red welts marring her leg from where Dani
shoved her to the floor. My girl looks on with concern. "I'm going
to walk Pru to the nurse."

"You go ahead." I deflect a little more for good measure.
"Besides, I've got second lunch today." Syl and Pru have first lunch
on Mondays, while mine is right smack in the middle of study hall.
We wouldn't be able to sit together anyway.

Syl shoots me a look like *why by all that's holy do you want to
hang out in a gym that smells like sweaty socks?* I give her my patented charming smile. I don't want to worry her. Because the plan
that's been forming in my mind all summer?

Yeah, it's some serious Bad Idea Theatre.

And today's the first day I can actually give it a shot. "Just want
to check something out," I say casually. I wish I could involve her,
but for a fair Fae, UnderHollow is deadly. If the brutal cold of winter doesn't kill her, then the deep wards cast by the arch-Eld will.

Syl can't survive in my winter barrens any more than I couldn't
survive in her summer wood.

I can't risk her. I won't.

"See you later?" She doesn't really buy my overly cool cool,
searching my face with those storm-grey eyes. Shivers play my
spine like a keyboard.

My girl turns me inside out.

I regret keeping my plan from her, but if this doesn't work,
there'll be nothing to tell. "Yes, later." I blow her a kiss, and she
giggles. Is it later yet?

Syl and Pru head out. I watch, a small pang of missing her
hooking in my guts.

Someday, I swear, we'll find a place where we can exist without
fear of our differences. A place where we can be together without
judgment. In Faerie, or in this realm.

Second bell rings, and the halls quiet down. The gym hushes, tomb-quiet except for my heavy boots *thud-thud-thudding* as I head over to the stage. There aren't any gym classes around lunch period. Admin probably doesn't want to risk kids hurling on their polished floors. I won't have to worry about being disturbed for at least a half hour.

It's just you and me, ley lines. Or whatever's left of you.

And thirty minutes is plenty of time.

Yeah, plenty of time to do something stupid, my inner grump snarks.

I brush it off. I've been thinking about this all summer—testing the Snickleways before trying to bring Syl along to heal the hearthstone.

It's the only way I'd ever risk her—if I knew it was safe.

I've come here more than once since the Winter Formal. Human locks and security measures don't mean much to a dark Fae. But even though I dowsed the area for ley line energy, with all the leftover Circuit Fae gramarye and backlashed Grimmacle magic, it was like trying to pick one radio frequency out of a wall of static.

I'm hoping today will be different. I can already sense that the ambient magic has faded. If there's any power left in the ley lines, I should be able to feel it.

I walk around the gym, remembering last year's Winter Formal. Here's where the prom council made an honor guard of icicle pillars. This is where the seats and tables were. Up there, on the stage, is where I was strapped to a fake ice castle like some bizarro figurehead, Agravaine casting his spell as moonlight shot down on me.

There are parts of that I don't remember.

All that pain… I kept fading in and out of consciousness. Once, I came to with Agravaine close to me, grinning his sharky grin. And then the agony in my chest—no, in my *heart*—stole my consciousness again. I remember him laughing as I blacked out, his voice following me down into darkness. *"In the end, you'll destroy everything."* Those words nag me late at night, gnawing at me.

Okay, Rouen, enough with the trip down bad memory lane. Back to work.

The ley lines…

Normally, dark Fae use them to travel, zipping through the Snickleways, across the Shroud, and safely into UnderHollow, but Agravaine ripped them off their natural course to forge his circle of magic.

Maybe the lines can be repaired…somehow.

In a single bound, I'm on the stage. My right hand prickles as I recall that night—Agravaine fueling the Moribund to infest my entire body, rewriting me as dark, hellish circuitry so he could blow the fuses inside me and consume me, body and soul, blood and spirit.

"In the end, you'll destroy everything."

Until Syl kicked the door in and saved the day.

Syl… She seems so fragile, so innocent, but she's a total badass. She doesn't even know it.

All right. Enough stalling, Roue.

I stop in the middle of the stage. Nothing about standing center stage should throw me off my game, but… My heart's pounding hard as a kick drum, my palms are sweaty, and my right hand aches as if remembering the pain, the anguish…

Clenching my hand into a fist, I squeeze until my knuckles crack. Above me, the ceiling's been patched where Agravaine had punched a makeshift skylight to let in the moon.

I'd like to punch him to the moon. Too bad he's dead.

Seriously, Roue. Enough stalling!

I close my eyes. It's time.

I sing a single note, pure and high. My gramarye flows out of me, licks of violet lightning leaping from my fingertips to the floor. They track the path of the ley lines, tracing the faded circle they made that night.

Faint blue lines and arcs glimmer and fade, glimmer and fade.

I push, trying to infuse the lines with my power, to strengthen them. The ley lines are there but so faint. They seem to retreat, drawing in, pulling the circle smaller.

If only I could activate them, forge them back to their original paths.

I only need one. Just one tiny Snickleway to travel so I can rouse Father and the arch-Eld from Winter's Sleep. They have powerful gramarye. Perhaps one of them could do something to heal the hearthstone.

We could rebuild the Winter Court. Start anew.

That's impossible, and you know it.

My father didn't trust me before. Why would he trust me now? I am still only a girl. Still a sluagh. *If only you'd trusted me, Father.* If only... I'm sure Syl and I could have found a solution. Is it too late?

I'll never stop trying. I'll never stop fighting. Neither will Syl.

I walk the circle, taking care not to step on the flickering lines. It took my blood to activate them a year ago. It will take no less to activate them now. If I'm lucky, the small amount of moon magic left will answer.

Blood calls to blood. Spilling mine should bridge the gap between the mortal realm and Dark Faerie. But last year, Agravaine's dark spell bolstered my power.

Is my blood powerful enough alone?

The blood of a sluagh, an outcast, dead to my people.

Only one way to find out. I draw my black-handled blade.

"I wouldn't do that if I were you."

I jolt like I've just been hit with a Taser.

Miss Jardin stands there, all prim and proper—pencil skirt and blazer, bright-colored top, her red hair pulled back into that severe bun, black chunky glasses perched on her nose.

She looks like the textbook hot librarian in every anime ever.

Okay, I haven't seen *every* anime, but I'm working on it.

"Wouldn't do what?" Her rose scent doesn't fool me. Beneath it, the burn-your-face-off hot and spicy smell makes my nose tingle, but Miss Jardin's just looking at me in that judgy teacher way of hers. I'm still not sure I can trust her. I mean, she did save Syl, but she also sent her into the Winter Formal to fight Agravaine and Fiann alone. Baptism by white fire.

I didn't approve then, and I don't approve now.

She nods her chin at my knife. "Try to activate the ley lines. You're smarter than that, right, Miss Rivoche?"

What am I supposed to do, say no? Sometimes teacher logic is infuriating.

She wrinkles her freckled nose. "Miss Skye would be upset if anything happened to you."

Okay, that is a seriously weird thing to say. I dial my glare up to full blast.

Translation: *I do what I want.*

She doesn't even bat an eyelash. "I'll just stand back."

"Or you could leave." I'm being rude, but whatever. This is off-the-charts weird.

"Or"—she ups the ante—"I could call your admin. I'm sure he'd be very interested in why you skipped study hall to hang out in the gym. Unsupervised."

Right. Check and mate. "Fine. Just don't get in my way." I stand back and cut the meaty part of my palm. Just a little nick—not like those gashes you see them do on those teen supernatural shows. I mean, really? Who just slices up their palm like that? You literally use your hand for everything.

Besides, I heal way faster than any mortal. A few droplets of blood hit the floor and the ley lines flash. Then the glowing blue races around the circle as though my blood is filling it up with blue fire.

Yes! The glows brightens. I'm filled with hope. And then, as fast as it came, the light starts to fade.

It's now or never. I've got to try to find an open Snickleway so I can push my way into UnderHollow. For my people.

I take a step toward the circle.

"I wouldn't do that, Miss Rivoche." Miss J's voice is calm as you please. We could be discussing fashion or the weather or her giving me a hundred detentions.

Whatever. Steeling my "I do what I want" confidence, I push with my gramarye and snickle-step through the Shroud. If all goes well, I'll end up in a Snickleway that's not too damaged and be able to squeak my way into UnderHollow despite the tangle of ley lines.

Fingers crossed…

The Shroud feels like a thick, oily membrane covered in sludge. I push, pouring more power into my snickle-step. The Shroud expands like a bubble, but it refuses to part. *Forget this.* I force myself in.

And…immediately regret it.

The gym fades away as I shove my way through the Shroud. Instantly, my guts drop out. I'm falling through dark, empty space, none of the passages strong enough to support me. And then I slam down, my body lodged awkwardly in a tiny, cramped space. Blackness surrounds me, sweaty, claustrophobic, creaking and groaning all around me.

Bloody bones! I thrash in the small space, unable to see, barely able to move. I can't get any purchase, my knees in my face, one arm wrenched above my head.

And my tiny bubble? It's getting smaller.

Hell and hue. Leave it to me to snickle-step right into a collapsing passage. *Should've listened to Miss Jardin.* I kind of hate her right now. Because of course she was right.

Duh, Roue. The librarian in all those urban fantasy shows is always right. I push with my legs, but the passage constricts more, falling in on me.

Tighter, smaller. Crushing me.

The passageway groans. It's not stones or rock that fall in on me. The Snickleways don't have floors or walls like a house. Instead, they're made of solid Faerie, an ever-changing, living, breathing labyrinth. At least, it should be living and breathing. This Snickleway is in its death throes—a dying creature whose organs are failing, veins collapsing, bones buckling, skin sagging…

And I'm trapped inside.

I push harder, straining with everything I have. A single note brings violet lightning, but the darkness swallows it, the passageway irising closed, squeezing me.

I'm going to be swallowed, crushed by the destruction of Dark Faerie. My hand goes to my pocket, and I touch the ring.

Syl…I am so sorry.

CHAPTER ELEVEN
SYL

The Moribund, an ancient, dark magic
Proximity to it can twist mind and body
Until the victim is nothing more
Than a Moribund zombie—a Circuit fiend
- Glamma's Grimm

Pru's going to be all right, and that's a total relief. The nurse cleans the court rash and puts some antiseptic on it. There's a huge bruise, too, so she orders Pru to stay off her feet and calls her mom to come get her. Pru'll be back in action tomorrow, but her injury is a reminder of my mortal life before I became fair Fae.

I tend to forget not everyone is as tough as me and Euphoria. For either of us, that rash would've healed within a matter of hours.

Being Fae has its perks.

After saying my good-byes to Pru, I snag the hall pass the nurse writes me and head out to my next class, Astronomy with Miss Mack. Most people can't stand Miss Mack because she's kind of a drill sergeant, but Astronomy is my fave class (after Advanced Art with Miss VB). We're learning about solar winds and the effects of other atmospheric events like lightning strikes. I'm twenty minutes late, and all classes are in session. I should be the only one out here.

Quiet footsteps behind me tell me different.

Warmth flows over my skin, like stepping out into the sunlight after being under a too-cold air-conditioner. The little hairs on the back of my neck prickle a warning. As much as that feeling is all warm and welcome, as much as it tugs at my heartstrings, promising me all the things I want—answer, acceptance, an end to wondering...

As much as I want to sink into all things fair Fae like a warm, soothing bubble bath, I can't.

There's something not quite right about Golden Guy.

"Syl." His voice is smooth as honey, and I feel him wanting to reach out and touch my shoulder. There's something possessive about that gesture, something that curdles like month-old milk in my stomach.

I whip around and step back. "What?" My voice comes out a little cold, but seriously? Dude has been stalking me, and I'm not one of those girls that finds that cute or romantic or whatever. Consent is very much a thing for Syl Skye, sleeper-princess of the fair Fae.

Euphoria would never invade my space this way.

He's standing there, studying me, those eyes warm as a buttery-yellow sun. He's so golden and perfect, I swear, he looks Photoshopped. And I still can't get a bead on him with my Fae-sight. Looking at him for too long leaves me with dark spots and halos. Not to mention a throbbing ache behind my right eye.

His look gets all glowy and intense. "I wanted to warn you."

Ruh-roh. There's something about his words, some kind of double meaning. Glamma always said the Fae were super-good at twisting words. I give him the side-eye. "About what?"

He leans against the lockers, a bright beacon even in the sunlit hallway. He looks for all the world like one of those old paintings of a saint, a halo around his head.

Too perfect, too radiant.

Black spots riot across my Fae-sight, and I shake it away to look at him as a mortal would. Instantly, my headache fades. I breathe a sigh of relief.

He chuckles softly, as if he knows the effect he has on my powers. I'll bet he does. Everything about him is scheming and oppressive, the way height-of-summer heat seems nice at first, but the longer you stay out in it, the more you realize you're getting burned.

I remember Glamma's words whenever she would speak of the Fae, *"Just because something is fair does not mean it is just and good."*

That fits Golden Guy to a T.

He makes a show of examining his flawless manicure. "You might find the ladies' room of interest." He flicks his gaze to the door at the end of the hall by the stairwell.

"Really?" I give him the raised eyebrow, a pretty good impression of Euphoria, if I do say so myself.

His lip curls like he tastes something sour. "Go look for yourself." He shrugs one shoulder. "Or don't."

Okay, I'm officially tired of his games. I put my hands on my hips. "What's next? Are you going to yell, *Behind you!* and then stick a Kick Me sign on my back?" Seriously, talking to this guy is like dealing with a ten-year-old.

He snorts. "Hardly." His gaze goes back to the door. "But you should check it out. That is, if you care about your fellow students." He pushes off the lockers and walks away, stuffing his hands in his pockets and whistling.

It's the same song the silvery pipes played in Fair Faerie.

It holds me for a sec, images of those wildflower fields and white birch groves, the emerald-green grass, the gold and ivory castle with its gleaming turrets—

Whoa! I yank myself from my trance. That's the second time I was almost faestruck.

What in the—?

He's up to something, for sure. Is the ladies' room somehow connected? I've got a hall pass, so there's no harm in just looking, right? I wait until he goes out the door and up the stairs. I don't want him knowing I take any part of what he says seriously. Then I stealth over to the door.

What are you doing, Syl? This isn't a spy movie.

But everything about what I'm doing feels super cloak-and-dagger. I reach out to push the door open. My hand's all trembly.

Get a grip.

Taking a deep breath, I push. The door gives way silently, and I step into the ladies' room. The acidic stink of antiseptic and bleach hits me. The custodian must've just been in here or something. The place is empty, the bank of kelly-green stalls sitting there all innocent, a few doors swung open…

A quiet sniffle from the far corner snatches my attention. There's a little alcove there, in the space between the stalls and the wall, where girls sometimes hang out and smoke. Another sniffle, followed by whimpering and scraping, like someone scuffing their shoes on the floor.

The sound is faint and…horror-movie sinister.

My throat goes dry, and then I scold myself. *For real, Syl? It's probably just some girl crying over her crush. Relax. Besides, you're a badass sleeper-princess. You got this.*

I straighten up and walk to the alcove.

My heart nearly punches its way out of my chest.

Sofie, one of Dani's basketball buddies, is lying there on the floor, her backpack fallen open, books, gel pens, and makeup scattered all over the floor. Her cell's broken on the tiles, the screen black. But that's not the worst of it.

Not by a long shot.

A gross black shadow is slowly eating up her arm like the necrotic tissue Miss Mack showed us in Bio last year. There are two things that immediately set off all my warning bells: one, it's definitely some kind of dark Circuit Fae woojy-woo, and Sofie can see it; and two, she's got an X-Acto blade from art class.

Okay, so that's three things. But who's counting?

She presses the blade to her skin and a red line appears. "No," she whimpers. "No, no, no, no…"

Holy—! My shoes squeak on the floor, and Sofie looks up.

She scrambles to her feet, her eyes eating up her face they're so wide. "Help me." She backs up against the wall, pressing the X-Acto harder. A small trickle of blood rolls down her arm. "Get it off." Her voice gets all creepy high-pitched. "Get it off!"

Without thinking, I spring into action, snatch the blade from her hand, and drop it, kicking it away. "It's okay. Don't worry. I'm here." The whole time I'm *there-there*-ing her, I'm checking out her arm. Is she infected? No. The icky-gross shadow isn't from a full-on Moribund infection. It's not black circuitry that's eating up her arm.

It's the ambient magic from an Ouroboros.

She's been in its proximity and more than once. It's started to drain her slowly, sucking out her life-force like a leech.

She's becoming a Circuit fiend.

And she can see it. *Great.* Sofie's one of those rare Wakeful people, like Fiann, who can sometimes see through a Glamoury. I'm super-relieved right now that sleeper-princesses look normal because yeah, if I looked like Euphoria—fangs, pointed ears, etc.—Sofie'd probably be running for the hills.

And she must've just become Wakeful since we all played basketball like an hour ago. I mean, she totally saw Euphoria and didn't freak, so…

"Help me, please!" Sofie's eyes are wide, tears ruining her makeup.

Head in the game, Syl. I shake off my stray thoughts and get my act together. All right. The only thing that can purify Moribund magic is my white flame. I've never used my magic in front of anyone but Euphoria.

Well, Fiann and Agravaine, but he's dead, and Fiann? She doesn't count.

I look back at Sofie. *You could Glamoury her, Syl.*

I could give it a shot. After I purify her. I've never tried that level of tricking a mortal's senses before, but… I look down at her arm. The shadow is growing. What choice do I have?

I can't let the Ouroboros drain her, hollow her out, turn her into a zombified Circuit fiend. My power should be okay. It shouldn't go wonky—not without Euphoria near, so…

"Hold still." I take her arm and run my fingers over it. The Ouroboros magic settles beneath the skin like ice in her veins. It crunches and writhes. It senses me and tries to pull deeper into her.

Nice try. I focus my power to my hands and light up. White flames plume from my fingers.

Sofie takes in a huge breath like she's going to scream.

"Don't!" I shush her. "Trust me."

She meets my gaze, and what she sees in my eyes must make her trust me because she doesn't scream and she doesn't pull away. She just slumps against the wall, resigned to whatever's going to happen.

My heart goes out to her, and I pour the white flame into her, across her skin and then deep into her arm. My sleeper-princess power flicks hungrily over her, eating up the Ouroboros taint, devouring it, purifying her.

It's over in a matter of a minute.

I let her go, and Sofie looks at her arm, turning it over and over, looking for the burn marks. There aren't any, of course. Her eyes are super-wide. "You... How did you do that?" She's breathless, her chest heaving as she nearly hyperventilates.

"My power is to purify the darkness," I tell her, knowing it sounds crazy, but I don't care. If there's an Ouroboros, I have to find out where. "Where did you see the ovo?"

"The...what?" She rubs her arm, the fear on her face turning instantly to distrust, wariness.

Crap. I only have a few moments to get answers and then Glamoury her before she tries to take off.

"The ovo, the egg..." I see she's still not getting it. "It'd be black and look part machine, part organic, all gooey and black. I know it's gross. I thought so, too, the first time I saw one."

Fear flashes red-orange through her aura. She backs up, but the wall stops her. "I...I haven't seen anything like that." Her eyes are wild now, and she's looking from me to the small gap between us and the stalls.

She's going to bolt, Syl.

And then I'll have real problems.

"I haven't seen anything, I swear. Please…" She begins to cry again. "Please let me go."

I saved her, and now she thinks I'm some kind of bad guy. That hits me hard, like a hammer to the forehead. *Is this how Euphoria feels?*

And it's so clear this girl didn't see the ovo. She doesn't know where the Ouroboros is. Heck, even me and Euphoria can't break the Ouroboros' Glamoury. How can someone who is barely Wakeful do it?

She sniffles. "Who are you anyway?"

"I'm Syl Skye, princess of the fair Fae." I meet her gaze, hold it, and summon my power. The temperature rises, and a summer breeze blows through the ladies' room. I pitch my voice low as I Glamoury her. "And you will forget about what I just did, my powers, our conversation, and that black shadow. You will go back to class and get like ten Band-Aids for your arm. You'll forget."

I sense she wants to believe all this anyway, to just forget about the black shadow, almost cutting herself, and the crazy girl who burned her arm but didn't burn it.

My sleeper-princess power leaps from me, a gentle push.

Her eyes dilate and go glassy. She repeats my words in a weird monotone, and then walks out of the bathroom. I hear her footsteps pick up into a run as she dashes back to class.

I blow out a deep breath. I have to tell Euphoria.

There's an Ouroboros inside the school.

CHAPTER TWELVE
ROUEN

Dark Fae, Unseelie, heed the call of your princess
Come forth from your slumber
In winter and darkness
- "Unseelie," Euphoria

All around me, the cramped, claustrophobic Snickleway buckles inward. The dark fabric of Faerie ripples over me, a cold second skin riddled with pinpricks of stars. In a rushing wave, the gravity of this place grows heavier, crushing down like an iron anvil on me, and then constricting, wrapping me up, trying to mash me into a tiny ball. My knees are in my face, my arms pinned to my sides. I can barely move, barely breathe. The darkling starts to twinkle, announcing my death…

My hand clenches around the ring that I wanted to give Syl.

I won't get the chance now.

Sudden fury sweeps through me, cold and wintry. *To hells and Harrowing with that.*

I might not be able to move, but I can use my voice. I take in a deep breath, ready to shear my way through the fabric of Faerie with violet lightning.

Wait.

If I call upon my gramarye, I could very well tear myself out. But if I rip the Shroud in the process...I could go spilling anywhere—UnderHollow, the mortal realm, even the Fair Fae realm of OverHill, where the scorching sun would blacken my bones.

I could leap from one death into another.

Not to mention, the damage to the Shroud would be irreparable. If Faerie ever bled into the mortal realm... Well, that would be a very bad thing indeed.

The pulsing darkness around me crumples inward. *Snap!* Pain shoots through my arm. My entire body jolts, a cold sweat breaking across my skin.

Do it. Do it now! I open my mouth, take in a breath. *Ancestors, guide me, protect me.*

A sudden furnacing heat lights up the darkness, blotting out the darkling stars. Smoke blasts me, stinging my eyes, steam singeing my skin.

Syl!

But no. This is not Syl's white flame. This flame is burning red and belching black smoke.

It's...hellish. And it smells...hot and spicy?

What in the unholy hells?

The velvety-black fabric of Faerie that's trapped my arms, my legs, glows yellow, then orange, then red-hot. In the next second, the temperature ramps up to sweltering, and the velvet darkness begins to *melt* like candle wax. Fighting for space, I scramble into a defensive crouch.

To say I'm regretting my decision to throw caution to the wind is a serious understatement.

A scorching wave of heat assails me. I throw my arms up to protect myself, but it only blasts around me, hollowing out the collapsing passageway like a hot knife coring an apple.

Someone is coming. And it most definitely is not Syl.

I stand, emptying my lungs for a deep breath in. If I have to defend myself here, in this fiery pocket of Faerie, so be it.

The sweltering darkness parts over a strange figure backlit in fire and smoke. A woman's silhouette.

The burning of her black spectacles imprints on the darkness. *Bloody bones. Miss Jardin?*

And then she...transforms, hunching down, skinning her human form and becoming a massive black horse with fiery eyes, flaming hooves, mane and tail streaking fire. A night-mare? But no... Night-mares don't help people.

But púca do. For a price.

If I'm a dark Fae princess, then Miss J is púca.

Mystery solved! But there's no time to celebrate because púca aren't exactly friendly.

The massive black horse paws the fabric of Faerie, sparks striking beneath sharp hooves. Fire blasts from her nostrils, her eyes a molten, fiery crimson.

As a guardian of the Snickleways, she's probably mad that I've been messing with them.

"Bring it on, púca!" And then I save my breath. When she gets closer, I'll strike.

In a burst of embers and fire, she comes galloping, burning away the darkness, burning the passageway open. The Snickleway shudders and melts around me, sloughing away in sheets now, trying to make my death shroud. I twist and sing a pure note, blasting it back with violet lightning.

Damn it all! She's on me before I can take my next breath.

A presence touches my mind. *"Having a bit of trouble, Miss Rivoche?"*

Crud. My mental shields have never been the best. "What do you want?"

She shakes her black-smoke mane, sparking embers. *"Get on."*

Oh, hells no. Riding a púca is beyond dangerous. Once on its back, you can't get off until it lets you. Púca have drowned people in lakes or bogs; they've taken them on wild rides across dimensional barriers, only to drop them in other realms.

They feed on their riders' fear until the rider dies or is aged beyond recognition.

In short, púca are dirty tricksters and not to be trusted.

"What choice do you have?" If night-mares could smile, she'd be grinning ear to ear.

The Snickleway shifts, threatening to pitch me into the darkling void.

All righty, then. I leap onto her glossy black back, the heat of her blasting me, smoke from her hooves choking. I barely have time to grip her smoggy mane before she surges forward through the collapsing Snickleway, burning it open as we plunge through…

Everything is smoke and fire, the stench of heat and spice tingling my nostrils. The Snickleway gives its last gasp, and like a tent with no poles, collapses into a suffocating shroud. Miss Jardin plunges on, hooves casting fire.

Darkness closes down around us, and then in a roar and rush, we burst into the gym, trailing smoke and fire. Miss J snorts and prances, flames licking in a circle she turns. *"Off you go."* She bucks, and I go flying.

I tumble out onto the gym floor, smoking, gasping, my lungs grateful for the cool gym air. But breathing is the least of my problems.

Miss Jardin whinnies, and it sounds suspiciously like a laugh.

Dirty púca! I stagger to my feet, ready to fight.

But Miss J just straightens up, skinning off her night-mare form. A moment later, she's human again, adjusting her glasses, calm as you please. The metal hinges glow red-hot and then fade, her eyes reflecting the hellish glow. "You can relax, Miss Rivoche."

"Relax? You funny." Because púca are greater Unseelie of the worst variety. Tricksters, grudge-holders, obsessed with a bizarre Fae etiquette that only they know the rules to.

It won't take me without a fight. I sing, and violet lightning crackles around my hands. "All right, Unseelie. Let's go."

Her soft laughter is not what I'm expecting. Púca are lowborn, Unseelie with no rank or renown. She should be quaking in her Jimmy Choos at the sight of a highborn dark Fae like me.

She's not, though. She's still laughing.

Fine. I rein in my temper. "What's so funny?"

"I have no wish to fight you, Miss Rivoche," she says in her *I am totally reasonable, pay no mind to all that hellfire* voice.

"A totally reasonable púca?" I give her the dark Fae princess glare. "Doubtful." Still, she did save my butt back there. I snuff out my violet lightning. For now. But I don't let down my guard. "What do you want? Why did you follow me?"

She wrinkles her nose, a gesture that makes her glasses slip down. She glares at me over them, flames in her eyes. "Rudeness will get you nowhere, Miss Rivoche."

I sigh. Right. Púca are sticklers for etiquette. They've been known to follow the most obscure rules to absurdity. A careless person caught at a púca tea party is sure to make a mistake and find herself dragged bloody on broken pottery or choked to death with macarons.

Still, I am a dark Fae princess. She wouldn't dare. Would she? *You're not exactly royalty anymore, Roue.* I clear my throat. "What brings an Unseelie of the Winter Court to the mortal realm?" And why would she stay? I have a million questions, but asking one at a time is the polite way.

She wastes no time correcting me. "Púca. My people don't prefer that name—Unseelie. So rude."

I clench my fists. "What brings a púca of the Winter Court to the mortal realm?"

She sniffs as though to see if her rose scent is hiding the spicy scent of what she truly is. "I suspect many of the lowborn Unseelie will escape to the mortal realm in the days to come."

In the days to come? The thought of Unseelie walking among mortals, Glamouried, gives me a chill. *She's trying to distract you, Roue.* Damn púca, always twisting words! I school my expression. "I didn't ask about them. I asked about you."

"I was not in UnderHollow. I was here." She readjusts her glasses. "I have been here for some time. Seventeen years."

Since Syl was born. But why? "You're here for Syl."

She levels me with that burning gaze. "Yes."

"Then why help me?"

"Because Miss Skye would be devastated if anything happened to you." She sighs and brushes the smoke off her skirt.

Okay, that raises some serious red flags. *Warning, warning...* "You almost got Syl killed last year. What do you want with her?"

"She wanted to save you. I helped her."

A chill runs down my spine, and not in a good way. Púca don't just do a thing for no reward. "And what did you ask in return?"

Miss Jardin's left eye twitches. Her voice comes tight and controlled. "Nothing."

Nothing? That is so very un-púca-like, it can only mean one thing. I take a step closer to her, studying her. "Are you...? No. You can't be."

A *pocket* púca? Oh, it sounds all innocent, but trust me, it's not. A pocket púca is still plenty dangerous. It's just bound to a certain place, a pocket dimension they can never leave.

At least, not until they fulfill their geis, a random number of rules set down by whoever defeated them in a battle of war or wits.

But that doesn't mean they're trustworthy.

With púca, there's always a loophole, a trick.

I press. "You are, aren't you?"

"I am a pocket púca, yes." Her left eye twitches even more.

Ha! Got her. "And your geis is to protect Syl."

"That's simplifying it, but yes, I am to protect Miss Skye. And by extension, you."

"But who...?" I have a million questions now. Who defeated her? Who forced her to make that vow to protect Syl? Who's crazy enough to challenge a púca to a battle of war or wits? And how—

"Hold on." I put a hand up. "If you're a pocket púca, then how can you move from here to the tenement?"

The bell rings for second lunch.

"You're late." Coolly, she adjusts her glasses again.

She's not going to answer that, and I have no way to make her. Fine. "How did you pull me out of the Snickleway?"

"I'm a pocket púca," she says simply. "I'm well versed in trans-dimensional physics and psycho- and physiomagical occurrences.

When the ley lines collapsed, they created innumerable pocket dimensions, all connected but untravelable."

"Great." I pace, ignoring the bell. "It sounds even worse than I'd originally thought."

"Maybe it is." She smiles, showing some very sharp teeth. "Should I tell you for nothing?"

"Well…" I push my luck. "Miss Skye would probably like it if you told me."

Her voice is mild, though her eyes flash molten crimson. "You needn't play games with me, Miss Rivoche. I'm on your side."

"Really?" I give her a suspicious look. Only a fool trusts a púca. They're crafty, always looking to twist your words round and break free.

She folds her hands in front of her. "For as long as you and Miss Skye are on the same side."

"And if we're ever not?"

Miss J smiles then. It's the sweetest, most sinister smile I've ever seen. And that's truly saying something. "Does that displease Your Highness? Only…" She reaches into her blazer and pulls out a red card. *Warning: detention, detention!* "You're not really noble any-more, are you?" She slaps the card into my hand, the dirty—

"As for healing the ley lines… Blood calls to blood, Miss Rivoche." She walks to the door. "Do make sure you get to study hall."

Then she's gone, leaving me cold. Blood calls to blood—*noble* blood.

But for me to become nobility once more, I have two choices: fight my father to the death or drain Syl's blood, her very life-force.

I can't—I won't—do either.

There must be another way.

What if there isn't, Roue? my inner grump whispers, sowing seeds of doubt.

Well, I'll burn that bridge when I come to it.

CHAPTER THIRTEEN
SYL

Poca púca, the Irish witches call them
Incredibly powerful
Despite the geisa that bind them
To their tiny, pocketlike dimension
- Glamma's Grimm

When a dark Fae bets you that their news is crazier than yours, don't take that bet. I know this, and yet, after school, I totally take the bait anyway.

"Ready?" I'm standing on one side of the kitchen. Euphoria's on the other, like some kind of Western standoff.

"Sure." Her smug smirk tells me she's going to win, but I'm a glass half full kind of girl, so I go for it anyway.

"On three. One…two…three!"

"There's an Ouroboros in the school."

"Miss Jardin is a pocket púca, geised to protect you."

Whoa, what? "Oooookay." I concede victory to Euphoria with a nod. "You first." I open the fridge, snag the packet of chicken thighs, then move to the stove to pull out the glass pan.

Euphoria grabs the chicken and a knife and goes to work. The blade flashes in the dim light as she cuts and fills me in on Miss Jardin, pocket púca, the ley lines, and her little trip into the collapsed Snickleways. She sighs heavily, finishing with, "Are you mad I didn't tell you?"

"No." I put down the spices I'm holding. Reaching out, I brush her fingers with mine then pull away before my power decides to go nuclear. "I don't blame you one bit for testing out ways to save your people."

"Yeah…" E's face goes all gloomy-broody, and she gets super-quiet. I silently vow to do whatever I can to help her and her people. But right now? At best, I have three percent of a plan.

Maybe less, since there's no actual way to get to UnderHollow.

"Now my news." I distract her with dinner prep and fill her in on Sofie and my theory that there's an Ouroboros in the school.

E whistles low, meeting my gaze with those serious sapphire-blue eyes. Try as we might, we've never been able to sense an Ouroboros before it started spawning. If there's one in the school, our best bet is to lay low and wait, then kill it with fire.

"One thing, though." I season the chicken after Euphoria lays it in the pan. The delicious smells of garlic and paprika make my mouth water. "Why did Agravaine hide them so well? I mean, wouldn't it make more sense for Fiann to be able to find them?"

Euphoria cleans off the knife and slips it back into the butcher block so super-easy it's kind of chilling. "Like everything with Agravaine, it's a game. A wild goose chase." She turns the oven on. "He liked nothing more than to torment people maliciously. Fiann's no different."

"So…" I put two and two together and come up with another year of me and E sneaking around the school, all cloak-and-dagger. "Looks like we've gotta keep Fiann in our sights."

Euphoria nods all solemn. "Agravaine promised to make her the dark Fae queen. She hasn't forgotten that."

"Rad." I think a moment. "She couldn't really do that, could she?"

Euphoria's eyes get even darker. "There's never been a dark Fae queen, but honestly, Syl? I don't know."

The gloom-and-doom in her voice makes me lose my appetite.

The rest of the night passes with us planning out Operation: Spy on Fiann, and the next morning, we head to school to put our plan in place. But that day and for the rest of the whole week, Fiann totally lays low—at least power-wise.

In every other respect, she's a total pain.

Thankfully, the weekend rolls around, and E and I trade being super-spies for being superheroes, running around the city, dowsing for Ouroboros and fighting/destroying Circuit fiends. Turns out, as cool as Mom is, she doesn't go for her daughter running around the city all night, every night.

Homework gets done first. And then saving the world.

Monday morning comes too fast, finding me all bleary and grouchy. It's only week two, and I'm ready for the school year to be over.

"Looks like your mom left early." Euphoria hands me a note as I step into the kitchen still in sweats and a tank top. I glance at it. Something about Jefferson High and smoke bombs. The emergency calls are good money, but I hate to think of her getting up at the butt-crack of dawn.

"Well…" I snag the box of sugar-coated awesome from the top of the fridge. "The one good thing about it is cereal for breakfast."

E grins, and we dig in. Soon enough, we're dressed, heading off, then at our lockers. I swear, Mondays are always a blur.

I yawn as I toss my books into my backpack. "Ugh. So tired." Last night's Circuit fiend battle had us crawling through my window at midnight. I yawn so loud my jaw cracks. "It's a good thing Mom doesn't check my room after curfew."

Euphoria gives me the sly side-eye. "Or, if she does, she never says anything."

"Whoa... You don't think..."

She tucks her lyric notebook under her arm. "You expect me to believe for one second that Georgina Gentry doesn't check your room after curfew?" She clucks her tongue. "Not even going there."

Wow. Yeah... She's probably right. I do some quick math: Mom + me breaking curfew a million times = me being grounded till graduation.

I groan. "How did I forget my mom's a total ninja?"

Chuckling, E turns her electric-blue gaze on me, and the butterflies in my stomach remind me I'm her biggest fan. She leans in.

Okay, we haven't *kissed*-kissed since my power started going haywire, only barely touched lips. Like now.

"Ewww!"

My face is on fire as I pull away from Euphoria. Fiann and her pony-tailed posse are leaning against their lockers, staring at us. Fiann's not the one who said, "Ewww." That was Becca, who stands next to her.

"Seriously, have you ever seen anything grosser?" Becca rolls her baby blues.

Casual as you please, Euphoria pulls her bow out of her case like she's drawing a samurai sword. "Ever see a girl with a violin bow shoved up her a—"

"Whoa!" I grab her and totally propel her toward class, giving Becca the stink-eye over my shoulder. "Keep staring. That's how we know you're jealous!" I call out, and her face reddens.

Got her.

E's still laughing as we make our way down Yellow Hall. I spot Lennon and wave. We've got Library Studies first thing today. Euphoria's got Music Theory, but she walks me to class. When we get to the door, I blow her a kiss.

She smiles, but there's such darkness in her eyes. Her hand strays to her pocket. I wonder what's on her mind. Before I can ask, the bell rings.

"Gotta go," she says.

"I'm here for you, you know," I say softly, toeing the floor with my sneaker.

"I know." Her smile goes genuine, her cheeks pink. I want her to grab me around the waist and kiss me breathless. For one sec, I think she will—just forget all the rules—but she only steps back. "See you after."

"You bet." My hand goes to Glamma's ring, and I have to fight myself not to chase her down. *Now's so not the time, Syl.* So I drag my butt off to Library Studies.

Miss Jardin. With all the Fiann drama, I haven't exactly had time to find out more about her, who put that geis on her and why.

Besides, how do you ask, *Hey, who kicked your butt and imprisoned you in a high school library* without sounding super-rude?

"Have fun in Library Studies, nerds!" Fiann flounces by with Becca and company in tow.

Ugh. I turn to say something smart-alecky, but Lennon's there.

"Don't bother. She's not worth it." Lennon smiles and opens the door for me.

I grin back. "Yeah, you're right."

We head in, the door whumps shut, and we're cocooned in that odd library silence, like the way the world gets quiet after a heavy snow. It's me, Lennon, and a group of girls in the giant rotunda, all tall stacks and cherrywood accents. There's a distinct smell of roses, even though Miss Jardin's rose garden is just turned earth and empty trellises.

I'm betting it won't be long before we see giant blood-red roses on those trellises. An Unseelie who…likes flowers?

Seriously. I need to spend some quality time with Glamma's Grimm.

If only I knew where it was.

"Earth to Syl." Lennon nudges me out of my space-out. We take our seats, and soon Miss Jardin comes in. She's perfectly put together as always, today all in red.

Red, ha. I think I'm getting trolled by my high school librarian.

Oh, wait. She's a Defense Against the Dark Arts teacher. Which means…she's totally evil.

"Take out your laptops, please," Miss Jardin says in that smooth voice.

While mine boots up, I look around the room and spot...

My own personal stalker, Golden Guy, right by the old card catalogue. I sigh as he tips an imaginary hat to me. Everywhere I go, he's there. He wasn't even in this class last week, and now, bam! Here he is.

I've given up trying to have a normal convo with the guy. He's all fake smiles and cheesy pickup lines. Clearly, me playing keep-away isn't enough. My stomach heaves as I contemplate something more...confrontational.

Euphoria's the get-in-your-face kind of girl, but I'm not.

The entire class shifts as Miss J starts her lecture, all the girls edging closer to him, making swoony faces, their auras sticky-pink like reams of cotton candy at the carnival. It's both funny and barf-worthy.

He smiles, all *let's play nice* at me. Yeah, right. Nice people don't stalk others—or Glamoury the entire female student body.

Lennon looks between us, her rounded eyes going wide. "That boy is...odd."

"You don't know the half of it," I whisper back.

Every time a girl fawns over him, I hear those silver pipes, I smell dandelions on a breeze, I feel the sun on my face, and I'm reminded of my dream—those white columns, that perfect summer day.

How much I yearn for the realm of my people.

I'm lost in thought, when...

"That's all for now, class." Miss Jardin wraps up her lecture on search engines. Everyone's getting up from their seats.

Whoa...I just spaced the whole class.

"Miss Skye, please remain behind." Miss Jardin looks up. The sun coming in through the filtered windows casts a weird red glow on her like fire.

"But she's a good púca, right?" I'd asked Euphoria.

She only laughed and said there was no such thing.

Lennon shoots me an apologetic look and files out with the others. I head over to Miss J like a girl getting ready to go before a firing squad.

"Syl." Miss Jardin leans on the counter, her chunky black glasses reflecting the red glow, giving me wild thoughts of hellfire. "You have a question for m—?"

"Oops, clumsy me," someone calls out, and a bunch of books spill over the desk. A few plop onto the floor on Miss J's side, making her eye twitch.

Golden Guy. What. The. Heck? "This is a private conversation," I tell him, trying to be nice but not too nice.

Miss Jardin only adjusts her glasses primly. "We'll talk later, Syl." Her gaze pins him a sec. "Fair winds are coming." She turns smartly on her heel. Like heading into the wardrobe in Narnia, she vanishes into the stacks.

Total. Ninja. Púca.

Golden Guy turns to me. "Beg your pardon."

Beg my what? Who talks like that? Not even Rouen, whose people are super old-school. "No worries," I say, but when I turn to go, he calls out.

"Wait." He catches my hand again.

Sheesh. What is it with this guy? I pull away, sighing. "Seriously, I'm not interested." I wave a hand. "There's about a hundred other girls who were totally drooling over you. Try one of them."

"I'm here for you."

Those words hit me like a ton of bricks. Here for me? Him? It's like every normal girl's fantasy. The supernatural dude who stalks you, watches you sleep… "No thanks." I'll wait for a well-adjusted nonpsycho fair Fae to find me.

That seems to throw him. "Wait…"

"What do you want?" It comes out meaner than I want, but seriously?

He tries again. "You've Awakened."

"So?"

"So I want to talk to you."

"Talk, then." I look at my bare wrist. "You've got two minutes before second bell."

He looks around. "Not here. Let's talk later. On the bleachers. After school."

106

"I'm meeting Euphoria after school." At the mention of her name, his eyes flash all hot and molten gold again, his pretty face screwing up into something ugly. I saw that very same look on ol' Aggy's face whenever he saw me and E together.

For real, what is it with these Fae dudes?

"It'll only take a minute." He sounds sincere enough, and I should find out what-all is going on. Maybe then I'll be able to head off the inevitable showdown between him and Euphoria.

"Okay, okay. But only a minute."

"Good." His smile is like a thousand suns bright. He walks away and looks back, shooting finger guns at me. Finger guns. "I'm going to change your life, Syl."

"I'll bet you say that to all the girls."

He's going to change my life? Yeah, right.

The bleachers are empty, a few football players running drills on the field below. Homecoming's coming up fast. I shiver and not from the autumn chill in the air. Last year at Homecoming, everything went from a hot mess to a total raging bonfire of suck.

I don't want to repeat the experience.

I tug my jacket tighter, even though, with my Fae blood, I'm not cold. Dang. Guy can't even be on time. I find myself toying with Glamma's ring on its chain beneath my top. I should just go find Euphoria and ask her—

"Syl."

I whirl around and see him standing there. It's a Fae trick—just appearing out of thin air like that. Euphoria can do it, too. Note to self: make her teach me that.

"All right, talk."

He steps forward, but I put my hands in my jacket pockets. "Stop trying to touch me, okay?"

He spreads his hands like he's surrendering. "My name is Aldebaran."

Definitely a foofy fair Fae name.

"You already know who I am." I'm pretty sure dude is an expert in all things Syl Skye.

He bows. Like…he *bows*. "Prince Aldebaran."

"Oooookay?" Like that makes a difference?

"Of the Fair Fae of the Summer Court."

"I guessed."

He seems pretty put out that I'm not gushing over him like every other girl in school. Whatever. He might be the first fair Fae I've ever met, but he's been a huge jerk. Not to mention a huge disappointment.

"I am a prince—"

"You said that."

"And you are my princess."

His words slap me in the face like a wet towel. "Wait, what?" I splutter. "No…no way. I'm *a* princess. A sleeper-princess. But I'm not anyone's. I belong to me."

He steps in, and he's looking for my hand again.

I want to smack him on the nose like he's a puppy. But you know, a puppy would've learned by now.

"You don't understand, Syl. We were meant to be. We're fated to be together. As king and queen."

"Fated?" Wow. Guy is totally delusional. "By who? By what?"

"Our hearthstone," he says, and okay, that gets my attention. The fair Fae have one, too? "Our hearthstone is powered by the energy the king and queen bring to it. As mated pairs. Soul-bound."

I don't know what "soul-bound" is, but I can guess, and uhhhh…ick. "No thanks." I turn, but he grabs my elbow, his grip super-strong.

"You can't just walk away from this." His golden eyes smolder.

Now I know a lot of girls would be all swoony for this "fated prince" stuff, but all I feel is dread, my stomach tight as a fist. My butterflies want zero to do with this guy. And what makes him think he can just stake a claim? I slap his hand away.

He looks startled. Never been rejected before, probably.

"Listen, dude." I step in and poke him in the chest. "First, keep your darn hands to yourself. Second, I've been trying to be nice since you're new here. But really? Buzz. Off."

"Your people need you, Syl. Our king is dying. The people need a ruler."

"Ooookay." I get the sense he's telling the truth about the king, but…something still rings out like a lie, clanging through my mind. I wish I could read his aura, but all my Fae-sight gives me is black spots and a headache. Is it because he's a fair Fae prince? Also, I'm starting to suspect that means he's super-powerful.

Also also, I'm seriously tired of his crap.

I square my stance. "What about the queen?"

"Queen?" He looks confused. "What about her?"

"Can't she rule?" Duh. It's a simple question.

His laughter echoes over the stands, so super-insulting I want to kick him in the shin. "Don't be ridiculous."

I give him the stink-eye. "What's so wrong with a woman ruling?"

Dude must realize he's overstepped because he backs off a bit. "Nothing, I suppose, but the rule of OverHill necessitates a couple. A soul-bound male and female whose mated love reflects the bounty of the land."

I almost choke. Mated love? Bounty of the land? And there's that word again. *Soul-bound.* Nope. Nope. Nope. All the nopes. I don't want to…mate—barf—with him. No way. "Sorry, not your girl."

His eyes go from smoldering to searing hot. "There is no other girl."

"Do it yourself."

"I cannot. If there is not a new king and queen on the Aureate Throne by next Midsummer Night, our world will begin to die."

Okay. I don't want any part of Faerie to die, but I trust this guy as far as I could donkey-toss him. "Look. I'm not going to mate with you, or whatever you want to call it, but I'll help if I can."

But…apparently that's not good enough because dude keeps right on going. "You're the sleeper-princess, you've begun to Awaken, so you have to be soul-bound to your prince. Me." He steps in, looming over me, bullying me with his posture and his words. "Only I, as your prince and soul-bound mate, can help you fully realize your Awakened power—so that we can fight together. You don't have any choice, Syl, so you might as well give up resisting. It's tradition. You're mine. It's how the magic *works*."

Okay, I hate every word he just said. It's up to some guy I've never met to help me control my powers? Is that what being soul-bound means—I'm his? Like, his *possession*?

Nope. No way.

I poke him in the chest again. "Listen up, jerk. I Awakened just fine without you, and I'll keep training my power until I gain the control I need. I don't need your help. And besides, what are we supposed to fight?" I gesture around at the empty field.

"Dark Fae."

"You mean Euphoria?"

"Rouen," he corrects me.

"Yeah, but I never call her that. It makes her all emo and broody. And she's not a problem."

"Really?" Now he's giving me the stink-eye.

"Yeah, really. Besides"—and I know this'll really get his goat—"she's my girlfriend."

"Your—" He looks like he's going to choke on all that masculine beauty.

"That's right. So step off." With that, I turn and walk away.

Now that's how you mic-drop.

CHAPTER FOURTEEN
ROUEN

Worship me
I'm no good for you
You're no good for me
Worship me, worship me
- "Worship," Euphoria

I'm standing at the end of the football field, on top of the scoreboard, a don't-see-me Glamoury cloaking me as I watch this fair Fae jerkwad hit on my girl. The wind blows cold, mirroring my emotions, whipping my dark hair about my face.

Every cell in my body *begs* me to go down there and knock him into next week. If he were a dark Fae, I would. But he's not. He's a fair Fae, one of Syl's own people, and I won't come between her and her people.

It wouldn't be fair.

Still, I watch as he gets pushier and pushier, fury building up inside me until I swear, the Winter's going to burst from my blood. I'm ready to explode, all my protective instincts on high alert.

I blow out a shaky breath and touch the ring in my pocket. *Let Syl handle it, Rouen. Don't go berserk...*

At least not yet.

I can hear every word they say, thanks to my Fae hearing. He makes it sound so easy. Just pair up with him. He tells her they're meant to be soul-bound. It's what every teenage girl wants to hear, right?

Except, Syl's not falling for his whole "fated mate" speech.

Good, because it's more than half a lie.

She turns to walk away, and he grabs her. And refuses to let go. The flex of his biceps tells me he's exerting his fair Fae strength.

I see red, my heartbeat pulsing so hard that time seems to spiral outward. In that moment, I know two things. One, he's a prince and that means he's powerful. Two, he's likely had hundreds of years in the Summer Court, maybe even thousands. I'm not a quarter of his age.

He could easily overpower me, even kill me.

Let him try. No one grabs my girl.

All my fury rushes in, cold and calculating. Boosting my Glamoury, I leap to the bleachers. My motorcycle boots slam down on the metal slats hard enough to shake the whole foundation. I straighten, slow, deliberate, giving him my dead-eye stare. "For a fair Fae, you're awfully pushy." I look at the hand he has on my girl. I want to snap it off and beat him with it.

He squares his stance, still gripping Syl's arm.

Wow. He's really doubling-down on the stupid. I clench my fists, getting ready to fight. "Take your hand off her. Now."

My threat rings out like the pounding of Faerie war drums. It hangs between us, a sharp and glittering thing, and I see him weighing his options, weighing me. Whether he can take me.

A smirk tilts his lips. He knows he can.

"Euphoria..." Syl's voice trembles, but I give her what I hope is a reassuring smile.

Then I turn the full force of my dark Fae glare on Mr Fancy. He might be stronger, but I'm willing to bet I'm more cunning. I won't go down without a fight, and he doesn't want to pick one. Not here.

Not when he thinks he can sway Syl's decision by manipulation alone.

Not on my watch, buddy-boy.

He lets her go. "Rouen Rivoche." His voice drips with scathing hatred.

I shrug one shoulder. "Prince What's-Your-Bucket."

Syl comes to my side, and I risk getting burned to a crisp by putting an arm around her. She leans in, the small, solid warmth of her body a balm to my ragged emotions. I keep her there longer than I should, already feeling the hum of her power firing up.

I let go and step away just in time.

"It's Aldebaran," he says. "Prince Aldebaran." He puts both hands in the pockets of his skinny jeans and slouches in that way some guys have of making it look casual while flexing his biceps.

Give me a break. Agravaine was twice as big as this guy, and he went down just fine. The bigger they are, and all that.

"The infamous Huntress." Aldebaran gives me a snotty once-over. "I wondered when you'd show up."

"Wonder no longer." I show him a flash of fang. "And I'm not the Huntress. Not anymore. The Huntsman is dead and the Hunt banished, masterless." It's true. Syl and I "killed" the hell-hounds, but their deaths in the mortal realm only banished them back to UnderHollow, to haunt the wintry Greymoors until all of Dark Faerie dies.

It's the only good thing about the Snickleways collapsing.

Aldebaran crosses his arms. "You shouldn't meddle in the affairs of Fair Faerie. Syl belongs with me. Soul-bound."

Over my dead body. "You shouldn't lie to your princess," I shoot back, my voice cold as ice splintering. "Why don't you tell her the truth about Fae princes?" Because he doesn't want an equal partner. He wants a battery, and Syl would be perfect—newly Awakened, not in full control, her power limitless.

That's the way Fae princes—and kings—work.

His lips lift in a snarl. "She is a sleeper-princess of the fair Fae. She is meant to do this, to be this. She—"

"Is standing right here, thank you very much." Syl tosses her red curls back from her face, her annoyance on display. "Tell me the truth."

He holds out his hand. "Come to Fair Faerie, and I will show you."

Syl's whole body jolts toward him, the pull of Summer in her blood a strong lure toward the realm of Fair Faerie. But she doesn't take an actual step. "I'm waiting."

He smiles at her warmly, but darkness slithers behind his eyes. "You can't realize your full power without your soul-bound mate. Me."

I want to scream, to shout at her not to trust dirty, lying Prince Fancy, but a tiny kernel of doubt coils in my stomach. She is a sleeper-princess of the fair Fae, a vessel of all their raw power. What if he's right?

After all, fair Fae power is as weird and rules-riddled as dark Fae power.

The wind tugs at my hair, and I brush it back. If she chooses me over him, she'll be an outcast just like me, dead to her own people.

I don't know if I can let her do it.

"We're leaving." Syl's voice is soft but resolute.

Aldebaran changes tactics, hitting below the belt. "She wants something much worse from you, Syl."

Damn it. He knows about the blood.

He laughs, shaking his head like a lion shaking its mane. "Everyone knows about you, Rouen Rivoche. You're something of a legend and a cautionary tale. The spitfire princess of the Winter Court who betrayed her own people and was outcast as a sluagh, turned into a Circuit Fae because of it." He steps forward, his gaze burning bright. "Do you really think I would leave Syl alone with you? Knowing what you need from her?"

A sinking feeling grips my guts. I'd hoped to break this whole *hey, I could be a dark Fae princess again, but I need your blood* thing gently to Syl. It's never going to happen anyway. No need for anyone to freak over it. My glare is ice and daggers. "I would never harm her."

Syl looks between us. "Harm? What's going on, E?"

But before I can answer, Mr Impatient butts in again. "You'd make a wonderful Mistress of the Hunt, Rouen." With every word, he mocks me. "You could go back to your old ways. Hunt the last sleeper-princess down. Use her blood to restore your nobility."

That's it. All my fury rises inside me—the thought of hurting Syl, the reminder that my people are trapped, that I'm a sluagh outcast, that this little maggot is hitting on my girl. It all comes rocketing out of me.

My fist pistons out fast. I crack him a good one, right in the cheekbone.

He falls to the bleachers. Fast as a snake, he coils and snaps to his feet, those golden eyes blazing hotter than the hottest sun. "That was a mistake, sluagh."

The pressure in the air drops drastically. My ears pop. The wind picks up, a late-summer breeze hot and oppressive. It surrounds us, whipping our hair into our faces, suffocating us in its heat.

A smile quirks on Aldebaran's lips, and he brightens, glowing with sunshine, a yellow beacon burning against the fading day. The air around him shimmers with heat.

Syl's eyes go wide. "What's happening?"

Dread curdles in my stomach, rising into full-blown panic. He wouldn't… But I feel him calling on the Summer in his blood to *manifest* on the mortal realm. Only the most powerful Fae can do it. I swallow hard. I will not show fear. "He's about to manifest—to open the gates to the Summer Court right here in the mortal realm."

Only a true-blooded noble can wield such power.

"Stop it!" Syl cries, stepping in front of me like a shield.

As quickly as the heat ramped up, it drops.

Aldebaran steps back, smug as ever. He waves off the last ripples of Summer heat. "Very well, then. I'll leave you to think on it." He turns on his heel. "But, Syl. Don't think too long." He leaps from the bleachers and is gone.

I shake off the brightness, the sun—every last vestige of the Summer Court that almost came crashing down. "I should've punched him twice."

"There's no need for that." Syl's voice is gentle as she touches my arm briefly before pulling away. "Let's go home."

I don't argue, but deep down, I know it'll come down to a fight between me and Prince Fancy.

We get home a little later than usual. Thankfully, Syl's mom isn't due back for another hour. Which means…dinner's on us. Again.

Normally, I'd drag my feet, but Syl's pretty upset. She sinks into one of the threadbare chairs in the living room. I go to the fridge and grab her a Coke.

"Catch." I toss it. She doesn't even crush it accidentally, so that's progress. But I know she's not thinking about that. She's caught up in all that Aldebaran's told her.

She pops the tab and takes a few sips, sets it down. I busy myself getting out pots and pans to make spaghetti.

"Rouen?"

Uh-oh… It's never a good sign when she calls me by my real name. I keep my voice casual. "Yeah?"

"Do you think what he said was true?" She picks up the can again, holds it like it's a life preserver.

Suddenly, my heart is hammering like mad. "Which part?"

"The part about me realizing my full power…" She clears her throat, uncomfortable. "With him."

I put down the pan I'm holding. Basically, everything that guy said was harmful garbage, but if I tell her what to think, I'd be just like him. My hand strays to my pocket. No. Now is definitely not a good time. And why am I even thinking about it?

Because you're territorial as hell, Rouen, and you want to claim her as your own. But no. That wouldn't be any better than what Aldebaran's trying to do.

So I forget the ring.

Instead, I cross the room, squat down, and look into her eyes. "Listen, no one gets to tell you that. That's for you to decide. You've grown, Syl. You're stronger, more confident. He doesn't get to just come in and tell you that doesn't count, that your feelings don't count."

She smiles gratefully and swipes at her watery eyes. "Thanks." She takes my hand, and I squeeze hers.

I look down at our entwined fingers. I've missed her touch more than I can say. Even now, I feel her white flame igniting within her, building up to lash out.

All my instincts scream a warning.

Reluctant, I pull away. "Only you can decide if what he says is true or not." I take a deep breath and let it out. There's one thing that's true no matter what either of us decides. "How much do you know about soul-bonds?"

"Between the Fae?" Syl's face furrows up adorably as she thinks. "Nothing, really. Glamma never brought up soul-bonds in her tales."

Gah! The first time Glamma doesn't have an opinion...

Syl's looking at me now, studying my face. She cocks her head. "Why?"

Because I want to soul-bond with you. I almost blurt it out. I almost whip out the ring. Down on one knee and everything.

But I don't. I can't.

I won't make her decide between me and her people.

I blow out a breath. "When two Fae bond like that, they become as one soul." Looking into her summer-storm-grey eyes, I want that more than anything. I swallow hard, and my throat clicks dryly. "They become immune to each other's destructive grama-rye. Some say they can even speak telepathically."

"Cool!" Syl's excitement sends a wave of love through me. My girl is so positive, so bright. I have to protect her light.

"Well, yeah." I toss my black hair back from my face. I wish I could hold her hand while I tell her this. "But it also means never being able to hide your thoughts, your emotions. It means being laid bare for that other person. It means when that whatever fate befalls that other person also befalls you."

Syl bites her bottom lip. "So, like, if they died, I would, too?"

I nod gravely. I'm not one hundred percent sure that would result in insta-death, but soul-bound pairs generally don't outlive each other.

I stand up, my hand straying to my pocket. "Look, I don't want to influence your decision, or make it seem like…" Gah! It's so important for me that she has choices without me swaying her. "Like I'm your only choice—"

"Euphoria."

"You could be an amazing fair Fae queen, Syl. You'd be—"

"Euphoria."

"Amazing. Just—"

"Rouen!"

I swallow the rest of my rambling.

Syl's grey eyes are serious. She stands, deliberately grabbing my hands and pulling me into an embrace.

"Syl, what are you—Your power!"

"Shhh…just enjoy the moment." She's warm and soft in my arms. The scent of her hair like sugared vanilla on a balmy summer day.

Ancestors, preserve me.

I melt into her, powers be damned. Wrapping her tight in my arms, I draw her in, reveling in her closeness, her scent—everything that is uniquely and awesomely Syl.

We're there for what feels like two seconds before her power surges. A wave of Summer heat washes over me, stinging my skin, prickling the Winter in my blood.

Don't be foolish, Roue.

After all, I'm the one with all the training, the discipline. But one look into her stormy grey eyes, and I'm almost a goner.

Then the heat ramps up. I push myself away. Every inch of my body aches at the loss of her touch, her warmth, *her*. I try to sound causal, but my voice comes out ragged. "We should get dinner started."

The pot's begun to boil. *I feel you, pot. I feel you.*

"Right." She's breathless and so adorable.

The last thing on my mind is dinner. I'm itching to pull her close and kiss her, to wrap her tight, protect her from anyone who would dare hurt her. I just want to be close to her, bathed in her scent. And my dark self wants more. So much more.

Maybe more than she wants to give.

On second thought, maybe it's good that her power wants to murder me.

Deliberately, I put the couch between us. My heart's pounding, needy and angsty, and I step on my dark self's throat. *That's enough out of you.*

"Okay, then." Syl's tense, too. She blows out a breath, and we take a few moments to get our acts together. I grab our backpacks and toss them on the hooks near the door. Georgina would have a total fit if she found us just throwing our junk on the floor.

"Euphoria?"

I turn and meet Syl's gaze. "Yes?"

"You're my choice." Her grey eyes are intense, fiery. "My one and only choice."

It's everything I want to hear—that she chooses me—but she might be making up her mind too soon.

We haven't seen the last of Aldebaran or my dark self.

CHAPTER FIFTEEN
SYL

The sleeper-princess is immune to
Mind-altering Fae gramarye
Except that of fair Fae royalty,
For she is one of them
- Glamma's Grimm

They say those who don't learn history are doomed to repeat it. Yeah, well…I *lived* through last year, and this year is shaping up to be a total repeat.

Weeks pass with me and Euphoria racing along the rooftops of Richmond, hunting Circuit fiends, her playing gigs by night, us going to school by day. I use my press pass to wander the halls, purifying any students who've strayed too close to the Ouroboros and had their life-force drained. E and I search and search the entire school, but the Ouroboros' Glamoury is too strong.

We can only hope it's the next to spawn.

So we can destroy it once and for all.

And then there's Fiann.

She doesn't go all Teen Wolf on us again, but she's laying low for a reason, I'm sure.

It's Homecoming week, and the entire school's abuzz. Last year, Fiann was hailed as a hero when she fake-saved me from the train accident. This year, she's talking about her "addiction." Before you know it, *Say No to Drugs* banners with her as the poster girl start popping up all over the school. Ugh. It's last year all over again. Except instead of *Real-Life Supergirl Saves Friend*, it's *Teen Role Model's Heroic Journey*.

Heroic journey? Ick. She practically killed everyone in this school.

It just goes to show that Glamoury is totally a double-edged sword. If not for that, everyone would remember almost being devoured by Agravaine's Moribund as Fiann played her violin like Nero while Rome burned. Instead, they're hailing Fiann as some kind of hero.

Double ick.

I try not to let it bother me. October's my fave month, and Halloween's coming up. Euphoria's playing the Monsters' Ball at the Nanci Raygun.

I'm still holding out hope for a date night.

But even at school, E and I are getting pulled apart.

The Friday before the Homecoming game, I head into the school paper's headquarters for my first assignment. It's early, before homeroom, and only a few people are there, milling about. Pru's leaning over her souped-up laptop, blue-green hair masking her face.

"Syl Skye, reporting for duty!" I sling my backpack and DSL camera down on the table.

She glances up. "Oh, hey, Syl." She straightens and heads over to her desk. Papers are scattered literally everywhere, and she shuffles through them. "Hold on a sec…" Concentration scrunches up her face. "A-ha!" She snatches up an assignment sheet and holds it out. "Here you go."

I take the paper. Yearbook duty. I glance down the list of shoots she wants. They're all band and Cheer-Cheer squad pics.

Excitement and dread fizz in my guts. "Wait. Since when is the band working with the Cheer-Cheer Squad?" Last year, there was a ginormous rivalry between the two, resulting in a competition that Fiann and her pom-pom posse lost. Hard. She's still miffed about it.

Pru gives me a weird look. "Um, Earth to Syl? Admin decided that on day one. The band plays Homecoming, and the Cheer-Cheer Squad"—Pru shudders at Fiann's dumb name for the varsity cheerleaders—"are doing their thing in the background."

"Wait, what?" My Spidey Sense is tingling. Fiann's behind this. Of course. It would mean she'd have to spend a lot of time with Euphoria.

"Are you...okay?" Pru looks like she's resisting the urge to feel my forehead for a fever.

I laugh, but it sounds super-strained. "Yeah. For sure. I mean, for a lot of people, the idea of their girl working with their most bitter rival would freak them out. But not me. Nope. No siree, Bob."

Pru's giving me the side-eye now. "I can assign someone else. Maybe Shoshanna—"

"Nope!" I hold up a hand. "Not letting Fiann win." I shake off the gloomies.

"That's my girl. Besides"—Pru tips me a wink—"it's a great excuse to get shots of your girl in her band uniform."

"Okay, since you put it that way..." I do like my Winter girl in uniform. She hates it, but I think the green-and-gold looks pretty damn hot on her. Even if it isn't really part of her goth-rock star image. I look down to hide my blush. "Thanks, Pru."

She nudges my shoulder. "Who loves ya, girl?"

Grinning like a loon, I head to band practice, super-excited, my DSL camera clutched in my hot little hands. On my way to the field, some football players jog by me. One looks back and winks. "Hey, Syl!" I catch a glimpse of golden-blond hair and golden eyes.

"Aldebaran. Wait, what?" The prince of the fair Fae *plays football*? He's cut his hair. Instead of the long Legolas 'do, it's short on the sides and stylishly messy on top, like he's just rolled out of bed looking perfect. And of course, he's wearing number 13. The QB's number.

He waves with two fingers. "Don't forget to get my good side."

"Do you have a good side?"

"Both, actually." He seriously says that with a straight face.

Ugh. He jogs backwards, smirking at me, and then one of his guys butt-slaps him, and he turns and heads onto the field.

I sigh. That guy is supposed to be my "soul-bound" mate?

Nope, nope, nope, all the nopes. I don't want to be soul-bound. From what I've heard, it sounds like the worst. I'll find some other way to help my people. I mean, it's not like all of Fair Faerie is going to collapse just because I won't date this guy.

Will it?

Earth to Syl. Pictures, remember?

Right. I busy myself warming up, snapping a few shots of the football players at practice. Pru can always use them as filler. Aldebaran tries to put himself in my line of sight as much as possible, but I'm a pro. I get shots of all the guys. Soon enough, the band comes onto the field, a wash of green-and-gold uniforms. The cheerleaders make it there first, Fiann looking as gorgeous and golden as Aldebaran.

Maybe he should soul-bond with her.

She's all flouncy, her high ponytail bouncing as she gives orders, her posse a pack of green-and-gold swans around her. Whispers of "She's so brave!" and "How does she do it?" echo across the field.

Right now, I'm kind of cursing my sleeper-princess hearing. Sometimes being Awakened isn't all it's cracked up to be. Like now—or like when a fair Fae prince stalks you, tries to gaslight you into thinking you need him, and threatens your girlfriend. I might need help to "fully realize" my power, but it ain't gonna be him.

No way, no day. I'll never team up with him.

And if I'm going to soul-bond with anyone, it's going to be E.

"What, are you asleep, Syl? Take my picture already!" Fiann snarls at me.

I snap a picture of her with post-snarl derp face and give her the thumbs-up. "That'll look super-good in the yearbook!" Right next to her duck-face pic from last year.

She gives me a farty face, and I snap that too. *Seriously, girl?* I shake my head. She probably messes with her waitress before she gets her food, too. *Dummy.*

And then the band heads to the fifty-yard line. Euphoria leads them, her violin's glassy surface reflecting the sun like a beacon in a sea of green-and-gold. They take up position, and I start to shoot the band playing, cheerleaders cheering.

Eleven lords a'leaping. That sort of thing.

Euphoria plays, concentrating and biting her lip in that way that drives me wild. She knows it, too, the little minx. I get some good shots of her all sexy and smoldering. Maybe I'll have to keep one or two for me.

In the interest of science and all.

For the first time in weeks, I'm almost relaxing. Me and my girl are flirting. My face is burning-hot, and I'm super-glad to hide it behind my camera.

Fiann's face is red, too, but for a different reason. She's clearly annoyed that Euphoria's attention is on me. She does a final split-jump dismount and paces around like a drill sergeant inspecting her troops. "Okay, girls. Let's mix it up. This Homecoming show is all about teamwork, right? Let's get some shots of that."

I sense a rat. A big Fiann-shaped rat.

The cheerleaders gather round, and suddenly, I'm in the middle of this gaggle of girls with their high ponies and spankies.

"What kind of shots?" I'm going to so regret asking.

"Group shots." Fiann's all wide-eyed innocence, which is how I know she's full of it. She turns up the sass. "If that's okay with you, Miss Journalist?"

I can't see any reason not to, so I nod. But my mouth is dry, and my heart is trying to Bruce Lee its way out of my chest. She'd definitely up to something. And while I'm a sleeper-princess and I can throw a Mini Cooper, I'm still so out of my league in social situations.

Yup. Total geek, no waiting.

She starts posing, draping herself on various band members. I have to admit, she's photogenic. Chuck almost swallows his tongue when she leans in and flashes her ten-thousand-dollar smile. Poor guy.

Fiann moves on to Octavia, and I get a nice shot of them posing by the drum set. Nazira just pushes Fiann off with a "No, thanks." Did I mention that I heart Nazira?

And then Fiann gets to my girl.

She smirks at me, and then she climbs Euphoria—like seriously climbs her, as if E's some kind of cheerleading base. My girl sets down her violin, looking super-uncomfortable, but there's nothing she can do unless she wants to dump Fiann on her sorry behind.

For a second, I kinda want her to do just that.

But despite the fact that my girl's a super-powerful dark Fae, she's also a super-softie. Like, we once did that Pottermore quiz, and she totally came up as a Hufflepuff.

Tell no one.

Fiann stands on my girl's shoulders. "Come on, Syl. Take the picture already."

The other cheerleaders pipe up. "Yeah, Syl. Hurry up."

"Do it. Come on."

"Great pic, Fiann."

The peer pressure bears down on me like an SUV's parked on my chest. I can barely breathe, and I'm sweating. Also, I feel like I'm acting like a two-year-old.

It's just a picture, Syl. Whatever.

So I lift my camera and snap a few pics. "All right, got it. You can get down now." My voice sounds strained even to me.

Fiann does the dismount with an innocent-sounding, "Catch me, Rouen!"

And my girl does. Because again, she's not a jerk.

Fiann lies there in Euphoria's arms, all sex-kitten smirky, and gives E a kiss on the cheek…except that kiss lands on the corner of my girl's mouth.

Hot, burning anger rushes up inside me. I swear to all that is holy, I'm going to—

The sound of silvery pipes cuts through my inner tantrum.

What the— Instantly, my hands are burning up hot. White-hot. *Oh, crap.* What is happening?

I've never lost control like this, but there's no mistaking the Summer heat pouring up from inside me, rushing to my hands. *Crappity, crap, crap, crap.* I'm about to burn down the entire cheer-leading squad.

Don't get me wrong. Most days I think Fiann and her silly squad are a stain on the planet, but some of them might grow out of their mean-girl phase.

They don't really deserve the scorched-Earth treatment.

I let my camera hang from its strap and stuff my hands into my pockets. No good. They glow, even through my jeans. I throw up a desperate don't-see-this Glamoury.

But I'm losing control.

Euphoria sees it, too. She takes a step toward me then stops. We both know that's not going to help.

I have to turn away before the white flames burn down my Glamoury and reveal me to the Cheer-Cheer Squad, the football players, Coach Blix.

Outing myself as a fair Fae sleeper-princess is not one of my squad goals.

"Gotta go," I blurt, all freaked out, and practically run off the field.

My face is burning hot as my hands as I scurry away to the sounds of Fiann's laughter. "Where are you going, Syl? Did you get that picture? Should I kiss her again?"

My anger blazes hotter than the sun, and I swear the white flames are going to leap from my fingers and scorch that smug smile right off her face. I run, tears of anger and humiliation burning on my lashes. I beeline through the parking lot back up to the school. I have to get to my bike, have to get out of here before I burn the world down.

And Fiann in it.

Aldebaran's words echo in my mind, *"You can't fully realize your power without your prince, your prince, your prince..."*

"Syl!"

I turn to see Euphoria there, her sapphire-blue eyes drowning in concern for me.

"Hey..."

"Rouen!" I want to throw myself into her arms, but...instead I jam my fists deeper into my pockets and rock on my heels. Tears start their hot, humiliating slide down my cheeks. "It... She..."

"It's okay." Euphoria's voice is soft, soothing. Her gaze holds mine. "Take a breath. Relax, Syl. You got this. Just relax, breathe..."

I do, and with the first breath, my white fire dies away a bit. I breathe out again, relieved that I'm not going to light the world on fire. At least, not right now. "She practically made out with you."

Her shoulders slump. "I'm sorry, Syl."

"It's not your fault. I'm not angry at you." I brush a damp strand of red hair from my face. My face feels hot and sweaty, tight with crying, and I know I'll be wearing this all afternoon now. *Thanks, Irish complexion.* "Fiann's just... She just..."

"She knows how to push your buttons." Euphoria waves away my apology. "It's okay. Come on, let's get out of here."

I look into her eyes. Her concern for me is sweet, but...I know how much band means to her. Last year she taught them how to be a team and defeat Fiann's mean-girl posse. Band is E's creation, and I want them to kick butt this year, too. But they need to practice.

I step back. "No, it's okay. You go back to practice. I have work anyway." It's true. She's got band. I've got work, then dinner with Mom, then homework and racing across the rooftops, hunting Circuit fiends.

Typical us stuff.

"Are you sure?" She looks at me, that one eyebrow cocked.

"Yeah. My bike's up at the rack, so don't worry. Go on." I'm pushing her away when all I want to do is grab her and hold her close.

"All right." She still seems dubious, so I dare to give her a little nudge. "Go. Nazira will kill me if you miss practice."

She breaks into a smile. "Text me when you get to work."

I lift my track phone from my pocket and wave it. "You bet."

Blowing me a kiss, she goes. She turns back like three times, and each time, I wave her on. Once she vanishes, I turn and jog around the building toward the bike rack.

It's empty.

Like…totally empty.

My lock hangs there, cut open and dangling. My heart sinks. Fiann. I smell her mean-girl stink all over this. She knew I'd get upset, knew I'd come back here alone… *Ugh. This is the worst.* I don't want to bug Euphoria any more than I already have, and I can't face those girls knowing Fiann's expecting me to come back in a huff looking for my bike.

My hands grow hot, the white fire rising inside me. I squinch my eyes shut. *Go away, go away, go away.* Last year, all I wanted was my power to Awaken, and now all I want is for it to go away. The irony is not lost on me.

Finally, the heat subsides, and I blow out a breath of relief.

I resign myself to walking the mile and a half to work. Check that—jogging, since I'll be late if I walk, and I sure as heck don't dare use my fairy wind in case my white flames go all crazy bananapants again.

"Tough day?" a voice behind me says.

I nearly leap out of my skin, turning to see Aldebaran there. *Great.* But I'm too tired to lie. "Yeah, I guess you could say that."

"I could help." He holds out his hand.

I look at it like it's a poisonous snake.

He laughs that bright laugh. "Come on, Syl. Trust me."

"Where are you bringing me?" I know the Fae have all kinds of tricks up their sleeves, and my gut tells me not to trust this guy.

"Where do you want to go?"

Don't trust him, don't trust him. But if I don't, I'll be late. I could lose my job. I give in. "Work. Elephant Thai near VCU."

"All right, then." He holds out his hand. "You have to take my hand, though."

"Okay." Far be it for me to look a gift horse in the gramarye.

I take his hand. There's this jolting sideways *shift* as he steps snickleways, using the fair Fae pathways set down by the sun. The brightness hurts my eyes. We're hurtling by at speeds I can't comprehend. I see only flashes of light and color. *Urgggg...* I half-expect to see the Wicked Witch on her bike. *Dun-dun-dun-dun-dun-dun.*

And then it stops, and I'm standing in a brilliant summer wood, the leaves all green and gold, perfect and sparkling. Nearby, a shining brook babbles, a family of tiny deer sipping from its edge. I turn to see white marble pillars rising up all around me. A pure white and gold castle in the near distance.

I'm in the place from my dreams.

"But where is this, exactly?" The balmy scent of a zillion wildflowers fills my nose, and I'm dazzled. Faestruck. Holy cats, I'm *faestruck* and...instantly in love with this place. At peace.

"Welcome to OverHill, my home." Aldebaran steps closer. "And yours."

CHAPTER SIXTEEN
ROUEN

The fair live by the sun
And the dark, by the moon
You and I are caught
Betwixt and between
- "In-Between," Euphoria

It's pure luck that I check out the bike rack after band practice. Something at the back of my brain keeps nagging me until I trudge up the hill and around the main building to the rack. That's when I see Syl's lock hanging there, cut open. Fury sweeps through me, cold as a winter squall, but worry wins out. I whip out my track phone and shoot off a text.

Are you okay?

Syl always teases me for writing texts out fully, but I can't help it. I'm as play-by-the-rules as she is free-spirited. As I wait for a response, I check out the scene. Someone cut her lock, and it wasn't high school security.

Of course I suspect Fiann.

So when she and the pony-tailed mean-girl posse come strolling up the hill, laughing and talking, all of them hanging on her every word like she's some kind of hero, I stride right toward them.

I can tell she's guilty because when she sees me, she brushes the other girls off. "I'll catch you guys later. Rouen wants to talk to me." She puts a hush-hush tone on it, as though I want some kind of secret rendezvous in a high school parking lot.

Maggie and Dani smirk at each other, and I know tomorrow the rumors will ignite around the school like wildfire. *Fiann and Euphoria. Gross.*

But right now, I'm too angry to care.

I stand there, towering over Fiann as the other girls hurry off, get into the cars their parents bought them, and drive away. Until it's just me and Fiann left in the parking lot.

My opening volley's a killer. "Give it back."

"What?" she asks, all wide-eyed innocence.

Her dumb act grates on me. Syl probably walked the mile and a half to work, and now Fiann's standing here, pretending to be innocent? Hells no. I'm tempted to grab her, whisk her to the top of the highest building, and dangle her off the edge to teach her some manners. But Fiann's a weirdo. She'd probably think I was flirting. Besides, the idea of touching her after she was flush with Moribund circuits… I mean, I was, too, but she actually invited it, *wanted* it.

I heave a sigh, running a hand through my hair. Syl and I still need to figure out just *how* infected Fiann is. After all, if it really is the Ouroboros, she should've gone up in a puff of black ashes and harrow-stitches by now.

Whatever. She's not getting away with this. "The bike." I glare at her, super-intense. I'm counting on the fact that she knows what I am. A dark Fae: unpredictable, dangerous, volatile. "Now."

"Oh, fine." She pouts, but she doesn't move. "So I took her bike. I was going to give it back." She flips her high ponytail over her shoulder. "Not like I'd want the grungy thing anyway." She stands there, flipping her hair like she's in some kind of shampoo commercial.

Full disclosure: dark Fae aren't known for their patience. I'm swiftly losing mine.

I step up to her car. "Nice ride." A brand-new Porsche, right off the lot. White leather interior, moon roof, power everything. I let my finger trail down the tinted window. "It'd be a shame if your car somehow...I don't know...ended up on top of the gymnasium."

I give her The Look.

Fiann pales, but then shakes her head to hide it. "Fine, fine." She pretends annoyance as she takes out a key fob and presses a button. *Pop!* The trunk clicks open, and lo and behold, Syl's bike is nestled inside.

Whodathunk?

Fiann makes no effort to help. Whatever. I push past her, trying not to inhale the scent of her expensive designer perfume. Lime and musk and something darker...like oil on asphalt. Agravaine's dark circuit. Gag.

Or is it the Ouroboros? A jolt of worry shoots through me. But how? It's literally impossible. She'd have been infected and then devoured. She would have turned other kids in the school into Circuit fiends.

She is, dummy. That girl Sofie, the other kids Syl's purified... remember them?

I do. I give Fiann the once-over with all my Fae senses while hauling the bike out one-handed. I don't see or smell anything other than the single tiny circuit of power Agravaine left in her.

Is she hiding her power somehow?

Maybe Syl should purify Fiann for good measure the next chance we get.

Syl... I set the bike down, the slight clink of it settling dread into my guts. I should've walked Syl to the bike rack, should've made sure she was okay.

Gah! I'm such a jerk.

I whirl on Fiann. There are a million things I want to say to her, but what's the point? Fiann's Fiann. She's never going to change.

Instead, I just turn my back on her and walk away.

She sniffs, calls after me. "Have you thought about my proposition? About teaming up with me?"

Yeah, about as much as Syl's thought about Aldebaran's proposition about teaming up with him. "No means no, Fiann." I keep going.

So does Fiann. "Join me. Be my queen-consort. I can help you, make you a noble dark Fae again."

"Not interested."

"But, Rouen—"

"You"—I whirl on her, jabbing at her with one finger—"don't get to use my real name. I'm Euphoria to you."

She flinches back, a hurt look in her green eyes, and then it fades into that crazed, lopsided smile I recognize from last year. Girl's got some screws loose. "Oh, come on, Rouen." She walks right up to me, hips swinging. She's trying hard to be hot, but her touch is about as sexy as spiders crawling up my arm. "We can be queens together. Me as high queen of the dark Fae, and you as my queen-consort. You wouldn't have to play by your father's rules anymore. That's what you want, isn't it?" Her gaze bores into mine as she studies me for the slightest flinch.

She's right. I do want to make my own rules, but challenging my father when he wakes? Killing him? Hells and Harrowing, no. I am a dark Fae through and through, loyal to the Winter Court, loyal to its king.

Even if he orders you to kill Syl? my dark self whispers, and my heart cries back, *No.* If it came down to that, I would challenge him, I would break our oldest rule and tradition: blood calls to blood.

Meaning, we don't fight amongst ourselves.

But for Syl, I would. I'd fight anyone.

"Well?" Fiann's all impatience and spite. "Are you going to join with me or not? There's this thing called a soul-bond. It'd make us more powerful. If I was queen, I could soul-bond you."

"Gross." There's so much wrong with what she just said, I use my rudest voice. That's all she seems to understand anyway. "I'm loyal to the king of UnderHollow." I jerk my arm away. "And if I did challenge him, I wouldn't need you to do it."

She flinches back from my intensity, but then recovers fast, snake that she is. "What if I challenged him for you? You wouldn't have to fight him, and…" She's really warming up now. "And you wouldn't have to resort to using Syl's blood. You'd like that, wouldn't you?"

I hide my shock. Fiann is too damn good at pushing my insecurity buttons.

Of course I'd like to know that Syl would be safe from everything, including me. And if that means there has to be a queen on the throne for the very first time ever, then, well…

A sharp realization hooks into my guts.

That queen is going to be me. Not Fiann.

You're thinking about challenging him, aren't you, Rouen? that rebellious part of me whispers. I try to stamp out my treasonous thoughts, but one slips free. *If he goes after Syl, all bets are off. Blood or not.*

I look Fiann straight in the eye. "I'm not teaming up with you. And soul-bonding with you? Get. Real."

Fiann's face turns an angry plum shade, nostrils flaring, eyes flashing. "Oh, I'm very real." She lunges for me and grabs my arm. "I hear her power's trying to kill you. With me, you'd never have to worry about that."

I give her points for persistence. As gently as I can, I take her arm off me. "You just can't let it go, can you?"

It makes so little sense to me that with all her wealth and popularity Fiann should care about destroying Syl, but she's still mad that Syl got the best of her last year, made her look like a fool—even if only a very few of us remember it, thanks to the Glamoury.

"Rouen—"

I'm already walking away, and this time, I'm not turning around. "Take no for an answer, Fiann." I can feel her temper tantrum building.

She's going to explode in three…two…one…

"You'll regret this, Rouen Rivoche! You and Syl. You'll both pay when I'm dark Fae queen!"

"Doubt it."

She lets out a frustrated snarl, and I just can't pass up the opportunity to rile her up. After all, maybe she'll spill some of her dastardly plan.

"No one's ever going to take you seriously as queen."

"You!" She stomps her foot like a toddler, and her voice rises shrilly. *Wait for it...* "You think you're so smart! You may have beaten me to the first four ovo, but there are three left, and that's all I need. Once I harvest the Ouroboros inside, I'll have enough power to—"

"To what?" I turn, fixing her with my dark Fae glare. Four ovo... She missed those by being in "rehab." Now there are only three left. Relief and dread flood me. Finally I can tell Syl that there'll be an end to our nightly battles.

Finally, I can...

My hand strays to my pocket. My mother's ring. *Soon, my sweet Summer girl.*

But first... "You'll have enough power to what?" I take a step toward Fiann, putting the pieces together. "I get that part of your plan—you want the Ouroboros that Agravaine left you. But no matter how much power you steal from Dark Faerie, they'll never make you queen."

So what's her endgame, then? I loom over her, hoping she'll spill.

Fiann's face is white, and she's trembling in rage and shock. Clearly she didn't mean to spill about the ovo. "You'll find out." She backs away like she's afraid I'll attack. Then she jumps into her car and peels out of the parking lot, leaving smoking skid marks.

I watch her go. "Yeah. Good talk."

I'm left standing there with my Harley and Syl's bike, reeling a bit at Fiann's confession. On a scale of one to ten, my urgency to get to Syl just ramped up to eleven.

Normally, I'd just snickle-step and come out in the alley behind Elephant Thai to return her bike. Or I'd snickle-step home and then go pick her up. But...all the pathways are collapsed, thanks to Fiann and Agravaine and their stupid circle of power that yanked the moon's ley lines off course.

I've learned my lesson after that incident in the gym.

Who knows if the Snickleways can ever be remade? Miss Jardin's words come back in a rush, *"Blood calls to blood, Miss Rivoche."*

Another interpretation of our oldest rule. But…I tried that and almost got crushed. So, the ley lines are a no-go.

I need to stow the bike and find Syl. I wheel her bike into Miss Jardin's rose garden. Despite a cool autumn and winter coming, the roses are growing, flourishing. Makes sense now I know that Miss J is an Unseelie and all. The scent makes me feel a little punch-drunk, but the trellises give me some cover.

Because there's only one place Fiann and her mean girls won't find the bike.

I leap to the top of the gym and lay the bike down.

Then I go back to my Harley, kick-start it, and speed off toward Elephant Thai to catch up with Syl, trying hard not to think of Fiann's promises, of my people slumbering in the darkness, the Harrowing abyss inching ever closer to them.

I try not to think of Syl's people coming to claim her.

Or of becoming the dark Fae queen.

CHAPTER SEVENTEEN
SYL

The beauty of OverHill is blinding
Intoxicating
Here, even the Fae can become
Faestruck
- Glamma's Grimm

It's official. The Fair Faerie realm is next-level awesome.

Dazzling sunlight cocoons me, warming me to my toes and welcoming me to this place. My birthright. The castle at the center of OverHill. I stand in a ginormous, open-air courtyard, white columns punching up from the polished white marble floors all around me. Jade-green ivy dotted with sticky-white flowers winds round the columns. The scent makes me feel all drunk and dizzy.

White benches with golden tracery sit beneath weeping white ash trees. Pollen floats in the air, and birdsong fills my ears—and the haunting silvery pipes.

"Come." Aldebaran's voice is hypnotic. I barely feel his hand in mine as he tugs me forward, through white rose hedges that tower over us. Golden thorns drip golden sap onto the rich brown earth. Everywhere I look, flowers and shrubs bloom.

"The Pleasance," he whispers in my ear. "The gardens of the Summer Court welcome you."

A white hare lopes into our path and then darts into the silvery underbrush. The babbling of a brook splishes and splashes to our left, and I glimpse it through the white trees, sunlit and glittering. Jewel-toned dragonflies dance over its surface. A flock of butterflies breaks from a bank of flowers, flittering around us, tickling my skin.

I find myself laughing, chasing them like I did when I was a child. Everything is hazy, beautiful. I could stay here forever. My heart is totally at ease.

Except…it's not.

Something is missing, beyond the fact that I haven't seen a single fair Fae aside from Aldebaran. That's definitely weird, but… that's not quite it.

Not exactly.

I stop mid-path, looking around. My hand goes to my heart. An ache swells there, and I don't know why. What is missing?

Aldebaran steps to me, touches my elbow. "What's wrong?" His voice is super-calm, but underneath, there's an edge to it. When I glance up, though, his face is still as a summer lake.

But something slithers beneath the surface.

That dark thought, here in this bright place, shocks me.

I touch my heart again, and something brushes my fingers. The ring!

"Rouen…" She's what's missing.

"Come." All the soothing tones leave Aldebaran's voice. "Now." His grip is steel-hard as he tugs—no, drags—me forward through the gardens. I have to run to keep up with him.

"Where are we going?"

He doesn't answer, only drags me, his face screwed up into a fiery snarl.

A bright splash of fear hits me. Everything that was warm about him turns harsh, searing. Is he trying to kidnap me, to force me to stay? Euphoria's always said that Fae can't force you to do a thing. You have to consent openly.

So what's his game?

The silvery pipes come again, breaking the stillness with their eerie, haunting melody. The sun bathes everything in dazzling warmth, the birds begin to sing, crickets chirp, and the brook babbles on.

"Where is everyone?" I ask, looking around at the beautiful landscape. But I already know. There are no people because he's chased them all away. They fear him.

"It doesn't matter where they are." Aldebaran's voice melds with the pipe-song, all smooth as honey. "When you return to us, they will as well."

"They...will?" I can't help the doubt and hope warring inside me.

He touches my cheek. "Yes. You are the princess. You will bring us back to a golden age." He smiles, and the warmth of the sun bathes us in that bright garden.

Aldebaran is the radiant prince once more, beautiful and gracious, warm and inviting. His touch is soft on mine, though he doesn't let go.

Everything returns to being so bright and beautiful that I wonder if I'd just imagined that slithering darkness.

We come to a stop.

"Here we are." Aldebaran's tone is gentle, coaxing. We stand beneath a white ash tree, its leaflets tinkling like tiny wind chimes, hypnotic. Seed pods float in the air, and the sunshine beams through the canopy in hazy rays.

Before us, a ring of golden mushrooms stands.

He steps into it, careful so as not to crush a single toadstool.

Glamma's ring is suddenly super-heavy, weighing me down, trying to hold me back. Frowning, Aldebaran tugs me harder.

I step into the circle.

"There now. That's better." He gestures, and the cap of one of the mushrooms appears in his fingers. He turns it over, and suddenly, it's no longer a mushroom cap. It's a golden thimble, bright and gleaming. I'm spellbound by the sunlight glinting off that tiny curve of metal. *So pretty.* He puts an arm around me, and the world goes super-bright, the sounds of silvery pipes filling my ears.

The thimble in his fingers glints, then turns molten-hot. Its shape seems to change. He takes my hand.

What is happening? I try to pull away, but the thimble holds me, transfixed.

My skin tingles. My vision whites out in a bright blare. The silver pipes howl, and my hand heats up.

Only one finger burns. My ring finger.

Panic shoots through me. I fight the weird spell, fighting against the thimble's brightness, the pipes, the soothing babble of the brook, the scent of dandelions. With a herculean effort, I yank away from him.

I stagger outside the mushroom circle, crushing a few as I go.

The faestruck spell breaks. But my hand still burns. He's placed the thimble on my finger.

But it's no longer a thimble.

A ring, made of golden light, cools on my left hand, on my ring finger.

An engagement ring.

No, this'll ruin everything! I whirl on him. "What did you do?" My heart rabbit-kicks my ribs. Suddenly, I'm sweating, panicking, filled with hot fury, one question blazing in my mind. How did he—? I'm supposed to be immune to Fae power.

He sees the question on my face and answers calmly, though a shadow slides behind those golden eyes. "Don't underestimate the power of where you come from, Syl. OverHill wants you here. With me. Soul-bound."

"No. No way." I back up. The ring's cooled from sunlight-bright moltenness to a warm metal band, and I tug and tug at it.

Stupid thing doesn't budge.

"You…" But there's no word disgusting enough for him. "What is this?" My mind races. I should be immune!

"It's a *torc*." There's zero guilt on his face, the jerk. "A ring made of OverHill. It obeys only the physics of Fair Faerie. Once you come to me willingly, once you accept that I am your prince, you'll be able to remove it. Until then, the torc will remain on your hand." His eyes burn with accusation. "To remind you of who you are—and who you belong to."

"I belong to myself." *And to Rouen, once we're ready.*

The warmth in Aldebaran's eyes goes out like a blown candle. Darkness clouds him, casting his golden hair and golden eyes in shadow, his gilded crown tarnished. "Syl, you should give it a chance. This is OverHill, your home. The SummerWood, the Meadowlands, the Pleasance, it's all here. For you." He moves to embrace me.

"Don't touch me!"

"You will do as I say." He grabs for my arm, but I'm faster.

I dart away, rage burning me up inside, hotter than this ring, hotter as my white flame. I want to get away, I need to get away, but I don't know how to snickle-step.

"Syl...you need your soul-bound prince to fully realize your power." Aldebaran steps in, cloaking himself in his Glamoury again. The shadow is gone, and the brightness returns, but it's oppressive—like looking directly at the sun. When you look away, all you're left with is black spots.

And Aldebaran is one of those black spots.

"Come. Let me show you." He reaches for me again.

The want to get away, the need, it rages inside me, and my blood—my power—awakens to the Summer all around me. I bring my hand up, licks of white flame trailing from my fingertips.

"What are you doing?" His eyes go all wide in disbelief.

I don't know what I'm doing. Getting away? But this seems like more.

With one downward swoop, I rip open the Shroud between OverHill and the mortal realm.

The calm breeze turns into a howling gale, blotting out the intoxicating scents of wildflowers and dandelions, roaring over the sounds of the silver pipes, and the brightness of the sun tilts and warps, my world narrowing down to a fine pinprick.

I hear Aldebaran howling in fury as I'm catapulted through the gaping tear.

All the Summer Snickleways pass by me, my tear like a golden seam ripping through them, slashing across the sun lines that mark the pathways to OverHill. My mind reels, my stomach drops out…

Then I fall to my knees, gasping, in the alleyway behind Elephant Thai.

CHAPTER EIGHTEEN
ROUEN

In the darkness I stand
And wait
For you
To come to me
- "Come to Me," Euphoria

Syl's not here. I pace the alleyway next to the Thai restaurant, looking up at the darkening sky. She's two hours late, and she didn't report in to work. I've already gone back and retraced the route she would've taken here. I've sent countless texts to her phone.

Nothing.

Someone has her. That cold thought grips my guts. But who? Agravaine's dead. Fiann was with me, and...

Why did it even take me three guesses? Aldebaran.

I smell his fair Fae elderflower stink all over this. The sun's ley lines weren't damaged last year in Agravaine's dirty coup attempt, so the Snickleways to OverHill are still open.

He took her there.

It's a leap in logic, but didn't Sherlock Holmes say once you discard the impossible, whatever's left, no matter how unreal, must be the truth?

Ancestors preserve me, I'm starting to sound like an English Lit textbook, and that is next-level broody.

And why would Aldebaran do that? Fae can't be forced, so he can't *make* her be his mate. He could keep her captive, but that's no way to win her over. Besides, he has to know I'd come after him.

Hells and Harrowing, I'd risk scorching to death in the merciless sun of the Summer Court to save her.

I'm pacing by my bike, imagining all kinds of awful things happening in OverHill, when I sense the ripple in the Shroud.

Someone is stepping snickleways. And yet...

Something's not right.

The shadows begin to warp and peel, then they blister, pinholes of blaring bright sunlight riddling the gloom, shredding it.

Bloody bones! That is not supposed to happen.

It looks like a thousand tiny harrow-stitches of sunlight hooking into the fabric of the Shroud, snagging it, tearing it...

I step back, shielding my eyes.

This is no manifestation. Hells no. A manifestation would coax open the Shroud, allowing Fair Faerie to shine through, like light hitting a target. This is not a gentle coaxing. The Shroud is tearing. Fair Faerie is breaching, *bleeding* out into the mortal realm.

Sunlight sears into me—pure sunlight from OverHill—and I stagger away from it, all my dark Fae instincts instantly hitting critical mass. I cloak myself in shadows, shielding myself against the killing heat and brightness. Already, my skin is starting to smoke. Still, I draw the line at hiding behind my bike. No way.

If something fair Fae is coming into this alleyway, I'll meet it head-on.

Especially if it's Aldebaran.

Shielding my watering eyes, I face it, steeling myself.

A silhouette appears in the brightness. I clench my fists, ready to beat Syl's location out of Prince Fancy, ready to beat him for daring to take her in the first place.

The figure staggers and then stumbles, falling unceremoniously into the alley. I see a flash of grey eyes, a cascade of red curls—

"Syl!" I go to her, scoop her into my arms. The sunlight washes over me, the sting instant, then amping up to a burning, searing pain across my body. With a growl, I pull us both back into the shadows.

Syl is almost limp in my arms, her grey eyes open and dazed.

Ancestors, she's been faestruck! I brush the hair from her face and pat her cheek lightly, hoping to break the spell. Her left hand feels hot as it brushes my thigh, but I pay it no mind. Of course she's hot. She just came out of OverHill.

No, not came out. *Tore out.*

I try not to panic at that thought of Faerie bleeding, try not to let my mind go wild. What did Aldebaran do to her? "Syl...Syl..." I shake her gently, cradling her.

You should have been there to protect her, Roue.

"R-Rouen?" She blinks, her eyes clear, and then she throws her arms around me and pulls me close, trembling.

I'll kill him. Murder lairs in my heart, but she's my first concern. I wrap my arms around her, allowing us a long moment before pulling away. "Did he hurt you? Syl?"

"No... Yes... He..." She shakes her head, bites her lip, her eyes filling with tears.

I'll kill him twice.

I can feel her, hot from Summer, her power right at the surface. I can't risk touching her again. "It's okay. Whatever happened, I'm here now."

"Rouen, I..."

Sunlight flares into the alleyway again.

"He's coming." Syl's face is stamped with hurt and fury.

"Oh, he is, is he?" I stand up. "Good. I can't wait."

She gets up, turns her back on the sunlit portal, and meets my gaze. "Rouen."

Okay, all this calling me by my real name is starting to freak me out, but I don't show it. I need to be strong for her. "I'm here."

"He..." She holds her left hand up.

That's when I see it. Aldebaran's ring. No, his *torc*. On my girl's hand.

In the mortal realm, the torc is just a ring. But in Faerie, it's a sign. It marks his ownership of her, that she will eventually soul-bond with him.

And somehow, he tricked her into putting it on.

A low growl rumbles from my throat. "That dirty…" A torc binds two Fae. He won't be able to control her with it, not like with a Contract, but she's tied to him.

He'll know where she is at every moment. He'll be able to track her, stalk her…and other Fae? They're supposed to recognize the torc as his claim on her.

Never. Rage sweeps over me so fast it leaves me shaking. Before, I was just going to kill him. Now? I'm going to eviscerate him. Slowly.

Once I get that damned torc off her.

The shadows peel back into a light so bright it fairly burns me. The Shroud parts the right way this time, and Aldebaran snickle-steps into the alleyway.

Anger, jealousy, rage—it sweeps through me, a freezing Winter wind. A scream of fury echoes in the alleyway. I don't recognize my own voice. In a flash, I'm on him, slamming him into the wall. Bricks crack and dust flies. The entire alleyway shakes.

"Hello, Rouen." His voice is steady, though I catch a thread of fear in those golden eyes—fear and a darkness slithering beneath the brightness.

"Hello, dead guy."

I cock my fist to take his head clean off—

"Rouen, don't!" Syl's cry stops me.

My hand shakes. I want so much to drive my fist into Prince Jerkwad's face. He's smiling at me, golden and beautiful. I want to break that radiant mask, to see the dark mess of his true soul leak through like oil and slime.

A torc. The mark of a soul-bond.

Everything Syl and I are denied.

My breathing is ragged. The temperature in the alleyway drops ten degrees.

"Rouen, please." Syl is suddenly there, easing my hand down.

I let her lower it, still glaring at him. I bare my fangs, gripping him by his T-shirt. "I see you. The real you."

A flinch in those gold eyes. "OverHill and UnderHollow will never allow a soul-bond between a fair Fae and a dark Fae." Aldebaran pulls away, straightens his shirt. His smile is bright on Syl, his expression calm. "Thank you."

"I didn't do it for you," she says, her voice cold in the darkening alleyway.

The torc glints on her finger, and I nearly lose myself to rage again.

But Syl gets between me and Aldebaran, which is probably good because I might snap at any moment.

Don't rip his head off, don't rip his head off...

Syl is flustered, upset. I take a deep breath and push my anger aside. I want to protect her, but Aldebaran is a fair Fae, one of her people.

I have to let her take lead.

She raises her chin, looks him dead in the eye. "You think this means you own me, but it doesn't. Rouen and I will find a way to break your crappy spell."

See? She can take care of herself. There's no need for me to Hulk-smash him. Still, I lay a hand on my belt. If I had my black-handled knives, I might just give him a taste of wintersteel. For good measure.

"If you say so, Syl." That arrogant, lazy half-smile rides high on his lips.

"You think we won't?" she challenges him.

He lounges against the wall. "I think you'll be really busy trying not to murder your girlfriend." He chin-nods at the torc.

Dread slicks my guts. Of course. "The torc." The last word deepens into a threatening growl. "It's going to make her power worse."

He winks at me. "Exactly."

"You—!" I lunge for him, but Syl drags me back.

147

Aldebaran clearly takes this as a signal to leave. "Don't forget what I said." His voice is slick as a car salesman's. "Your true home is waiting for you, Syl. And so am I." And then he's gone, snickle-stepping on the sunlit paths through the SummerWood.

I wince back from the brightness, the Summer heat sapping my fury. I focus on Syl. "Are you all right?"

She's trembling, tears filling her eyes again. "I'm sorry, Rouen."

"Sorry?" I shouldn't touch her—not now, not with the torc. *Screw that.* I brush away the first tear that falls. "Don't you worry about it. None of this is your fault." But the slightest glimpse of Aldebaran's torc on my girl's finger fills me with cold rage. My heart aches. Every instinct tells me to follow him, to tear him apart.

That'd be one way to get his ring off my girl's finger.

But no. This is her fight.

Just like saving the dark Fae will be mine.

I will support her, be there for her, a shoulder to cry on, a rock to lean on. But I will not decide her course of action. "I'm here for you," I say, but it doesn't seem like enough.

"Thank you." She reaches for my hand, but then pulls away. "I... shouldn't." A few more tears slip free, and she wipes them angrily with the back of her hand.

You can't help her with this, Roue. You won't survive it.

My heart collapses. The torc is of the Summer Court, with its deadly brightness, its white gleaming towers, its poisonous gardens, the very air a fume of toxic dandelion fluff and wildflower stink. A dark Fae cannot step one foot there without suffering, sickening, dying, burned to death in the sun's brutal rays.

All of OverHill is deadly to me.

That torc most of all.

Her power. My death.

I step as close as I dare. "We'll find a way to remove it." I glare at the damnable ring, glimmering brightly with Summer power. It will only intensify her own gramarye.

The power within her that wants to kill me.

Yeah, things just got even more complicated.

CHAPTER NINETEEN
SYL

A torc is a sign
Of a serious commitment
A desire between two Fae
To bind their souls
- Glamma's Grimm

I've been in some awkward situations in my life, but this one? It takes the cake. Heck, it takes the cake, eats it, and comes back for seconds.

Euphoria's super broody-quiet as we race from the alleyway behind Elephant Thai toward home. I want to be my usual cheerful self, but what is there to say? *I'm sorry the prince of my realm tried to make me his girl.* Ugh. Even the thought of it makes me want to barf.

Magic ring or not, there's no way I'm ever going to be with him.

We speed toward the VCU campus, summoning our fairy winds so fast we're barely even a blur.

My face is tight and hot from crying, my nose is stuffed up, and my heart feels like it's being crushed in a vise. I just want to be with Euphoria, to have peace between our people, and to find our rightful place in Faerie and the mortal realm.

But I can't even control my own powers.

Winter and Summer winds zip us past the VCU parking lot, Euphoria letting me lead. There's this weird, awkward tension between us, and I hate it. Was tonight only a taste of what our future holds?

Both of our peoples trying to tear us apart.

My heart hurts when I think of OverHill, how I belong there, the warm, welcoming feeling like the homecoming I've been dreaming of for so long. OverHill is in my blood. It's part of who I am.

And its prince is a horrible bullying tyrant.

The golden ring has cooled, but my hand still feels hot, burned by Aldebaran's touch, by this bogus physical claim he's forced around my finger.

I can't even look at the torc. With every move I make, it glints and catches my eye. I want to tear it off and throw it as far as I can.

But of course, it won't budge.

I'll have to find another way.

We whip past two students getting out of their car, juggling grocery bags and backpacks. This late at night, there are only a few people on the streets, so I throw up a quickie don't-see-me Glamoury. After all, I don't even look like a Fae.

Aldebaran's words come back to me. *"You need your soul-bound prince to fully realize your power."*

Something about that seems half true and half a lie.

But which half is which?

Just the thought is enough to send me into a rage, all the Summer in my blood ramping up to boiling hot. I need to scream, to punch a wall, to throw something. To run and run and just keep running until I'm too tired to think.

The ring seems to tighten on my finger, cutting off my circulation.

Cutting off my possibilities, my choices.

It is one of two that I wear.

My right hand goes to the other ring on its chain around my neck. Glamma's. I wanted to give it to Euphoria. I can't now. I might be ruined for rings forever.

Because of Aldebaran.

I remember that calm look on his face as he stole my choices.

"That's it!" I jerk to a stop near Monroe Park. A wind blows through the trees, making the leaves flitter-flutter until it seems like we're surrounded. But the park is empty, just us and a bum sleeping on a far bench.

I've seriously had enough. "I have to get this thing off. Now."

Euphoria stops near me, her aura a light blue cloak of worry. Her eyes meet mine. She doesn't ask if I'm okay. She knows I'm not. "Syl..."

"I have to get it off." I tug at it, but it's no use. Stupid thing is stuck. It won't budge.

"Once you come to me willingly, once you accept that I am your prince, you'll be able to remove it."

No. Way. I shake my head, tears of anger blurring my vision. "All right." I wave her away. "Stand back."

"Syl, what are you—?"

I step way back from her, put up my for-real Glamoury, and flame on! I call upon my sleeper-princess power.

Whoosh! White flames erupt.

They come hot and fast, raring to go after being cooped up for so long. As always, a wild, runaway joy sparks in my heart. But... I'm not exactly joyful in this moment. More like angry. I pour more and more heat into my hand, hoping to burn the ring, imagining it melting off into sludgy molten gold.

Come on, come on.

But no, the torc only glows. It doesn't even get hotter.

Darn it all! Sweat trickles down my face. From the corner of my eye, I see Euphoria throw up her own Glamoury to bolster mine. After all, I *am* using fair Fae power right here in the middle of the city. My head spins. I should not be doing this. I'm sure it's against some kind of Fae rule, but I don't care.

The gloves are off.

Until this ring comes off.

My flame fights me, trying to burst from my hands—toward Euphoria.

"Syl…" E's gentle voice breaks into my thoughts.

I'm in danger of losing control, but I push a little more power at the torc.

Nothing. No effect.

White sparks fly like fireflies racing along the ground, bursting into tiny flames. I step on them before they can ignite into something bigger.

Euphoria's a good ten feet from me, a frown crinkling her pretty face.

I want to push more, but warning bells go off in my head. *Easy, Syl.* My power is like a wild, white tiger fighting to get free, with me grasping it by the tail. I'm barely holding on.

"Syl." E's voice is stricter this time.

"Just…another second." I tense every muscle and push hotter, *please hotter.* I have to get this thing off. I can't stand looking at it, feeling his claim over me. It's like I'm trapped in some crappy romcom, only I'm totally not into the hero. Like a thousand percent not into him. Nope, nope, nope. All the nopes.

My power flares again, straining to get free, yanking in white tendrils toward Euphoria. Her bronze skin looks pale in the glow.

Her eyes flash a warning. "Syl, the Glamoury…"

I feel it, too. Our Glamouries will fail if I don't stop.

"Okay." I try to ease off, but easier said and all that. The white flames are out now, and they do not want to be snuffed out. My power fights me, the white tiger twisting, writhing, roaring to get free, but I tighten my grasp, using my fury to smother it instead of strengthening it.

Whoosh! Finally, the flames die down, leaving us in darkness again.

And that stupid torc. It still shines on my finger. I drop to my knees on the pavement, gasping in exhaustion, my head and heart hurting.

Euphoria squats down near me, her aura blazing light blue, though she keeps her game face. "Let's go home, princess."

Love swells in my chest. My Winter girl, so stoic and strong for me. I feel terrible. I brought this on myself by wanting to find out where I came from. Didn't I?

"It's my fault," I blurt out.

E's look gets all gentle. "No, my sweet Summer girl. It's not your fault at all. It's his."

I push myself up and start pacing, all these thoughts whirling in my mind, making my head ache, my heartbeat a pounding mess. "It's too much," I say. "It's just too much."

But when I turn, she's there. "I know," she says simply. "I'm here for you." For a sec, it seems like she'll open her arms to embrace me. But then she just stuffs her hands into her pockets.

I can't even touch her without fear I'll hurt her.

I grab the torc again, tugging on it, my hand hurting. Good thing for my Fae healing, or I'd have probably yanked my own finger off by now.

"I want it off." I look at her, desperate. "Is there anything you can do?"

"I…"

I know she wouldn't hesitate if there wasn't a very good reason, but I don't want reasons. I want results. "We have to at least try. Please!"

"All right," she relents. "I can try."

I hold out my hand.

"Here?" She looks around, but we are hidden from the streets by giant trees and a huge construction fence. The one bum in the park's asleep. There's no one out here but us.

"Please, Euphoria."

She hems and haws, but I see the exact moment she gives in. "I suppose it's safer out in the open." Her sapphire-blue eyes flick to mine. "Just in case."

In case anything goes wrong. Both of us have crazy-powerful gramarye. If we tried this in my bedroom, we'd probably light the entire tenement on fire.

And then Mom would officially kill me.

"The Glamouries should shield us." Euphoria holds out her hands. "Put your hands in mine."

"Are you sure?"

"It's only for a moment."

"Okay." I lay my palms across hers, like you'd do in that game where you try to pull your hands away before your opponent slaps them. But this time, she's going to slap me with dark Fae power.

And I'm not going to pull away.

She bites her lip.

"What is it? Are you going to use the lightning?" Part of me is terrified of that raw dark Fae energy. Seriously, I've seen her destroy hell-hounds and Circuit fiends with a single bolt.

"No." She shakes her head, her face grim. "I'm going to try to call upon the Winter in my blood to...freeze it off." She sounds doubtful.

I cheer her on. "Okay, great."

"I've only tried this once before." Her blue eyes are super-intense. "I could hurt you."

"I don't care."

"I care." She lets go of me and walks a few feet away, flexing her fingers until her knuckles crack. Silhouetted by the streetlights, her pretty face is all concern and confusion, but fury rolls just beneath the surface. Hers is an icy anger, cold, terrifying, sharp as her win-tersteel blades. Mine is hot and passionate.

We are two opposites. Her power, my weakness.

This should work. It has to work. "Please. Please, Rouen."

"I remember..." Her voice catches and she clears her throat. "I remember what it was like when Agravaine first spliced the Mori-bund into my hand. Aside from the pain, it didn't feel like my hand anymore. It felt like..."

"His," I finish for her. "Yes." That's exactly how I feel.

"Okay." Resolve steels her gaze, and she takes my hands again. She closes her eyes, concentration making her face all frowny. With a breath, she summons her fairy wind, and a cool breeze blows across us, chilling the sweat on my skin, making me shiver. Her hands tremble as she holds mine.

The chill in the air turns biting. I can see my breath.

Sweat freezes on her temples. She bites her lip over a gasp. Of pain? I want to pull away, but the chill feels good on my swollen hand.

"It's working…" Hope sparks in my chest.

With a sudden icy breath, Euphoria's eyes snap open, glazed over with frost. She pushes more power. I feel the chill intensify. The temperature drops again.

Zap! A cold blue spark jumps from her hands to mine, the Winter in her blood attacking Aldebaran's ring. In answer, the torc lights up, a brilliant fiery gold, Summer against Winter.

Without warning, a jolt of sunlight leaps from the ring at Euphoria.

Her blue eyes go wide, and an icy shield appears, the bolt crashing into it. The ice shatters. She's blown backward.

She crashes to the ground near a park bench and rolls once, her leather jacket, her leather pants, every part of her smoking.

"Euphoria!" I race over.

She sits up, coughing, shards of ice melting all around her. Her sapphire-blue eyes are dazed. "Did it…?"

Her gaze falls to my hand, where the ring still glints.

Tears threaten to turn me into a blubbering idiot, but I dash them away. I won't give him the satisfaction of crying. I stand up, sniffle once, and get my act together. "Let's go home."

Once more, I touch Glamma's ring on its chain. I promise myself, and I promise Euphoria.

I will find a way to remove this ring.

CHAPTER TWENTY
ROUEN

Daughter of the Winter Court
I am cold, emotionless
But with you
I burn and burn and burn
- "Burn" Euphoria

All night, I can't get Syl's face out of my mind—that pale, shattered look she gave me when we couldn't get the torc off her finger. That look haunts my nightmares. It haunts me in the shower and at breakfast, on the ride to school, Syl holding onto me, glum and quiet.

I should have been there. When Aldebaran forced that ring on her finger, I should have been there to stop him. And I wasn't.

Just another thing to be gloomy-doomy about, Rouen, my inner critic scolds.

Guilt swells inside me. Worse, my dark self rises, urging me to take her, possess her, steal her away and keep her for my own. Now, now, now, now.

I crush those voices down deep.

Still, they gnaw at me as I escort Syl to her class. "Hey…" I give her hand a quick squeeze. "It'll be all right. I promise."

Syl nods. "Okay." Her voice is strained, and she's trying so hard to give me that bright smile of hers. "Have fun in band." But there's no teasing today.

I risk a quick kiss to her forehead. I want so much to linger, but I can't. "I'll see you after." It takes every ounce of my willpower to walk away from her. The last time I left her alone…

By the time I get to the band room, I'm filled with cold fury.

"Hi, Euphoria!" Octavia is her usual cheerful self. She, Naz, Marcus, and Chuck have their heads together about Battle of the Bands stuff, but I'm in my own funk.

"Fiann's going to cheat," Octavia is saying. "Because she's Fiann, right, E?"

I only grunt, taking out my violin.

My girl is hurting. I have to do something.

All class, that thought pulses coldly inside me. I'm going through the motions of playing, but for once, it doesn't bring me solace or pleasure.

I can get it out of my head—Syl's face… Shattered.

Just the thought of someone doing lasting harm to my girl makes my Winter blood sear with icy vengeance. All class, that cold fury inside me builds and builds like a snowstorm picking up wind and sleet and brutal speed. I've sworn not to butt in. I've sworn to let Syl make her decisions.

And I will. But I have to do *something*.

By the end of band, I know what I must do.

When lunch comes, I slip out into the west quad, a courtyard of sorts with four walls and only rafters but no roof. I hear it was part of a historical building before Richmond E was here, so they built it into the school itself. Six green picnic tables line the area, three on each side with a wide lane down the middle. Yellow umbrellas sit atop each table, casting long shadows in the early morning sunshine.

And there, beneath the last umbrella on the right, sits one lone figure—Aldebaran, his golden brightness not at all dimmed by the shade.

He sees me, too.

Be careful, Rouen.

Despite my control as a nobleborn princess of the Winter Court, despite my cold calculation, all my feelings—love, protectiveness, guilt—boil up inside me.

I am a powder keg, waiting for a lit fuse.

I walk toward him slowly, sizing him up. *Hello, fuse.*

The quad's deserted at this time of day, everyone piled into the cafeteria or at class. I pass by the comic book murals, amused that the image of Gotham City looms behind him, the Bat Signal a yellow beacon in a dark sky.

He watches my every move with those golden eyes. He's as attractive as any superhero's alter ego, on par with Bruce Wayne and Clark Kent.

But I know the truth of him.

"The worst villains are the ones who don't look like villains."

He's the very picture of calm. "Rouen."

"Prince Fancy-Pants." I want so much to punch his head clean off his shoulders, but I rein in my cold anger. Barely.

There are rules when noble Fae want to shed blood.

I straighten to my full height. When I speak, my voice rings across the open rafters. "Aldebaran of the fair Fae, I challenge you to a duel. To the blooding. By the fádo, the old laws."

He leans against the table, his posture relaxed, his eyes hooded as he contemplates my challenge.

Then he utters one word, "No."

All my control threatens to snap. I clench my fists. "You can't refuse a duel."

He sighs, running a hand through his short spiky locks. "Only a royal Fae can invoke the traditions of fádo. And you"—he smirks—"are no longer royalty, Rouen Rivoche, sluagh, outcast."

My fury swells inside me, a snow squall raging out of control. "Too bad, buddy-boy. You picked this fight the second you staked your claim on my girl."

"Your girl?" He scoffs. "How can she be yours when she belongs to OverHill?" His words shock me, and he keeps right on going.

"You don't have the power to claim her. Not unless you take the throne."

"I don't want it." But even as I say it, I know it's not true. Not really. If I were queen, I could stop this war, stop the fighting, the hatred, the prejudice. I could keep Syl truly safe.

Nothing like this would ever happen again. Ever. Not on my watch.

He chuckles, unfolding his long legs across the picnic table's bench. "Your father or your girl, Rouen?"

There's no contest. I know it in my dark heart. And when my people wake from Winter's Sleep, I'll have to choose.

"Here's the thing, Rouen." He steps away from the picnic table and toward me, the outline of Gotham City looming large over his shoulder. "You'll need that crown if you ever want to duel me for her."

He's right again.

"If I want to duel…"

"Yup." He smirks.

I smash him in the face, the meaty *smack!* so, so satisfying as I knock him right off his bench. "How about I just kick your ass, then?"

He sprawls on the ground, those gold eyes wide in shock.

Winter's fury roars inside me as I step over him, throwing up an extra layer of Glamoury—my *it's about to go down* level. "Forget duels. Forget the fádo. No one touches my girl."

"You'll regret that." He stands, wiping blood from his split lip.

Now I smirk. "Doubt it."

He ducks my flying punch, and my fist shatters Gotham City, the brick beneath crumbing into dust. I whirl around…

Just in time for his kick to slam into my cheek. I sprawl against the brick, crushing it into a spiderweb of cracks. *Sorry, Batman.*

"I wouldn't underestimate me if I were you." Aldebaran stands between the picnic tables, his stance loose and fluid like a snake about to strike.

Before I can answer, he dashes in, a golden blur. I dodge punches and kicks, him flowing around me like a Summer breeze. The heat chokes me, threatening to sap my strength.

159

I pour on the Winter. Cold and heat warring it out in the quad, steam rising from the cobblestones. I block; he counters. We trade blows in the early morning, the sun rising, casting shadows of the umbrellas across us.

"Haaaaaa!" With a battle cry, he lunges.

I sidestep, grabbing his leg, and hurl him at the wall. This time, Gotham City PD crumbles to dust. I'm on him fast, punching, driving him into the wall again and again.

The impacts feel so good, my dark self revels in every one. *Hit him. Hit him again.*

He falls to the ground and I step back. I may be dark Fae, but I don't kick people when they're down. He wipes blood from his mouth, a look of disbelief in his eyes.

He didn't think I could hurt him.

Think again, pal.

"You want to take this to the next level, do you?" He gets to his feet, staggering a bit.

I smirk. "Sure, why not?"

Aldebaran raises his hand. A brilliant glow sparks there, so brilliant it hurts my eyes.

Hell and hue. Is he trying to manifest again?

No. He's—

A bolt of pure sunlight leaps off his hand. Barely, I dodge, and it sizzles past me, searing my cheek. A lock of my black hair falls to the ground.

Blast and bloody bones! Maybe I spoke too soon about that next-level thing.

He is older, faster, and he has access to his full power. The Fair Fae hearthstone is still alive, still healthy. I see his ties to it, threads of heat shimmering around him the way heat shimmers off the pavement in the dead of summer.

He fires again, and I dive behind a picnic table.

The golden bolt blasts it in two, and I'm showered in wood dust.

He snarls in frustration.

I snicker. "Aww…is the dark Fae princess giving you too much trouble?" Snatching up a slab of wood as a shield, I dart away.

He fires again, and my makeshift shield goes up in a flare of sunfire.

"No trouble at all. I can do this all day." He laughs and blasts away.

I dive behind another table. Grabbing it by the legs, I yank it up from its moorings. Nuts and bolts patter to the ground.

He advances, his hand glowing so bright I can barely look. He seems a creature of sunlight and sunfire.

I hurl the picnic table. "Here, catch!"

He doesn't. The table smacks him dead center, plowing him into another table. He upends over the top like a Cirque du Soleil performer making his first-ever mistake. He crashes to the ground. I leap over the table with a double stomp.

He rolls, and my boots crash down where his head just was, breaking the cobbles.

He gets to his feet, panting, readying his next sunbolt.

Only one of those would gravely wound me, perhaps kill me. *He's not playing around, Roue.* He's practically burning up with rage. *Good. I can work with that.*

I call out in my most mocking voice, "So you do want to duel?"

"Never!" He spits the word like foulest poison and fires another flare.

I dodge it, reaching for the table behind me. "Then why use your full power," I taunt, "unless you think you need it, prince?"

His face turns red and he blasts at me. "Shut up!"

I yank the umbrella from the picnic table and sweep it in front of me like a shield. The sunlight hits the yellow canopy, burning through it. As it turns to ash, I shove the burned pole like a javelin at his face.

Crack! It smacks him in the chin. He hurtles back, crushing the Bat Signal this time—*Wow. DC is sure taking a beating*—and goes down like a ton of bricks.

I stand over him, pointing the burned pole at his throat. "Yield to me. Take your blasted torc off Syl. Remove your claim on her."

"Why, so you can have her?" he snarls, blood on his teeth. "She is my princess, to be soul-bound to me. Mine to use as I will."

My cold fury matches his hot anger. "Really?" I'm just about to reeducate him about girls, consent, why no means no—all at the end of a sharpened stick—when he sits up and touches my hand.

He *manifests*.

All that was warm and bright in him intensifies, the power of Summer turned up full blast into an oppressive, scorching heat. His golden eyes flash molten-hot, his touch burning, burning, burning…

Sweltering heat envelops me, chokes me, saps my strength as the Gates to OverHill loom, dragged forth from Fair Faerie at the behest of its prince. The golden radiance blinds me, waves of heat blasting me.

"Gah!" I stagger to a knee.

He grins at me. "You recognize this power, yes?"

Even now, my body is burning up at his very touch.

He leans in. "I could kill you, but I won't. I want you to watch me take her away from you."

I bare my fangs at him. It's all I can do, my entire body racked with agony. Smoke begins to rise from my skin, like I'm a vampire caught in sunlight.

"Goodnight, Rouen." A spark jumps from his fingers, jolting into me, and blackness rises to take me.

"Rouen…Rouen?"

Urgggg… I groan as consciousness swamps me, my entire body a sweaty mess, throbbing with pain. I've got the world's worst third-degree sunburn, every inch of me stinging sharp. But my pride hurts more.

I'm a dark Fae. I have standards.

"Rouen!"

My eyes snap open, and I'm staring into Syl's beautiful face lined with worry.

See the trouble you cause her, Roue?

I sit up, scattering my traitorous thoughts. "Syl...where?" I'm still in the quad, the ruin of the murals all around me, the broken, burned umbrella, the upturned picnic tables. The ground beneath me is scorched black, the cobblestones melted.

It comes rushing back to me, challenging Aldebaran, throwing down, his sunfire power, and then—

"Aldebaran! He manifes—"

"What? Rouen...you're hurt." She almost touches my cheek, then thinks better of it. Even the heat from her nearness burns me. Aldebaran's torc doesn't kid around. I wince in pain.

"It's nothing." I get my legs under me, but I'm shaking like a newborn faun. My veins feel like they're on fire, every part of me hurt and aching.

"Come, sit." Syl moves a bench over and coaxes me to it. She has to restrain herself from reaching out to me, finally stuffing her hands into her pockets.

I know the feeling. I just want to hold her. If only for a moment...

"What happened?" Her storm-grey eyes are concerned, grave.

I blow out a breath and get her up to speed. Okay, I kind of gloss over the part where Aldebaran refused my duel because I'm no longer royalty. I mean, no sense pouring gasoline on the Dumpster fire, and definitely no sense reminding her about the whole *sleeper-princess blood can purge my sluagh taint/make me royalty again.*

"I'm glad you're okay." Syl's looking at me like I'm made of spun glass.

"I'm all right." And to show her just how all right, I get to my feet. Pain rockets through my body, and I barely bite back a scream. My vision greys. *Uh-oh.*

Syl jerks to catch me, but white flames spasm across her palms.

"Don't!" I hold up a hand, grab the edge of the table until the wooziness passes.

"Rouen..." She sounds so miserable I want to kick myself.

I've failed her twice now.

As if sensing my gloom and doom, she gentles her voice. "It's all right. We'll figure this out. We'll find a way. Together."

Did I mention that I love this girl?

"Together." I straighten. "What time is it?" My head rings, and then I realize…it's the bell.

"Well, lookee here." A too-familiar voice cuts through my headache. As if on cue, Fiann stands at the entrance to the quad, Principal Fee behind her. "Look at this, Daddy. It looks like Rouen and Syl destroyed the quad, but why?" She looks right at me. "Why would you do such a thing?"

I step forward. "It was me. Syl had nothing to do with it."

Syl opens her mouth to deny it, but a bright figure moves into view.

Aldebaran smirks." I saw the whole thing, principal. Rouen's telling the truth for once."

"Miss Rivoche." Principal Fee drops the bomb. "You've just earned a month's detention, and I'll be calling your guardian about paying for the damages."

I blow out a heavy sigh. Could today get any worse?

CHAPTER TWENTY-ONE
SYL

The SummerWood
So beautiful it haunts you
Men have died
Faestruck and dreaming
- Glamma's Grimm

Halloween's on a Saturday, but E and I decide to skip the high school parties. After all, last year was a hot mess—Fiann's party, her trying to sabotage my costume. I mean, yeah, I got the hang of my Glamoury that night. But Fiann's pretty much the worst, and I see enough of her at school, so…

This Halloween night, Euphoria and I are spending it more wisely.

First, we head into Richmond center for training. Now that I've mastered my fairy wind, E's going to teach me how to windwarp the way she does.

She makes it look easy.

One minute, she's on the ground, and then next, *whoosh!* In a gust of Winter wind, she vanishes then appears on top of the Omni Hotel in a puff of violet mist and ice.

She looks waaaay down at me, all smirky cat that got the cream.

I jump up and down, getting loose, psyching myself up. "Okay, Syl, you can do this. It's only…what? Eighteen stories." *Two hundred and seventy feet,* the mathlete in me calculates. Still, I've never been one to back down. I summon a fairy wind, and the warm breezes of Summer wrap me up, ready to speed me through the city.

But speed's not what I want.

Relax. Euphoria mouths the word.

Try as I might, I am so not grasping the concept of being able to use the wind to freaking *teleport* like Nightcrawler. I've tried a million times. By now I should be all like *bamf!* Except with less ozone smell.

I sigh. Glamma would say it's time to try a million and one times.

I relax and call my fairy wind. *Zoom!* I zip down the street, but up? Not so much.

At least Euphoria's patient with me. I glimpse her way up there, that sexy smirk curving her lips, and my heart gets all fuzzy and swoony.

She seems no worse for the wear after her fight with Aldebaran, and I'm hoping that playing the Monsters' Ball at the Nanci later will cheer her up.

As for me, I'm holding out for Halloween date night.

I touch Glamma's ring on its chain beneath my cute top.

Come on, date night!

Forgetting wind-warping for a sec, I take three giant leaps up to where E's standing. The autumn night is cool, and even though days have passed since the whole Aldebaran/ring thing, everything still feels super…uncool. First, Aldebaran manages to faestrike me in OverHill, which is supposed to be my home turf in Faerieland, and then he taunts Euphoria with the fact that I'm wearing his ring.

No, not his ring. His *torc*. Some tricksy fair Fae spell meant to… to what? Lull me into accepting him? Really? I might be an introvert, but I'm hardly the docile "mate" material he wants.

And then there's Euphoria.

"You okay?" It's like the gajillionth time I've asked.

"Yeah." Her smile shows she's trying, but her eyes? There's the same look as when I showed up in the alleyway, Aldebaran's ring on my finger. Betrayal. Hurt. I know she doesn't blame me, but I blame myself.

All my instincts told me that guy was bad news.

"Are you sure?" I ask her, because I know she can sense it— OverHill's gotten under my skin, wedged my heart wide open.

How can I find my place when my heart is split between Euphoria and my people?

"I'm good." She steps to the edge, the wind blowing her black hair all wild, and gestures at the city. "Shall we?"

"Sure thing!" I step up next to her. I'm so ready to tackle that million and first try. I'm bound and determined to learn every Fae power I can.

That'll teach jerkface Aldebaran that I don't need him.

"Remember: call the wind, ride the wind, be the wind." And then E's off like a bullet from a gun, *flying* across the buildings, windwarping so fast all I see are bursts of icy violet mist against the night.

It's like she's trying to outrun something.

I get it. There's no sense in rehashing things until we have a solid plan to get this stupid torc off my finger. Even now, it's all glitzy and in our faces.

No wonder she's having a hard time.

She stops on top of the new Dominion tower and waves me on. Her sapphire-blue eyes flash with mirth and mischief, pulling at my heartstrings so hard I almost step right off the building.

Whoa…head in the game, Syl. I take a deep breath, ready to summon my fairy wind, ready to put the weirdness behind us.

But can we? Aldebaran's torc, his promise that my power would actively try to murder her…

It's a lot.

Still, E and I are a team. I need her stoic strength. She needs my hopefulness, so I put on my bravest face. *Call the wind, ride the wind, be the wind...* So far, I've managed to nearly fall to my death at least three times.

Doing great, Syl. Ha, ha, yeahhhh...

I'm ten stories down on the bank building, looking up at her. She waves at me, and that slow smirk curves her lips. I'm relieved to see it, even though she's being a cheeky minx.

At least that's still the same between us. *Okay, then. Challenge accepted.*

I leap from the roof, pushing off hard and sailing into the night. *Call the wind, ride the wind, be the wind...*

I feel it whipping past me, but catching the wind is like trying to grab a greased piglet.

Lucky for me, my fairy wind speeds my leap, and I don't fall this time. Instead, there are a few spinning seconds as I sail into the night, the wind on my face chill and whipping my red hair around.

Still can't catch it... I flail, like I'm grasping at straws falling through my fingers.

And then I land, my boots whomping down on the rooftop. "Darn it all!" Frustration makes me all hot and sweaty.

"Catch me if you can, princess!" Euphoria's off like a shot.

I try to cut her off by darting through the leftover construction on top of the tower. I race through the scaffolding and between partitions. She's out of sight for a sec, but I'm suddenly filled with gutsy confidence.

I can do this.

It's because of her that I can do this.

I remember all those nights last year with her pushing me harder, pushing me faster, pushing me to Awaken.

I finally did.

And now Aldebaran wants to say I'm still "not there"? That I somehow need him to fully realize my power?

Ha! Jerk. I'll bet I could catch him without breaking a sweat. As for Euphoria...

She's fast, but clearly my guerrilla tactics have confused her. Usually, I'm a straight shooter, playing it fair, which…pretty much explains why I keep losing to a dark Fae.

Tonight, I take a page from her playbook. I get sneaky.

I stop just at the inside of the scaffolding, hidden from her sight.

She's on the edge of the building, looking down, probably watching the kids in their costumes trick-or-treating down Main. I have her back.

My heartbeat is a pounding wreck. I'm totally going to get her.

I might not be able to windwarp, but who needs that when you're a sneaky fair Fae princess-ninja? I take two quiet steps, then I'm running, throwing myself out in a flying tackle.

It's at the last second I realize my mistake.

She turns, a gleam in her eye. She knows!

Crap. Crappity, crap, crap, crap.

She sidesteps, dodging and kind of olé-ing me like a bullfighter pulling the cape up. Only, this bull is going straight down, down, down…

I plummet, seeing her snarky little wave as I fall. "Don't forget to windwarp, princess!"

Darn her and her dark Fae tricks!

The wind blurs by now, burning my lungs, gravity sucking me down. Normally, I'd freak, but since I've Awakened…

I freak and then I try to windwarp.

Call the wind, ride the wind, be the wind…

Nope. Nothing. Still falling to my death.

The pavement rushes up fast. Glimpses of jack-o'-lanterns and orange lights, trick-or-treaters flash closer and closer. I hope my Glamoury holds.

Because I'm about to become roadkill.

At this point, I fall back on Old Faithful: my fairy wind. Because if I don't, I'm totally going to go splat.

And that would be one thousand percent uncool.

Come on, come on…

Finally, with a burst of Summer breezes, my fairy wind comes. *Yes!* It swirls around me, buoying me like a bobber on a lake, ten feet from the asphalt, and I whoosh over a group of kids dressed like the Power Rangers. Whew! They notice the wind, but don't see me. Double whew.

Go, go, sleeper-princess!

I glance way up at Euphoria. It's on now.

Get ready for it, Miss Smarty Pants.

Using my fairy wind, I leap upward. This time, I don't overshoot my target. I zoom straight for her.

With a flash of a smirky-smile, she bolts off the rooftop, her fairy wind an icy violet cloak swirling around her. I can't keep mine going for as long as she does. She's faster, *and* she can wind-warp, but I'm getting there.

In half a mile, my fairy wind gives up. As it fails, I put on a burst of speed, burning it out in a final surge. And everything comes together like the perfect storm.

The last burst of fairy wind catapults me toward her. She zigs when she should zag, and… Got her! I tackle her around the waist, and we both fall to the rooftop. She twists midair, taking the brunt of the impact because, yeah, my girl's chivalrous like that.

All my love for her swells inside me, my internal butterflies doing the cha-cha. I wanted to talk, but now, with her in my arms, warm and soft, I don't want to talk at all.

There's something far better we can be doing with our lips.

By unspoken agreement, we come together, our lips brushing, and then we are tangled together on the rooftop. Her breath is warm, her kisses wild. Her touch is heaven. My hands are everywhere, on her sides, on her hips, sliding up to run through her hair. I'm lying on her, our bodies pressed together, burning, burning, burning…

This. This is what I've been missing.

And for some ungodly reason, I totally forget why this is a bad idea.

My body is on fire. My left hand is on fire, my ring finger blazing. The sudden blare of silver pipes fills my ears. *No. Oh no, no, no, no…*

The torc constricts, and now, I'm really burning.

My hands ignite in white flame. "Rouen!"

Panic lights her eyes. Hissing in pain, she shoves away from me, black smoke rising from where I was touching her. I jerk away, too, freaking out, shaking my hands, trying to douse the flames.

But this is different.

There's a shadow that burns blue-black on the edges of my flame—the torc's magic twisting my own.

Calm down, Syl, calm down, calm down!

I exhale hard, and the flames whoosh out as quickly as they came, taking that blue-black shadow with them. *Rouen...* I'm afraid to look, but the stench of burned leather stings my nose. *Please tell me I didn't...*

Please tell me she's not...

When I turn, Euphoria stands there, her shoulders smoking. Her leather jacket is burned away, the skin beneath black and blistered.

"No!" I jerk toward her, but then stop. I can't go to her.

I'd only make it worse.

I look down at my hands like they've betrayed me. The golden torc glows hot, just beginning to fade. My stomach bottoms out, and I feel like I'm going to hurl.

And Euphoria...usually she heals super-fast, like Wolverine, right on the spot, but she's...not.

"I..." What can I say to her? Sorry I nearly burned your face off?

But in an instant, she's right there next to me, close but not touching. "It's all right," she soothes me. "It's not your fault." Her gaze drops to the torc, her eyes narrowing.

"It is." I shake my head. "My power's been trying to kill you all summer!" I swallow hard over a lump in my throat. "And now..."

Now, it's intensified by a factor of a gajillion.

Aldebaran's threat races through my mind. *"I think be really busy trying not to murder your girlfriend."* I lost control at the football field when Fiann kissed my girl, but this is so much worse.

Euphoria meets my gaze.

We say it in unison. "The ring."

It's faded from a hot glow to a cool gold. Pretty, innocent-looking. For a wild moment I consider chopping my own finger off.

"How can he just control my power like that? What's wrong with me?"

"Nothing." Euphoria moves closer, and I see that she wants to touch me, comfort me. We don't dare. "Your power comes from Fair Faerie, from OverHill. The very realm where Aldebaran rules as prince."

"So he can just use my power however he wants?"

"No." E shakes her head. "He's intensifying it." Her voice is tight. "Using the torc."

It's too much. The silvery pipes, Aldebaran, the torc. "I hurt you!"

I throw myself into her arms, grateful when no part of her flinches or jerks back. She stands, solid and warm and real, an anchor against all my guilt and fear and doubt.

At least for a second.

When my white flame flares up inside me again, hot and burning, when I hear those silvery pipes, I jerk away. Fast.

Euphoria steps back, too. She blows out a breath and fingers her burned jacket, her burned skin. A wince crosses her pretty features.

I hover like a mother hen. "Are you...? Will it heal?" Last year, we totally teamed up to defeat Agravaine, and tonight, I practically burned her to ashes.

She nods quickly, dropping her hand. "Yeah. I'll be fine."

My beautiful Winter girl. I know her *I'm just saying that* face. Guilt nearly wrecks me. My voice cracks. "How do we stop it?"

E's the hurt one, but she's super-gentle with me. "We find a way to get that ring off you."

"How? I mean, I could ask the king of Fair Faerie, if I could even find him." Doubt's having its way with me—doubt and crazy, wild ideas. "Plus, I can't even get to OverHill, and you can't teach me to walk the sunlit Snickleways."

"Syl." Euphoria takes my face in her hands. "You are a fair Fae princess. Within you is a power every bit as strong as Aldebaran's. We just need to unlock it."

"Aldebaran says I can't do it without him." Panic swirls in my chest. "And now, he's upped the ante. What if I really can't?"

Euphoria smiles softly at me. "Since when have you needed anyone?"

"I need you." My voice shakes, and tears fill my eyes again. *Aw, crap.* "Rouen, I'm—"

"Don't you dare say you're sorry. You are not to blame for this. Aldebaran is, and we'll find a way to defeat him. Together." She looks me in the eye, all fierce beauty and determination.

That's the best thing about us. When one weakens, the other is strong. We support each other.

E's been super-cool about all this, but she's hurt, physically and emotionally. At least I can do something about the physical part. "Come on." I nudge her. "Let's swing by home and patch you up before we head to the Nanci. It's almost time."

"All right." She nods and wastes no time wind-warping away, toward home. I leap down, fall in step with her. She switches to her fairy wind, and in a burst of Winter and Summer, we rush past the interstate, throwing up our Glamouries up so the humans can't see. In a passing car, a ten-year-old girl dressed as Alice in Wonderland points, but her mom sees nothing.

Nothing. That's what I owe Aldebaran.

I don't owe him a stinking thing. Not friendship, not dating privileges. Certainly not my kisses or embraces. My body is mine until I choose to give it.

The universe seems to want to pair me up with him, but you know what?

Forget the universe.

I watch Euphoria leap to the next building, all badass grace and strength.

When I give myself, I want it to be to her.

CHAPTER TWENTY-TWO
ROUEN

What is fair cannot survive in darkness
What is dark cannot survive in fairness
- "Star-Crossed," Euphoria

Everything hurts.

But I don't let on as Syl and I climb up the tenement's fire escape and slip back through her window. She heads to the bathroom to grab the first aid kit, and I sink into the beat-up chair by her vanity table.

I take that moment to drop the tough act.

A glance in the mirror tells me the truth: I look like ten miles of rough road. Sure, my hair's still wavy and styled, and my eye shadow and liner's on point, but there's no mistaking the dark circles under my eyes—or the fact that my shoulders are burned to hell.

My jacket's toast, so I shrug out of it. A hiss of pain escapes my lips, and I grit my fangs, swallowing the rest of it as Syl comes back with bandages and peroxide in hand. "Here you go."

Our fingers brush as she hands me the stuff, and she jerks away, terrified to even touch me. Cold rage sweeps through me, and my fist tightens around the bandages.

If only this was Aldebaran's throat...

"Rouen?" Syl's watching me, ready to fret over every wince and gasp of pain.

"I'm good," I say, injecting reassurance into my voice—maybe for both of us, because this is going to hurt like hell. I pour the peroxide onto the bandages and press them to my wounds. The pain goes from *this sucks* to *unholy hells and Harrowing, I'm dying.*

I manage to keep my cool, though. Barely.

All right, maybe I whimper a little.

Syl's wringing her hands by the time I'm done.

"Come on." I stand up, silently vowing to do everything in my power to take away the pain and doubt I see in her eyes. "After the show, how about I take you out? A real date night."

That gets a smile, the storm clouds lifting from her features to reveal that bright smile of hers, a shine in her eyes. "Really?"

It's been months since we had any time to ourselves, what with the Ouroboros and Circuit fiends, and now Fiann and Aldebaran. I smile back at her. "Yeah. Let the world wait for a night."

But will it? *Rue and wrath, I hope so.*

By the time we arrive, the Nanci Raygun is packed, the Monsters' Ball drawing a massive crowd. Ghosts and ghouls and super-heroes pack in with Disney princesses and horror-movie icons, everyone rowdy in a good-natured way.

The energy of so many people jammed into a small space, united in their love of the music, rushes over me. I breathe it in—the musky tang of excitement and adrenaline mingled with the scent of coming autumn. I revel in it as I lean back against the wall in the backstage area.

My shoulders are still sensitive, my healing power working slower than usual since Syl's white flame is my complete and utter nemesis. I haven't let on about that, either.

Still, I know Syl knows. My girl's nothing if not perceptive.

She leans in. A quick kiss to my cheek makes me yearn toward her, wanting more. I see it in her eyes. She wants more, too. But for now... "I'll wait for you by the stage."

"After," I say, and we both freeze. "After" was what I promised her that night we very first met, way back when I was ordered to kill sleeper-princesses. I didn't keep my promise that night.

I look her right in the eye. "Syl, I swear by all that's dark and unholy, tonight, I'm going to keep my pro—"

"Nope." She shushes me sweetly. "Don't promise. Just in case."

My answering sigh is heavy, but I nod in agreement.

She's right.

These past few weeks have been tough, with Fiann coming back, catching us off-guard with her ties to the Ouroboros, then Aldebaran showing up and making Syl's powers go crazy.

"You know," I tell her, only half-joking, "we could take the direct approach and beat the stuffing out of Prince Fancy."

Her smile is just as sweet as the rest of her, though there's summersteel in those grey eyes of hers. "I want to beat him at his own game."

One look at her, and I can't deny her anything. "All right, princess. We'll play your way."

At least for now.

"See you soon." She blows me a kiss and heads out to the main club area.

I wait in the wings backstage as the house music blares, bumping and thumping through the speakers, fake fog rolling across the stage, the orange jack-o'-lantern and purple skull lights bobbing spookily.

"Euphoria." The backstage guy holds up three fingers. Three minutes. I inhale deeply, taking all the energy of the crowd into myself.

I'm ready. So ready for this. I need it.

I cradle my violin, its glassy surface glinting. My shoulders still hurt. I need escape, need this moment on stage to lose myself, to play, to forget, to just *be.*

I draw the curtain back an inch. Syl's out there now. My heart rate kicks up a notch. I love seeing her there, watching me play. I love having that connection with her.

It's like the whole world goes away, and I play only for her.

Syl... My heart aches, the hollow left by the shattered hearth-stone cranking open wider, but it's the thought of losing her that sinks desolation like knives into me.

Great lyric, Roue. You should write that down.

I touch the winter topaz ring in my pocket and vow to carve out a little time for us.

Somehow.

The stage guy gives me the thumbs-up, and all the lights go down. There's that hush that ripples over the crowd, that swelling moment right before I step onto the stage. I savor it, my nerves jittering pleasantly.

And then I step out, a dark figure silhouetted against the light. In the swelling pause, I lift my bow to my strings and hold it there.

The crowd is waiting, holding their breath.

I bring the bow down. The first note is like crystal spiderwebs being plucked. It strikes the air, shattering the stillness. Cheers and shouts erupt from the crowd, and suddenly, they are all moving, dancing, swaying to the sounds of my violin. The stage lights come up, blazing across the crowd in a sheet of white. The house band comes in behind me, the music cresting in a wave. The bass and drums pound, reverbing through the amps and over the crowd.

"Eu-phor-i-a! Eu-phor-i-a! Eu-phor-i-a!"

I play hard, and the band backs me up as we roar into a string and synth version of "Monster Mash." It's hokey, but we own it. I play, bowing away at the violin, its glassy surface flashing. I'm filled with the energy of the crowd, the fog machines pumping out smoke, the bass thrumming, bodies moving, bumping and grinding in the stage lights.

Syl's hair is a red halo in the crowd. She waves, and I move to the edge of the stage.

I play for her, my bow flashing under the lights.

Her eyes are on me, and I revel in her attention.

I wish this moment could go on forever—just me and her and the music.

"Euphoria!" she calls out, grinning, playing up being a fangirl.

I wink at her as I move to the mic. My voice comes out rich and powerful. Dre, the lead guitarist, backs me up, his baritone giving the lyrics a deep, spooky thrum.

The crowd cheers as we finish the first song.

"Thank you." I look out over them. "This next song is for my girl, my princess. For Syl."

I can see her blush from here as I bring the bow down on the first shimmering note of "Everywhere." The crowd goes crazy. It's always the most popular song, and I've decided to play it now, when I'm on my high from performing.

I relax into the song, become one with the flow of the music around me, and my heart aches a little less as I play. Song after song goes by, and I feel lighter and lighter.

So far so good, and date night after this.

I touch the ring in my pocket. Do I even dare?

Finally, I reach the encore.

My blood pulses in time with the music, the bass reverbs—*boom, boom, boom*—up through my boots and into my chest.

Boom...boom...boom...

Ping!

I feel it in my chest first. That dreadful ping that tells me—somewhere, an Ouroboros is spawning. *Ping!* Then a deep, thrumming vibration. My fingers falter on the bow before I pick up the song again. Em, the bassist, gives me a side-eye look, but then nods when I get back on track.

Ping...ping...boom...boom...boom!

I lean forward, clutching my chest. *Boom! Boom! Boom!*

The Ouroboros. It's near.

Suddenly, I'm thankful down to my bones that Syl stopped me from making that promise. Because there's no "after" for us tonight, either.

It looks like date night will have to wait.

It's showtime.

CHAPTER TWENTY-THREE
SYL

Among the Fae
There are those who are soul-bound
Dedicated to each other
By blood and bone and soul and heart
Together, they are unstoppable
- Glamma's Grimm

I swear, the Ouroboros are trolling me. Another date night totally wrecked. I'm glad I stopped Euphoria from promising me the "after" we both want. She'd have only felt bad.

We live such crazy lives. It's hard to find even a second for ourselves. More and more, I want that—to spend time just talking, to ask her favorite color (besides black), her favorite movie, what kind of books she likes.

But not tonight.

With no time to lose, I follow E out the back of the Nanci and into a night bursting with Halloween craziness. Trick-or-treaters throng the sidewalks, spilling into the streets, bags of candy clutched tight in their fists, parents chasing after them. Laughter and shrieks fill the night air, some from the kids, others from spooky decorations rigged up to the small smattering of houses here.

The night air smells like autumn and mischief. Everything is orange and glowing and festive, all fake spiderwebs and Frankenstein's monsters, eerie screams and fog machines.

For just a sec, my heart sinks, and I wish Euphoria and I were out here, dressed to the nines, having fun instead of heading into battle. Then I shake off the gloomies.

We'll have our moment. As soon as all these Ouroboros are destroyed.

We cross West Franklin, throwing up our quick don't-see-me Glamouries. I might be a total fail at windwarping, but I've pretty much mastered Glamoury. The magic tingles, settling like a blanket over me. We speed through the trick-or-treaters, hidden. Good.

Because we're not actually going to stay streetside.

At the corner, Euphoria leaps to the top of a taco shop. I follow, my mouth watering at the spicy scent of pico de gallo and guac. Hunting Ouroboros always makes me hungry.

Come on, Syl. Get it together.

Euphoria's quiet, looking out over the night like a hawk. I watch as her blue irises bleed to that ghastly green. She's clutching her heart, and I know she feels the Ouroboros pulsing there like the hearthstone used to.

"E?" I hover close. "Do you sense where it is yet?"

"Almost..." She's all black leather and badass attitude. I know she's bummed about our "after" going kablooey (this makes twice now), but if we find the ovo, it'll more than make up for it.

"It's near the water." She shakes off the trance. "Ready?"

"Always."

We dart off into the night, E leading as we race down North Laurel. It's mostly businesses here, the Altria Theater, and the cathedral, so not too many trick-or-treaters. The streets are covered in autumn leaves, and our boots kick them up in colorful waves.

I grin at her over the spatter of leaves, and she smiles back.

Our footsteps fall in sync. Even our arms move in the same motion.

Most people see only the super-intense rock star or the ruthless Fae assassin. But me? I see the hint of gentleness. The curve of a smile. That's all mine.

We're a team.

I just hope… I swallow hard as a cold sweat shivers over me. I hope I don't have to use my white-flame power tonight.

I don't want to risk hurting her again.

Atop Sacred Heart Cathedral, Euphoria stops to dowse again. The city spreads out below us. Lights, cars, people, kids in crazy costumes—it all comes together in a deep, rumbling thrum. A sense of urgency pulses off Euphoria.

Urgency, danger, desire…

My heart is racing, and where I was cold before, my skin is suddenly hot, flushed. The things this girl does to me. I want to grab her and kiss her right here on the domed cupola.

A slow grin curves her lips. She knows I'm staring. "Catch me if you can."

"Oh, it's *on*, princess."

"That's my line." She winks before she dashes across the cathedral's roof and leaps across to the Altria.

I chase her across the top of the theater. It looks like an old-school mosque and is totally *gorgelous*, as Glamma would say. Hazy light shines from below, the vibrations of music coming up through the soles in my boots.

Euphoria and I race to the edge and drop off.

A light drizzle starts, and she reaches for her hood midstride. Note to self: bring a hoodie next time. By the end of the night, my curls are going to be a frizzled, frazzled mess.

We stop under a restaurant awning, and Euphoria whips off her leather jacket, pulling the hoodie off over her head. The action causes her black tee to ride up, showing a strip of dark skin.

Holy—! Swoooooon. I swear, I'm going to pass out right here in the street.

"You're staring." She tosses me the hoodie.

It's still warm and smells like her—all crisp autumn leaves, amber, and bourbon-vanilla. She smells like incense and sin. *Mind on the mission, Syl.*

But the butterflies in my stomach are doing Zumba. I'm flushed as I tease her. "I bet I find the ovo before you."

Her eyes light up, the golden rings bright. "You're on."

"What do I get if I win?" I pull the hoodie up to hide my furious blushing. Wearing her clothes, being armored in her scent, I love it.

"Hmmm…" She darts off while thinking. I keep pace, and together we leap. We're heading toward the canal, toward Shockoe Bottom. I wonder where the Ouroboros is this time. We land and keep running.

"Well?" I press her.

She doesn't break a sweat, not even as we run. "What do you want?"

She knows what I want. I think she just wants to hear me say it. "A date night. No Moribund, no training. Just you and me, a movie, dinner, dancing." I mean, why not? That's what couples do, and I want us to be a real couple, to share everything.

The ring on its chain bumps gently against my skin.

I want to ask her—

"Deal." Euphoria smirks. "And if I win?"

"You won't."

She laughs. "You're so sure, princess?"

"Yup."

"Good. Then I'll name my price later. When I win." She nudges me. "You're good with that, aren't you, Little Miss Cocky?"

"Sure am." But I'm sweating it out a bit. She could ask for anything, and Euphoria's crafty, cunning. Messing with her is a fool's errand.

And yes, I am that fool.

"Okay, then." Euphoria's eyes reflect that green glow again. "The Ouroboros is that way." She points as we speed down Dock Street. Headlights streak past us, but we're going just as fast, dodging cars. We jump from the viaduct to street level and race through the night.

Almost there.

We come over the rise, and Euphoria slows down, wincing back instinctively. A weird aura warps the air, sharp and metallic.

Iron.

Ahead, jagged silhouettes poke up against the night sky—abandoned buildings and the giant, ironwork gasometer of the Fulton Gas Works. It was built in the 1800s to provide gas to the city, but a ton of flooding and the fact that it could literally explode shut it down.

Now, all that's left are a few buildings, all gutted and graffitied up, and the circular frame of the gasometer, which totally looks like something out of a Mad Max movie.

Thunderdome. Except made entirely of iron.

Good times.

Iron is terrible for the Fae. Euphoria will be weaker here. We'll have to be extra careful. With my power on the fritz and Euphoria weakened, we can't afford an extended fight.

Lucky for us, the Ouroboros hasn't created any Circuit fiends in the area.

This is too easy, Syl.

Hushing my inner killjoy, I follow E, leaping over the barbed-wire fence.

I totally get why Agravaine chose this place. A lot of the more powerful, permanent magics—like the Grimmacle he tried to cast and the advanced Glamoury that hides the Ouroboros—require iron as a focus.

And here? It's all iron, iron everywhere. The ginormous gasometer registers as a black smear to my Fae-sight, and when the wind blows off the James River, I can smell it—rust and the heavy tang of metal.

Imagine if the Ouroboros infected that thing.

A giant Erector-set version of Thunderdome, wheeeee!

Euphoria must be thinking the same thing because she picks up the pace. We double-time it across the overgrown grass. The abandoned buildings loom over us, black against the night.

The Ouroboros could be in any one of them.

Okay, showtime, Syl. We're on the verge of battle. Not to mention, I'm going to win our little side bet.

Date night, here we come!

"It's here." Euphoria touches her heart again, her voice all smoky. She skirts the buildings and heads toward Thunderdome, her eyes that creepy glowy-green as the ping inside her leads toward the Ouroboros.

I want to call that out as an unfair advantage, but Glamma didn't raise a Miss Whiny-Pants.

Euphoria heads around the gasometer counterclockwise, and I go the other way, getting the wider scope, just in case. Our enemies are the sneaky kind, so it pays to be ready. She's on the other side when I hear silvery pipes.

Ugh, not now!

"You should team with me." Aldebaran's voice comes from behind me. "Only we can stop this."

Double ugh. Could this guy quit stalking me for like, a second? "Stop what?"

Aldebaran points. In the shadows by the biggest building, a flash of blonde. My heart seizes against my ribs.

Fiann.

"She's here for the Ouroboros." His breath tickles my ear, hot and icky. "You should pair with me to stop her."

I swat like I'm shooing away a gnat. "Are you helping her with this?" Whatever *this* is. I'm still holding out hope that her plan isn't to infect herself with Ouroboros circuits. It doesn't get more stupidly reckless than that.

E tells me people get addicted to dark magic, but I always thought Fiann was smarter than that. She flips her high pony and heads right toward us and Thunderdome.

Apparently not.

Aldebaran chuckles. "I'm not helping her. That dirty Circuit Fae Agravaine is, even from beyond the grave."

"Because he set the Ouroboros for her to find."

"Mm-hmmm. She was his failsafe, his revenge against the dark Fae."

185

"What?" I look him straight in the eye, but for once, he shuts his mouth.

I want to warn Euphoria, but she's already seen Fiann and tucked herself down beside one of the gasometer's giant girders. My girl is tall, but she's also limber. I've seen her fold herself into a kitchen cabinet. Of course, that was to avoid doing the dishes. My mom's a whole lot scarier than Fiann, but whatever.

Fiann walks to the center of the gasometer.

Seriously? If the Ouroboros is right there, I'll—

She lifts her hand. A ghastly green glow shimmers from her chest. With my Fae-sight, I finally see it—a single Moribund circuit embedded in her heart, glinting and snapping with spitting green lightning.

A master-key circuit. Dread grabs my guts. *That's what Agravaine gave her.*

With a gesture, the green lightning zaps from her fingers, hitting the girders, weaving a glowing web around it. The entire skeletal structure shudders and shifts. It warps blackly, circuits flashing to life all across its surface.

Oh, craaaaaaaaaaaap… We're too late.

The whole thing is a giant Ouroboros. And Fiann's controlling it.

It's go time.

"Come on, then," I say to Aldebaran.

"I'll only fight with my soul-bound mate." He examines his perfect nails. "You want me to fight? Team with me."

Seriously? "You know, I'd barf, but I've got better things to do." Like kick Fiann's sorry behind.

Euphoria and I close in, careful, quiet.

Fiann sees us—because of course she does. "Have you come to witness my rebirth?" She's creepily caressing the gigantic gasometer as green lightning zaps over it, lighting up like the gothiest Christmas tree ever. "With this master-key, I can control the Ouroboros. I can finally be reborn into a Circuit Fae. As I should have one year ago."

Wait, what? That's her plan—to infect herself with Ouroboros?

"Fiann." I try a shred of reason. "You'll die."

She laughs, all high-pitched and maniacal. "Die? I'm going to be reborn. Just you wait. You might have won the battle last year, but I'm about to win the war."

So much for reason.

As one, E and I lunge for her, but at her slightest gesture, all the circuits whine and whir, green lightning lashing around the gasometer in a ghastly halo.

The topmost ring of girders shivers and explodes.

Euphoria and I are blasted back.

A thousand-million-gazillion black circuits pour out like tiny black Lego pieces, puking Ouroboros across the ground in a spreading black pool.

Fiann laughs, raising her hand, the master-key circuit glinting in her heart. "Check this out, biznatches."

I sit up, my head ringing. Oh, this is so not good.

The chittering dark circuits leap onto Fiann, melding with her skin, splicing into her. She shudders and shakes, her eyes rolling back into her head.

Disgust and terror well up inside me. I scramble to my feet. Euphoria's picking herself up on the other side of the gasometer. We rush together and meet in the middle beneath the lashing lightning.

"We have to stop her!" I shout over the brewing electrical storm.

Fiann writhes, and her flesh runs like water as she's infected at such a rapid rate she looks to be drowning in black circuitry.

Euphoria clutches at her chest but gives me the nod. "Showtime."

"Stand back." I breathe out to summon my white flame.

"No, you don't!" Fiann gestures, and a wave of Ouroboros circuits surges up like an anvil and smashes down.

"Syl!" Euphoria tackles me out of the way. The impact takes the wind from my lungs. My white flame goes out. We fall to the grass as the Ouroboros arcs around and around Fiann like black DNA strands wrapping her tight, rewriting her.

Her body is warping, swelling, revolving... Her Glamoury bursts into being, hiding her from normal eyes, stinking up the

Gas Works in a sicky-sweet sugary smell that makes me want to hurl.

She's wearing that crazy Harley Quinn smile she wore all last year.

Yup. Fiann is officially crazypants, gone around the bend, two sandwiches short of a picni—

"Let me show you the true power of the master-key." She raises her hand.

I get to my feet. "You know, that's totally not necessa—"

"Oh, it is. I assure you." She gestures, and tendrils of Ouroboros circuits eject from her fingertips, pouring onto the ground, forming giant hulking forms. "I warned you, if you crossed me, I'd unleash the full power of the Wild Hunt."

I call her on her bull. "You know, I don't remember you saying that at all."

"Didn't I?" That sick smile stretches wider. "Whoops. My bad."

Ugh. There's nothing worse than a cheeky bad guy.

The Ouroboros takes three shapes, then splits to six, then nine. The hell-hounds of the Wild Hunt. Impossible. I admit to catching some flies with my open mouth, but seriously? She's *recreating* them.

The Ouroboros giving her the power of creation? It can't be.

But it is. The hell-hounds burst into being, black circuitry fusing into thick shoulders, lean bodies, massive clawed paws, muzzles jammed with jagged fangs. The night explodes with green miasma, the hell-hounds bathed in it, their bristling fur smoking.

With a burst of violet light, Euphoria sings her gramarye into being, purple electricity crackling around her fists.

All right. No more kidding around.

And no avoiding it. I need my white flame.

I've seen plenty of master-keys to know we can't destroy the Ouroboros without burning that down first.

I'm careful as I summon my gramarye. Instantly, my hands ignite in white, but the echo of silver pipes blares in my ears.

The torc on my finger burns sun-hot. *Oh crap.*

My power swells brighter, burns hotter—and then that weird blue-black shadow writhes over it. I struggle to hold it, but the ring on my finger glows liquid gold.

In a flash of bright sparks, my power snaps free.

Suddenly, the grass around the Gas Works is on fire, blazing high and hot.

Oh, no. No, no, no, no, no!

"Too bad, so sad." Fiann clucks her tongue. "Can't control your powers, Syl? Maybe you should learn where you belong. And who you belong to."

I smell Aldebaran all over this. The two of them have teamed up. Aldebaran wants me, and Fiann... I see the way she's always drooling over Euphoria. "Screw you, Fiann."

Fiann smiles, all sweetness and saccharine. "Screw me?" She gestures, and the hell-hounds snarl, black and bristling, all teeth and claws and burning green electricity. "No. Screw you."

The Ouroboros wraps her in a shiny circuitry-black. Just like Agravaine. Only worse.

My Fae-sight already detects at least nine harrow-stitches forming, hooking their dark claws into the Shroud, tearing it. Tiny wisps of Faerie magic leaks out, bleeding...

Suddenly, the burning buildings are much less of a priority for me.

I square off and face her, realization hitting me, a punch to the gut. "That's it, isn't it? The harrow-stitches, the master-key, the Ouroboros. You're trying to tear the Shroud, to get into Dark Faerie."

Go on, spill the beans, Fiann. You know you want to have diarrhea of the plan.

"So, you figured it out." Fiann's triumphant look turns to a simpering puss. "The harrow-stitches are the key to my legacy. To becoming Queen of the dark Fae." She's wild-eyed as the Ouroboros teems over her, twitching, jiggering, settling into place as her armor.

"It's not too late to win my loyalty," Aldebaran puts in from aside.

"Shut up," I hiss at him. As much as I can't stand the guy, he's definitely dropped to Number Two on our list of priorities.

Fiann lifts a hand. It elongates, black circuits running like water over it, forming sharp and jagged claws from her fingers. "Agravaine promised, and I will be queen."

"You have no right," Euphoria says calmly. "The birthright is mine."

"You gave that up. When you saved her." Fiann nods her chin at me, contempt in her green eyes. "Now I will be Queen, Queen of the Wild Hunt, and soon, Queen of all the dark Fae."

This is bad. No, forget that. This is bananapants, super, über-terrible, cannot-measure-with-existing-technology bad. Fiann's gone Moribund-crazy, and all that stands between her is me and Euphoria—and my power that's totally freaking out, threatening to burn the world.

Our odds are somewhere between *you so funny* and snowball's chance in hell.

Still… "I'm not quite ready to bow and kiss the ring." I flick a glance at Euphoria. "Are you?"

"Nope." She straightens to her full height. "Do we have a plan?"

"Nope."

"I thought you might say that."

I smirk at her. "Every couple has their issues."

As one, we leap at Fiann.

CHAPTER TWENTY-FOUR
ROUEN

Master-key, master-key
Elude me. Take me down
With your dark, killing magic
Bring me
To new and terrible life
- "Master-Key," Euphoria

I stand in the center of the massive gasometer-turned-Ouroboros, black-magic circuitry and iron all around me, a ring of Syl's flame outside that.

Weakness and infection on one side. Death on the other.

Not a great place for a dark Fae to be.

The rusty tang of iron chokes me, weighs me down. All around us, the Ouroboros chitters as it spawns, wrapping Fiann in black carapace armor, rewriting her, making her into a dark Circuit Fae. The bitter taste of ozone floods my mouth.

In my chest beats the *boom, boom, boom*—my heart resonating with the Ouroboros.

This is all sorts of bad.

"I will be queen." Fiann's mad laughter splinters the night, the black circuitry racing over her, the master-key in her heart humming with a gruesome green current. "The Ouroboros is mine to command."

Meaning: it won't devour her when it's through remaking her, and she can create as many harrow-stitches as she likes until it finishes spawning.

Lucky for us, she has other things on her mind.

"You will both watch me be reborn. Right before I kill you."

Reborn. Into a Circuit Fae. Heh. Seems like Agravaine kept his promise to her after all. The word of a Faerie is binding.

But the one thing Fiann doesn't know?

That all of this will cost her. Dearly.

Dark Fae magic always comes with a price.

I step forward, but Syl holds me back.

Syl, my beautiful Summer princess. She tries again to reason with Miss Crazy Town. "Fiann, you have to stop. The only one you'll kill is yourself!"

Predictable as a comic-book villain, Fiann ramps up the laughter. It's not quite *maniacal* laughter, but it's damn close. "Why stop when I've already put myself through all this?" She waves vaguely at the Ouroboros shivering over her body in a living swarm. "Do you even know the agony? All those long days and nights I spent in that rehab facility, writhing in pain, *craving* this?"

I recall the night of the Formal, her sawing away at the violin… She was faestruck, and faestruck mortals often develop an addiction to Fae power. No wonder she was so ravaged. No wonder she's gone mad.

We must stop her.

I step forward, looking for an opening in the bristling black wall of hell-hounds. "Mortals are not meant to become Fae."

"Not meant to?" Her green eyes flash, crazy-bright against all that teeming black. "Women weren't meant to rule, either, according to your old, tired-out traditions. But one of us will, Rouen."

Her words unspool something inside me. If I were queen, I could protect Syl, stop the war. I lift my chin. "It will be me."

Her smile is warped, twisted by hatred and jealousy. "I'll so enjoy making you kneel."

Syl shakes her head, red curls bobbing. "Agravaine's dead. You don't have to do what he wants anymore."

My girl, always so empathetic and kind. My heart swells with love for her.

Fiann doesn't deserve it, but Syl tries anyway. "You've got parents who care about you, good grades. You're the most popular girl at school. What more could you want?"

"More?" Fiann's hand clenches. Green electricity writhes under her fingers. "No, Syl. I don't want *more*." She straightens to her full height, Ouroboros armor glittering darkly. "I want it all. Power, popularity, the dark Fae crown." Her gaze settles on me, and I get what she doesn't say. *You, Rouen.*

"Ha. Fat chance."

"Oh, really?" she shoots back. "I'm already the Mistress of the Hunt."

Fiann, the Wild Hunt. She's used the master-key circuit to call to them, pull them across the Shroud, and recreate them in the mortal realm once more.

And they've come back, bigger and badder than before.

More gargoyles than hounds, their massive circuitry wings unfurl, every inch of their bodies burning with green electricity. They form a bristling black wall, flanking Fiann, each one ready to spring at her command. A choking green miasma smokes from their jaws. Already, the air is tinged with its poison.

Syl and I have fought hell-hounds and worse, but these *things*…

Who knows what they're capable of?

"You like my Môrgrim, do you?" Fiann rests her hand on the biggest gargoyle's head. "Wait till you see all the tricks they can do."

As one, the Môrgrim lower their heads and growl deep in their throats. They lash their mace-like tails, slamming the ground. The very earth shudders beneath them.

Instinct makes me shield Syl with my body, though I know she's just as capable as me. This is unchartered territory we're in. Fiann's infecting herself with Ouroboros. She's got the master-key…

Goodbye, frying pan. Hello, fire.

Speaking of which… Outside the gasometer, the ring of white and blue-black fire blazes and burns. I feel the heat at my back. "We're running out of time."

Syl spreads her hands in a universal gesture of peace. "Fiann—"

"Enough talk!" Green lightning snaps around Fiann, amplifying her words, her anger, sending the Môrgrim howling and growling. Wrapped in black carapace armor, electricity arcing around her hands, she's brimming with power.

She is the Mistress of the Hunt now, and powerful.

But she is not and will never be one of my people. Much less queen.

I step forward. "You want the crown—my crown?" I gesture at her. "Come take it."

"Oh, Rouen…" Her smile is smug, the glow of electricity ghoulish on her face. "Kill them."

The night comes alive with snarling and growling as the nine "hounds" of the Hunt leap, all flapping wings, snapping teeth, slavering jaws. Green smog plumes from their maws, filling the air with choking miasma.

My front kick blasts the first Môrgrim in the muzzle, crushing it from the air. A lash of my voice and violin sends violet lightning searing across its burning body.

The Môrgrim smashes into the side of the gasometer with a yelp. Green lightning bursts up over the girders, zigging and zagging, jolting over the iron, rattling it in its fastenings.

Hmmm…that gives me an idea. But I'll have to hurry.

Already, my strength is flagging.

But no way will I let on. Not in front of my girl.

Speaking of my sweet Summer princess… Syl's fighting, too, using only her physical prowess. She doesn't want to unleash her white flame again, doesn't want to risk it with the torc just waiting to twist her power.

I pray she doesn't have to.

The fire is already raging out of control. The one plus side? It's keeping the Ouroboros infection from spreading to the cement, grass, the buildings, everything. But on the wind, I hear the faint wailing of sirens.

"Rouen!" Syl cries.

I whirl to see another Môrgrim attacking. I step back and palm its head, slamming it down into the ground. "Down, boy!" Cement shatters, kicking up plumes of dust into the miasma-ridden air.

Everything is ozone and choking smog.

Desperate, I hold my breath. But for how long? *Gah!*

I search for Syl in the foggy, fiery night, but I catch only a glimpse of flying red hair—and then pain shoots through my forearm.

The Môrgrim savagely shakes its head, dragging me a few steps, its teeth piercing my jacket. *Damn it! I just replaced that thing.*

I punch down with all my might—which, if I do say so myself, is pretty badass. The satisfying *crack! pop!* resounds through the night. I crush the thing's skull like an egg, and oh, crap...

Ouroboros circuits pour out onto the ground. The rest of the gargoyle's body collapses into burning-dark circuitry, chittering, jiggering, racing toward Fiann to become one with her again.

Oh. That is so not good.

I duck, and a Môrgrim goes sailing over my head to land snarling on the other side. A fourth snaps, tears my sleeve. *Grrrr...* My poor jacket's taking a beating, but I have more pressing problems.

Like Fiann respawning her killer gargoyles *at will.*

The stench of iron is thick in my nostrils now. My limbs feel like jelly, and my strength drains like I'm a Coke bottle left open, contents fizzing out...

"Having trouble, Rouen?" Fiann's grinning like a loon now, walking toward me as she sends the Môrgrim to wear me down.

I grit my fangs. "You. Wish."

The night is filled with dark wings. Black forms rush toward me, surrounding me, snarls and growls blotting out the rest of the world.

Next to me, Syl backs up, her hands in front of her. Hesitation and fear tenses every line of her body. She's weighing our options.

But we're running out of good ones.

The Môrgrim we've "killed" respawn, burning, chittering circuitry racing from Fiann's Ouroboros armor to rebuild them. A never-ending army.

My strength is failing, the air poisonous, suffocating…

I hate to do this, but… "Syl, we need your white flame."

"But, Rouen—"

A gargoyle leaps at her, spitting green lightning and fire. Syl dodges the bite, but the noxious fog blasts over her, and she staggers back, coughing and spluttering.

"Don't *but Rouen* me!" I breathe shallowly. We're slowly being poisoned. "Snap to it, princess."

"Are you saying you need help, Your Gothiness?" Syl lands a killer side kick on the miasma-spewing Môrgrim, sending it hurtling into the girders. One of them rattles loose and falls from its base with a heavy *clunk*.

Well, it's good to see her witty repartee isn't lacking.

Even if we are about two seconds from getting our butts kicked.

"Me? Need help? Hardly." And then I do something totally dumb. Dodging and ducking hell-hounds, I race to the girder and pick it up. Instantly, the touch of iron on my skin sinks a sick nausea into my guts.

But hey, in for a penny and all…

Three Môrgrim zoom in at me, and I swing the girder wide, smashing them aside like tenpins. One hurtles into Fiann. It shatters on her armor.

Boo…

But it does knock her tuckus over teakettle, as Syl would say.

Yes!

"That'll teach you to think you're queen!"

The seven remaining gargoyles rally around Fiann, the two "dead" already respawning, but this time, as they're rebuilt from flaming green circuits, their heads split into one, two, three…

They've got three heads.

Awesome.

I drop the girder like it's a hot potato, my hands burning, tingling. My strength is really failing now. That was a dumb stunt. But hey, I proved I didn't need help, right?

Idiot, Roue.

Syl comes to my side as Fiann scrambles to her feet.

Fiann's eyes dilate shark-black. She's spitting mad. "Kill the sleeper-princess," she orders the Môrgrim because, of course, Fiann Fee isn't the type to get her hands dirty. "Bring me Rouen Rivoche."

The gargoyles growl. A few race in, a few take to the air, corralling us in from all sides.

I pull Syl close to me, and we go back to back. "Anytime now, sleeper-princess."

She's trembling like a ghost in a gale.

I glance back over my shoulder. "I trust you."

She holds up her hands as the burning black Môrgrim surround us, hemming us in. Tiny wisps of white fire spark at her fingertips. "You shouldn't, Rouen. You really shouldn't."

"She's right, you know," says a too-familiar voice.

Aldebaran's standing between the gasometer and the ring of fire, calm in the knowledge that he's safe in his alliance with Fiann.

I want to punch him in the face just to prove him wrong. *Tool.*

Our entire world is green lightning, white fire, and oncoming sirens.

Three of the Môrgrim wing in, howling. I step back, shielding Syl with my body. My strength is flagging, but screw it. I'll go down fighting.

"Bring it on!" I sing my gramarye to me. Violet lightning ignites around my fists, and I lash out at them.

Electricity arcs and snaps, zapping them, catching them in a net. They shudder, caught in a localized electrical storm. Violet arcs tear over them, through them. I see the brightness of their skulls through their skins, lightning-struck.

And then they burst apart, raining black circuits.

I stagger a bit, smirking. I'm running on empty, my body racked with fire and fatigue, but I can't let Syl down.

Fiann's face is purple in anger. She stomps her foot like a spoiled child.

"Oh *no*," I taunt her. "You might actually have to get into this fight yourself."

And hoo-boy, she does not want that.

But she's nothing if not smart. She backs up toward the edge of the gasometer. She won't risk stepping outside, not with Syl's white flame raging.

"Syl!" I call. "Use your fire again! We have to keep her from escaping."

Syl's face is as white as the flames I want her to conjure.

Fiann scoffs, an ugly sound. "Having a little problem with your powers, Syl? I can't believe I wanted to be a sleeper-princess like you." Her laughter winds up.

She's going all classic supervillain on us again. Good times.

"Why? When I can be the queen." She gestures, and the fallen circuitry jiggers and zigs, starting to recreate the dead Môrgrim.

She sends a gargoyle at me, all flashing teeth and snapping jowls.

I sidestep and flick my wrist. A flare of lightning zaps over the black mastiff, flash-frying it into a crispy critter. I look over the short-circuiting Ouroboros at Fiann. "That all you got?"

She bares her teeth. "And you, Rouen. I'll make you suffer the most. When I'm the Queen of the dark Fae, I'll take your place and make your exile permanent."

Leave it to Fiann, teen Queen of Mean, to make it personal.

"And how do you propose to do that?" I leap, snagging a gargoyle from the air and wrestling it down, fangs bared as it snaps and whines. With the last remnants of my strength, I tear it in half.

Burning circuitry rains down around me.

Hmm, probably should have left some gas in the tank, Roue.

Still, I glare at Fiann. "You might be able to create enough harrow-stitches to tear through the Shroud and into UnderHollow, but my people will never follow you. Even if you could wake them."

She smiles, Moribund circuits crawling over her face like tribal tattoos. "Oh, I'll do more than just wake them." She clenches her fist over spitting green lightning. "I have the master-key now, and I will have their allegiance. And yours."

I call my lightning to my hand. "Keep dreaming, Moribund Barbie."

Fiann steps forward, that crazy light in her pale eyes. "In the end, you will serve me. At my side or by my feet." Fiann's smile is a knife thrust in the dark. "With all your people."

In the end... Just like Agravaine said. "*In the end, you'll destroy everything.*".

I shake my head to dispel those thoughts. *With all my people.* She might be able to tear her way through to UnderHollow, but controlling my people?

"That'd take some serious power," I fire back at her, but she only smug-smirks and draws closer to me.

"You think I don't have that?" She waves a hand in a *look around you* gesture.

All around me, green lightning flashes and flares, arcing over the iron gasometer. The Môrgrim respawning in blazing green circuitry, their miasma clogging the very air. The harrow-stitches wisping into being.

Fiann moves closer, that ghastly green glow lighting her eyes. "I'll tear right through to UnderHollow. You'll see. I'll be Que—"

"Shut up already." White flames ignite the night. *Syl!*

She looses a sheet of white fire from her hands. The edges curl with that blue-black shadow.

Still, that gets Little Miss I'm Going to be Queen's attention.

Desperate, she throws up a hand. A wall of Ouroboros circuits shoots up between her and the flames. White fire strikes it, eating through it in a second.

Fiann backs up, wild-eyed as my girl advances, sleeper-princess fire bursting from her hands. She's having trouble controlling it, but she's got Fiann in her sights.

The tables turn lickety-split.

Now it's Fiann who looks around for an escape.

She lashes out, a tangle of black circuitry arcing in from all directions.

Desperate, Syl and I dodge one, two, three… I dodge a fourth. Syl rocks back, a cry escaping her.

Blood splatters to the ground.

And that is when the tide turns back.

Terror strikes through me. Blood…the Wild Hunt. *No…no, no, no…*

The Môrgrim growl, and as one, their eyes flash from green to a deep furnacing red.

This is not good. Not good at all.

They've got Syl's blood-scent. She's become their ultimate target. The Wild Hunt is engaged. They will never give up until she's dead.

I grab Syl by the arm. "Run."

"No, we have to stop her!" She takes a step toward Fiann.

I love that my girl wants to beat Fiann around the landscape, but right now, that's not the best idea.

Last year, when Agravaine set the hell-hounds on Syl, they could be killed, sent back to Dark Faerie until they absorbed enough dark energy to reform and return.

Now? Now they can't be killed at all.

I grab Syl by the shoulder, a desperate plan forming in my mind. There's only one way to throw the Môrgrim off the scent, and that is more magic. "We have to get to the school." We need a safe haven.

"What? Why?"

"I'll explain on the way."

The howling, growling behind us ramps up, mixed with Fiann's maniacal villain laughter and the flapping of dark wings on the air.

"Run!"

CHAPTER TWENTY-FIVE
SYL

The Wild Hunt
Once it has the blood-scent
It will not stop
Until its prey is dead
- Glamma's Grimm

We run through the night, me and Euphoria, the hunters become the hunted. Thick, growly howling and the heavy *flap, flap, flap* of wings tells us Fiann's gargoyles aren't far behind. In fact, they're gaining on us.

The Môrgrim are no garden-variety beasties.

Okay, the fact that I can differentiate between "garden-variety" creatures and super-über-max-power ones is officially weird.

Seriously, Syl, there are easier ways to prove your geek cred than fighting everything in the D&D Monster Manual.

Our fairy winds speed us through the city. I hate running away. Ever since I Awakened, I swore, no more running from my problems. And looking back over my shoulder, glimpsing the nine Môrgrim gargoyles all blazing with green lightning and fire…

Yeah, that's definitely a problem. With a capital P.

I turn to make a stand, but Euphoria nudges me on. "We can't fight them."

"B-but…" I splutter, falling back in step. "We've fought them before." Okay, not exactly. The hell-hounds we fought last year were puppies compared to these winged killers. Still, I've never seen her so freaked. Not even when Agravaine had her bound to that fake ice castle at the Winter Formal.

"Not this time." Her brow's all frowny, her voice grim. She pours on the speed, her fairy wind gusting high and cold.

I trust her. If she says we should run, then hauling butt is what we'll do. She knows way more about this Fae stuff than I do.

And considering my powers are all wonky…

The torc tightens on my finger, glowing, threatening to twist my white flame if I summon it. Threatening to make me a menace, out of control, as bad as one of the Circuit Fae.

Maybe even worse.

Is that why E's so keen on running?

She swerves off the street into an alleyway. We trade asphalt for broken cobblestones, splashing through shallow puddles. "We'll be safe at the school."

"Will we?" I have my doubts.

"Trust me."

It's not even a question. "You know I do."

We clear the alley, back onto the street, heading toward the Fan. Most of the trick-or-treaters are up on Hanover Avenue, so we luck out that the side streets are empty. With every step, the gnashing of teeth, the flapping of dark wings, the bursts of miasma-breath chases us.

My heart is pounding hammer-hard, my white flame surging up inside me like crazy, wanting to break free.

I edge a little farther away from Euphoria.

Don't want to take a chance.

I pour on the speed, trying to leave all my uncertainties behind, trying not to feel Glamma's ring bobbing on its chain beneath my shirt.

We jump a convenience store and run along the rooftop. Euphoria's ahead of me, raven-dark hair flying, her body all sinuous strength as she drops off into an alleyway. I follow. The lights for the gothiest goth club in Richmond flash past me.

A quick glimpse behind us tells me…

The gargoyles haven't given up. They flash past cars, clubs, people—shadows in the night. The Hunt's Glamoury is über-powerful. It warps the air around them with blackness and confusion, fogging people's perceptions as they rush past. Even the Wakeful can't see them, but they'll feel a goose walk over their grave, as Glamma would say.

I feel like an army of geese just walked over mine.

The Hunt is relentless. And I'm pretty much out of commission.

The streetlights streak as we blast past them. There aren't a lot of cars out this way at night. School's closed, so there's no reason for anyone to come down this street. Except maybe the cleaning crews.

Aaaaand…just like clockwork, my phone goes off.

I've got two ringtones, and this one's Mom's.

Euphoria gives me the side-eye. "Don't answer."

"No kidding! I can just imagine trying to explain: *Yeah, Mom, Fiann's gone totally Moribund-crazy, and now we're running from killer Môrgrim, no biggie. Home for dinner!*

Euphoria snorts. I want to face-palm myself, but I'd probably take a digger and fall flat on my face. That'd just make my night complete. I slow my speed and check behind me. No Môrgrim. The baying's stopped.

I turn toward Euphoria. "Whew! Looks like we lost them!"

"Syl!"

A huge gargoyle smashes into my chest with the force of a Mack truck. *Bam!* The wind goes out of me with an embarrassing *oof!* And I'm tumbling tuckus over teakettle with a thousand pounds of angry, burning Môrgrim on my chest.

Everything is crushing weight and green fire and smog as I wrestle with it.

"Ugh." I grab its muzzle. "Brush. Your. Teeth." Every word is punctuated with a punch of my fist. I can hear Euphoria shouting my name. I turn my head to the side to avoid its snapping jaws.

A chorus of howling sends shivers down my spine.

Crap. We've been ambushed.

Dark forms surround Euphoria. The Môrgrim snaps at me again, froth flying in my face. I'm slowly choking, green electricity snapping and zapping around me.

I'm about to become a crispy critter. No choice.

"Bad gargoyle!" I call my flames to my hands, bright and burning white, edged in the torc's shadow.

And, oh, how the tables turn.

The Môrgrim decides he wants exactly zero to do with me. While he's pondering the finer points of being on fire, I kick him off. He howls, goes skittering into his pals—a wall of bristling, growling black.

Euphoria windwarps over next to me.

"Seriously?" I give her the stink-eye. "When are you going to teach me that?"

"When you're able to learn, young Padawan."

"That's it." I scramble to my feet, ready to fight. "No more Star Wars."

Euphoria goes back-to-back with me. "Anger leads to the Dark Side."

"Gah!"

But the Môrgrim back off.

Before we can start celebrating, though, E points, a grim look darkening her face.

Sure enough, the two jerkiest jerks in the world are coming up on us fast. Aldebaran keeps pace easily with Fiann, his golden-boy looks totally at odds with the Evil Queen look Fiann's trying, unsuccessfully, to rock.

Although…I've gotta admit, her special effects are on point.

Ginormous black wings unfurl from her back, like a cross between bat wings and dragon wings, all glittering with circuitry. More dark circuits make up her cloak and black body armor.

She's flying.

"Hey." I look at Euphoria. "You don't have wings."

"Of course not." She keeps one eye on the villains and another on the Môrgrim. "I'm not a Circuit Fae."

"Looks like these two losers have teamed up," I say, hands on my hips. It figures. They couldn't get at us separately, so they've joined forces. "Why are bad guys always so predictable?"

"I think it's in their contract," E deadpans.

Fiann glides up, her wings all smoky and flap-flapping. I brace for the impact of cheesy villain lines.

"Get them!" Fiann orders.

Let it not be said that Fiann Fee disappoints.

"You know," I say, taking a few steps back as the Môrgrim crouch to attack, "I was almost expecting you to yell, *Magic wand! Make my creature grow!* All Rita Repulsa style."

Her face turns a hilarious shade of purple.

"Wow. All that power and still, super-sensitive."

"Okay, princess." Euphoria grabs me and drags me back.

The Môrgrim charge, reminding me that the better part of valor is running my butt off. E and I rush toward the school, killer gargoyles hot on our heels. One flies in and snags my jacket. Crap. I throw an elbow back, catch it in the jaw. *Crunch!* With a yelp, it lets go. "Stay. Heel. Roll over!"

All the stress has gotten to me. I think I've cracked a bit. I'm laughing, and I can't stop. I mean, it's absurd, right? I'm running away from the legit Wild Hunt like I read in Glamma's books when I was ten. As much as I studied the folklore, as much as I loved it, I never believed it was real.

Now I live it.

We get to the doors. Fiann shrieks in anger.

"We must be on the right track because"—I glance back—"she mad."

Euphoria puts a hand on the security panel.

The Môrgrim streak across the parking lot at us.

I dance around like a kid who has to pee. "Anytime now."

"Don't mess with me, princess." Violet lightning leaps from her fingers, licking across the surface, lighting all the circuitry up like a Christmas tree. The panel shorts and smokes, and the door clicks open.

I yank it open. We duck inside and shut it fast. The lead gargoyle slams into the glass.

Ha! No opposable thumbs. *Too bad, sucker!*

We rush through the darkened halls. It's weird being here after hours. The spooky stillness of the hallways creeps me out.

"Come on." Euphoria takes a left, heading to the gym.

"What's the plan?" I finally ask her.

"The Hunt can be kept away by the ley lines."

"Ooooooookay. I thought all the ley lines were wrecked."

"I know a way," she says grimly. "I think."

I don't like the "I think" part of this equation, but...the shattering of glass and claws clattering onto the polished floors decides me.

I do not want to be a Môrgrim's dinner, so we race to the gym.

Euphoria beelines to the far end, where the Winter Formal stage was set up last year. A shiver runs down my spine. I remember it all. The ley lines, the Glamoury, Agravaine trying to leverage his Circuit Fae power through it, to steal Euphoria's life-force. To rewrite Richmond into a dark Fae paradise.

Is Fiann going to try a similar power-steal?

Probably. Girl is not exactly original.

Euphoria's walking in a circle, biting her lip. "Agravaine pulled the ley lines into a circle. I should be able to activate them into a shield." She paces, dowsing, and her eyes take on a faint blue glow, the color of moon magic. "They're still here, but faint."

"How will you do that?" Already, I can hear the gargoyles tearing up the hall. Maybe we should've tried to trick them, but if they have my scent, what's the use?

Smooth as silk, Euphoria pulls her black-handled knife. Ice and frost plume off the wintersteel blade.

"Wait, what are you doing?" And where exactly was she hiding that?

"Blood calls to blood," she says. "Last year, Agravaine used the power in my blood to activate the ley lines. That same power should reactivate them now."

Should? "Wait. If you spill your blood, the Môrgrim will get your scent, too."

She levels me with a serious gaze. "Yes."

"No." I shake my head vehemently. "It's too dangerous."

She looks at me all serious, her sapphire-blue eyes on mine, the tip of the knife poised to cut her palm.

I put my hand out to stop her. "I have an idea." My mind flies back to the Winter Formal. "Remember my white-flame shield that deflected all Agravaine's power. It should keep the Môrgrim at bay, and—"

The torc tightens on my finger and glows golden-hot.

"Aldebaran's here," she says warily.

I smile. "Good."

"Good?"

The Môrgrim are at the doors now, leaping against them. Giant dents slam into the doors. *Thunk! Thunk, thunk!* The hinges creak, and the doors buckle inward. Soon, opposable thumbs won't really matter. It'll be all teeth and claws and two dead Fae.

Euphoria's giving me the side-eye, but we're desperate.

"Yeah, good. Trust me." I push the knife away. As usual, I have about eleven percent of a plan. "Stand back."

She does, stepping way out of reach.

I close my eyes and call my power. Summer heat builds up inside me, hot, sweltering, and white flames burst to my hands. The torc tightens painfully, and my power surges, trying to leap off my hands and fry Euphoria where she stands.

I hold it back. Sweat drips down my temples.

If only I could control it, I could take down Fiann and all her Môrgrim.

But I can't risk taking out Euphoria, too.

Head in the game, Syl. I breathe out and try to calm my rabbiting heart. I envision a circle drawn in white around us. *White, hot, the power of the sun. A shield...*

Fiann and Aldebaran bust into the gym, looking all villainous and mustache-twirly. They head our way, the Môrgrim charging at us to tear out our throats.

"Come on, come on..." I whisper, coaxing my power to do what I want. "Shield, shield, shield..." I can feel the Summer in my blood boiling, wanting to burn everything down.

I don't need a bonfire. All I need is a pure spark.

The biggest Môrgrim leaps.

A spark leaps from my fingers, hitting the ley lines.

Whoosh! "Got it!" White flame shoots up in a column around me and Euphoria. The blast slams the gargoyle back, white fire trailing across its burning body.

In seconds, it's consumed, Ouroboros circuits burned to ashes. I smirk.

"Cute," Fiann says and gestures. Her arm grows thick, black circuits whirring, splitting, reproducing... Paws dangle, then jaws, then a muzzle forms, the Môrgrim *dripping* from her arm. She shakes the swollen limb, and the circuits pull apart in a spatter of green lightning and fire, the gargoyle now freely moving away from her.

Crap.

It joins its pack, pacing outside my white shield.

We're trapped. They can't get in, but we can't get out. Not yet.

Aside, I whisper to Euphoria, "Get ready," and then taunt Fiann. "Looks like your evil minions are in time-out. What was it you said?" I cock my head and pretend to think. "Oh, right. Too bad, so sad."

On cue, her face goes red to the tips of her very pointed ears. "You little bi—"

"Now, now," I tut. "Language."

"Let me." Aldebaran steps in, and the sound of silvery pipes fills the air, his annoying torc tightening on my finger. He steps closer, pouring on the power.

Perfect.

Because that's when I reach across the white flame barrier and grab him.

"What the—?" Shock widens his golden eyes.

I have the satisfaction of smiling right in his face as I steal his power. I did this once before with Euphoria. That time it was a mistake, but this time?

Oh, yeah. I mean to do it.

His gramarye pours into me, silver pipes filling my ears, the scent of elderflowers and dandelions rioting around me as his power to intensify everything ripples through me.

My white flame flares up, and Euphoria flinches away.

"Don't!" I call, and she hesitates. "Trust me."

Aldebaran yanks away and fights, using his power against mine, trying to get me to lose control. The torc on my finger tightens, my white flame flaring and flashing. Gritting my teeth, I force it back, force it into the shape I want.

I use his intensify power against him.

The flames move outward in a column, pushing him, Fiann, the Môrgrim back.

Yes!

The circle moves out and out, and soon, they are all shoved out of the gymnasium by an invisible force, my shield expanding outward.

"Stop it!" Fiann screeches at Aldebaran, but he can't.

My power combined with the gramarye I've stolen from him is too strong.

Fiann screams, and the gargoyles attack. They smash against my shield, bursting into ashes. She remakes them and sends them again, again. I feel the battering of their bodies against the shield, each one sucking a little more of my strength.

I'm exhausted. "Roue, I can't…"

For all my plan, I don't have the power to make my shield permanent. The only thing that can create a permanent barrier is a Grimmacle.

But we don't have any iron.

We could call on the ley lines.

But to use moon magic, we need to spill dark Fae blood.

"I've got you, Syl." Euphoria's voice is gentle, resolute as she steps up. With a flash of her wintersteel blade, she cuts herself.

As her blood falls to the floor, I push what's left of Aldebaran's stolen gramarye at it, intensifying the effect. The ley lines flicker, then flare into being. They cross my shield, mix with my own magic, and then…

Fwoosh! My shield explodes outward in a burning, circular wave, smashing into Fiann and Aldebaran.

They fly back down the hallway and crash out the doors.

I fist-pump the air. "Whoa. Home run!"

The glowing line of my shield stops ten feet outside the doors. It's covering the entire school now, a faint ghostly outline of white imprinted on the grass.

Fiann stands up. She charges, but the shield makes her bounce back.

I grin at Euphoria as a wave of tired hits me hard. "We did it."

"You did," she says proudly.

Fiann stands as close as she can get, and Euphoria and I walk down the hall to the edge of the shield. We don't want to miss her parting villain threat.

"So you're trapped. Good job, Syl." She paces at the edge of the shield, and I think back to all those Bugs Bunny cartoons where the cheeky rooster set up those "Rope Limit" signs and then taunted the barnyard dog from the other side.

"For someone who's got us trapped, you seem awfully upset."

"Fine." She flounces, pushing her high pony off her shoulders. "Stay in there. But if you come out, my Môrgrim will devour you."

She gestures, and the Môrgrim hunch down, their bodies solidifying into gothy gargoyle statues, making a circle in the lot outside the gym. "Meanwhile, I'll be hunting down the next Ouroboros."

Now it's my turn to be like, *crap.*

She turns and flexes her wings. In a flash, she's gone, a black speck in the sky.

Aldebaran stuffs his hands into his pockets, all *aw, shucks*, as if he's not part of Fiann's rotten plan. "Anytime, Syl. I can take the spell off that ring anytime."

"Oh, really? And what would you want in return?"

"For you to become my soul-bound mate."

"You're a regular comedian."

"You should talk to her, Rouen." He turns to her now. "Convince her this is best."

Euphoria shakes her head, mocking him. "Fat chance, Prince Fancy."

"Seriously, guy. I'd rather stay in here forever," I add. And with that, we turn and head into the school.

One thing's for sure, we're not kissing Fiann's ring, and we're not bowing to Aldebaran's bullying.

Not even if we are trapped in high school hell.

CHAPTER TWENTY-SIX
ROUEN

And if I had to be trapped
In an eternity with only one person
My Summer princess, it would be you
- "Eternity," Euphoria

It's been a hell of a night. Syl and I stand at the cracked windows of Richmond E High, looking out over the quad. The nine black statues stand there, a grim reminder of what'll happen if we step outside. Or should I say a Môrgrim reminder?

Har har, Rouen. You so funny.

The Wild Hunt has both of our blood-scents.

We're well and truly trapped. It's enough to make a Fae lose her mind.

At least I'm trapped with Syl.

My poor girl's exhausted, the faint shimmering of her gramarye shield like a curtain around the school. "That was some pretty smart thinking, stealing Aldebaran's intensify gramarye."

She smiles shyly, dark circles beneath her eyes. "Thanks, but now what? We're locked in here, and Fiann's out there. With the last two Ouroboros." Her grey eyes meet mine. "At first, I thought there was one in the school, but now... Now I'm pretty sure it was her."

I begin to pace. "The last two are out there somewhere, and we can't let her get them." If she sucks up the last two Ouroboros, she'll increase her power, maybe even create enough harrow-stitches to tear her way through to UnderHollow.

I stop. "Is that her endgame—to turn all of UnderHollow into a massive, sprawling Ouroboros, and rule it all as queen?"

"Whatever her plan is, we'll stop her." Syl sways against the door.

I want to scoop her up in my arms and hold her close, comfort her, but I slam those thoughts down deep. I can barely touch her, thanks to Aldebaran.

Instead, I pace, my brain whirring in Sherlock Holmes mode. "She'll need a night of special power to pull off her plan. The harrow-stitches aren't powerful enough by themselves."

"Are you serious?" Syl does some quick math and then rolls her eyes heavenward. "Not again..."

"The winter solstice," we both say in unison.

"Not to mention," I add to the garbage pile of our evening, "the Battle of the Bands is that night. I'm sure that figures into her plan. Somehow."

Syl, my positive Summer princess, gives me a reassuring smile. "We have until then. We'll figure something out."

Her positivity is infectious. "Yes. I mean, does she really think we'll sit around and do nothing? Even your mom would—" I snap my fingers. "That's it!"

"What?" Syl looks up, her face open and honest.

I know she's not going to take this well. "Your mom."

"What do you mean, my mom? What are you plotting, E?"

"Hey, now..." I fold my arms across my chest, playing indignant. "I don't plot. I plan. There's a difference."

"Oh, really?" She's partway teasing me.

My body awakens in tingling heat. So near to me, that vanilla scent of hers sends my mind spinning, my want for her pulsing in my heart, my soul. Every inch of me is strung with fire and need.

But she's also partway serious, so I swallow hard and put my raging teen Fae hormones aside for the moment. "Listen." I resist the urge to take her hands. "We're trapped in here, but your mom isn't. She could help us track down the Ourob—"

"No." Syl turns her back. "The last time she helped us, Agravaine nearly killed her."

"But, Syl, this time—"

"There's not going to be a this time!" The panic in her voice tells me there will be no arguing with her. Not right now, at least. I don't blame her for wanting to protect her mom, and Georgina… Well, she did renounce her power as a sleeper-princess so she didn't have to deal with this stuff.

I sigh heavily. "Okay, okay." I step close to Syl. She's trembling, sweaty. I am, too. Running across town, fighting Môrgrim, the panic of trying to summon Syl's power, futzing with the ley lines—a desperate plan if ever there was one.

We're both bone-tired.

I turn toward more practical concerns. "Let's at least call her and have her bring us some supplies." I look around at the lockers and the long halls. "We're going to be here a while. We'll need clothes, food, that kind of stuff."

She looks reluctant.

I press, gently, logically. "We only have a few hours till school opens. Fiann's going to be putting whatever next step of her plan into action. We need to be rested and ready."

Finally, Syl relents. "Okay…" She pushes red curls from her face as she goes into planning mode. "We can shower in the gym." She makes a face. "And the caf's got food. I'm sure we can dip into that, and the nurse's office has cots."

"We could make our own." It feels good to have a plan—even if it's only for our basic needs. "The mats in the gym. We can have your mom bring us some blankets."

"But where are we going to sleep?"

"Hmmm…" I worry my bottom lip with a fang. "The nurses' office is too small; the gym is too unprotected. I don't want us out in the open in case Fiann or Aldebaran decides to sneak attack us. But *above* the gym…"

I look at Syl, and she gets me immediately. "The attic!"

The "attic" is actually a big crawlspace above the gym. It was originally used so construction workers could fix the roof Agravaine destroyed, but then they just covered it up and left it. For a while, kids were sneaking up there to skip class, but then administration found out and moved the access ladder so no kid could make the ten-foot leap to it.

No kid. But a Fae…

Syl's grinning. Yup. Easy-peasy.

"We could set up shop there. It'll be warm, even when the winter comes." And then her shoulders slump. "Are we going to be stuck in here forever?"

I try to channel her positivity. "Your shield and Aldebaran's Glamoury should last until the winter solstice, but then…" My sunny outlook wilts. "That night is the height of dark Fae power. The spell will likely break."

"Great." She toes a locker. "Now what?"

"Now we do what we've been doing. We watch and wait for Fiann and Aldebaran to make their next move."

"But we're stuck here!" She kicks the locker, and the entire thing dents in. "And we know they're going after the next Ouroboros to spawn. What are we supposed to—?"

"Stop right there!" A flashlight hits me from behind, and I freeze like a bug pinned to a card. *Blast it!*

That's what we forgot in our brilliant calculations. The security guards.

"Hands up!" he shouts from about twenty paces away.

I can't see into his eyes, so there'll be no Glamouring him. Instead, I put my hands up.

Syl turns slowly. "It's okay. We were just…" She glances at me. I love my girl. She's such a straight shooter, it makes her a bad liar.

Still, she looks way more wholesome and white bread than me. This guy's going to believe her over me.

"Track team," I whisper to her, remembering a flier I saw yesterday.

Syl clears her throat and speaks up. "We've got an important track meet, so we were just—"

"Don't give me that crap." The guard pulls his walkie-talkie off his belt and clicks the button.

Damn it. If he calls for help, it's game over.

Luckily, a breeze is coming in from the cracked doors. In a flash, I windwarp over there. At the last second, he registers me, lifts his flashlight like a club. Poor guy. I dodge easily, grab him by his lapels, and lift him off his feet. Glamouring a weak-willed human can do permanent damage, so I push gently.

"We're fine. You don't see us. It was a cat."

His eyes dilate and then glaze over. "Just a cat."

"Yes. That's right." I set him on his feet and turn him about-face. I give him a little push. "Off with you now."

He toddles away in a stupor, lifting the walkie. "It's okay. Just a cat."

Static sounds on the other end. *"A cat? Reg, I told you to lay off the wacky tobaccy."*

"Yeah, yeah." He takes his grumbling around the corner.

I breathe a sigh of relief. "That was close."

"What about the other two?" Syl asks.

Good call. My girl's always thinking. "Yeah. I'll go hunting. You go call your mom. Tell her what's up."

She nods, and we slip into *Mission: Impossible* mode. "Meet back here in a half hour?"

"Yup." I dash off to find me some security guards.

An hour later, I've Glamouried all three of the security guards, and we're standing at the back door to the cafeteria, watching Syl's mom pull up in her SUV. I get a few flashes of that night at Homecoming when she rolled up and popped off at Agravaine.

Took him totally by surprise. Idiot.

Georgina gets out of the car. Uh-oh. She's all wearing her leathers and Docs. Her face is pale and stony, and she is giving me the mom death-glare.

I brace for impact in three...two...one...

"What did you do?" she asks us both, but her eyes are on me. Of course. Georgie's smart enough to know Syl's no angel, but when your daughter's bestie is a dark Fae, well... Guess who gets blamed.

I reach out to take the bundle of blankets from her hands. She gives me a frosty look before turning back to the car for a few crates of food, clothes, my violin.

Her remembering my violin kind of softens the glare she's giving me.

Meanwhile, Syl's trying to explain about Fiann, Agravaine's plan, the Ouroboros—you know, normal stuff you keep from your parents. I busy myself looking through our supplies: blankets, sheets, two pillows, some sweats and school clothes, snacks.

Mmm...snacks.

I crack open a bag of cheddar and sour cream chips and stuff my face. Hey, all this running and fighting Môrgrim has me starving.

Syl comes in with her mom following, looking none too pleased. At least she's been briefed. She seems a little less accusatory, but she's still is giving me the almighty mom glare.

I sigh and shove another handful of chips in my face. The salty, cheesy goodness takes the edge off.

"So what're you going to do about all this?" Georgina puts her hands on her hips in a typical mom pose.

I swallow and shrug one shoulder. "The same as we'd do if we weren't trapped here—look for the last two Ouroboros." I brush crumbs off my hands and lift my violin case out of the crate. "This is just a temporary setback."

Syl's mom gives me a look that says, *Are you effing crazy?*

Maybe I am. But I meet her glare head-on. "Look. Aldebaran's power isn't supreme. He's a fair Fae, in tune with all things Summer.

Once the winter solstice comes, it'll be the height of dark Fae power. His will fade." *And then we'll have to do something about those Môrgrim.* "Hopefully, by then, we'll have found the Ouroboros."

Syl's mom looks at me. "Who's going to destroy them with you two stuck in here?"

"That is the problem, isn't it?"

Syl looks between us. "No." She shakes her head. "Oh, no, you two are not going to decide this without me."

"Syl…" Georgina and I both start, and then we glare at each other. I give in first, though I don't drop my gaze. After all, Georgina is Syl's mom. She's got more clout in the "you're gonna do this thing" department. I knew Georgina wouldn't be able to just sit back and do nothing. Even though she's not a sleeper-princess anymore, that doesn't mean she wants the entire world to burn.

It kills me to see Syl so upset, but we are trapped. Options are limited.

"I don't want you anywhere near the Moribund, Mom! Especially not the Ouroboros." Syl's face is red in anger and worry. She turns and walks away.

Georgina looks at me. Translation: *Your turn.*

I go after Syl.

She's leaning against the caf's walk-in fridge, her shoulders shaking. She's crying. *Blast and bloody bones!* I am so not good with crying girls, but I try because this is Syl, and I love her more than anything else in this world or any other.

I would never let anything hurt her. Not even me.

I shouldn't touch her at all, but I risk it—just a bit. "I've got you," I soothe her, rubbing circles on her back. "Just let it out. It's okay."

I rest my chin on her head and look at Georgina. Neither of us wants to upset Syl, but the fact is, this is war, and we're stuck in it. Fair Fae against the dark Fae. That's how Aldebaran wants it. That's how Fiann wants it.

That's how it's been since time immemorial, and it's only gotten worse since Agravaine turned me into Circuit Fae and started going after sleeper-princesses.

Syl and I didn't choose this, but we're in it now.

I step back and let her cry, feeling like a complete heel since I can't hold her. Georgina bustles around mom-style, hustling our supplies to the attic when I give her the green light.

Finally, Syl swipes at her tears. "Sorry." She sniffs mightily. "What now?"

"Your mom's setting up the attic for us." Because if any human can navigate the leap to the ladder with a ton of supplies, it's Georgina Gentry. I smile gently at Syl. "We could go check it out."

"Okay."

We get to the gym, and sure enough, up in the crawlspace, Georgina's set us up two cots—distinctly apart from each other on either side of the attic. I don't have the heart to tell her we're just going to move them, but hey, A for effort.

We do our best to make it cozy. The place is cramped, and in some places, I have to duck, though Syl can stand up fully. There's no way anyone's going to find us up here.

Not to mention having to jump an Olympic distance to reach the ladder.

I eye Georgina, wondering how she did it, but the lady is stoic.

Finally, she sets the crates down and brushes a strand of silver-streaked red from her face. I know she wants to find a reason to stay, to protect Syl, but instead, she looks at us. "You girls going to be okay?"

She goes over to Syl and wraps her in a hug.

Jealousy rears its ugly head. I want to be the one holding Syl, comforting her. My dark self grumbles, but I shut it down.

Syl hugs her mom tight. "No heroics," she tells Georgina.

"No heroics."

But I know that look. Georgie's no slouch. She'll do what we have to do, to make the world safe, to make Syl safe. She says her goodbyes and goes.

Syl sits on the corner of her makeshift cot and looks at her feet.

I drag my cot over next to hers. "It'll be like a sleepover."

She smiles and dashes the tears away, fluffing the blankets, the pillows. "It's kind of like having our own little apartment up here."

There are even electrical outlets. Tomorrow, I'll hunt down some extension cords and power strips so we can make use of the outlets. But for now, I gotta cheer my girl.

I pull out my cell.

"Who are you calling?"

I smile. "Isn't it obvious? I'm calling for pizza."

She smiles, and that's worth all this.

An hour later, I'm standing at the front of the school, paying the pizza guy with the money Syl's mom left us. I watch him walk past the black statues, but the gargoyles don't move. Not even a twitch. I'm sure if I stepped past the glimmering line of fair Fae magic, that it'd be a different story.

They'd eat me and my pizza.

I take the pizzas, including Syl's gross Hawaiian, and head back upstairs.

Syl drops the ladder for me. I make the leap and hand her the pizzas.

"Oh, wow." She smiles when she inhales the scent of salty goodness. I hand up the sodas.

A few minutes later, we're stuffing greasy pizza into our faces, and Syl's outlook seems sunnier.

"There's not much that pizza can't fix," she says, licking the grease from her fingers in a way that makes me stop breathing. "I mean, sure the last two Ouroboros are still out there, and Fiann's gunning for us. And there are killer Môrgrim in the quad, ready to chew off our faces if we step one foot outside..." She winks at me. "But hey, life's not perfect."

"No," I agree. "It's not."

Syl grins around a gooey bite of pizza, cheese and grease smearing her fingers.

Life may not be perfect, but my girl is. And though we're trapped, at least we're together. We'll find a way to defeat Fiann. We always do.

It's just the cost that's got me worried.

CHAPTER TWENTY-SEVEN
SYL

All Fae, fair and dark,
Are at times
Given to whimsy
- Glamma's Grimm

The next morning, I wake up as dawn leaks in through the shuttered windows, slanting light across the whole attic. Golden beams wash across my girl's face, and her beauty hits me like whoa…

I'm a total goner for her.

She doesn't even have bedhead. Me? My curls are a rat's nest. "You know, if I wasn't totally into you, I'd kind of hate you."

She cracks one eye open, mutters, and drags the blankets up over her head. "It's early."

I reach for my track phone. 6:15 a.m. *Ugh… Whyyyyyy?* It's Sunday, for cripes' sake. I try to close my eyes again. But no, this place is too unknown, the sun too bright. And for some reason, I'm raring to go.

"Euphoria…"

A groan muffled by covers. "Mmm?"

"We have the school to ourselves," I say, trying to tempt her. Okay, it sucks to be trapped in here, but I've always wondered what it would be like to roam around unsupervised in an empty school.

Do whatever I want. "E?"

She shuggles around beneath the blankets.

I do my best impression of Dr. Frankenstein. "She's alive!" I poke her shoulder, barely resisting the urge to leap on her and tickle her fully awake.

I shouldn't. My power, the torc... But before, I could touch Euphoria as long as I didn't, you know, *touch her* skin-to-skin.

I go for it.

A startled "oof!" comes from her blanket fort as I land on her, and then she attacks back, sweeping me up in a blanket embrace until we're rolling around, laughing and smacking each other with pillows.

My power plays it cool. For two seconds...

Because when we pause to come up for air, blushy-faced and breathing hard, she moves closer, those sapphire-blue eyes super-intense, the autumn scent of her making me all swoony...

A surge of fire ignites across my palms.

"No!" I jerk away, and Euphoria windwarps just in time.

Panic surges in my chest, but I close my fists, luckily snuffing out the flames. I'm gasping, all the deep breaths, to get my heart back down from DEFCON 1. "I'm sorry! I'm sorry..."

E smiles gently. "It's all right, princess."

My whole body is tingling from all that crazy-hot contact with her. I blow out a breath, trying to calm my thudding heart. *Down, girl.*

My girl is killer hot. Literally.

E comes to my side slowly. "You know," she says, smiling to distract me, "it's Sunday. We have the place to ourselves."

"Ooh." That gets my interest. I'm thinking hall sports, chair races, plastic wrapping all the toilets—

"We need to check out Fee's office."

Being a dark Fae, my girl goes right for the jugular. The principal's office. "We'll have to break in."

She stretches, catlike and so sexy my head nearly blows clean off my shoulders. "It's as good as done."

I get up and stretch myself, and then I get a whiff of me—all girl sweat from running from Môrgrim and fighting. "But first, I need a shower." Mom brought us some shower stuff and even a helpful little bucket to hold it all in.

But…

Euphoria's smile widens, part outrageous, part shy. She grabs the bucket and tosses me a towel. "Come on, princess."

I swallow hard, just the idea of showering in the stall next to Euphoria nearly giving me a nosebleed. A blush creeps up my neck, and my butterflies start *Dancing with the Stars*.

Maybe I should be thanking Fiann for trapping us here?

Enough stalling, Syl. Time to bite the bullet.

In minutes, we're down the ladder and in the girls' locker room. The entire place is empty and chilly. Not to mention creepy. It doesn't seem to bother Euphoria. Not much does. She's a dark Fae, stoic and fearless as they come.

She'd be more put off by someone forgetting proper duel courtesies than by finding a bogie in the shower.

My gaze travels over her in that tank top and adorable boyshorts. Aaaaand I'm staring.

Her lips curve upward in that smirky tilt. She steps into the shower stall and shuts the door.

Real cool, Syl. Feeling like a total idiot, I go into the one next to her. There's a small spot to undress and a tiny bench to put clothes on. I shuck my cami, and then…I hear the rustling of her *taking her clothes off.*

Can she hear me, too? I spend a second touching the wall, but instead of dowsing for magic, I'm dowsing for her—for a sense of her, for that connection we have—and I'm trying not to imagine whatever beautiful dark Fae girls do in the shower.

Oh, wow… Stuffing my angsty teen angst down deep, I strip down and get into the shower. The spray is lukewarm. *Ack.* I like my showers to practically scald my skin off, so I crank the dial up to hot. It never quite gets there, but I'm hot enough, hearing Euphoria in the stall next to me, humming a little tune.

"Pass me the shampoo?" she asks. "I've got ashes in my hair."

Trying to keep my hand steady, I pass it to her beneath the stall. Our fingers are slick as they brush.

I want to linger, but I don't dare.

The water pounding on me is nothing compared to my heartbeat going wild. And then she squeezes and pulls away, leaving me missing her touch.

I finish up, and by the time we step out of the shower, I am sold on this *trapped in the school together* thing.

Giggling and laughing, we run through the halls in towels and back to the attic. And that's where we discover…

"Ummm…" I look around. There is zero privacy here.

Euphoria just grins over her shoulder and drops her towel. I get a glimpse of perfect dark skin, the muscles in her shoulders and back, the curve of her hip. She's got a cute little mole on her—

Whoa! I turn around fast, my face hot and beet red. "Don't do that!" I scold her, my heart totally freaking out. "You almost gave me a stroke."

"Too much for you, princess?" she teases.

"Yes," I breathe. I hear the rustling of her getting dressed, and it hits me.

I am in the same room with a naked Euphoria. It flashes in my mind's eye like a teenage-dream marquee.

"I'm good now," she calls out.

I turn around, and she's sitting all primly on her cot, lacing up her tall boots. She cocks an eyebrow at me. "Your turn."

I'm pretty sure my blush is going to burn my face off. "Turn around."

She smiles, and a slight blush pinks her cheeks. So, I'm not the only one. She turns her back, and I drop my towel and nearly kill myself tripping into my bra and bikinis, then jeans and a tee. I'm a sweaty mess by the time I'm done. I could probably use another shower.

A cold one.

I turn in time to catch the power bar she throws at me.

"Gotta keep our energy up." Euphoria winks. "It's time for school shenanigans."

"Oh, you are such a Cheaty McCheaterface!" I sputter, spinning in my borrowed office chair as Euphoria crosses the makeshift finish line at the end of Yellow Hall. She's a blur of flying dark hair, black skinny jeans, and artfully torn tee riding Principal Fee's thousand-dollar rollie chair.

I cross a half second later, putting my foot down to keep my chair, the one Miss Hawklin uses in her office, from spinning into a bank of lockers.

Euphoria's all smirky. "That's three-to-one in my favor."

Ugh. Leave it to me to pick the chair with the one wonky wheel. "I should've known Fee would have the best chair," I bemoan my loss, grinning at her.

"Well, you did beat me at bouncy handball."

It's true.

I glance back at the hall strewn with Frisbees, basketballs, and about a dozen bouncy balls scattered all over the place. Winging them against the lockers and watching them bounce was a blast. Watching Euphoria run after them was even better, all long legs and athleticism. Yum.

I have no idea how I kept my mind on the game long enough to win.

But playtime's over now. I give E a meaningful look. "We should put these chairs back. In the offices they came from."

Euphoria nods, playing along. "It's the responsible thing to do."

Ha! That's a lark. We've totally shirked any responsibility today. After being chased by Moribund Barbie and her giant killer Môrgrim, we deserve a little R & R. Plus, we're still noodling around in our minds ways to get out of this.

So far, we've drawn a big fat zilch, but...the day is early.

Fee's office might hold some answers.

Euphoria wheels the chairs down the hall, my one wonky wheel squeak, squeak, squeaking all the way. I'm relieved when we drop it off at Miss Hawklin's desk.

I eye Fee's door, shut tight. Earlier, we found his chair in Hawking's office with a note about fixing the arm. E fixed it in a jiff, and here we are.

Standing in front of his door.

Euphoria tries the door. Locked. She lays a hand on the panel and hums a bit. Electrical circuits light the wall and shoot into the security panel. It glows violet, and a moment later, *click*. The door opens.

She gives a bow and flourish. "After you, princess."

"Thanks." I step into the dark office. It's cooler here, and a shiver runs down my spine. This is where I met Euphoria last year.

The day my whole life changed.

For a sec, I'm caught up in the jarring hugeness of that. If I hadn't met her, I'd be... Well, probably dead. My blood used to crack the dark Fae hearthstone.

"You okay, Syl?"

I shake off my thoughts. "Yeah. Let's toss the place."

Hours later, we're sitting in a pile of paperwork, studying a map and some other official-looking docs we found at the bottom of a locked (not anymore) desk drawer.

"Nothing," Euphoria says, wrinkling her nose in disgust.

I blow out a breath. "I figured Fee'd at least be hiding something juicy in here. Seriously, Fiann's a total daddy's girl."

"I think we're looking in the wrong place." Euphoria tosses a ledger aside.

"What do you mean?"

"Well, if we want to find something to help us with the Ouroboros or Aldebaran's torc, we shouldn't be looking in the very mundane principal's office."

"Riiiiiight..." I want to face-palm myself. "But where—?"

Euphoria fixes me with her sapphire-blue gaze, and *bam!* It hits me.

"Miss Jardin. The library!"

An impish glint sparks in her eyes. "Beat you there."

Flash! She's gone in a burst of violet mist.

"Oh!" I summon my fairy wind and chase after her, but Summer winds are only so fast, and windwarping… Well, it's instantaneous, almost as fast as teleporting.

I burst into the library to find E standing before the floor-to-ceiling stacks. "I'll check down here. You try the second level."

"Got it." I head up the spiral ladder to the second floor that rings the bottom half of the library like a balcony. The books are older here, mustier. My nose tickles, but thankfully, becoming Fae has pretty much cured my allergies.

We search for hours, both of us dowsing for Glamouries, but we come up empty.

"We must be missing something," I say as I come back down the ladder. "I mean, where else would a pocket púca stash all her magical tomes if not the library?"

Euphoria blows a stray lock of black hair from her face. "Or there's some trick to her Glamoury. And considering she's a púca, there's probably a weird rule to it that we haven't figured out."

"Sounds about right."

Miss J has been cryptic as all get-out about everything—about helping me last year, about saving Euphoria from the Snickleways. She's definitely hiding something. "We'll figure it out," I say.

But for now?

It's Miss Jardin: 1, Team Fae: 0.

Sunday day passes into Sunday evening. Euphoria goes to the auditorium to practice. The Battle of the Bands is coming up.

Word on the street is Fiann has something up her sleeve. Because of course she does.

Winter solstice, the Battle, Fiann, the Ouroboros.

It'll all come down to that one night.

Again.

Truthfully? This is a tradition I'd rather see die in a fire.

Meanwhile, Mom comes to help us cook dinner. Our first at school. She's bustling around the giant caf already, pulling out boxes of spaghetti and ginormous cans of sauce. She's quiet, and that can't be good.

Does she blame Euphoria for everything that's happened?

"Here." Mom tosses me an apron as she fills a pan with water and plunks it on the massive stove. She gives me a bit of the side-eye, but she looks tired. She's yawning, and her eyes are red-rimmed.

"You okay?"

"Another late call." She shrugs.

I nod and tie the apron around me. "Here. I'll make coffee." I grab one of the pots and a coffee packet, make sure it's not decaf, and set it to brewing. "What happened?"

"Thanks, bug." She gives a little sigh. "Some kids broke into Richmond Public last night. Trashed the place." She yawns so hard her jaw pops. "Good money, though."

I take a seat. "School...yeah." It hits me in a wave, all the things that've happened. Fiann, the Ouroboros, Aldebaran... I can't help but look down at the ring on my finger. It shines like liquid sunlight.

I want to yank it off and throw it as far as I can. Which...considering I threw a Mini Cooper last week, I could probably throw this ring into space if I wanted.

I wish I could, and then I'd throw Aldebaran after it.

"Syl?" Mom sees my frowny face. Great. Euphoria's gloominess is rubbing off on me.

"Yeah, Mom?" The coffee finishes in record time, and I get up, pour some into her travel mug, and hand it to her.

She keeps me pinned with that mom stare over the rim of her mug.

I fidget. I've been wanting to ask her about the fair Fae since this whole thing with Aldebaran started, but I didn't want to remind her of a past she tries so desperately to forget. My stool squeaks as I fidget some more.

I only have few minutes before Euphoria finishes practice. It's now or never.

"Mom, what do you know about the fair Fae?" I almost cringe because my mom was a sleeper-princess before I was. And the fair Fae put her up to poisoning the hearthstone of their enemies, the dark Fae. I know she regrets that, and I also know she doesn't regret renouncing her power. Not one little bit.

"What brought this on?" she asks in her Socratic mom method.

I sigh. "There's this boy in school—"

My mom raises an eyebrow.

Oh heck no. She does not think...

I make a disgusted sound. "Please, it's not like that." I shudder. So very totally and completely not like that. "He says he's the Prince of the fair Fae."

"Do you believe him?" She goes to the pot and pours the box of spaghetti in.

"Yeah. I can...sense the power radiating off him, the way dark Fae power radiates off Euphoria." I skip the part where Aldebaran brought me to OverHill and spelled me with his stupid torc.

No sense having Mom go on a rampage. At least, not just yet.

Back to the matter at hand. "When you were a sleeper-princess, did they...?" I wrap my hands around my mug, hoping for a little warmth. "Did they tell you you had to...marry the prince?"

Mom spends a moment examining me. I see her calculating how many bullets it'd take to ruin Aldebaran's day if it came down to it.

Side note: do not mess with Mom. Ever.

"No," she says. "I never got that far. After they had me poison the hearthstone, I..." She clears her throat. "The very next day I renounced my power." I see she wants to ask me why I'm asking, but she waits.

My mom is like that. Patient.

But me? I squirm like a toddler. "Because this guy, this Aldebaran, he's saying that I should be with him. Soul-bound." The words feel gross coming out of my mouth, and I know I've got a squicked-out look on my face. "He says I can't fully Awaken without him."

Mom laughs. It jolts me because my mom's kind of a play-her-cards-close kind of lady. But clearly this one gets her goat, as Glamma would say.

I stare at her. "What?"

Mom puts her hand on mine. Her hands are chapped and red from janitorial work. I make a mental note to grab her someone of that Burt's Bees lotion from the nurse's office. Her green eyes are serious. "Do you like this boy?"

"No. I mean, I don't hate him or anything, but I'm not that into"—guys—"him."

This is the closest I've ever gotten to talking to Mom about the me and Euphoria thing. I get up and grab the can of sauce. I tackle it with the industrial can opener, taking out all my aggression on it.

"Syl," Mom says gently. "You should be with who you want."

It's everything I want to hear, but… "I'm a princess. Shouldn't I be…? I mean, what about my people?" On my finger, the ring seems to tighten.

Suddenly, I find it hard to breathe.

"Your people? Syl, you are seventeen years old. You were born here in the mortal realm. You have a duty to yourself first." Mom's look is honest and direct. "Remember what Glamma always said? *'Put your own oxygen mask on before assisting others.'*"

Her words floor me. "But what if I…?" *Want to be with Rouen?*

Mom already knows that, doesn't she? So why am I too freaked to say it? I never thought coming out to my mom would be hard, especially with me-and-Euphoria staring her in the face.

But suddenly, my heart is rabbit-kicking me in the ribs.

I choke the words out. "Isn't that what I'm supposed to do, though? Pair with him to defeat Fiann and the Ouroboros?"

The oven gives a sad little *ding* as I turn it on to heat the garlic bread.

Mom raises an eyebrow. "Who says that's what you're supposed to do?"

Okay, now her Socratic mom method hits me hard. I sit down heavily, spaghetti, sauce, garlic bread totally forgotten.

Yeah. Who said? Game. Changer.

"You didn't need Aldebaran to defeat Agravaine," Mom says, then casually takes a sip of her coffee. "But you did need Rouen."

Wait, what? Did my mom just give me permission to date Euphoria?

She gets up and stirs the spaghetti. "It's almost ready. You should go get her."

"Okay."

"Love you, bug." She kisses my cheek and strains the spaghetti.

And me? I'm left feeling totally floored as I head down the hall to grab Euphoria. I wouldn't trade my mom for anything.

And if Fiann hurts her, I'll never forgive her. Or myself.

CHAPTER TWENTY-EIGHT
ROUEN

As long as you're on
My side
Baby, I'm winning
- "Winning," Euphoria

Days pass, and we're still trapped in the school and going a lit-tle stir-crazy. We've figured out part of Fiann's plan—to gather the power of the Ouroboros, create harrow-stitches, and tear her way to UnderHollow to become queen—but unless we can find a way past the Môrgrim, there's no chance we can stop her from getting the last two Ouroboros when they spawn.

We rack our brains, but I know the Hunt. I used to be one of them, the premiere Huntress.

There is no escape.

And I won't risk Syl.

Not to mention, Aldebaran's torc makes her lose control of her white flame, and that is dangerous in the extreme.

Especially to yours truly.

There must be a way to sneak past the Môrgrim, or at least nullify the effects of his stupid ring. Some spell. Something I don't know of.

And where do you go to find stuff you don't know?

The library. *Miss Jardin.*

As much as I hate the idea of enlisting the pocket púca, I've got no choice, really. I trudge down Yellow Hall, the emergency exit lights bloodying the canary-colored lockers. It's late, Syl's upstairs doing homework, and I'm supposed to be doing my last pass around the school, making sure the security guards are Glamouried appropriately.

Note to self: send them all gift baskets when this is all said and done.

I stop in front of the library and steel myself. *All right, Roue. You got this.*

Tangling with a pocket púca is not for the faint of heart, and I'm sure there's some kind of elaborate (and probably embarrassing) way to ask for her help, but deciphering that would be harder than figuring out Fiann's endgame.

Fine, then. I won't ask. I shove the door to the library open.

"Looking for something, Miss Rivoche?"

Of course she's right there, sitting on the desk all prim and proper in her librarian power suit like she's been waiting for me. Her hand rests on a stack of books, her eyes glinting crimson.

Suddenly, the library takes on an eerie gloom, all deep dark reds in the emergency lights. The spicy scent of hot peppers stings my nose. The hair on the back of my neck stands up, and all my dark Fae instincts scream, *Warning, warning, warning!*

I'm about to enter a pocket púca's demesnes, the tiny dimension where she reigns supreme.

This is for Syl. So I step across the threshold. "We need your help."

Miss Jardin's glasses flash in the red glow. "I know."

"Well, if you know"—I try hard to swallow my cold anger—"then why aren't you helping?"

"How do you know I'm not helping?"

Great. Just what I need. A passive-aggressive púca. "Because Syl and I are stuck in this school and Fiann's out there hunting down the last two Ouroboros."

"Yes." She leans forward, her eyes twin burning embers, her voice edged in steel. "It is terrible to be trapped in a school, isn't it? Stuck between this library and that tiny apartment in Jackson Ward."

So that's it. I fold my arms. "I wouldn't set you free, even if I could."

A slow smile stretches across her lips like poured honey. "I know this, but there is something you could do for me, yes?"

"I don't know." I'm losing my cool. "Is there?"

Damned púca and their damned double-talk! I know she's hiding her cache of magical tomes in the library. Púca love knowledge almost as much as they love rules and etiquette.

She could help us if she wanted to. *If…*

Crossing her legs at the knee, she folds her hands over them. "Promise me something."

"What?"

"A favor. To be named later."

Now it's not just warning bells blaring in my mind, it's air-raid sirens. Every inch of me tenses. Entering into a pact with a púca is beyond stupid.

I know it. She knows it.

"Well, Miss Rivoche?"

Do I dare? I flex my right hand. The last time I jumped into something with both feet, I got infected by Moribund and bound by a Contract of Blood and Bone. "We're through here."

Miss Jardin's right eye twitches, but her voice is calm. "We'll speak again, Miss Rivoche."

"Maybe." I back away slowly, not wanting to turn around until I'm at the door. The second I step back across the threshold, the heat and spicy smell lessens, and I feel the air pressure return to normal. I blow out a breath.

Something tells me Miss Jardin has a bigger part to play, but only a fool bargains with a púca. Syl and I will simply have to find our own way. I slip from the library, doubt filling my heart.

So many questions, and I'm not sure I'll ever have the answers.

November moves onward, and I have to admit, aside from our frustrations about Fiann, it's kind of...fun. I mean, if there was one person in the whole wide world I'd like to be trapped in a high school with, it's Syl Skye.

And if Aldebaran wins, these might be the last days you spend with her, Roue.

I revel in every moment we get to spend together. Even though I don't sense any Ouroboros, we're still super-busy practicing, training. Band practice for me, windwarping for her, classes during the day, and running around the school at night doing office chair relays, hallway sports... You name it, we do it. The school is our playground, and we make the most of it.

She still doesn't get how to windwarp.

It's a hard concept, using the wind to speed you so fast you literally become mist, vanishing at one point and reappearing at another within line of sight. And it's one thing to get it intellectually. It's another to make your body do it.

And Syl would get there eventually, if it wasn't for the torc throwing off her every power. I soothe her and encourage her, but inside I'm seething like a winter storm.

I can't decide who I want to beat the stuffing out of more—Fiann or Aldebaran. And my girl is so brave. She sets her chin and tries and tries and tries. Even when she windwarps, slamming into the walls or falling twenty feet to the gym floor... I encourage her and support her, as many times as it takes.

December is swiftly coming.

As for Fiann... She's found a way around Syl's shield—some kind of Glamoury that tricks the shield so she's not immediately ejected from the school like a spit-take. At least she can't use her Ouroboros power openly.

That doesn't keep her from snarking at us in class, in the hallways, every chance she gets. Aldebaran, for his part, stays on the sidelines, watching, waiting...

Georgina trails Fiann at night, but our theory seems to hold: Fiann doesn't know where the last two Ouroboros are.

As for me...

I lie awake most nights, unable to shake the weird feeling that the one of them is closer than we think. Every time an Ouroboros has spawned, there's been that pulse inside me, throbbing in my chest like a living thing.

The way the hearthstone used to. Calling to me, pulling me...

My mind catapults me back in time to that night at the Winter Formal, Agravaine standing over me, his voice filled with a deep dark chuckle as he lead in, his breath hot and gross on my ear. *In the end, you'll destroy everything.*

Those words haunt me. I was in such agony that night, such white-hot pain, I can barely remember... I recall his hands on my heart and then a searing-hot pain.

Did he...? Did he do something to me?

"E?" Syl's voice calls me gently out of my reverie. "You okay?"

I snap back to reality, sitting on the attic floor in the midst of all our blankets. Syl's tied her red curly hair tied, wisps of it falling into her face. Her grey eyes are filled with concern. For me.

She bites her bottom lip and for one dizzying moment, I forget about Fiann, the Battle, the Ouroboros, everything...

My girl is breathtaking.

You could lose her at any second, Roue. That realization hits me with the force of a fae-bolt. I want to sweep her up in my arms and kiss her senseless.

But the torc...

I can see she's frazzled, too. What with us being trapped, her mom trailing Fiann, the torc and Aldebaran, her powers going haywire...

I want to lift her spirits. "I have an idea."

"Oh?" She senses the mischief in me.

I smile around my fangs. "Let's prank Fiann."

In the end, it's nothing like the prank I wanted to play on Fiann. That involved some breaking and entering, defying physics, and a big ole glitter bomb. Syl talked me off that ledge. In the end, the prank turns out to be pretty tame.

The Diet Coke of pranks. Still…

After first period the Monday before Thanksgiving, we're leaning against our lockers, opposite from Fiann's. Syl and I are in super-spy mode, pretend-talking about what we're going to order out for tonight.

Fiann flounces to her locker, her mean-girl posse in tow. "So like I was telling you girls, you better dress up for the Battle of the Bands. It's gonna be big." She does her combination lock.

Wait for it.

She yanks open her locker.

Wait for it…

About a million dirty gym socks tumble out of her locker, plopping down on the floor around her feet. "What in the hell?" Her face twists in rage. Fists clenched, she whirls on Becca, Maggie, and Dani, but they're stunned, too.

Dani's hand twitches, and I see it in her eyes—she's almost to the point of accusing Becca.

Perfect. I love dissension in the ranks.

Syl snickers. "It's going to take forever to get the smell of gym socks out of there."

"That's the general idea." I raise my voice and call to Fiann. "You know, you're supposed to wash those after every class."

As pranks go, this one's tame, but Fiann treats it like it's World War III. Of course.

She comes high-heel clacking over to us. I lounge against the locker. Syl's trying her best to look innocent, but me? Nah. Not my style. I smile in Fiann's face.

She jabs me in the shoulder with one perfectly polished finger-nail. "You'll regret this, Rivoche."

"What are you gonna do?" I challenge her. "Trap us in the school? Oh, wait…"

Syl can't hold it in anymore. She collapses in a fit of giggles against the lockers.

Fiann slams my locker closed. She leans in, her eyes dilating shark-black. "You'll regret this. Both of you."

"Careful." I straighten, lowering my voice to a dangerous growl. "Your Moribund is showing."

Fiann's grin slides back over sharp teeth. I can see the dam-age the dark circuitry has wrought in her, how she hides behind the Glamoury and strains to keep the Ouroboros from running rampant.

"Go ahead," I taunt her, loud enough for only her to hear. "Use your powers. See how fast Syl's shield pops you out of here. Like a pimple."

Syl's got tears in her eyes now.

Diet Coke or not, this prank's worth it.

"I'll get you back." Fiann's seething now. "You wait."

My smile gets wider, colder. "Should we synchronize our watches?"

"Just. Wait."

"When you're queen?"

Her face turns ten shades of purple. She whips around, her high pony flying, and stalks back to her gal-pals—a black-circuited snake sliding through the school hallways wearing a human skin.

"Wow. She mad." Syl's still trying to get her giggles under con-trol. Some of the other kids are having a laugh at Fiann's expense. She'll never forgive us for that.

She lives and dies by her rep.

"She'll get over it." I put my arm round Syl and we head to class.

Turns out, Fiann does not get over it.

It's Wednesday, the day before Thanksgiving break, before she gets us back.

I'm sitting with my bandmates, sheet music and mechanical pencils scattered around us like offerings to the music gods. It's been hours, and we've barely made a dent in our set for the Battle of the Bands.

This is always the hardest part—picking the perfect lineup.

Octavia leans back, shoving a pizza box out of her way. "Couldn't you just ask the Nanci's band to back us up?"

"Nope. Nada." I shake my head. "The rules specifically state that all members have to be high school students. And those guys…" I think of Nico and Vic, Em and Hayley. They're young and all, but, "Definitely not high school age."

"But they're hot," Octavia says in her defense.

Nazira wrinkles her nose. "Could we get back to this?"

"What?" Octavia shrugs. "Can't a girl enjoy a little eye candy?"

"You're impossible." Naz just shakes her head.

"No." Octavia grins. "I just don't discriminate between boys and girls."

"Naz is right," Chuck chimes in. He does a little spindle of sound from his keytar. "If we don't pick the perfect set list, we're gonna sink fast."

"Hey, have a little faith." Octavia twirls a drumstick while Marcus scribbles away in his notepad, pencil in one hand, fidget spinner in the other.

"You don't need faith," a voice from the door snarks. "You need a miracle."

I don't even have to look.

Fiann clack-clacks her way into the room. "Hey, freaks and geeks!"

I was hoping to scrape by without any crap from her until the Battle. But no. She just can't help herself.

I shift around in my chair. "What do you want?"

She's standing there in her designer jeans and Louboutin heels, her thousand-dollar sweater. She tosses back her blonde ponytail. I wonder what she's doing here without her usual train of popular girls.

Something's up.

Fiann preens a bit. I think she thinks it's sexy.

I kind of want to punch her.

"The Battle of the Bands is only a month away." She's playing innocent, like she's not the one who trapped me and Syl in the school and has killer gargoyles out to get us.

I really, really want to punch her.

"So?" I take out my rosin, start treating my bow.

"So…" Fiann looks back over her shoulder. "You can come in now."

Three guys with alabaster-pale skin, blue eyes, and blond hair walk in. They're striking, like guys out of a men's fashion mag. I recognize them immediately as the triplets called Triiiad (yes, with three I's), a super-popular boy band from LA. They've been blowing up the college airwaves.

Clearly they're with Fiann because they stop next to her. The one on the left kind of waves shyly. The other two stand there like a pair of Viking statues.

Well, if Vikings were popular pretty boys.

Normally, I'd welcome the competition, but there's so much wrong with Fiann's plan, it hurts. First off, the triplets are in no way high school students. Second, they're professionals with a record deal, sponsors—the works.

Of course, the band kids are freaking out. Octavia practically snaps her drumstick in half, and Nazira is scowling beneath her hijab. Marcus blats out a *wop-wop-wop* sound on the tuba. Chuck hides behind a Batwoman comic book.

Fiann smiles at us, that cruel smile that says she knows she's got the upper hand. "This is my backup band."

"No way!"

"That's not fair!"

"Come on!"

The band kids all explode into complaining, but Fiann only preens.

"It's against the rules," I tell her.

"They're going here."

I stand up. "For what? Steroids 101?"

Fiann laughs, an ugly sound. "If you actually went to class, Rouen, you'd realize some of them are worth college credit. And those credits are transferable."

I glare at her. "So?" It sounds super-fishy. I'm sure her father's in on it, too. A twinge of jealousy hooks my heart. Must be nice to have a father who backs your plays.

"Fine," I say. "I'm not going to fight you."

She gives me a blank stare. "You're...not?"

"Nope. We're going to beat you."

Anger sweeps across her face. "Just you try!" She turns on her heel. "Daddy said we could practice in the auditorium. You know, where the actual Battle is going to take place." She smirks, secure that she's got home-field advantage. "See you, freaks and geeks!"

She flounces out, snapping her fingers. The guys from Triiiad look amused, but follow. The guy on the left waves meekly.

And then they're gone.

I glance over. Chuck, Octavia, Marcus, even Nazira, they all look totally defeated.

"We'll never beat those guys," Chuck grumbles, plinking on his keytar.

Marcus toes his tuba case, scowling.

"Yeah." Octavia slumps in her seat by her drum kit. "That's not fair. We should be able to get her disqualified. Those guys are pros."

They all start talking at once, and I see they're spiraling down the hole of self-defeat.

I whistle to get their attention. "Look, we beat Fiann last year, right? Well, this is no different." Actually, it is, but I don't want to tell them that. Their confidence is already shot.

They look dubious, and as of right now, I don't have a plan beyond practicing like hell.

Nazira pulls herself up. "Euphoria's right. We can do this."

"Okay." Octavia hunkers down over the sheet music, and we settle in for a long haul of set production and practice.

One thing I swear...I'm not letting Fiann win.

Not the crown. Not the Battle of the Bands. And certainly not me.

Fiann's trying to intimidate us, to make us even more off balance than we are. Leave it to her to ruin a holiday. Tomorrow's Thanksgiving, but me and the band kids? We'll all be sweating out how to beat Fiann and Triiiad.

And Syl?

We've spent a lot of time being angry, frustrated, scared. I look over the band. "Hey, listen. I have an idea."

It's time to break this cycle.

CHAPTER TWENTY-NINE
SYL

The Fae believe
That a holiday is worth
Celebrating to the fullest
- Glamma's Grimm

You know how they say the waiting's the hardest part? Well, they're right. It's Thanksgiving, and we're still trapped in the school. Leave it to Fiann to ruin a holiday. Last year, Euphoria and Mom and me were in the kitchen, making turkey with all the fixings. I wish…

I roll over on my cot, look out at the thin autumn sun setting, and swallow back a sigh.

All this waiting, all this worrying…

We totally strike out on finding the Ouroboros ovos, so we're stuck. Fiann's endgame happens on the winter solstice, the night Fae power reverses from fair Fae to dark Fae. She's going to try to tear open the Shroud, get to UnderHollow, and steal Rouen's crown.

That's one thing I can say about Fiann: it's always personal.

I won't let her hurt Euphoria or her people. Okay, I know it's crazy to want to protect the dark Fae who would murder me in a heartbeat. But, one, they're pretty helpless, snoozing away in Winter's Sleep; and two, someone's gotta be the first to stop all the violence.

It might as well be me.

And then there's Aldebaran's stupid ring. Using my white flames is off the table. Ever since the night at Fulton Gas Works.

Villains: 2. Team Syl/Rouen: 0.

My track phone buzzes.

It's E. *Meet me in the auditorium.*

She probably wants to run another arrangement by me for the Battle of the Bands. She's been working hard, day and night.

I drag myself up and head on down. The auditorium is dark. I slide along the side, skimming my hand along the wall until I touch a switch. I flick it on to see—

Chuck, Marcus, Naz, Octavia. Prudence and Lennon. Euphoria. *What the what?* Everyone's dressed up all fancy, bags and casserole dishes in their hands. Scents, sweet and savory, fill the auditorium. Smiles light their faces, and they all burst into talk at once.

"I brought apple pie!"

"Sweet potatoes here!"

"Snagged some of Pop's famous spaghetti bake!"

I take another step into the auditorium. "What…what's going on?"

Euphoria smiles softly. "Happy Friendsgiving, Syl."

"Happy Friendsgiving!" everyone calls, their cheerful voice making my spirits soar.

"Wow. Thanks, everyone." I'm overwhelmed, even more so when everyone comes in for a hug.

Lennon holds up a glass dish. "I brought *chè trôi nước*." At my blank look, she giggles. "Vietnamese dumplings? My mom's specialty."

Oh my… They smell amazing, but what's more amazing is that Lennon's here. I pull her into a hug, and that's when I see Pru behind her. "Come here, you!" I grab them both in a giant hug, trying not to spill their food.

Pru laughs and hugs back tight. "All right. Let's get this Friendsgiving on the road."

"Oh my God, you guys. This is perfect!" I gush, helping them off with coats and gathering everyone's things. "This is going to be the best Friendsgiving ever."

"Are you guys really camping out in here?" Nazira asks, looking around.

"Yup." I smirk, falling back on the story E and I have concocted. "We're really that dedicated."

Octavia turns to me, a very serious look on her face. "Syl, is something going on? Like, at home? Did you guys…" She lowers her voice. "Run away or something? Like from your mom?"

"From my…" Wait, what is she talking about?

"You know, because you're gay."

Uhhhh…

"Hi, everyone." Right on cue, my mom shows up behind them. They jump like she's some kind of boogie-mom. She's got bags and bags of food. The band kids move to help out, and I grab some bags, too.

Octavia's face is a little red. I mean, for all she knows, she almost outed me in front of my mom, but…I nudge her to let her know I'm not mad.

Anyhoo… We bring the bags of food to the kitchen. Euphoria's already got the oven warmed and starts taking out pots and pans. My girl is wearing an apron with her dark hair tied back. She looks so cute and…domestic. It's adorable, and I have a flash of us as little old ladies sitting in our rocking chairs on the porch.

It hits me like a fist. I want to spend the rest of my life with this girl.

I'm staring at her like a dummy when Pru nudges me. "Right."

We fan out and get to work. Mom starts unloading everything onto the counter. Everyone adds in their leftovers.

"Here we go." Mom takes out a giant ham and a can of pineapple. "Figured you kids already had turkey today." She turns to me, an apologetic look in her eyes. "Is this okay, bug?"

"Okay?" I have to wipe away a sudden tear. "It's perfect." I'm not one bit disappointed.

We all help, Mom giving us chores like a drill sergeant. Octavia turns on the caf's old radio, and it crackles to life with 80s music. Hoo-boy. Euphoria is in her element. She belts it out to some old-school Bon Jovi song. I give her a teasing stink-eye, and she just smiles and smiles.

Soon enough, the food is on the warmer plates and the ham's in the oven. Mom passes out bottles of sparkling cider and we toast to a perfect Friendsgiving. We all head to the auditorium, and I watch the band practice.

Their set's pretty awesome, including the lights, which Octavia and Naz have worked really hard on, rigging them up to a remote so they flash and whirl at key points.

"It's gonna be awesome!" Chuck crows. Even Marcus is excited.

Soon enough, we sit down to a delicious meal, Chuck and Marcus serving everyone while Mom pours more cider. The delicious smells of baked ham and pineapple sauce, the spaghetti bake, Naz's apple pie, Lennon's dumplings. I cram as much food in my face as I can, but really? It's my heart that's overfull. I look at all these amazing people. At my amazing girl.

I touch her hand across the table. Not too much, since I don't want to fry everyone.

And then, it's time to clear the dishes. I grab one, but Pru slaps my hand away. "No way, Skye. We got this."

"Thanks." I stand up and suddenly, I'm overwhelmed by my emotions, this night, everything. I won't let anything happen to these people. It doesn't matter that I only have Mom, that I have an absentee father. This is my family.

And just like that, I'm not crying—you're crying. I duck out while everyone makes short work of the dishes. We've gotta clean everything so the kitchen staff doesn't know there was a

Thanksgiving meal cooked here today. Pru and Mom are on it. Lennon tips me a wink as I step out the back.

The cold air hits me like a fist, but I'm okay with it. I take in a deep breath, my face hotter than a dozen suns. I lean against the wall.

The snow spirals lazily down, not committing. I probably shouldn't be out here, what with the Môrgrim and everything, but technically, I'm still touching the building, so…

Still, I wait for a long second. No baying, no snarls, no growls.

Okay, I deem this space safe. For now.

"Penny for your thoughts."

Euphoria comes out of the shadows. As a fair Fae, it should freak me out that a dark Fae just appeared out of nowhere, but it doesn't.

Euphoria would never hurt me.

Although, if our people had their way, we'd be at each other's throats.

I toe the ground. "Just…thinking."

She comes and leans against the wall next to me, her shoulder brushing mine. The scent of her wafts over me—autumn leaves and bourbon-vanilla, sin and heaven.

"What happens if Fiann wins?" I hate saying it, but spending time with everyone, seeing a flash of my desired future, it makes me realize just how much I stand to lose.

"She won't." E's matter-of-fact. As always, with my Fae-sight, I see beneath her Glamoury. Her electric-blue eyes becoming deep sapphire-blue ringed with gold and filled with love and concern for me. "I'll protect you, Syl."

"Me, too." I clear my throat. "I'll protect you, too."

"I know you will. We're a team."

She leans back, her breath rising in icy curls from her lips.

"You know what I want?"

"No."

"Snow. I want it to snow for real. Not just a dusting. I want to have the most epic snowball fight ever."

She cocks an eyebrow. "Really? That's what you want?"

I can't help the blush that comes to my cheeks. "Well, not everything."

A startled light shoots through those blue eyes of hers, and then she lowers her head, waves of black hair falling into her face. Her chuckle rolls through me, pleasant thunder. She holds her hand up.

It's still spitting, as Glamma would call it. Fits and starts of small flakes falling from the sky. A tease, a taunt.

Euphoria's eyes flash ice-blue, and she breathes out. There's a single note, so high I can barely hear it, and her breath crystallizes into ice and then breaks apart into…snow. The temperature comes up a bit, and suddenly, it's snowing.

Like full-on snowing.

"H-how…?" I know in Glamma's Grimm it says the Fae can control the weather, but to make it snow? "How'd you do it?"

She shrugs one shoulder, now embarrassed. "It's not that hard, really. The snow was already in the air. I just coaxed it out."

"You just…"

"I called on the Winter in my blood. Dark Fae used to be able to do a lot more of this." Her expression glooms over. "Before the hearthstone shattered."

The snow spirals down between us, landing in her hair and mine. It melts, leaving diamonds her hair on her cheeks. I lean in, overwhelmed by her beauty, my every instinct saying *no, no, no,* and *yes, yes, yes* at the same time.

Our lips barely brush before the door pushes open.

"Seriously, get a room." Pru's good-natured voice breaks us apart.

"So pretty!" Lennon slips past Pru and dances out into the back parking lot. It's then that I realize the snow's seriously accumulating. E and I are standing in two inches of fluffy white. I don't feel cold, and I chalk that up to me being Awakened.

Being Fae definitely has its perks.

Octavia and Marcus pile out with Naz and Chuck.

"Wow." They all rubberneck, Naz falling down to make snow fairies.

I'm laughing when the snowball hits me.

Euphoria's already packing another snowball, a gleam in her eye. "Well, princess, gonna take that lying down?"

"Oh, heck no. It's on!"

I scoop up a handful of snow, pack it down, then lob it at her. She can't windwarp, too many witnesses. It hits her in the side.

We're laughing. And then it's really on.

Naz and Pru are the first to duck behind the old Dumpsters and start packing snowballs. Chuck and Octavia and Marcus fade back to the golf carts the staff uses to get around.

The next thing I know, I'm in the middle of a snowball fight. Whipping snowballs, hitting people, getting hit myself. I'm a sweaty, snowy mess, and I'm loving every second of it.

Euphoria and I stray a little ways, but not too far from the building. There's that nagging in the back of my brain that tells me we're testing my shield, but it appears to bubble out here, making a safe space for us to play in. *Ghouls*, as the dark Fae call it.

Good deal. I'll take it.

The snowball fight heats up until Euphoria's team pins mine down by the Dumpsters and rains icy death down upon us. Octavia fist-pumps and high fives E, and Marcus stands there like King of the Hill.

"Okay, okay," I say, getting up. "You guys win. Good job."

The door to the back opens, and Mom comes out. At first I think she's going to yell at us. My hair is a wreck, my clothes soaked through, and I'm away from the building. She can't see the bubble.

But she only breaks into a smile. "Who wants hot chocolate?"

Oh yeah. I share a look with E as everyone goes rushing for the door, crowding in with cries of "Me! Me! I want mini marshmallows!"

I laugh, shake the snow from my curls, and then Euphoria spins me toward her. Our bodies press against each other's. And suddenly the cold is the furthest thing from my mind. She's warm and gorgeous, and—

My white flames surge up, flaring dangerously. Sparks leap to my hands.

I push myself away, shoving my hands into my pockets. "Sorry."

"It's all right," she says gently, coaxing me toward the building, toward our family.

The most perfect Friendsgiving ever. But for that one small thing.

I'm still buzzing on Monday, wondering how I can continue to ride this high. And then it hits me in study hall. I sit up straight, nearly snapping my pen in half. *Date night. I should set up a secret date night.*

My heart pounds, and I swear everyone can hear it.

The plan races in my mind, forming rapidly. I could make dinner while Euphoria practices for the Battle. I'd have it ready, then lure her secretly into the caf... A romantic dinner for two! By the time the bell rings, I've got my master plan in place.

Operation: Date Night is a go!

School can't end fast enough. I even ignore Fiann when she flounces past me with her posse and Triiiad in tow because whatevs.

I'm a girl on a mission.

First thing, I get with Lennon and ask her for the biggest favor ever. Euphoria loved those dumplings, and so...could Lennon make some, and maybe, just maybe, pretty please could she deliver them tonight?

Lennon says yes because she's a true friend. Phase One: Complete!

On to Phase Two.

I wait until the school empties out. I should be doing my Astronomy report on solar winds and lightning, but I just stare at the page, the same sentence burning into my brain: *"Solar wind can accelerate particles in the atmosphere, making lightning strikes more severe. Solar wind can accelerate particles in the atmosphere, making lightning strikes more severe. Solar wind..."*

You get the point. Finally, Euphoria heads to the auditorium to practice.

Normally, this is where I'd throw in some TV dinners.

Ha! Not this time.

Proud of my sneaky self, I hightail it down to the caf. Like a total ninja, I whip through the pantry and the huge walk-in. Hmmm... looks like there's a stash of steaks back here. Probably for some PTA barbecue or something.

Not anymore.

I snag two steaks, a bag of frozen crinkly fires, and a hunk of cheese to make our own snotty fries. They make those at the Nanci—fries with gooey melted cheese—and seriously, I would murder for them. I dump everything on the counter and get cracking. The oven goes on 400°, the fries go in. I root around until I find a pan to cook the steaks. A little bit of butter and garlic.

I check the clock. E should be done in about fifteen minutes.

While I wait for the fries to get all crispy, I head out to the soda fountains and get me a soda and E a lemonade. I drink half of mine and refill it, enjoying the way the tiny bubbles make my nose sting.

Yum. I love me a good fountain soda.

Then I set up a table by the windows. It looks out over the quad, but at least from here we can watch the sunset. The cafeteria is empty, echoey without anyone else in here. But there's a crappy jukebox that some class gifted the place back in the 90s. I plug it in and hit Play on "Tainted Love" by Soft Cell.

They have Christmas lights already strung up, so I take advantage and change the setting to low-light flicker. The soft white glow is super-romantic, and my heart starts pounding again.

Me and Euphoria. A quiet dinner.

I'm practically losing my mind, I'm so excited. My thoughts go to the ring on its chain around my neck. I want so much to give it to her, to show what she means to me...

But how can I when I'm wearing some guy's torc?

My anxiety starts in, but I take a deep breath. *Relax, Syl. Start small.*

Date night. I can handle a date night. Dinner, some TV...

Five minutes till E's done.

All right, Syl, head in the game. I dash back to the kitchen.

Soon enough, the steaks are sizzling in the pan, and the entire cafe smells like delicious meat and garlic. I glance at the clock.

No minutes. Euphoria should be here any second.

Normally we eat TV dinners and have office chair races down the hall waiting for it to arrive. Tonight, though…

We'll totally have date night.

Take that, Aldebaran, Fiann, all your Moribund and Ouroboros! We're having a night off. A night to ourselves. For once.

I'm just taking the steaks out of the pan when my phone rings. Lennon. Yay!

I grab it. "Hey, Lennon, you can come in the—"

"Meet me on the quad." Fiann's voice is epic levels of cold. "Alone."

My breath goes out.

And now I hear Lennon's voice, whimpering. "Syl! Syl? She's says she's going to—"

"You have five minutes, Syl." Fiann hangs up.

Craaaaaaaap. Euphoria should be here any minute now. I don't want to be stupid about this, but I have to go alone or Fiann will hurt Lennon.

That doesn't mean I can't leave a clue for Euphoria.

I look around for a sec. And then I grab a handful of crinkly fries. I tear out of the kitchen and down the hall, dropping a few fries as I go.

A trail of breadcrumbs…

To bring a dark Fae.

I get to the front door just under the five-minute mark. My heart's pounding in my ears. I swallow hard and push the door open with a shaky hand.

Fiann's there, holding Lennon, her giant Moribund bat wings unfurled over them, a sharp wing-barb at Lennon's throat. "Hello, Syl."

I want to smack that smugness right off her face. I cross my arms to make myself look bigger. "What do you want?"

Lennon squirms a bit, and the wing-barb presses harder to her throat. Fiann smiles wider. "An Ouroboros is spawning."

Darn it all. Was that what was keeping Euphoria—because she sensed it? I fix Fiann with a glare. "So?"

"So. You're going to get it for me." Her eyes glint that ghastly green. "Or Lennon dies."

CHAPTER THIRTY
ROUEN

Princess, how you complicate my life
But I wouldn't want it
Any less complicated
- "Complicated," Euphoria

Syl! My heart jolts against my rib cage as I burst out the door, nearly shattering the glass. Moments ago, I started to sense the Ouroboros. But I wasn't expecting to find…this.

My Summer girl stands, a gleaming beacon against Fiann's black-circuitry wings. Fiann's jagged wing-barb is at Lennon's throat, her hand clamped on Lennon's shoulder. Tears stream down Lennon's face, and she sniffles quietly.

What is she even doing here at this time of night?

My gaze goes to the broken casserole dish on the cobblestones, dumplings spilled out over the quad. Dumplings…the trail of crinkly fries I followed from the kitchen…

Syl's eyes, stormy with worry, meet mine. "We have to help her."

My sweet girl. She tried to give us a secret date night. Now, she's putting herself at risk to help her friend. My heart swells with love.

And cold rage. Fiann's going to pay for this. For everything.

In a flash, I windwarp to the edge of the quad. The nine gargoyle statues don't move, don't transform. *Thank the ancestors for small favors.* I move to stand behind Syl. "What do you want, Fiann?"

Her wings ripple in the night's wintry breeze, her voice cruel. "What do you think I want?"

"Some manners? A group of real friends? A spa day? A sparkly pony?" I angle for a better attack position. There has to be a way to rescue Lennon.

Fiann's smile is sharp enough to cut glass. "The Ouroboros, Rouen. I know you can feel it about to spawn. And you're going to get it for me."

"Ha." I cross my arms over my chest. "Fat chance."

"Euphoria…" Syl's voice cracks with concern. She leans in to my body as much as she can without touching me.

"You don't know where it is, do you?" I go with our hunch, and bingo!

Fiann's face twists with frustration and hatred. Her grip on Lennon tightens, and a trickle of blood runs, bright scarlet, down Lennon's throat to seep into her cute Pusheen scarf.

"Euphoria." Fiann mocks Syl's tone. "You'd better do as I say."

"Please." Syl turns to me, summer-storm-grey eyes pleading. "She'll hurt Lennon."

She'll hurt Lennon anyway, I want to say, but when I look at Syl, the words die on my lips. I can't deny my girl anything. I give Fiann my most withering stare. "You'll let Lennon go?"

"Once I have the Ouroboros."

Of course she's lying. But what choice do I have?

I hazard a brief touch, brushing stray curls from Syl's face—and fully ignoring Fiann's jealous huff. I pull away gently. "I'll be back soon."

"Be careful."

"I will." I glare at Fiann. "If you harm even one single hair—"

"Puh-leeze." She rolls her eyes, her wings rippling. "If I wanted to hurt her, I would have already." She rests her free hand on one of the gargoyles for emphasis. "I won't even send the Môrgrim after you."

I don't even twitch. "One hair, Fiann, and I'll tear you apart."

She smiles sweetly at me. "Time's wasting, Rouen. You'll want to get the Ouroboros back to me before it spawns."

I stare a moment longer, give Syl an encouraging nod. Then I'm off like a shot, summoning my fairy wind. In a burst of chill air, it wraps me up, speeding me through the city, through northside and Highland Terrace, following the pulse inside me—all the way to the local baseball stadium, the Diamond.

It's just about two miles away, but it seems to take forever.

Finally, I tear up North Boulevard to the turnoff. I windwarp to the top of the bleachers, the entire stadium quiet and blanketed in darkness, save for the maintenance lights. My heartbeat is slamming against my ribs. I close my eyes and try to calm it. I reach out for the Ouroboros.

Boom! goes my heartbeat. *Boom…boom…boom…*

Ping! The pulse opens up inside me, swelling my heart, making it ache. A prickle of awareness shivers across my skin.

The Ouroboros. It's here, all right.

Summoning my fairy wind, I speed around the place, windwarping, dowsing until I get to the home team's dugout. Behind a stack of bats, I find it.

The Ouroboros' ovo.

An oblong, sticky-black egg, part organic, part machine, circuitry running along its soft, squishy surface. *Gross.* But I have more important things to think of.

Like Lennon. Like Syl.

I tuck the ovo under my arm like the grossest, gooiest football ever, and speed back.

It's like I never left—Syl and Fiann still in that standoff, Fiann holding Lennon. If this were a Western, there'd be tumbleweeds blowing between them. Lennon's stopped bleeding, thankfully. My girl is glaring at Fiann, and I know she's run through every possible scenario to avoid giving Fiann the Ouroboros.

But…

I alight next to her. "There's no other way." My words are a small comfort, I know.

Syl rolls her shoulders, her smile forced. "I know." Her gaze falls to the ovo tucked beneath my arm.

"You want it?" I hold it out one-handed toward Fiann. "Give us Lennon."

Fiann doesn't bat an eyelash. "Throw it over."

My laugh echoes across the dark quad, humorless and cold. "No. Way."

She presses the wing-barb tighter, and Lennon gives a small cry as it pierces soft skin. Two more trickles of blood rush down her throat.

"E…" Syl puts a hand on my arm. I sense her urgency.

I relent. "Fine, but if you try anything, anything at all—"

"You'll tear me apart." Fiann's mocking tone makes me want to punch her a good one. She holds out a hand. "Give it."

I start to head over. If I can get close enough, maybe I can grab Lennon.

"Nuh-uh." She shakes her head, blonde ponytail swishing. "Toss it."

With no other choice, I lob it at her. She catches it, the ovo squishing into her hand with a disgusting sucking sound. Fiann's eyes dilate, the green becoming glowing rings. "You want her?" She indicates Lennon. "Have her!"

With one thrust, she hurls Lennon at us. Syl steps forward and catches her. "Oof!" They both fall to the quad in a tangle.

I step in, but Fiann raises her hand. Black-circuitry claws shear from her fingertips. She tears into the ovo, and Ouroboros circuits tumble out in a gushing pitchy wave. The master-key circuit in her chest glows that ghastly green, and the Ouroboros obeys. Wave after wave of black circuitry crawls over her skin, adding to her black carapace armor, wrapping her in darkness. All around her, I see the shadowy hooks, the harrow-stitches forming.

But right now, that's the least of our worries.

Because the black statues begin to shiver.

I grab Syl and help her and Lennon up. "Run," I breathe, my eyes on Fiann. This isn't over. "Run back inside. I'll hold them off."

"No way am I leaving you." Syl raises her chin, stubborn as hell.

Fiann's command echoes across the quad. "Kill them."

On three sides, the statues shudder and shake. Green lightning and fire licks over them as their circuits waken. We have precious few seconds before the Môrgrim break free.

"Don't argue. Run for the school."

Syl huffs. "You'd better be right behind me."

"Don't worry, princess."

She gives me the side-eye, and I wink. Then she takes Lennon and runs.

I turn just as the alpha Môrgrim leaps, all three heads snarling, slavering jaws gaping wide. Flecks of foam hit me in the face, my world lights up with growls. Fangs snap, grazing my arm—

Whoosh! I windwarp around him. Silly gargoyle.

I land at the far edge of the quad, drawing him and all the Môrgrim away from Syl and Lennon. Electricity snaps, and green fire flares. As one, the gargoyles break free of the stone, flexing dark wings, shaking multiple heads, growling as they smell their blood-scented prey.

The Wild Hunt—they won't stop until I'm dead.

There's no way I'm giving them that satisfaction. Hells no.

They charge, black wings flapping, circuitry whirring with fire and lightning.

I sing a note, flick my wrist, and a lash of violet lightning strikes one solid, blasting its head clean off.

Yes!

And then the hole begins to heal, black circuitry pouring from the beastie's neck, recreating one, two, three, *four, five* heads, each of them belching poisonous miasma.

One bite from their jaws, and I'm infected.

And they just keep growing more heads. And teeth.

The better to bite you with, Rouen.

Fiann's chuckle rises over the growling. "The Ouroboros gives me powers beyond your wildest imaginings." She steps toward me, black circuitry crawling, chittering across her, casting her in a ghoulish green light. "Come with me, Rouen. It can make you powerful, too."

A bolt of fright jolts through me. Let myself become infected again? "No way, Miss Crazy Town."

"All I need is the last Ouroboros." Her eyes glint, and a wolf-ish smile slides across her lips. "That one…I do know where it is. Would you like to know?"

The Môrgrim creep around me, crouching, snarling, waiting for their mistress to stop monologuing already. *I feel you, Môrgrim.*

"It's in the school," I guess wildly, hoping to stall long enough for Syl and Lennon to get to the doors.

"Ah, but where?" She's enjoying this way too much. "Do you know where?"

Something about her words chills me to the bones. "No." *We thought Fiann was the one in the school, but now…*

"You'll find out." She smirks, green electricity snapping and popping off the Ouroboros as it spawns blackly across her body. She strokes the nearest Môrgrim. "Bite her. *Infect* her."

Fear tightens my spine.

The alpha raises his head with a blood-curdling bay, its eerie howls lighting the air, signaling the Hunt. My blood goes cold.

The Hunt is engaged.

I force myself to stand my ground. Syl and Lennon are nearly at the doors.

As one, the Môrgrim leap.

Screaming a battle cry, I slam into the alpha and take him down. I sing, and my fists light up with lightning, electricity zapping between us. Grabbing the alpha by the scruff, I swing him around.

Like bowling pins, I knock four of the others down.

They crash back across the quad, but the other five dash in. Dodging those flashing fangs, I strike, lightning crackling violet around me.

And then…Syl's safe. A faint white shimmer tells me she's over the line.

The Môrgrim know it, too. Their eyes narrow, furnacing on me, miasma dripping from their jaws. They surround me.

I crack my knuckles. *Bring it on.* I won't be infected again.

Hells and Harrowing, no.

"Catch me if you can, suckers!" I bolt toward the door, Syl and Lennon inside, shouting at me to run faster.

The air shudders as the Môrgrim take flight, the beating of their wings throbbing in my chest. The gargoyles fly after me, the sounds of their baying chilling my blood, hot breath on my neck, Fiann's screams to "Get her! Infect her!" ringing like firebells in my ears.

Môrgrim, Ouroboros, crazy high school mean girls…

Just a typical day for Rouen Rivoche.

I'm in trouble, but I won't call out. I won't put Syl in more danger than I already have.

Almost to the door.

"Come on, E!" Syl's waving me on, scared. I see the torc glowing on her finger. She's thinking of using her white flame.

"Don't you dare, princess!" I shout, losing precious breath, my feet pounding the quad like the pounding of my heartbeat.

Almost there…

The alpha is right behind me.

Blast it!

"Rouen!" Syl steps over the line, back into the quad, and my heart seizes. "Get back!"

Her hands are glowing now. Her emotions are so high I can smell her fear. The Môrgrim can, too, like blood in the water. She can't stop herself. Her hands are lighting up in white flame…turning blue-black with shadows…

"No, don't!" I pour on the speed. If she loses control here, we'll all be toast, and then the Ouroboros will be the least of our worries.

The torc is glowing. White sparks snap around her fingers.

I'll make it. She won't have to use her power.

Three Môrgrim plus the alpha are on my tail. They're too close for me to windwarp—they'll just be dragged along with me—but

I can summon my fairy wind. In a breath, it wraps around me, buoying me up, blasting me ahead.

But the alpha is a beast that never gives up. Its dark chuckle burbles in its throat.

It leaps.

Dread and pain slice through me as it clamps down, powerful jaws seizing me, piercing my skin. Instantly, my leg goes cold, numb. I slam my fists down, lightning blasting it in the face.

It lets go, and I stagger backward. My vision goes grey, but I hear Syl scream my name.

Her hands are on me. White fire flares up as she drags me through the front doors, across the shield line, and then she lets go.

The Môrgrim smash against the shield, scattering white sparks down around us. The alpha paces, throwing his head back and baying. They redouble their efforts to smash through the shield. I'm fearful the barrier won't hold, but it does. It's Syl's magic twice over, and it's as powerful as she is.

I glare at the alpha, its jaws dripping with my blood. "Ghouls, buddy-boy." I'm safe. For now. I turn over, my leg on fire. My black jeans are burned away, my thigh a torn and bloody mess.

And then I feel the writhing on the surface of my skin, trying to burrow inside.

The Ouroboros.

My heart goes out, and I lose my cool. I scream, thrashing, digging at my leg. "No, no!"

Syl is calling my name—my real name—so now I know things must be bad.

By the ancestors, I'll be infected again.

"I can't." I look desperately at Syl struggling with her power. "Please. I can't…" The words clog my throat. I can't be infected again. "You have to burn the Ouroboros out. With your fire."

Her face goes white as a sheet. "I…I'll kill you, Rouen."

"Better to die than become a Circuit Fae again." I look toward Fiann, a rictus grin on her face.

Syl's a mess, the torc glowing, threatening to make her power spiral out of control. I hate putting this kind of pressure on her—

"I'll let you do it," a honeyed voice comes from our right.

Dread lairs in my guts. Aldebaran.

He steps from the shadows, a golden idol. "I'll let you purify her, Syl."

"Don't." I put my hand out to stop her. I want to soothe her, but the Ouroboros… It infects me, infests me, black circuits splicing into my flesh.

"You don't have much time." Aldebaran looks calmly at me. "I will let you purify her," he tells Syl. "Without fear of burning her to ashes. If…"

If. That dirty—

"If what?" Her voice is strained, her face pale, hands trembling.

"If you agree to be my date for the Battle of the Bands and the following dance."

Icy-cold rage fills me, shoving down the pain from the Ouroboros. "Over my dead body."

His smirk slides into a grin. "That is also acceptable." To Syl, he says, "You will be my date. You will stand next to me, be on my arm. You will attend me, dance with me. You will laugh at my jokes, and you will obey me in all things that evening."

"Screw that," I growl, trying to rise.

"Rouen!" Syl cries, tears welling in her eyes. "I'll do it," she tells him, but her gaze is on me. "I'm sorry, Rouen. I can't let you die."

"You agree to all the terms?" Aldebaran asks mildly.

"Don't do this, Syl!" I'm nearly out of my mind with pain and fury and fear of losing her.

"Yes! I agree."

Aldebaran straightens. "The deal is struck." He waves a hand.

The torc stops glowing.

Syl sniffles back tears. My brave, brave Summer princess. She raises her hands, and the white flame ignites, leaping up before me, stinging my eyes, stabbing instinctive fear into me. Instantly, it hungers toward me. It's all I can do not to jerk away. I feel the heat and the purifying warmth of it.

I want to shirk away. The Ouroboros infecting me wants to shirk away.

Outside the barrier, Fiann's called off the Môrgrim. They surround her in a wall of bristling black as she watches, that sick grin
stamped to her face.

"I swear to all that is unholy…" I dial my glare up to a thousand.
"I will wipe that grin off your face before this is over."

"We'll see." She tosses her ponytail smugly. "Remember what
I said, about the last Ouroboros. It's closer than you think." She
summons a fairy wind—all green and gross—and takes off.

Good riddance.

Syl's white flame bursts, raging around her hands, showers of
sparks singeing my skin.

I grit my fangs. "Just do it."

I don't know whether or not her white flames will purge me—
all of me—or just the Ouroboros. I don't care. Already my leg is
numb to my knee.

I meet Syl's gaze. "You can do this."

She touches me, and my world lights up in white flame, my
thoughts graying out, wildly going to the ring in my pocket.

Maybe now?

My vision goes dark, darker…

Of course not now, Rouen. Maybe not ever.

"Syl…" My eyes roll back in my head, and I go out like a light.

CHAPTER THIRTY-ONE
SYL

With the Fae,
A promise made
Is a promise kept
- Glamma's Grimm

I'm a hot mess, hovering over Euphoria's unconscious body, terrified to touch her again, trying not to lose my mind—until Mom
comes. Finally, she arrives, SUV screeching to a halt in the parking
lot. She rushes over to me and Lennon, Mom-concern in every line
of her body.

I'm half afraid she's going to scold me, lecture me—something.
But when she sees Euphoria lying there, she doesn't say anything.
She just squeezes my shoulder then helps me and Lennon carry E
inside.

My poor Winter girl! She's unconscious, her leg torn up from the
bite, from where the Ouroboros tried to force its way into her flesh.

But at least, she's been purified. She won't become infected.

Thank God, Buddha, and all the cosmic nice guys.

Lennon and I stand off to one side while Mom gets busy treating Euphoria's wound. "It's not bad," she says, eying me in that way that tells me I've got exactly two seconds to come clean.

Now that the immediate danger's passed, she wants answers.

Apparently, so does Lennon. After all she's seen, she's wide-eyed, clutching her bloody Pusheen scarf.

I tell them everything.

My heart pounds like I'm trying to run a marathon instead of recap this crazy situation. My palms are sweaty, my throat dry. I run through everything: Fiann, her plan, her kidnapping Lennon, the Ouroboros, Aldebaran and his crappy deal.

Mom listens all stoic-like. Her expression tells me I'm looking at being grounded till I'm thirty. Meanwhile, Lennon's mouth hangs open, catching flies. It's a lot to take in, so I give her a hug.

Then I sigh, pushing back my sweaty red curls. "It's complicated…"

"I'm sure it is," Mom says without sarcasm. After all, she was once a sleeper-princess of the Summer Court, too.

I look at the torc on my finger. *Ugh.* Aldebaran turned off its power earlier, but I can already feel it coming back.

If I try anything, it'll be right back to Sucksville.

And now I have to be his escort for the Battle of the Bands. I lean over, brush a stray lock of dark hair from Euphoria's face. *I'm sorry, E. But there was no other way.*

I'd do whatever it takes to save her.

Mom rests a hand on my shoulder. "Things are getting dangerous."

I nod. I can't bring myself to look at her. Last year when things "got dangerous," she ended up in the hospital. Now Euphoria's hurt. And I have to let Jerky McJerkface take me on a date. Barf. I clench my hand into a fist on my thigh.

Fiann's the real mastermind here. She's got the Ouroboros and the master-key. She's manipulated Aldebaran to her side.

I swear…I'll make her pay for all this.

"What do you want to do?" Mom's voice is gentle. This is unchartered territory for her—having a daughter who's a fair Fae princess and all. She renounced her power way back when so she'd never have to deal with this stuff.

What *do* I want to do? I mean, I'm Awakened—the fair Fae princess, just like Euphoria is the dark Fae's. Like her, my duty is to my people. Aldebaran said they would die without a new king and queen on the throne.

But...I look down at Euphoria. My heart's duty is to her. It always will be.

I sigh, wishing with every ounce of my being that those two things were not complete opposites.

"I'm going to fight. For me. For her." I put my hand close to Euphoria's without touching her. "For us."

Mom's gaze is steady. "I'm here if you need me."

"I know."

"Okay, bug." Mom stands up. I hear the small chair creak. She motions to Lennon. "Can I bring you home?"

Lennon nods, and Mom gives me a look over her head—the *are we Glamouring her?* look. I shake my head subtly. I can't do that to Lennon.

Lennon seems to get it. "I won't tell anyone," she whispers, playing with the fringe on her blood-stained scarf.

Mom takes it gently from her. "Why don't I take this and wash it?"

Lennon smiles gratefully, and I go give her a huge hug. I know she'll keep my secret. We've been friends since the sixth grade.

Still, I squeeze her extra tight. "I'm sorry for what happened tonight."

"It's okay, Syl. Really. I'm glad you told me the truth."

"Me, too." And I am. All the hiding from my bestie really sucked. We break off hugging, and Lennon goes with my mom.

Mom hugs me and gives me a kiss on the forehead. "I'm here for you, Syl. Let me know what you need, when you need it."

"I will. Thanks, Mom." I watch her leave with Lennon, a part of me super-relieved that she's moving *away* from all the insanity that has become my life. Fiann's not crazy enough to attack my mom outright—not after what I did to Agravaine last year.

"Did you get the number of that troll that ran me over?" Euphoria deadpans, cracking an eye open.

I rush to her side and mother hen all over her, as much as I can without actually touching her. "No," I say, swallowing back tears. "But you're going to be okay."

"So you have to go to the Battle with him."

"I—" My throat closes painfully. "Yes."

She nods, her blue eyes dull. She's trying to look tough, like she hasn't just been through the Moribund wringer.

"Mom came and patched you up." I gesture to her leg. "It's a poultice. Dried yarrow and lavender, a dash of cayenne pepper to stop the bleeding. She said it'll help you heal faster. An old recipe from Glamma's Grimm."

She smiles, but it's thin like March ice.

"This is all my fault." I sit down heavily, putting my face in my hands.

"Syl…" Euphoria brushes my hand, her fingers blessedly cool. "You saved me."

"I…I…" Maybe I did, but at what cost? I want so much to throw myself into her arms, but I can't. Because of Aldebaran. "I don't want to go with him!" To be his arm candy, to dance with him to… obey him.

Euphoria sits up, shifting as close to me as she dares. "It's all right," she says over and over as I cry, getting it all out, like getting sick.

Finally, I sit up, my face hot and tight.

She brushes a stray tear from my face, the soft touch of her fingertips a healing balm to my ragged emotions. "It's only one night. One silly high school dance." Euphoria smiles at me, love in her eyes. "What is that compared to what we have?"

The positivity shining in her blue eyes jolts through me. If my Winter girl can look on the bright side… "You're right. It sucks, sure, but it'll take more than Aldebaran's crappy drama and Fiann's threats to defeat me. Especially when I have you." I straighten, wiping the last of the tears from my cheeks. "Can you walk?" I look at her leg and wince.

"It'll take more than a little Môrgrim bite to keep me down." She levers herself up, limping a bit.

"Come on." I hover as I lead her slowly to the caf, to the huge walk-in freezer. The cool air blasts me, but I dig in, pulling out two great big boxes of ice cream sandwiches. They save these things for special occasions, like field days and parent-teacher workdays.

I'd say cheating death and Moribund infection is a pretty special occasion.

"Here we are." I grab a box and lead her back down the hall to the A/V room. The theater tech people have huge screens set up to watch the stage at all times. I'm busy hotwiring the thing to play Netflix when I sense it.

Or should I say smell it? Habaneros.

I whirl to see Miss Jardin standing in the doorway, silent as a church mouse and a thousand times more intimidating. The dim light flashes off her glasses. "Miss Skye."

"Whoa, don't you ever knock?"

"What do you want?" Euphoria cuts right to the chase. She's sure Miss J is hiding books and other intel from us, and she hates having one put over on her.

But I get it. Miss J is a púca. Being an international Fae of mystery is kind of her job.

I put out a hand, staying E's wrath. Glamma always said it was best to be polite to strange Fae, and you don't get much stranger than Miss Jardin. "Can we help you?"

"You mean, can I help you?"

"Oooookay, sure." At this point, yes, any help would be good, and Miss J did bail me out last year. But from the look on her face, I can tell I'm out of freebies.

Euphoria's the one who says it out loud. "She wants something."

"I do." Miss Jardin sweeps into the room. In two seconds, she's hotwired the screens and broken through the firewall. The Netflix home screen pops up.

"Show-off," Euphoria huffs.

Miss Jardin only leans back against the A/V setup, crossing one ankle over the other. "I can help you stave off the effects of Aldebaran's torc."

My heart soars. "Yes! Let's do i—"

"There's a catch." Euphoria's voice is as cold as winter. Her gaze is icy as she glances at Miss J. "Isn't there?"

"Not a catch so much as a price."

"No." Euphoria says at the same time I say, "What price?"

"In exchange for my help, Syl will consider one of the conditions of my geis met."

It sounds so innocent, but from the grim look on E's face, it's not. Glamma always said that geisa have a number of conditions. Once they're met, the geised Fae is free. For one hot second, I think of Miss Jardin free, all that firepower and dark magic...

"How many conditions do you have?" I venture carefully.

Miss Jardin's right eye twitches. "That is a very rude question." She peers at me over her glasses. "And I can't tell you."

Euphoria hobbles over. "She's trying to trick you into freeing her."

I sigh. E's right, but... "We're running out of options. What other choice do we have?"

"Or Miss Rivoche could promise me a favor," Miss Jardin offers casually. "To be named later, within a year and a day."

Well, that doesn't sound like a good idea. I glance at Euphoria. Every inch of her is tense. I shake my head. "E's not making some kind of random deal with you."

Miss Jardin's eyes flash a burning crimson, and the spicy pepper scent ramps way up, until my own eyes water.

I hold up a hand. "But I'll agree to remove one condition of your geis."

"Syl, no!" Euphoria steps between me and the púca librarian. "We don't know how many conditions she has. You could free her, and we don't know what she'd do."

My girl's on a hair trigger. I can't blame her. We're stuck between two bad choices: Trust Miss Jardin to nullify the torc's power over mine, possibly freeing her. Or doing nothing while Fiann and Aldebaran find the last Ouroboros and gain even more power.

Winter solstice is next month.

We're running out of time. We have to do something.

"I can't stand around and do nothing." I give E my most sincere *forgive me?* look. "We have to trust her."

E meets my gaze, uncertainty in her sapphire-blue eyes. She knows it's true. Finally, she nods.

I look to Miss Jardin, that slow, Cheshire Cat smile stretching across her lips. "You've got a deal."

Miss Jardin lifts a perfectly arched red brow. "And you agree to my terms?" I can feel her triumph. I see it in her aura.

"Yes." I struggle to keep my voice steady. "If you help take away the effects of the torc, I'll consider one condition of your geis met."

"And you realize that this power is…not absolute."

"What do you mean?" Euphoria's eyes narrow suspiciously. "If you're trying to trick us…"

Miss Jardin looks at her coolly over the tops of her spectacles. "I am insulted you would think so, Miss Rivoche. No." She shakes her head. "It is the mere nature of the Prince"—she means Aldebaran—"and his power. I can only trick his power into thinking it is working."

"Like you did last year with the Moribund?" After Fiann stabbed me with a Moribund dagger and infected me, Miss J placed a Glamoury on me, tricking the Moribund into thinking it was under attack and keeping it from infecting me fully.

Yeah, eventually her Glamoury shattered, and all hell broke loose, but hey?

What's a little deadly risk between friends?

"That is correct." She adjusts her glasses. "This will buy you some time to use *your* powers, Miss Skye, as you see fit, but…"

"But?" I press, holding Euphoria back with one arm. Darn, my girl seriously does not trust púca, particularly this púca.

Meanwhile, Miss J levels a serious gaze on both of us. "But that time is finite, and it may be precious few minutes at a time."

"Oooookay." That doesn't sound great, but it's not the worst. "How many minutes?"

"I don't know."

Okay, it's the worst.

Still, I shore up my resolve. At least, with Miss Jardin's help, I can stave off the effects of Aldebaran's torc for a short time.

E and I exchange glances. Slowly, I nod. "Agreed."

"Good." Miss J hops down, her glasses flashing. "Let us go to the library."

"Yes, let's," E says, her sarcasm evident. But we go, because without Miss Jardin's help, sketchy as it is, our odds of beating Fiann and Aldebaran are terrible.

Worse than terrible.

As we get close, Miss J leading, the doors to the library swing open on their own. Euphoria tips me a look that says she's so over this "Miss Jardin helping us" thing, but we're in it now. I already promised.

Miss Jardin strides into the library. Without even looking, she waves a hand and the shelves behind her shimmer and blur. The Glamoury falls away to reveal—stacks and stacks of tomes, grimoires, magical texts.

"I knew it!" Glamma always said never trust a púca.

Too late now.

Miss Jardin smirks. "Shall we begin?"

CHAPTER THIRTY-TWO
ROUEN

We are meant to be
My sweet Summer princess
No one will come between us
Meant to be
With me
- "Meant to Be," Euphoria

It's one high school dance, and it comes far faster than we expect. While I'd love to say that we spend the rest of December kicking butt and taking names, we...don't.

We spend our time trapped inside Richmond E, hunting for the last Ouroboros. Turns out, our theory about it being in the school was right, and it's beyond frustrating that its Glamoury is too strong for us to pierce.

We'll have to wait for it to spawn, but when it does?

It's game on. For sure.

Meanwhile, Syl and I track down at least half a dozen students in danger of becoming Circuit fiends.

At least, Miss Jardin's Glamoury-spell holds. Mostly.

After some trial and error, Syl and I discover she's got anywhere from one to three minutes to use her white flame before it amps up to murder yours truly. And while that's all we need to purify the Circuit fiends, I'm about a thousand percent positive we'll need longer than three minutes of full white-flame sleeper-princess power on the night of the winter solstice.

The night of the Battle of the Bands. It arrives before we know it.

"Soon" becomes "tonight." And it all comes down to tonight.

One high school dance.

Just one. I can survive that, even if I want to murder Aldebaran if he so much as looks at my girl the wrong way.

Syl and I walk down the hallway, close enough to touch without really touching. And hoo-boy, do I want to touch. She's beyond adorable in her black gothy minidress, cute mesh sleeves and lace in all the right places, her red hair spilling over her shoulders in soft curls. As for me, I went with Old Faithful: motorcycle boots (polished), a long burgundy dress shirt with lacy sleeves, black hair artfully tousled, and just a little more eyeliner and shadow than normal.

It's my warpaint

"You look beautiful," I say for the hundredth time since we left the attic.

She blushes prettily. "Thanks. So do you."

I lean in, letting her vanilla scent wash over me. I want so much to be with her, to dance with her and show her the world. After all, hasn't that been what all this date night stuff's been about—us carving out a place for ourselves among all the craziness of Moribund and Ouroboros, fair Fae and dark Fae?

This seems like our last shot. And Aldebaran took it from us.

I wilt a little.

But Syl's such a "glass half full" kind of girl, she finds little things to get excited about.

"Look!" She points.

The Battle of the Bands committee has decorated the hallways with banners emblazoned with bands' logos and streaming pennons everywhere. There's the smirky rainbow kitten of the pop duo Smooshy Kit on a black background, the Nordic-metal hammer of Odin's Beard, silver on copper. The bright teal-on-white K-pop silhouettes of Supernova Tinkerbell.

"It looks like *Game of Thrones* threw up in here," I say, but my sourness is mostly an act. I can't help smiling when she's near.

"Check this out." Syl snorts a bit as we stop beneath a hot-pink banner with a silhouette of a girl with a high pony, holding a violin. *Heiress* is emblazoned on it in that gross, Ouroboros-green.

I shake my head. "Real subtle."

Syl points again. "There's you guys.'"

The F's & G's (short for Freaks & Geeks—take that, Fiann) is a picture of me and the band in front of a wall of diversity flags. I'm in the foreground with my violin while Octavia has her drumsticks twirling and Chuck's striking a "rock on" pose with his keytar. Marcus leans on his tuba, and Nazira holds up her cello bow like she's conducting an orchestra. It's goofy and serious and cool all at once.

"I love it." My girl took the picture, and it perfectly captures our band and banter, our kooky energy.

She meets my gaze, love shining in her storm-grey eyes. "You're gonna be great."

When she looks at me like that, I feel like I can do anything. I could become the dark Fae queen if she wanted me to. I can certainly defeat Fiann in the Battle, find the Ouroboros, and somewhere along the line, punt Aldebaran's sorry behind into a Dumpster.

Syl looks back at all the banners—the kitten, the hammer, the silhouettes. I know what she's thinking about this *Game of Thrones* setup combined with the solstice.

She smirks at me and recites a line from the books. *"Valar morghulis."* All men must die.

"But we are not men," I return solemnly.

Her smirk turns to a smile. "Damn skippy. Let's do this."

We turn the corner, and there's the auditorium, all decked out. At least it's not an ice theme this year. I shiver, remembering being bound to the ice castle.

Definitely not my finest moment.

"Say *moneeeeeeey*!" Prudence steps out from behind the cheesy inflatable archway that bounces and sways precariously around the entrance. Already, a few stray green and gold balloons have fallen off and drunkenly float around the floor.

She kicks one out of her way and raises her camera. "Come, you two."

Before I know it, she shuffles us underneath the arbor and starts snapping away. Syl and I do a few serious poses and then get right to making faces and glamour shots.

I laugh as Syl jumps into my arms for the last picture. I hold her as though I'm carrying her across the threshold, like the mortals' wedding tradition. Pru snaps the pic, and I reluctantly put Syl down.

She's facing me. We're both breathless. My hand goes to the ring.

Now, Roue. Do it now.

I'm pulling it from my pocket when—

"I believe you have my date," a calm, honeyed voice says.

Aldebaran. Talk about awful timing.

He's standing there in a white suit coat and slacks, white shoes. Not a blemish anywhere on him. Students part to let him by. A few girls fawn over him as he passes. He crosses the floor toward me and Syl, smirking the entire time.

I let the ring drop back into my pocket.

He offers Syl his arm, but his gaze is on me, molten and volatile. "Rouen."

I dial my glare up to eleven and break the knob off. "Aldebaran."

He sniffs. "I see you have my date," he repeats, and then, when I don't budge, he looks at my girl. "You gave your word, Syl."

At the risk of sounding like Syl, could he be more of a whine bag?

With a rueful smile, Syl uncouples from me. I let her go. Aldebaran unceremoniously shoves his way between us under the arbor.

Barely, I resist the urge to schoolboy-trip him.

Instead, I step back, watching him with an eagle eye, willing Syl to interpret the look on my face as, *Say the word, and I'll tear his head off like a piñata.*

She gives me a patient look and stands as far away from him as the arbor will allow.

Aldebaran clears his throat delicately. "I believe the agreement was 'on my arm.'" He shakes it for emphasis.

Syl wrinkles her nose, but steps in. Even in her black dress against his white suit, she looks brighter than him, purer. My heart swells with love.

"You." Aldebaran chin-nods at Pru.

She pauses, finger pointed at her chest. "Are *you* addressing *I*?" she asks archly, flipping back her mermaid green-blue hair.

Ancestors, I heart Prudence.

"Who else?" He snorts in disgust. "Take our picture."

I roll my eyes. He might as well have added *loser* to that.

Prudence clearly feels the same way. She raises the camera slowly, and when she takes the shot, I notice her thumb's over the lens, blocking him out. I stifle a chuckle.

Aldebaran preens as Prudence takes half a dozen pictures. Of course, he won't show up in any of them. It'll be all Syl and Pru's thumb.

Come to think of it, her thumb would be better company.

We move into the auditorium. This time, the place is decorated with the band banners, cutouts of instruments, and the logos of various music TV shows and YouTube stations. There are flashing TVs hung up in each corner, showing videos on Mute. Kids mill around, everyone dressed to the nines for the semi-formal after this, with the winning band playing the music for the after-dance.

I spot Fiann and her mean-girl posse at the center of attention, as usual.

Tonight, she's going to try to take everything important away from me: the Battle, my crown…Syl.

She'll try, all right, her and Aldebaran.

Fat chance, girly.

Aldebaran tugs Syl by the hand. They move through the crowd, everyone stopping to look, to ooh and aah over them. I have to admit, if I didn't know better, I might think they made a cute couple. Him all in bright white, golden like a lion, and her, a sharp contrast of light and darkness, her red hair a fairy halo.

She belongs with him, Roue, my inner grump whispers.

But the rest of me fires back, *Like all the burning and freezing hells, she does.*

I can hear Fiann from here. "Where did you get that dress, Syl? Oh, it's just divine. And, Al, you look so crisp and fancy. Like a character out of *The Great Gatsby*."

She's so phony it makes my fangs ache.

All her mean girls surround her, Dani, Maggie, and Jazz each on the arm of one of the Triiiad guys. The other girls, Becca Buchanan, the softball team captain, and Bella Carver, the richest girl in school (well, except for Fiann) stand around. For contrast, I guess.

And then Fiann spots me.

Speak of the she-devil...

She flounces up to me, all pretty and perfect in her thousand-dollar dress. "Rouen." She takes my hand, and before I can protest, drags me down the stairs.

Normally, I'd just pull away, but this is new and improved Ouroboros-Fiann with super-strength action. If I fight her, we'll cause a scene, and that's probably what she wants more than anything—for her to be seen as my girlfriend while Syl's with "Al."

"Let's go talk to everyone." She hauls me toward the group. Cat-quick, I duck when she tries to put an arm around me. "Oh, come now, Rouen. Why fight it? When tonight's over, you will be my queen-consort."

"How many times do I have to say no before it sinks into your thick head?"

She smiles at me, but it's cutting. "Did you find the last Ourob-oros?" she hisses beneath the din of the crowd. "No?" She tsks, shaking her head. "The solstice is tonight. You'll find it, I assure you."

"We'll get to it before you do," I tell her.

Her smile widens to Harley Quinn-creepy. "I'm counting on it."

A sinister dread tightens my chest, and then she drags me into the fray.

"Everyone, you remember Rouen. She cleans up nice, doesn't she?" Fiann doesn't try to put her arm around me again, but she sidles close, working the whole "I'm with Rouen" feel.

I take a step back as everyone nods and mumbles hello.

"Well, this is awkward." I look around, hoping to distract myself from high school dance hell. I spot Syl and Aldebaran by the punch bowl.

As fast as I can, I escape the mean-girl posse.

"Save me a dance." Fiann blows me a kiss, and their laughter chases me all the way to the buffet table. Whatever.

Lennon's there, and she looks at me shyly. "Hi, Euphoria."

I nod. "Lennon. You look pretty." She does, in her cute goth-Lolita pink-and-black outfit with ribbons everywhere and cute Mary Jane's.

She leans in. "Let me know if I can help." Her gaze darts to Syl then to Fiann. "With anything."

"Thanks." I snag a handful of Takis and shove them in my face. Maybe nacho cheese death-breath will keep Fiann away. Lennon joins me, and then Prudence meanders over in between taking pics. I hand over the bowl of nacho-cheesy goodness, and we munch away.

The auditorium is filling up now, the first band's equipment already on stage. We drew lots before the show, and Odin's Beard is up first. I glimpse them behind the curtain, their cloak-and-giant-horned-helm-costumes like something out of a Disney movie. Maybe it's supposed to be ironic?

Pru's the first to broach the subject. She chin-nods at Syl. "How did that happen? Did you guys lose a bet?"

"You could say that."

The lights dim, and the crowd goes from chattering all at once to a hushed whispering and clapping. A few "woos!" echo.

A brief flare of green electricity in the darkness, and the stage lights come up, haloing a silhouette.

I know that figure.

Fiann.

She steps into the spotlight, her hands curved around the mic, blood-red nails flashing. "Hey, Richmond E!" she shouts, "I'm Fiann Fee of Heiress, and we've got an awesome lineup tonight. We're gonna rock your world. Are you ready?"

Seriously? Rock your world? That's so not a thing.

Still, the crowd cheers, and people grab their drinks and head back into the crush to watch the beginning of the Battle.

This is our chance to sneak away and find the Ouroboros. We're fairly certain it'll spawn tonight. If we can find it while Fiann's distracted…

"Let's do it!" Fiann shouts to the crowd. She meets my gaze, her green eyes bright.

"This should be good." Suddenly, Aldebaran is at my side, Syl on his arm, looking for all the world like she'd rather be anywhere else. "Let's sweeten the deal a bit, shall we?" He gestures, and I smell the sickly elderflower stink of his gramarye. He's intensifying everything, the way his stupid ring intensifies Syl's power, makes it go out of control.

Poisonous little maggot.

But the joke's on him. Miss J's special Glamoury gives Syl at least a few minutes before his cruddy torc turns her white flame power against us.

Still…soon, everyone's arguing, fighting over who's going to win the Battle. The crowd is rowdy, shouting, hollering, demanding the first band. Dread grips me.

I give him a wicked side-eye, studying him. What's his deal?

Whatever it is, Odin's Beard takes the stage. They waste no time screaming into their set, all shrill guitars and thumping drums and too much bass. The lead singer, a skinny kid that looks more like Hiccup from *How to Train Your Dragon* than Thor, does his best to make it sound like he's trying to swallow the mic and vomit it back up.

Everyone is dancing and shouting, fist-pumping. An impromptu mosh pit starts up, and I step closer to Syl. Aldebaran's momentarily distracted, so I mouth the word, *Ouroboros.*

She nods, her storm-grey eyes serious as she watches the crowd get rowdier and rowdier. She pitches her voice low so Aldebaran doesn't hear. "Let me know when you feel it."

"Right on."

Not soon enough, Odin's Beard finishes their set, and Fiann practically grabs the mic out of Hiccup's hand. "All right, Richmond E! Let's hear it for Odin's Beard!"

People clap and stomp.

"Woooooo!" Fiann seems almost punch-drunk. She grips the mic in a bloodless hand, waving it around.

She's gone totally woo-woo girl. I can't…even…

And then she intros the next band, and the Battle gets underway for real. The F's & G's aren't up till after Fiann's set, so I take my opportunity to slip away. "Keep an eye on Syl," I tell Lennon and Pru, and then I head out of the auditorium and take what's probably my millionth zoom round the school, dowsing for the Ouroboros.

Fiann's words, *"I'm counting on it"* ring in my head, a threat and a warning. She's got something else planned. Something we didn't count on.

Damn her.

Zipping around the school takes a while, and by the time I come back, it's Fiann's turn. She flounces onto the stage with her red-lacquered violin matching her nails and the guys from Triiiad behind her. "All right, Richmond E. Are you ready to rock?"

Who does she think she is, Taylor Swift? She's obnoxious as ever, but buoyed by Aldebaran's intensify gramarye, the crowd cheers and claps, hoots and hollers.

Fiann cracks her knuckles, and I see through her Glamoury to the tiny licks of green lightning around her hands. She's going to use her Circuit Fae power to cheat, because of course she is.

Does she think using her power's going to beat me?

Ha! I settle in to watch and wait for our turn. Nazira, Octavia, and Marcus sidle up. Even Chuck leaves off with the boy he's ogling, and we watch, quietly supporting one another.

Fiann's smile is shark-bright. "Want to bet I win twice tonight?" she asks. The crowd goes wild again, but they don't really know why.

I don't waver. I just give her my most superior smile.

Translation: *Bring it on.*

Fiann takes the spotlight as she goes to town on her violin with Triiiad backing her up. Their vocals are smooth like honey. She's not half-bad. Her fingering is solid, her bow-work decent. I mean, she's not going to be auditioning for the London Philharmonic anytime soon, but still.

Tiny licks of green electricity arc across her bow. She's got a Glamoury up, so no one notices except me and Syl. Oh, and Aldebaran, but who's counting him?

Not me.

An eerie grin lights her face as she starts with Mozart's Violin Concerto No. 5 and then jumps into a jam by a local punk band, Mary Maudlin. Her bow-work is on point but Ouroboros-infected, so her sound is overly technical, synthed up, and warped. Still, when she steps up to the mic, her voice is powerful.

Damn. Girl's got some pipes.

Doesn't mean I'm not going to kick her sorry butt, but I recognize talent when I see it.

The crowd shouts approval, and from the corner of my eye, I see Aldebaran, that smug grin on his face. The scent of elderflowers and sunshine amps up. He's using his gramarye to rile the crowd, to intensify their reactions to Fiann. The shouts become screams, the gentle swaying wild gyrating and pogoing.

I meet his glare. *Don't think I don't know what you're doing, buddy-boy.* He's here to instigate all of this: Fiann, the duel, the crowd, hunting down the last Ouroboros.

Which you should be worrying more about, Roue.

Right. Note to self: it's only half about beating the pants off Fiann in the Battle.

She finishes her set, bowing to all the clapping and hollering. She steps off the stage and flounces past me and the band kids, high pony swishing. "Good luck, losers. You'll—"

"Yeah, yeah, we'll need it," I interrupt her. "Do you have to practice to be so cartoonishly evil, or does it come naturally?"

That leaves her gaping like a fish out of water.

Burn level: inferno.

After all the fanfare of people clapping and the "roadies" switching out equipment, I nudge Nazira. "Come on. We got this."

We step up to the plate.

I take my place center stage. Tension knots my shoulders, but I let out a deep breath, letting it go as I raise my violin. The crowd is quiet now, hushed in the moment. I'm holding them all as I hold my bow over my strings.

Ready, waiting…

I let the pause swell, the anticipation build, and then I draw down on my bow, the first notes shimmering. I play, bright and swift, letting the music flow over the crowd even as I keep tight hold to my gramarye. I could let loose, get everyone under my sway, but I'd be no better than Aldebaran.

And you know what? I'm definitely better than that guy.

I'm better than Fiann, too, and it's about time she learned that.

Here on the stage is where I am the real me.

Royalty. At least, of a kind.

And I don't need anyone's approval. Here, on stage, I can take my crown.

CHAPTER THIRTY-THREE
SYL

Never cross a Fae
All Fae, fair and dark
Make an art form of revenge
Never cross a Fae
- Glamma's Grimm

My Winter girl is a dark angel, singing her heart out, playing and stomping the stage like she rules it. I could get lost in her.

The last Ouroboros, Syl. Stay focused...

We have to stop Fiann before she succeeds in her endgame.

The last Ouroboros is the key—that, and tonight's solstice. With the power of Dark Faerie at its peak, she'll use the harrow-stitches to rip through the Shroud to UnderHollow. She'll cause a catastrophic bleed of Faerie energy into the mortal realm.

All in the hopes that she can set herself up as Queen of the dark Fae.

Sure, that doesn't explain how she's going to wake the dark Fae from Winter's Sleep *or* get them to obey her, but...if I know

Fiann, she's got some sinister plot brewing in that blonde head of hers.

That is bad with a capital B, and we need to stop her.

But the last Ouroboros hasn't spawned yet.

All I can do is watch and wait.

Euphoria's well into her set. I check my track phone. 10:40pm. Close to the height of the solstice. At 11:11.

Any time now, Ouroboros…

I step away from Aldebaran, from Fiann's posse, from everyone, and watch Euphoria.

On stage, she's every inch a queen. So beautiful my heart aches.

I want to sweep her up and carry her off, not share her with anyone. But I'd never take this away from her. On stage, she's truly alive, vibrant.

I've gotta let her shine.

She takes a power stance, bowing down on her violin so fast, I swear, smoke rolls off the strings. The band comes in behind her, elegant as all get-out as they rip from classical strings right to moody, bassy old-school goth, slamming into Siouxsie and the Banshee's "Cities in Dust." Chuck rocks out on his keytar, Nazira backing him up on her cello. Octavia lays down a thumping drumbeat, and Marcus has traded his tuba for French horn, giving it an epic battle feel.

The crowd surges toward the stage, Euphoria calling them like some gothy Pied Piper. They're just as loud for her as they were for Fiann. Louder.

I smirk at the Teen Queen of Mean as she stands in the wings, waiting with the three identical Triiiad dudes. She does not look pleased. When she catches my eye, I wink.

My girl is kicking Fiann's sorry patootie. And I love it.

On the downbeat, Euphoria nods to the band, and they take her cue, changing the deep gothiness of Siouxsie into the rolling reel of an old Irish tune from the Old Rovers before switching to REO Speedwagon's "Can't Fight This Feeling."

It's smooth as silk, and the 80s cheese of the power ballad *resonates*.

Shouts go up from the crowd. Everyone's dancing, and not because of Aldebaran's gramarye. He stands close to me, clenching his fists.

Go on. Use your gramarye now, jerk. He can't. He'd only make the cheers louder.

Check and mate.

By the time The F's & G's are done, you can't hear anything in the auditorium but the roar of the student body. I yell and clap, cup my hands by my mouth and shout, "Freaks & Geeks! Freaks & Geeks!" I get the crowd cheering it until it shakes the place to the rafters.

"Freaks & Geeks! Freaks & Geeks!"

My girl's the best.

Aldebaran suddenly shoves off, pushing his way through the crowd and heading toward the doors. I guess he's had enough, maybe? I'm not sorry to see him go.

That's one big problem off our plates.

It's too easy, Syl, my inner killjoy whispers. And it is. Still…I can't be in two places at once, and everything hinges on us keeping Fiann from getting the last Ouroboros.

I watch him go.

Off to the side, I see Fiann biting her lip. She knows she's lost.

I wait for her to throw a tantrum. *Go for it, Moribund Barbie.* I want her to know that coming after Euphoria—that's a mistake. *I'll bury you,* I let my gaze say as I look at her. *I'll burn you down and bury you. Just like Agravaine.*

No one's going to try some Moribund takeover of Richmond on our watch. I mean, seriously? That's so last year.

"F's & G's! Freaks & Geeks! F's & G's!"

The whole auditorium is shaking from the stage to the rafters. The roar and rumble of the crowd vibrates the floorboards. I can feel it in my chest, reverbing.

Euphoria comes to the edge of the stage, shading her eyes as she looks for me. I hold my breath, my heart pounding, anticipating the moment her gaze finds mine.

Now that's she surrendered the spotlight, I want nothing more than to leap onto the stage and go to her, to kiss her breathless and steal her away for a night on the town.

A real date night. No hunting Ouroboros. No high school drama. No Aldebaran. No Fiann. No nothing. Only us.

The ring lies heavily around my neck. I want to give it to her.

To commit myself to her even amidst all this craziness. For better or worse.

Octavia steps to the mic, flushed with excitement. She twirls a drumstick over her head. "How was that, everyone!"

The crowd goes full-on bananas.

"Who's the winner?"

"F's & G's! Freaks & Geeks! F's & G's!"

On stage, Euphoria tips an imaginary hat at Fiann. "Thanks for playing."

Hoo-boy, is Fiann flustered! She stomps her foot like the little girl in that Willy Wonka movie—you know, the one who wanted it all. I think she got turned into a giant blueberry or something.

I look at Fiann. *If only.*

But...I gotta admit, it's Syl and Euphoria: 1, Fiann Fee: 0.

I am totally waiting for the other Louboutin heel to drop.

Fiann rushes onto the stage to confront Euphoria. She's close enough to the mic that her voice comes over the speakers. "You won't win in the end, Rouen Rivoche. I'll have the crown. I'll have it all." Her eyes are wild, practically flashing with green sparks.

"If you say so." Euphoria kind of shakes her head as Fiann shoves her way past Octavia and Nazira to center stage. The other band kids take that moment to vacate.

Because seriously...

There's going to be another showdown, and I'm guessing this one's gonna be less *Glee* and more *Mad Max: Fury Road*.

"You'll pay," Fiann snarls in Euphoria's face. She's right on top of the mic now. Her voice echoes over the auditorium. The crowd hushes. Nazira and Octavia stand behind her, staring at her open-mouthed. "You'll all pay! Just you wait and see!"

Whoa. Fiann's really gone off the deep end. Like, she dove in and is splashing around.

Euphoria steps between her and Nazira and Octavia. "If you're done throwing a two-year-old temper tantrum, we've got a dance to get to."

And an Ouroboros. I check my watch. 11:00.

Only eleven minutes.

"Really?" Fiann smiles now, and it's that sick Joker smile she wore last year. Oh, right. This same thing happened last year. On the same night.

Happy Anniversary, Miss Crazy Town.

She stalks over to the amps and starts pulling plugs. Nazira tries to stop her, but Fiann shoves her away and keeps yanking. The screech of feedback blares loud over the mic and through the speakers. People put their hands over their ears, and the lights dim.

Fiann makes a clawed hand gesture. With my Fae-sight, I see the air warp with her Circuit Fae gramarye.

No worries. My shield will stop her.

She must be thinking the same thing because instead of just unleashing her power, she leverages it through the amps, through the cables and wires and lights and instruments.

Uh-oh...worries. Definitely worries.

Everything lights up in that weirdo green, glowing like it's all been possessed, *Ghostbusters*-style.

Smirking at Euphoria, Fiann clenches her fist and pulls electricity from the amps in horrifying green bolts.

Crap.

The power forms a massive ball of green lightning in her palm. The crowd jerks back. Some people run. Some people, the dumb ones, whip out cell phones and start taking vid. The band kids crouches behind the drum set.

Double crap.

I throw up my own Glamoury as the feedback loop screams higher. Over the crowd's cries, I hear Euphoria shouting for me as she moves toward Fiann.

My brave girl…

She takes a step, and that's when the ball-lightning blasts her in the chest. She's hurtled back into the drum kit. *Bam!* Drums and cymbals crash every which way.

"Euphoria!" I bolt toward her.

It's on now. My shield's no help, what with Fiann using mortal tech to disguise her gramarye.

11:05.

I push my way through the wave of people surging toward the auditorium exits. They shove me back. I throw an elbow and then an apology after it. *Darn it all!* I'll never get to the stage at this rate.

Should've learned to windwarp, Syl.

Shut. Up, I tell my inner overachiever.

Euphoria gets to her feet, looking like she's going to bust some heads.

Starting with…I'm guessing Fiann.

Little Miss Moribund is already pulling the electricity from the entire room. Lightbulbs pop and shatter, sending glass spraying over the crowd. All the sockets in the room hum and hiss, glowing that bizarro green. Tendrils of electricity crawl from the sockets, leaping across the walls, the ceiling. Banks of lights on both sides of the stage shatter—*pop! pop! pop!* like gunshots.

The crowd screams, and now, everyone—even the ones taking video—decide the better part of valor is running the heck away.

I leap to the tops of the seats and run across them toward the stage.

Fiann's laughing, that crazed, maniacal, supervillain laughter that winds up and up and up. I swear, girl is seriously unhinged.

"Fiann!" I shout over the ruckus.

She whips around and flicks her fingers. Lightning rips off the walls and streaks toward me.

I duck behind a bank of chairs, and the lightning smashes them into flying slivers of plastic. "Now, now, temper, temper…" I hurdle a row of seats and race toward the stage.

How I wish I could use my white flame, but… The torc on my hand glints as if in warning.

Do I dare? I only have a few minutes of white-flame power.

I clench my hand into a fist.

No. Not yet. Not until the Ouroboros reveals itself. 11:06.

Fiann's the center of attention, just the way she likes it, standing in a storm of green lightning, lashing out with her captured electricity. She strikes the stage lights overhead, and several more bulbs explode, raining glass, their erector-set rigging swaying dangerously back and forth over the band kids.

They run for it, Chuck bringing up the rear.

Euphoria grabs him. "Octavia, catch!" She throws Chuck—like, for real, throws him. Octavia, Marcus, and Naz step up and catch him. Staggering, they beat a hasty retreat.

And then the ginormous bank of stage lights comes down.

Right on top of my girl.

I lunge, leaping the stage in a single bound and tackling her out of the way. The light rig smashes down, the remaining lightbulbs exploding in a shower of jagged glass.

The stage floor is a smoking crater, floorboards all jutted up like broken ribs around a dark hole. Euphoria and I lie on the floor, arms around each other. If everything wasn't going to hell in a handbasket, it might actually be nice.

But with the torc, Fiann, all this craziness… We're racing against the clock here.

11:08. Three minutes till solstice time.

Fiann steps to the edge of the stage. "Are you ready, Syl?" In the green glow and the red of the emergency lights, she looks dead— or worse. "Are you ready to find the last Ouroboros?"

I meet E's gaze. "Do you feel it yet?"

Euphoria looks around and then shakes her head. "No."

11:09. No time for messing around.

Where—? Sudden agony rakes across my shield like red-hot claws. But it's not fire. It's electricity.

Someone—some*thing*—is trying to break through.

"My shield..." I gasp, trying to straighten through the pain.

"What?" Euphoria's eyes flash wide.

About that other Louboutin heel? Here's where it drops.

The burning claws sear against my shield again, and I stagger. From down the hall comes a nerve-tingling howl.

Then another...and another. Nine in all.

The Môrgrim.

Suddenly, I put it all together—Aldebaran leaving, the shield, the claws... "He's intensifying the Môrgrim! Helping them break in."

"Give that girl a prize." Fiann's grin is sharp, filled with fangs. "Wait for it..."

11:10.

My shield shatters.

"They're coming for you," Fiann says softly, all mean and menacing.

Now, I hear them, the flap of gigantic leathery wings, the *shing!* of claws unsheathed, coming down the hall.

I step back to E's position. "We'll stand and fight. We've defeated them before."

Fiann laughs. "They've been intensified by Aldebaran, but okay. Sure." She cocks her head, those green eyes bright. "But aren't you wondering where it is, the last Ouroboros?"

Euphoria stops, her hand trailing violet lightning.

Fiann's face is ghoulish, triumphant. "Aren't you, Rouen?" She lays a hand over her heart, and the master-key circuit glints, embedded in her chest. "Want to see who's the real winner tonight?"

The master-key flashes.

Euphoria gasps in pain and doubles over, clutching at her own chest. Her eyes go that bizarro ghastly green.

"E!" I crouch down to where she's gone to a knee, but I don't dare touch her. Not yet. I can see a pulse jumping like crazy in her neck. "Rouen?"

"Syl…" She looks up through a curtain of her dark hair, her eyes bleeding that weird green.

"Syl…the last Ouroboros. It's me."

11:11.

CHAPTER THIRTY-FOUR
ROUEN

At the end of all these nights
When winter burns
And summer freezes
I want to be with you
Only you
- "Only You," Euphoria

Boom! A searing pain lances my chest. *Boom!* A blow to my heart, it takes me to my knees, sweat breaking out on my skin as pain shoots through my every nerve ending.

The Ouroboros. It's spawning...inside me.

Boom! Agony shoots through my limbs, and I crumple to the stage.

"No." Syl's voice comes from faraway, even though I feel her hand on my back. "No, Rouen!"

Now I remember... My mind hurtles me back to that night, Agravaine standing over me as I was tied to the fake ice castle. The pain blasting through my senses, dulling everything into a grey haze.

His hand on my heart.

The agony a white-hot sear through my chest, my blood, my bones. And his voice rumbling in my ear.

"In the end, you'll destroy everything."

So... *Boom!* This... *Boom!* This is what he meant.

"Gah!" I grab my heart, hand clenched tight in my dress shirt. *Boom!* My fingernails pierce my skin through the fabric. If only I could tear the ovo from my chest.

Boom after pulsing *boom* shudders through me, racking my body. "Ngh!" I double over, fingers digging into my skin as the ovo opens up inside me. *No...Ancestors, please no. Anything but this!*

"Rouen..." The pain swimming in Syl's storm-grey eyes undoes me. It's been me all along. Me who's been putting her—keeping her—in danger.

I am the seventh and last Ouroboros.

Fiann's laughing. She steps in, looming over us. "Didn't guess that one, did you, Rouen?" She smiles. "You'll be mine one way or the other."

Hers...what? I struggle to rise. "Never."

Syl scrambles to her feet. Barely, I grab her before she can lunge at Fiann. "Don't." I see how she clenches her hands. I know she's thinking of using her white-flame power, but there's nothing to purify. "No." I let my eyes say what I don't dare say aloud. *Not yet.*

"Such spirit!" Fiann's voice is laced with venom. She's grinning like a death's head, that malicious glint in her green eyes. "I'd save your energy, losers. Al has a surprise for you."

"Al?" I chuckle through the pain because the idea of Aldebaran, Prince Fancy-Pants, being called "Al" is just too funny. "Could you get any more ridiculous?"

Fiann grinds her teeth, and her voice comes out clipped. "Last chance, Rouen. Join me as my queen-consort."

"Get. Stuffed."

A disgusted huff escapes her. "Typical." She turns toward the doors expectantly.

Right on cue, Aldebaran appears in the archway and leans there, folding his arms across his chest. "Having trouble, Rouen?"

I swear, I'm going to rip his face off his face.

Boom! Boom, boom! My heartbeat picks up, and the agony expands white-hot inside my chest. The ovo opening up, cranking me open, spilling its black-magic circuitry through my system.

I can't keep the scream from pealing past my lips.

Once it finishes spawning, once it's rewritten me completely, I'll ask Syl to do the unspeakable, to—

"Rouen!" Syl throws herself to her knees in front of me, her grey eyes filled with tears, seeking mine. "I could…I could purify you." Even as she says it, the torc glimmers, growing hot.

We both know the truth.

If she tries to purify me, she'll burn me to my bones.

"No, Syl." Agony shoots through me like vises clamping around my ribs, trying to pull me apart. I imagine all those black circuits chittering, jiggering as they splice through my body.

Fiann fakes a yawn. "Bored now." She flicks a gaze at "Al." "Is it done?"

He inclines his head, though I see the disdain for her in his eyes. "The Môrgrim will be here soon—the new Môrgrim. You'll be pleased."

The new Môrgrim? Dread coils inside me. Oh no. He did not.

The heavy flapping of wings grows heavier, more powerful, pushing great gusts of wind down the hall and into the auditorium. They're coming. I count nine sets, then eight…then seven…

What is happening?

The crack of bone and snap of sinew echoes. Howls go up from the hallway, pained and hollow, blending, becoming…

One massive beastie.

"You hear that?" Fiann asks. Ha. As if I can't. "You're out of your league, Rouen. Are you going to be my consort or not?"

Forget this. I'm not going down without a fight. I struggle to my feet and breathe out in a single note, calling my violet lightning to my hands. It crackles and zaps.

Fiann steps back. "You know that can't hurt me."

"That's your problem." I grin, flashing my fangs. "You always think everything's about you." I exhale hard, pushing the power out into arcs. And then I breathe in.

I take the lightning into me.

The pain is excruciating. It doubles me over, Syl screaming my name. Aldebaran steps closer, sick fascination stamped to his face.

He doesn't see Fiann rise up behind him, doesn't see the Moribund dagger in her hand.

Syl screams a warning, "Aldebaran!"

Too late.

Chunk! Fiann stabs him in the back. Aldebaran screams and flails, but he can't reach the dagger between his shoulder blades. Fiann leaves it there and steps back. With a sneer, she kicks him toward Syl.

Syl, my sweet Summer girl, dashes forward to grab him. He's the only tie to her people, so I get why she wants to save him. He slumps into her arms, the dagger already melting into black circuitry, infecting him with Moribund.

In seconds, he'll become a Circuit Fae.

And that's when it hits me. She's going to do this to all of us, to every single one of my people.

She'll rule them by enslaving them.

Starting with me. *Boom...boom...boom!* With every passing beat of the ovo inside me, I am being rewritten into dark machinery, becoming a Circuit Fae again.

Fright spears me, and I ramp up the lightning, humming with it until my whole head lights up in vibrating agony. My vision greys out.

"Rouen...Rouen!"

Syl. Only Syl helps stabilize me. I have to be strong. For her.

"In the end, you'll destroy everything."

It's true. I am a dark Fae. We are more given to destruction than creation.

Be strong, Rouen. Be strong for Syl. Shaking my head, I look up through the pain shrouding my senses. Syl stands before me confronting Fiann, a white beacon against the darkness.

"That's your plan, isn't it?" Syl's breathing hard in fury. "To infect Euphoria with the Ouroboros and then use the master-key to control her. To make her your slave."

Fiann's laugh is jagged and cruel. "That is soooo last year. She had her chance. Now I'm just going to use her, and then let the Ouroboros devour her, body and soul."

Body and soul. My panic swells, terror clawing at my insides.

She waves a hand, and the master-key circuit embedded in her heart flashes gross green. "Let's speed this up, shall we?"

The next thing I know, Syl's leaping toward her. She cocks her fist and *bam!* punches Fiann right in the mouth. With a sharp smack, Fiann goes down like a ton of bricks.

My girl's standing over her, anger flashing in her grey eyes. "Stop the Ouroboros," she demands. "Right now." She takes a step. "Or you'll find out just how powerful a princess of the fair Fae is."

Fiann glares, getting up slowly, wiping the blood from her mouth with the back of her hand. "That'll be the last time you touch me, Syl Skye. Just you wait."

"You keep saying that." Syl's a bit cocky now. "Are you sure?"

Fiann licks her split lip. "Oh, I'm sure." The master-key circuit fires, and everything inside me pulls tight. "Remember those harrow-stitches?" She grins, shark-bright. "Well, there's one forming inside Rouen right now. And when I pull on it, I'll tear her open just like the Shroud."

She makes a yanking gesture, and yup, like a puppet on strings, I'm yanked toward her. I fight, dig in, but it's no use. The harrow-stitch has hooked deep into my heart. I stagger toward Fiann.

Syl holds me back. "You can't have her!"

"I don't want her." Fiann's hand clenches tighter, and I shudder, thrust up to my tiptoes in pain. The pulling swells, pain ripping through me, my chest expanding until I'm sure my breastbone, my ribs will crack. "I want what's inside her."

Another tug, and everything pulls to a point inside me, the harrow-stitch boring through me like a drill, cracking me open psychically so Fiann can use the master-key to rifle around inside my thoughts, my mind, my very soul.

At least she doesn't mean tear me apart physically, a tiny part of my brain offers, and I step on it for daring to be positive now, of all times.

Because I feel her using the master-key to dig around inside me, a clawed hand scraping over my guts, my bones. She digs into my mind.

Syl starts toward her, but my scream stops her.

I'm held captive as Fiann rifles my mind, images of UnderHollow speeding by—the Greymoors, the Willowwacks, the castle. Her claws close over the castle. No. I try to pull back, try to fight, to eject her.

I feel Winter's chill in my blood, the cold, the ice.

And then the gravity of UnderHollow...I feel that, too. She's trying to pull it toward us, to use me as a conduit. "No." I try to hold back. She just pulls and pulls.

Between her and UnderHollow, I'm being torn apart.

The temperature plummets, sudden cold in the air sharp and crisp. Icy breath plumes from my mouth, the power of Winter thrumming through my veins like cables.

In my mind's eye, the gloomy Gates of UnderHollow loom up, their wintersteel and adamantine metalwork heavy, dark, jagged.

That's what she's after!

She wants me to *manifest*.

"You see now, don't you?" Fiann's voice is in my ear, her breath hot against my face. Her touch is repulsive. I want to shove her away. "The Ouroboros will make you manifest."

I fight it, drawing back from the gates. "I won't."

"You will. You'll bring the Gates of UnderHollow here, and I will go through them, infect the shattered hearthstone, and rebuild it with the master-key. Everything will become Ouroboros, and

I will become queen." A dark chuckle. "I'll just walk in and take what's mine."

"The Ouroboros will devour itself—and you!" Syl tells her, but Fiann only laughs.

"No, Syl." Fiann curves her hands around me like claws. "You see, the master-key gives me total control. I can keep it from turning on itself. It's good insurance, too, against any who would defy me. Only…" She cocks her head, pretends to think. "It's not like anyone'll be able to. Especially not with Rouen, their precious princess, under my command."

"In the end you'll destroy everything."

I have already, and all because of who I am.

All my people are going to die and be reborn as dark machinery. As Circuit Fae controlled by Fiann and her vile master-key.

I fight, ramping up the violet lightning within myself. It's like every nerve ending is bathed in battery acid, attached to a metal coil and left to burn…

My vision goes black. I hear Syl screaming, hear Aldebaran calling for her, shrill and desperate as he turns.

"Aren't you done dying yet?" Fiann asks rudely.

But no, he isn't.

His voice is thin, reedy as he reaches out to Syl. "Soul-bond…" His limbs spasm against the floor, bony thuds and sickening smacks. "Syl, soul-bond with me."

All right, that gets me fired up. I try to battle back the darkness, but Fiann is too busy picking me apart with her blasted master-key. It twists and turns in my psyche, in my soul. The pull yanks and tugs inside me, the Ouroboros running rampant through me.

Not to mention…

A chill slides down my bones. The flap, flap, flapping of dark wings has stopped. Now… *Pound! Pound! Pound!* The entire auditorium shakes, the banners shivering overhead.

Syl looks toward the sound. She hears it, too.

The Môrgrim are coming.

Aldebaran reaches out to her. "Syl…" The black dagger has become a black stain, circuitry splicing through him, Moribund taking him over. "If I become a Circuit Fae, OverHill will suffer. All of Fair Faerie will die."

That stops my girl cold.

"Soul-bond with me," he begs, those golden eyes of his seductive, that honeyed voice drawing her in, all sticky-sweet.

Syl's gaze is on me. *Please, Syl...* But what? Am I supposed to ask her to choose me over her own people? Over the destruction of Fair Faerie?

I can't. I won't.

I'd rather be devoured. I'd rather be enslaved to Fiann forever.

But Syl's hesitating.

Aldebaran tries to sweeten the deal. "You could purify Rouen. You could save her. With my power helping you."

Arrogant jerk. How dare he promise her that?

"Aw, how sweet." Fiann trails a finger down my cheek. "She's going to sacrifice your love...to save you." Her eyes glint cruelly.

"No...Syl!" Not for me. The pain in my body is nothing compared to the pain of this.

"It's almost too late," Fiann prods. She grabs my arm and holds it toward Syl.

Darkling circuits wink like dying stars beneath my skin, the pattern of black circuitry running in necrotic veins, the Ouroboros infecting me, hooking its claws in deep.

"No, Rouen." Syl holds up her hand as if she's going to call her white flame.

"Don't!" I stop her. I meet her gaze, telling her without words what she already knows. The Ouroboros is inside me. She'd kill me, burn me black down to my bones, before she could purify me.

She whirls on Aldebaran. "Take the torc off me," she tells him. "Take it off, and I'll purify you both."

His laughter is a sick, wounded thing. "I can't. That's the blasted irony of it, Syl. I can't take it off. Not until Midsummer, when the power of the fair Fae returns."

Syl's face goes pale. Dread curdles inside me.

"You have no choice but to soul-bond with me." Despite his pain, Aldebaran sounds triumphant.

Fiann sighs. "As much fun as this is and all…" She gestures casually, and the pain intensifies a millionfold. "Manifest for me, won't you, Rouen?" She pulls and tugs, trying to drag UnderHollow closer.

I'm being torn apart. I jerk and writhe, my gaze never leaving Syl.

She stands, torn between me and Aldebaran.

"Do it, Syl," he pushes. "It's the only way to save her, to save OverHill."

She looks away, tears in her eyes. Her voice is soft, resigned. "I'll do it."

That black gleam shines in Aldebaran's eyes. "You have to say yes," he coaxes her.

The light goes out of my heart. "Syl, please…not for me."

She comes to me and cradles my face in her hands. She kisses my lips softly. The balm of her touch soothes the pain for a brief moment. "I'm sorry, Rouen. I will always love you."

She turns to him. "Yes."

"No!" The scream is torn from me, and I lose the fight—against the pain, against the Ouroboros, against Fiann.

The Gates to UnderHollow slam open.

I manifest.

CHAPTER THIRTY-FIVE
SYL

A soul-bond can only be formed
By true love
- Glamma's Grimm

"Yes." That one word tears my heart in two.

I don't even feel the freezing cold of UnderHollow opening all around us. Snow blasts me, the sting prickling across my skin, but I'm numb, hollowed out by that one word.

Yes. All my freedom, my hopes and dreams—my love—crushed. By one simple word.

I will become Aldebaran's soul-bound princess, his mate.

The very thought makes me sick at heart.

I've just sacrificed everything Rouen and I have been fighting for all this time—our place in the mortal realm and in Faerie, a place where we can just be.

A dark Fae princess and a fair Fae princess. Together.

It's impossible now. I will be soul-bound to Aldebaran. I will purify him and save our people. I'll become his princess, and at Midsummer, his queen.

My heart cries out against it. But what choice do I have?

I have to save my people. I have to save Euphoria.

Desperate, I look for her in the sudden storm of snow and sleet blanketing the auditorium. Everything is white and whirling. Everything awash in Winter's chill and snow.

She's a dark figure against all that white. Tiny violet arcs leap across her skin, her fangs gritted. Fiann's got her. She's summoned her black-circuitry wings, and they fold around Euphoria like she's a dragon's prize, captive as the Ouroboros ravages her body.

As she *manifests.*

The Gates of UnderHollow blast open, the wind howling from Dark Faerie into the mortal realm, bringing with it brutal cold and Winter. Snow coats the stage, frost glazes the curtains, the floor turns to a sheet of ice.

Already, I feel the sharp pull of Dark Faerie's gravity.

I have only seconds before we're all catapulted into UnderHollow.

If I don't do this right now, I might not.

I hold out my hand to Aldebaran. His fingers slide into mine, too hot, too sweaty. He struggles to get up, golden eyes burning on mine. He drools—actually drools like some starving dog.

I want to run, to hide, but I've given my word.

And when you're Fae, your word is binding.

"S-Syl…"

My heart bleeding, I meet Rouen's gaze though the snow. Even now, her violet lightning is failing, her strength fading as the Ouroboros infects her. Her face is pale, dark circles bruising her eyes. She is losing the fight.

My brave Winter girl. Her heart isn't in it.

Please, Rouen. I'm doing this for you. "Fight, Rouen! Please!"

I don't even know if she hears me. Aldebaran grabs my hand and spins me toward him. An awkward bride at a wedding she never wanted.

I want to run. I want to scream. Instead, I do my duty to my people.

Aldebaran takes my hand, the one with the torc. "By your binding word, you are made mine."

In answer, the torc glows red-hot, pain searing through my finger, lighting my whole body up. It rushes through me, up my arm, to my neck.

I stagger under the weight.

He lets go. "There. Now you're perfect." The torc has split. It's now both a ring and a collar. One binding my finger, the other heavy around my neck.

He thrusts my hand at his chest. "Purify me."

I'm all woozy at the tightness of the collar. With a shaking hand, I reach up, touch my throat. The metal circling it is already cooling. It doesn't hurt. Not physically.

But my heart... That's a different story.

I remember Euphoria telling me what being soul-bound to a prince is like—being used for my power.

Suddenly, I feel like I might throw up.

"Never mind," he says, his smile sharp as his golden eyes begin to glow. "I'll take what I need." His hand slaps onto mine, all possessive.

Pain rocks through me as he yanks the power from my body, siphoning my white flame to heal himself.

I am his conduit now.

This isn't how a soul-bond should be!

"Syl!" Rouen's cry reaches me, but I am suddenly so weak, so tired.

All around us, the wind picks up, the howling of Winter beating at the edges of the auditorium.

My white flame flares across Aldebaran's chest, licking across the circuitry infecting him. He closes his eyes as the sunlight's radiance bathes him.

Don't think of him. Think of OverHill.

My people. I'm doing this for my people...

The power surges inside me.

But something is very wrong.

I don't love him, my soul doesn't sing for him, and my power senses it. My white flame fights him, thrashing, pulling back. It doesn't want to purify him.

I yank away. White fire falls to the floor in sheets, racing along the snow, hissing in steam and smoke.

"You. Are. Mine!" Aldebaran screams, lunging for me.

I step back, but in a flash of Summer heat, he windwarps, grabs me, the gold in his eyes molten. "You are mine, and I will take what I want." His hand tightens on my arm. The torc tightens around my finger, my throat.

I promised him, and now I have to live with that.

He yanks more power from me, sending it against Euphoria's manifestation. Suddenly, the auditorium is awash in fire and snow, warring it out, steam rising as my Summer flames battle the Winter blast of UnderHollow. But tonight is the solstice, the height of dark Fae power. Winter blasts me, coating me in ice and freezing sleet. My white flames die like a candle blown out.

The Gates drag at us. We're being pulled in.

Euphoria struggles in Fiann's arms, in her wings. "Kill me, Syl."

"Wh-what?" I stagger in Aldebaran's grasp. Even as my power is being drained, I could do it. It would only take a flick of my wrist. She is the dark Fae princess. Even now, the Ouroboros infects her, rewriting her.

Just a touch of my white flame...

I won't even think of it. "There has to be another way!"

Aldebaran's claws latch on to me. I punch at him, striking him in the chest, but he siphons my power at a rapid rate. I stagger, nearly fall.

"Kill me! Syl, do it before I finish manifesting!"

"You should really do it, Syl," Aldebaran whispers in my ear. "Before she drags us to UnderHollow and we die frozen in the snow."

"No!"

His grip tightens as he pulls more power from me, siphoning the Summer in my blood, my body. "Do it now. UnderHollow is coming."

And that's not all.

With a massive snarl, a shadow falls on the auditorium entrance. The inflatable archway bounces crazily, the green and gold balloons bobbing in a cheerfully sinister manner. *Pound, pound, pow!* A huge impact from the other side cracks the wall. Spider web cracks run along the wall, the doors buckle.

The balloon arch wobbles wildly.

Wham!

The doors tear off their hinges, and the wall collapses inward, a huge muzzle and sword-length fangs ripping through wood and plaster. Drywall and dust pepper the SUV-size head and jaws of a single ginormous Môrgrim. Its eyes roll as it shakes its head, pushing its leathery wings through the hole it just made. Balloons rain down, half the banners fall, crumpling to the ground like dead birds.

The Môrgrim tears apart the wall like tissue paper. It has five heads, each of them as wide as a Dumpster, the teeth big as swords, green fire and lightning zapping over its body.

Rad.

It takes one step into the auditorium—

And then we're all catapulted into UnderHollow.

Freezing cold winds blast at my face, tear through my dress, sending shivers clawing over my skin. There's a gut-wrenching feeling of falling and then…

Dead-of-winter cold stings my cheeks. I open my eyes, already coated with frost.

We stand in the castle of the dark Fae beneath soaring pillars and arches, buttresses heavy and dark all around us. Winter has us in its grasp. Cold, wet silence broken only by the grating stone creaking of the castle all around us.

The castle is…moving?

"Rouen!"

Her voice is shaky, panicky. "It's the deep wards. They're activating! They sense the Summer blood in your veins. Syl, run!"

I would. I really would. But I have more immediate problems.

Aldebaran is still latched on, my power blazing like the sun as he siphons it away.

I shove at him. "Let go!"

"If I do"—his golden eyes fixate on the castle revolving, turning into an array of jagged spears and swords all around us—"the deep wards will kill us both." His grip bruises my arm, and he pulls more power from me.

"Ngh!" The weight of the torc and collar takes me to a knee.

He smiles sweetly. "I am your prince, and I will do with you what I will. It is my right."

His words burn inside me, igniting my fury. Do what he wants? Oh, really? I am suddenly burning up with rage, with Summer's passion and fury.

Enough.

I take in a deep breath. "This isn't a soul-bond. I'm not your equal." I straighten despite the torc that wants to drag me down. "No. You're not *my* equal."

The shadows of the castle fall around us. Euphoria has gone limp in Fiann's arms, sagging in her wings, the Ouroboros nearly done transforming her into a Circuit Fae.

What a pair we are!

Both held captive by our courts, by our people, by enemies disguised as allies. All this time, we have been afraid of being separated, and now...

Now it is happening.

And there is nothing we can do to stop it.

To all the burning, freezing hells with that.

"Rouen Rivoche!" I call to her name—to her very soul—and her eyes brighten with the force of her true name. I meet her gaze. I hold it.

And in that moment, I hold on to her, but I also let go—of all my fears, my doubts, the worries that have plagued us these past months.

"Whatever comes," I say to her. "Whatever happens, I want to give everything of myself. To you. The two of us together. Forever."

A sliver of hope flickers in her eyes. "Syl..."

Aldebaran hisses as if burned. He pulls more power from me, and I buckle. But looking at Euphoria, I find the strength to stand.

"Even if we don't ever find our place. Even if we never find peace between our peoples. Even if we have to fight every single day of our lives…I want to be with you."

Us against the world.

"I will fight for you."

I will fight for us. I push that thought and all my emotions— love, admiration, desire, yearning, fear of losing her… I push all that toward her as hard as I can.

Please fight. For me. For us.

Understanding shocks through her blue eyes. A calmness comes over her, an aura of serenity and love and surety.

I *will* her to hear me. To *feel* me. *"Fight for us, Rouen."*

I hear her in my mind as clear as day. *"Yes."*

Yes. That one word to bind us freely.

And something in my soul, beat-up and drained as it is, reaches out to hers—reaches out…

And locks in.

Summer and Winter come together, unafraid, trusting, loving, our energies flowing around each other in a natural give and take.

One surges and the other gives way.

The chill winds howl, but I feel none of it. The deep wards activate the castle defenses, spears and swords made from broken pillars and shattered turrets. An entire turret like a battering ram levels at us.

No, not us.

Aldebaran.

Desperate, white-faced, he strains to pull my power, to protect himself.

The torc glows hot, trying to make my power surge and rage out of control.

"Not this time, buddy-boy."

I hear Rouen's voice, her *thoughts*, clear as day.

I feel her in my bones, my very blood. My soul soars, Summer heat backed by Winter's chill. I meet Rouen's gaze. One word falls from my lips.

"Yes."

A word to bind myself willingly.

In a flash of white flame, the torc melts away, dripping from my finger, burning away from my throat.

"Rouen!" With a sudden surge of strength, I tear away from Aldebaran, lunging toward her.

At the same time, she rips away from Fiann.

Aldebaran grabs for me, his hands wrapping around my throat. Fury flashes up inside me. I half-turn and elbow him in the face. Hard. *Crunch!* His nose snaps in a shower of blood.

Ooh, that's gotta hurt.

I shove him off, and he flumps to the frozen courtyard, dazed. If this were a cartoon, there'd be a bunch of tweeting birds circling his head.

Fiann sweeps one of her massive wings around Rouen, a barb slicing in. My girl grabs the wing and tears. Fiann screams, striking Rouen across the face. Rouen staggers.

Something bright falls from her hand.

Aldebaran grabs again, fingers snagging the chain around my neck. Glamma's ring. The chain breaks.

Glamma's ring pings to the frozen cobblestones.

Next to it lies a bright white ring, so white it's nearly lost in the snow but for its brightness.

Two rings. Two of us.

Even though UnderHollow rises up all around us, my Summer powers activating the deep wards—I don't care. I run to her.

We meet in an embrace.

She's cold, her body shivering with the Ouroboros. I stagger in her embrace, weak, drained.

But we are together.

At our feet, the two rings gleam and glint.

I bend, scooping up Glamma's ring even as Rouen picks up the brilliant white ring. I face her. "I've kept this ring around my neck since the beginning of summer."

She smiles, blushing and holding out the white band. "I've had this ring in my pocket since summer began. I want to give it to you."

308

My heart soars, and I nearly swoon right there. "And I want to give you mine. But…"

Her blue eyes glint with mischief. "But?"

"But first." I look at Fiann and Aldebaran. "First, we're gonna kick some Fae patootie."

CHAPTER THIRTY-SIX
ROUEN

Summer and Winter
Together, as one
Is this a dream, my princess?
Or can we make it real?
- "Real," Euphoria

Oh yeah, we're gonna kick Fiann's and Aldebaran's sorry behinds, but first things first.

Time seems to spiral outward. Syl and I stand in the courtyard of my ruined castle, each of us holding a ring to give to the other, as UnderHollow opens up around us, an oyster for Fiann's plucking.

I was giving up. I was content to die here in my homeland.

My girl stolen, my crown stolen. Nothing left to live for.

The Ouroboros eating me alive.

And then Syl.

"I belong to you." She takes my hand, the one that is becoming Ouroboros. Darkling circuitry glints beneath my skin, rewriting

me. The last of my lightning is eaten away by the black-magic circuitry deep within me.

Soon I will be fully infected. Soon I will be devoured.

Or worse, enslaved to Fiann. Even now, she watches us, drink-
ing in our misery…

"I want a life with you, Rouen Rivoche," Syl says softly. "Even
if it is only for these last few moments before our world comes
down."

My voice comes, hoarse and husky. "I want that, too. With all
my heart." I touch her face. She's real and warm and alive, and the
Summer in her blood calls to the Winter in mine.

"To be soul-bound with me?" Syl's face is so open, so vulnerable
it tears at my wounded heart.

When I speak, it's from that raw, aching place. "Yes."

"I belong to you." Syl's voice is steady. "But…"

"But?" Confusion racks me. Will she pull away? After Aldebaran, how can she want to be bound to anyone? Especially me,
her mortal enemy?

"But I can't have you like this." She smiles softly. "I won't share
you." White flames flare from her hands, and where my dark Fae
instincts would have once made me jerk back in fear, I yearn for it.

For her. For every touch, every look, every breath—everything
that is her.

"No!" Fiann screeches, leaping forward, but the white flames
flare up, and she has no choice but to pull back, terror on her face.
She doesn't dare get any closer, lest she be purified.

And that would not be good. For her.

She'd be left human in the Winter Court of the dark Fae.

Snarling, she backs up, shielding herself with behind the leathery wings of the giant Môrgrim.

And then the white flame sears through me, and I think no
more of Fiann. Only of Syl. Syl, my beautiful Summer princess.

My bright beacon.

The flame rushes through me, a blunted pain, dull, like pulling
off a scab to find what was once wounded flesh pink and fresh

beneath. The Ouroboros wilts and dies away, Syl burning, burning it out of me until nothing remains.

We stand in a column of white fire, UnderHollow shivering around us, shirking back from the Summer power laid bare in the Winter Court.

Just me and Syl. In a place of Summer and Winter.

A place we can call our own. Even if it's only for a few moments.

My hands lay in hers, my eyes closed. The pain is pleasure, bliss. Cleansing. And then she gently pulls away and closes her hands, snuffing out the white flames.

We look into each other's eyes, breathless and smiling. And now, I feel her—really *feel* her—at one with me, her every thought, every emotion running parallel and in sync with mine. She is everything to me, and I am everything to her.

Our souls in sync, merged, bound.

"My soul-bound princess." I pull her close.

She laughs brightly. "Mine."

We lean toward each other. Our lips barely brush—

"Listen up, beeyotches!" Fiann breaks the moment. Because of course she does. "That's just round one. Wait till you see round two." She looks to the massive Môrgrim. "Kill them!"

Seriously, Fiann?

The snow falls all around us, and the giant beast lurches forward, a fresh wave of burning green fire and electricity blazing from its black circuits.

"Enjoy," Fiann calls, and then she windwarps.

"Where—?" Syl's face goes white. I meet her gaze, and the realization slams into both of us.

Fiann's heading to the hearthstone chamber.

If she gets to it before us, if she infects the hearthstone, this will all be for nothing. She'll remake it into a dark heart of Ouroboros circuitry under her control.

And all my people with it.

"We have to stop her!" I start to windwarp, but a massive black wing swipes me, crushing me to the ground.

I crash to the cobblestones, my head ringing.

Not my finest moment.

I push myself up, the cobbles cold and frozen beneath my hands. The way to the hearthstone chamber lies beyond the broken ebon arch.

But the Môrgrim stands in our way.

Fine, then. I nod at Syl. "We got this." I take a step toward the beast. "It's on, puppy chow."

As one, Syl and I charge the snarling, fiery, twenty-foot-tall gargoyle. I sing my violet lightning to my hands, and she calls her white flame. The snow-blanketed courtyard lights up in purple and purity.

At first I think the giant Môrgrim is going to be slow, but no, it darts in, its huge maw opening to snap me up. I sidestep, Syl dodging the other way.

Zzzzap! My lightning cracks off its hide, searing through its flesh, but the Ouroboros heals it almost instantly, green flame and black circuitry rushing over it in spiky waves, knitting it back together.

Blast and bane!

It swipes at me, swordlike claws raking in. I evade, and the claws slam down, the entire castle shuddering as the huge beastie tears great gouts through the black marble floors, the shrieking of stone and adamantine loud in my ears.

Syl leaps into the air and brings both fists down, smack-dab on one of the Môrgrim's five muzzles. The great beast staggers, wings folding, and I see it now... Having five heads makes it top-heavy, off balance. It teeters toward her.

I attack from the other side. Syl blasts it again.

The white fire eats up along the Môrgrim's side, and it howls in pain and fury, shaking its five great heads. The white flame flickers across the beast's bristling fur, shivering, burning bright, fighting against the wave of green fire and blackness trying to heal it.

"More. We need more, princess!"

"I-I'll try!" But she's starting to flag a little. After being drained by Aldebaran, after purifying me of the Ouroboros, she doesn't have much gas left in the tank.

We circle, staying out of reach of those massive teeth, claws, wicked wing barbs. The Môrgrim lunges. It swipes and snaps, but we are too fast. We blast it, but it heals quickly.

We can't defeat it by playing keep-away.

With every passing second, I'm more and more aware of Fiann racing to the hearthstone chamber. If she takes the shattered pieces, if she rebuilds it with Ouroboros…

There's no more time for playing it safe.

Time to do something reckless.

CHAPTER THIRTY-SEVEN
SYL

Windwarping, like most
Fae powers
Is more art than science
- Glamma's Grimm

We're not losing this fight, but we're not exactly winning, either.

We need to get to the hearthstone chamber, like, now, and the five-headed Môrgrim stands in our way. I can blast it, but my white fire is weakening.

All Aldebaran's meddling, his stupid torc and him draining me... It's all taken its toll. My white flame only distracts the ginormous gargoyle.

We need to find another way.

"Target its heads!" Rouen shouts as she rushes the beast again.

I nod, and flame on! Fire bursts from my hands. I shoot trails of it over her head, the heat beating back the chill in the air, making the frozen castle walls sweat and weep.

Howling, the Môrgrim jerks back as the flames sear its muzzle, but black circuitry sparks with that gross green fire, knitting it back together, looping synthetic circuitry-muscle and sinew on top of healed flesh.

With a rumbling growl, it lunges at Rouen.

"Rouen!" I pour on the heat, blasting the thing in the face.

No good. It strikes.

Rouen throws herself to the floor. The shadow of teeth and jaws falls on her—*No!*—and then *cha-thunk!* Swordlike teeth ram into the marble all around her, trapping her in a cage of tooth and fang.

The super-loud smack of cracking marble shakes the castle, the beast trying to pull back. Its fangs are stuck. It pulls and pulls, the groan of stone echoing.

"Bye-bye." Rouen's voice is muffled from inside the maw. Violet lighting flashes.

And then, its head explodes in a shower of gore and raining fangs.

Relief hits me as she gets up, brushing off the goo, and meets my gaze. "See? Easy-peasy."

Another shadow falls on her.

White flame leaps from my hands as the Môrgrim's second head slams into her with the force of a Mack truck. She's lifted off her feet and hurtled into the wall.

I race toward her, the knowledge that I won't get there in time shooting bright panic through me.

The wall shatters beneath the impact of Rouen's body. I hear the breath *whoosh* out of her in one gasp. But before she can fall, the beasts pins her with a ginormous paw, crushing her to the wall, holding her there.

It snaps in to bite.

Oh, heck no.

Flame on! My white flame power blasts it full in the face, turning it aside as I stride toward it, pushing more and more power.

Come on, come on…

Rouen fights free, grabs the Môrgrim's fangs as they spear in. Turning hard, like hauling on a wheel, she spins the thing's head, slamming it into the ground.

The Môrgrim howls, struggling.

Her hands slip on the drooling fangs, the other three heads whipping in. "Any time now, princess!"

"Oh, ye of little faith." My voice is calm. I am anything but. My girl is in danger, and my power is totally sucking right now.

I dive in front of her, blasting the gargoyle square in its ugly face, pouring on the power. My fire races along its Dumpster-size muzzle, searing into its eyes.

That's the trick! Its skull lights up and burns like paper from the inside out, turning into ash.

Head number two down!

"That's one for one," I say snarkily as I grab her hand and pull her up.

"Don't get cocky, princess."

For one breathless moment, I'm looking into those deep sapphire-blue eyes. I lose myself in them, in her. I just want to—

"Syl!"

"Right!"

We dodge slashing fangs, hot, sweaty breath blasting us as we dodge swiping paws, snapping jaws. One, two, three...

Bam! The fourth swipe sends us sprawling.

We crash to the ground, breath whooshing out. *Craaaaaaap.*

The third head whips down to bite. Flecks of hot drool splat onto my arm.

Ick, ick, double ick!

Rouen and I meet gazes for a sec, and it might be the soul-bond, but I totally know what she's going to do.

I roll to my back as she blasts it with violet lightning, her voice rising in a vicious aria. The bolts crash off the Môrgrim's muzzle, the thing chuckling darkly. It knows we can't hurt it that way.

At least not permanently.

My power's all flare and sparks, the flames flickering, dying.

Darn it!

The Môrgrim strikes. I dive on top of Rouen.

She freaks. "Syl, what are you—"

"Trust me!" I throw up a white shield, pouring all the power of Summer into protecting us. Fangs scrape it as the beast tries to bite it, to snap it in two.

Cruuuuuunch!

Fangs come around us on all sides, like drooling spears. The heat of its mouth surrounds us, choking us, all gross and slimy.

But it can't bite down.

My shield is wedged in its open mouth.

Rouen smirks at me. "Not bad, princess."

"You know it." I'm warming to our flirty banter, the soul-bond racing through me, letting me feel her adrenaline, her sexy confidence. "Watch this." I blast white fire down the Môrgrim's gaping maw.

The third head explodes.

Three down, two to go.

"That's two to one," I tell her ever so smugly, because why not?

If you can't joke when your life is in danger, then when?

The Môrgrim yanks away, staggering, bleeding green fire onto the floor. It's cautious now, mincing around us, keeping its three remaining heads well out of reach.

Three more. But how to kill them?

"I've got an idea." It's crazy, but it just might work. Pushing my thoughts, my plan across the soul-bond to Rouen, I scramble to my feet, wave my arms—"Hey, ugly!"—and then run away, giving the Môrgrim a shot at my back.

Of course, it can't resist.

It lunges, and I do a backflip over the flashing teeth, landing on its back. "Nailed it." The thing freaks, thrashing and howling, but I blast it in the back of the head again and again.

Okay, I know I can't kill it like this, but making it mad is all part of my strategy. And my strategy is eeeeevil. Oh, yes, it is. Muwahahahaha!

I blast and blast until the Môrgrim is super-crazy, hopping mad. It snarls and then rears up on its hind legs. It towers over some of the smallest turrets, paws clawing the air, and then crashes down on its back.

Whoa! I leap clear.

Rouen darts in and grabs me. "*Gotcha!*"

I feel her voice in my mind—a *sending* that's familiar, soothing. I *send* back, "*My hero.*"

My pretty Winter girl blushes to the tips of her pointed ears.

Note to self: tease her about that later. When we're not fighting an oversize, roid-raging gargoyle.

She sets me down, and we square off again.

The Môrgrim is smart now, playing keep-away while it swipes at us with its claws and blasts us with sickly green smog. Miasma spews across the snow-crusted courtyard, sending up ginormous gouts of steam.

Is it too much to hope a stray shot will melt Aldebaran?

I glance at him, sprawled out cold on the stones.

At least he's quiet. For once. *Jerk.*

I flame on, burning the miasma as it falls like a cloak around us. We barely breathe to avoid being weakened. The Môrgrim is just playing the last of its cards now. It's desperate.

Two heads to go.

The castle shudders and rocks. A weird, stony moan gasps from its every seam. Rouen suddenly racks, pitching forward to a knee. "Fiann's reached the hearthstone chamber."

All around us, the castle shakes like crazy, the black marble shivering beneath our feet. Slowly, a green, ghastly glow begins to bleed over everything.

"The master-key!" Panic speeds my heartbeat. "Rouen, she's infected the hearthstone."

Rouen's voice is pained. "I know."

Everything in UnderHollow will be rewritten into dark circuitry.

Even now, the glow bleeds outward, black circuitry racing up the walls, up the towers and turrets, racing along the deep wards where they loom over us.

Crappity, crap, crap, crap...

I look up at the Môrgrim, swaying, wounded, but still gate-keeping us.

Two more heads.

"We have to kill it." Rouen's face grows hard, and her determination hits me like a fist.

"I know." Time for part two of my plan. I send my thoughts to her, *"Stand back and support me. I got this."*

I feel her concern, but then she nods. *"I got your back."*

I don't like, but we're running out of time.

I only hope my desperate plan doesn't blow up in my face.

I race toward it, and she blasts the thing to distract it. Violet lightning bursts and slams into it, but it heals and heals. Hawking back, it vomits miasma again. I blast back, burning the poison to steam around us.

And then…

I stop dead. Right in between the two heads.

"Syl!" Rouen's voice rises in fear, the panic in her sending bright and sharp. *"What are you doing?"*

"Get ready."

I see her wanting to windwarp, I read it in her mind, but I stay her with one hand.

The two heads spear in, one from either side.

I breathe out. I relax.

Feel the wind, ride the wind, be the wind.

"Get out of there! Syl!"

A breath before they both crush me with force and fangs…

Whoosh! I windwarp.

One second I'm there, and then, in a burst of prismatic mist like sun refracting through rain, I'm gone.

The Môrgrim heads crash together, a sickening, bone-smacking crack. Blood and foam fly, and it staggers like a drunken sailor, eyes rolling up into its heads. Green sparks fly, trying to ignite, to heal it, but my windwarping has sucked all the air out for a split-second.

And in that split-sec, the Môrgrim dies.

It crashes to the floor.

I fist-pump. "Yes! Take *that*, you Cerberus wannabe!"

"Syl!" Rouen windwarps to me, sweeping me up, kissing me breathless. We're both sweaty and breathing hard, but I don't care.

"Now we only have Fiann to worry about," she says, her sapphire-blue eyes grave.

"You'll never defeat her," comes a voice from behind us. "Not even soul-bound."

Ugh. Aldebaran. Seriously, this guy is the worst.

I give him the stink-eye. "And why is that, Debbie Downer?"

He sniffs, picking himself up with all the dignity he can muster. "She has the master-key of the Ouroboros, and the hearthstone is infected." He gestures to where the walls, the floors, where everything has begun to take on that sickly green glow.

UnderHollow is being rewritten.

"We're going to try," I tell him.

"Come with me." He reaches out. "You'll never belong here, in the Winter Court of snow and ice, its people with hearts cold as Winter. You are a fair Fae of the Summer Court. Fire and passion are in your blood. Not this cold existence."

His lies ring hollow.

"Come with you so you can drain my power?" I clench my fists. This guy lied to me, practically enslaved me. He tried to kill Rouen.

Time for a little payback. I reach out through the soul-bond, reaching for Rouen. She reaches back. Aldebaran is talking fast now, begging, saying some junk neither of us is listening to.

This time, when I borrow Rouen's powers, I don't need to touch her.

The spark that leaps between us is instant, psychic. I feel her power slam into me, cold and bright as a wintersteel knife.

"No." I shut him up with that single word. "I don't think so."

I use Rouen's power, tapping into the Winter in my girl's blood, her royal ties to the land, to the castle, to Dark Faerie itself. There are activations in the deep wards. Words that one can speak to set them on a target.

I speak them now. *"Vao val mordu."*

Protect us from the enemy.

321

That enemy is Aldebaran.

"If you're really fast and really lucky, you could escape." I look at him in amusement. "Maybe."

He stares back, his mouth open, gaping like a fish's.

"If I were you, Al," I emphasize Fiann's silly nickname for him, "I'd start running."

The castle shudders, and even as it is being rewritten, it shifts and creaks toward him, all the spears and swords and towers jutting in at him as the deep wards activate and attack.

I take Rouen's hand and turn my back on him. "Good-bye, Aldebaran."

As his screams start, we windwarp away.

Time to face Fiann. Time to put an end to her crown-coup once and for all.

CHAPTER THIRTY-EIGHT
ROUEN

Hearthstone,
Serve your true mistress
Open to me
Your dark Fae queen
- "Dark Fae Queen" Euphoria

Our windwarp takes up deep into the castle, Syl and I chasing the ghastly green glow into the darkness. All around us, dark stairwells and passages—no, all of UnderHollow—shivers and shudders, caught in the grip of the Ouroboros that Fiann's unleashed. The very stones groan and grate, bleeding over with that green glow.

We have only minutes before every stone, every wintersteel arch, every tower and turret is overwritten, turned into black-magic circuitry. Only minutes before every dark Fae man, woman, and child is drained, hollowed out, turned into a Circuit Fae.

And Fiann will rule over them all.

As Moribund queen.

We'll see about that, Miss Fancy.

We pick up the pace, our footfalls echoing down empty, ruined halls. The passageways warp as we pass, flashing green circuitry overhead and underfoot. The sickly stench of ozone clogs the air, thicker and more disgusting than even the Môrgrim's miasma.

It's all I can do not to choke on it.

If Fiann gets her way, we'll eat, sleep, and breathe Ouroboros.

We'll be nothing more than slaves to her every whim. My worst nightmare come to pass.

Over my dead body. My resolve is as cold as the Winter in my blood.

The castle's tremors get worse and worse. We're racing against time.

And losing.

Finally, the hearthstone chamber looms ahead, bathed in a sickly greenish light. The gross, warped power of the Moribund.

Dread lances me, and I know with sudden certainty. This will be the last confrontation with Fiann.

It's her or us.

Me and Syl, my soul-bound girl versus whatever foulness Fiann's unleashing in the hearthstone chamber.

For the first time, we will see what we are made of—soul-bound and together.

The threshold looms out of the gloom, a glowing green archway dripping with ice and melting snow. Syl's small hand folds into mine. *"Together."*

"Yes," I say it again, and it feels good, right.

Whatever happens, I belong to Syl, and she to me.

We step across the threshold together.

Instantly, sadness and loss pierce me. I almost don't recognize this place, where I spent a good chunk of my childhood curled up against the font of the hearthstone. Everything here is in ruins, the stained-glass oriels broken, the vaults skeletal and pulsing with green circuits, stone being rewritten into machinery. The pedestal itself—the font—is no more than a broken, jagged hunk of black volcanic glass.

On it stands the hearthstone.

But it's a mockery.

A pathetic, splintered hunk—a thousand broken pieces jammed back together and filled with green circuits, pulsing like an ovo.

This is what my realm will become if we don't stop Fiann.

"Welcome."

Speak of the she-devil. Fiann stands there, an ice queen in a winter realm, snow eddying around her feet from the cold draughts, making a white carpet for her to walk on. The master-key glints from her chest as she sends wave after wave of black and glowing green Ouroboros splicing through the castle.

But that's not the worst of it.

Not by a long shot.

Flanking her is my father's Adamant Guard, the seven most powerful warriors of the dark Fae, their armor whorled with adamantine and wintersteel, their glaives and swords gleaming darkly. I recognize Morudain the Whisper, a killer, silent as fog; Vao Virago the Day's Death, her shield black as night, her scimitar pure wintersteel; Harkariel of the Crystal Fist, every inch of him glittering; Alystin and Aimsir, the Darkling Twins whose cold, angular beauty is matched only by their deadliness; Liriel of the Twilight Sword, haloed in gloaming grey, my mother's bodyguard when she was alive; Digitalis, Winter's Bite, his double knives gleaming frostily.

Our finest warriors.

My heart leaps in joy at the first sight of them—the first dark Fae wakened from Winter's Sleep. With a cry, I start forward, but Syl holds me back.

"Don't," she whispers in my ear. "Look."

I do, and this time I see the truth. Their skin, both pale and dark, is lit through with darkling circuitry beneath.

Our finest warriors. Infected by Ouroboros. Turned into Circuit Fae.

Fiann's puppets.

"Rouen, Syl." Fiann greets us like we're coming for high tea. She wears that lopsided smile, the green glow making her look even more villainous. Her body is encased in her black-carapace armor, but it *writhes*, the Ouroboros teeming and spawning across her.

Only the master-key circuit embedded in her heart keeps it from turning on her.

Devouring her.

She's got everything. She looks like the cat that ate the canary and went back for seconds.

"Fiann." I step square to her, the hearthstone between us, the Ouroboros spawning, spilling down the dark stone to turn the floor a sick, igneous green.

On either side of her, the Adamant Guard stands stock still, their armor glinting, adamantine and wintersteel platemaile pluming with cold. The Winter in their blood is strong.

Who knows what powers they've gained from becoming Circuit Fae?

Syl steps up next to me. Her sending is gentle but resolute. *"I'm here. I'm with you."*

"And I with you."

Fiann sneers at us. She sees I'm no longer infected—I watch that knowledge flicker across her face, watch her mouth pull into a disgusted snarl.

Still, her voice is saccharine-sweet. "I'm so glad you could make it."

Translation: *I'm going to kick your butt, Rouen.*

"Oh, me, too." I give her the dark Fae glare.

Translation: *Bring. It. On.*

It's a total royalty standoff. Moribund Queen versus the dark Fae princess.

Only, she's the one with an army.

She breaks the silence first. "This is your last chance. Bow before me."

"No. I don't think I will."

She sighs like she's just so put-upon. "Kill them."

Hells and Harrowing, she really loves that phrase.

As one, the Adamant Guard drops into fighting stances.

Crud.

They move forward, a wall of swords and scimitars and jagged-edged glaives, corralling me and Syl away from the hearthstone, away from Fiann. More Ouroboros circuits light up the gloom, the chamber around us pulsing with black-magic circuits.

How long before all of UnderHollow is overtaken, overwritten?

"Rouen?" Syl looks to me as the twins move toward her, glaives gleaming. Their eyes are dull, as though dark scales have grown over them.

But their movements are not dulled.

They slash at Syl, and she dances back. Her hand comes up, trailing white flames. The Adamant Guard are fully infected, flush with circuitry. If she tries to purify them, she could kill them outright.

"Don't hurt them!"

"I know," she sends back gently.

And then they're on us.

Aimsir and Alystin strike as one, driving Syl away from me. I lunge to her side, but Vao Virago cuts me off with her shining scimitar. Cold trails burn in the air, chilling even me.

I'm forced back. "Syl!"

"I'm all right."

She's holding her own, windwarping around Aimsir, engaging Alystin, the twins moving around her in flashes of darkling adamantine.

Bam! Morudain kicks me in the side, and I go down hard.

That'll teach me to get distracted. *Head in the game, Roue!* I roll as Vao Virago slashes down with her scimitar. The wintersteel rings off the stones.

In a breath, I'm back on my feet.

Lightning flares around my hands, but I don't dare.

These are my people. I use only my strength.

When Harkariel charges, glaive hooking in to tear out my guts, I sidestep and strip the weapon from him. Whirling, I whack him on the back. Down he goes. Spinning the glaive, I clear the area, the Adamant Guard stepping away from my reach.

Fiann claps as though we're at a production of *Hamilton* or something.

I swear, I'm gonna kick her a—

I lunge at her, but Liriel is there, her Twilight Sword slicing the gloom in silver trails. Our weapons clash, her face impassive. This is the woman who guarded my mother, who protected her to the last.

I see an opening, but I can't take it.

Liriel twists her blade, cuts in at me. I parry, and she strips my glaive away.

It clatters to the floor.

Weaponless, I backflip out of the way, seeking Syl.

She appears in a burst of Summer wind near me.

"No good," I send to her. *"We have to get to Fiann. To stop her."*

Fiann stands back, her armor a living thing writhing around her. She tosses her high pony. "Look." Beneath us, the floor flares gross green, and then the green fades away, leaving a glassy black that's partway see-through.

We can see the chamber below where dozens—no, hundreds— of sarcophagi stand on end. Their lids are made of ice, thick and clear, gleaming. And inside them…

My heart seizes. My people.

The Winter Chamber.

Fiann holds the Adamant Guard back with a gesture as she steps across the glassy floor toward me, the Ouroboros writhing around her, black and sinister. "This is what you've always wanted. For them to wake up, right?"

I take a threatening step, a single note bringing violet lightning to my hands. The electricity cracks, sparking off the floor.

Revealing…

Figures that move, sluggish, beginning to wake from Winter's Sleep.

Ouroboros circuitry rushes over their sarcophagi, licking at the ice, boring its way inside. Thousands of teeming black circuits, ravenous, insatiable. My people—they will all be infected as I was.

They will all become Circuit Fae.

Forced to serve Fiann lest she let the Ouroboros devour them, blood and bone, body and soul.

"You see now, don't you?" Fiann asks softly. "Once the Ouroboros infects them, they'll all be mine." She straightens, raising her chin. "My people. And I will rule them."

"There has never been a dark Fae queen," Syl tells her.

"I will be the first."

"You can't have them." I stand forth to challenge her. "And it is I who will be queen."

"Oh?" She laughs cruelly. "You're going to take Syl's blood, then? You're going to take her blood to wash away your sluagh taint?"

It's my old conundrum—hurt Syl or let my people die.

"Bring them to me," Fiann commands the Guard. "On their knees."

The Adamant Guard charges. Syl and I clash with them again, and again, we are forced apart, forced back. Vao Virago's scimitar slices in, cutting a stinging line across my cheekbone.

Blast and bane!

Blood trickles down my cheek. It's the least of my problems.

The castle shudders, my people wakening from Winter's Sleep—wakening to become Fiann's slaves.

I have to find a way to stop her. To free them.

Morudain feints and then drives in, slamming the butt of his glaive into my ribs. *Snap!*

The impact sends me reeling, Fiann's words cruel and cutting. "Take her blood, Rouen. Drain her down to death. It's the only way."

"Never," I snarl, backing away.

Harkariel is up now, his glaive gripped in mailed hands. He circles me on one side, Digitalis on the other. Vao Virago waiting, waiting…

"Shall I have them blood her for you?" Fiann asks casually.

"N—"

"Do it!" she commands, and they all rush Syl.

My girl's eyes widen for a second and then she windwarps, Summer breezes kicking up, making the frozen walls weep.

She's fast. The Adamant Guard is faster.

They hem her in with bristling blades, Vao Virago lunging in at the same time as Digitalis. She'll be skewered!

"Syl!" I don't think. I just windwarp.

In a burst of violet mist, I appear before her.

Chunk! Cha-thunk! Thunk! The meaty sounds register a second before the agony. A scimitar stabbing through my shoulder, two knives thudding into my sides.

I fight through my graying vision, lashing out with a kick. I take Vao Virago in the stomach, knocking her back.

Ka-thunk! To my side, Syl cries out, Harkariel's glaive sticking out of her shoulder. He's pinned her to the wall, but I can't get to her.

We're both pinned, trapped.

"Slay them," Fiann screeches.

"Ugh, make up your mind already," I gasp as Digitalis presses in, his face close to mine. I feel his chill breath on my face, cooling the blood trickling down my cheek.

The Adamant Guard rears back.

"Stop!" My voice rings out, and they hesitate at the sound of it. "I know your faces. I know your names. Harkariel. Vao Virago. Digitalis. Morudain, Alystin and Aimsir." I nod to each in turn, the slight movement shooting pain through me. "Liriel, you protected my mother. You all saw the vaults come down when the sleeper-princess poisoned the hearthstone hundreds of years ago."

Their faces are blank, but I see a flicker—just a flicker—in their eyes.

"They serve me now, not you." Fiann steps level with Liriel's shoulder. "I am their queen."

I draw them in with my voice. "You all saw the vaults come down. You protected UnderHollow then." I look Liriel in the eyes. "Protect it now."

The Adamant Guard slowly begin to lower their weapons.

"I am your queen!" Fiann screams, clutching her chest where the master-key circuit lairs. A green glow begins there, like some disgusting heart-light, and the Adamant Guard's eyes glow green.

They pull back to kill us.

"I am Queen of the dark Fae." Fiann meets my gaze, smiling her crazy villain smile. "I am queen, not you. Not even if you did take Syl's blood."

"Syl's blood, Syl's blood," I mock her. "Damn, Fiann, you are a broken record, aren't yo—Ohhhh…"

The words ring back to me—one of our oldest traditions: *Blood calls to blood.*

"Whatever." Fiann gestures, and the bright glaives and swords draw back and back and back. "Ready to die, Rouen?"

"Not even close, Moribund Barbie."

Fiann screams in rage, but it's like time spools out, dragging the scream on and on, dragging the moment open, dilating it. I feel Winter's chill on my skin, the bite of blades in my flesh, the roar of my own blood pulsing, pulsing…

Blood calls to blood… That's it!

I reach inward, digging deep to tap the Winter in my veins, to tap the essence of me, of Rouen Rivoche, princess of the dark Fae.

My heartbeat speeds up, blood pounding in my ears, singing, pulsing, like it did in time with the hearthstone only…

Now, I feel something else. Seven pulses, cold, chill…the Adamant Guard.

All this time, I've been told I needed Syl's blood.

But here, in UnderHollow, blood calls to blood.

Mine, nobleborn, calling to the blood of my people.

"You are no queen," I tell Fiann. "I'm going to knock that crown right off your head, girly."

"Kill her first!"

Aimsir draws back his sword.

I reach up, touch my torn cheek, and blood my hand. "I am your rightful princess. You will remember me."

He stabs in at me. I windwarp away, then back toward him. My bloody hand grazes his cheek, and I press it there, leaving my mark on him.

I call upon the Winter in my veins—not to manifest, not to create lightning or shield. But to call to my people.

"Blood calls to blood. Remember me."

331

Aimsir jolts, and the others step back. He shakes his head, his dark curls bobbing.

I see it in his eyes as the dark scales fall away. He remembers.

He lowers his sword.

"Rouen…" Syl breathes.

A flash of triumph bursts inside me.

I don't need Syl's blood to be royalty. I am royalty.

The power of my blood proves it.

I windwarp around, flashing in and out, between and among them, marking each with my blood, calling to them, pulling them from Fiann's dark spell. They are still Circuit Fae, but my blood—the power of Winter within it—wakens them.

Fiann is losing her mind. She's practically gnashing her teeth and tearing at her hair. "Kill the fair Fae, then!"

The Adamant Guard tense. They might be loyal to me, but the fair Fae are our sworn enemy. They move toward Syl pinned against the wall.

My poor girl! I feel a flare of guilt from leaving her so long.

I windwarp, get there first.

Seven gleaming edges press to my chest, every member of the Adamant Guard hell-bent on ending Syl's life. "You will have to kill me."

They hesitate, and then Vao Virago lowers her sword. "I would rather die." The others follow suit.

Their weapons clatter to the floor.

"You'd rather die? Well, you can have your wish!" Fiann snarls. She gestures, and green circuitry flashes over them. They all scream in pain, racked.

"Syl! They need you." I wrap my hand around the haft of the halberd pinning her to the wall, and meet her gaze. *"I'm sorry. This will hurt."*

"It's okay." Her lips curve in a wry half-smile. "Do it."

I yank, and the halberd comes away in a spatter of blood. Syl drops to the floor.

Fiann's still lighting up the Adamant Guard, her face twisted and ugly. They spasm and jerk, and as they fall, Syl lights them up, too.

In white flame.

The Adamant Guard are swathed in a bright blare, blotting out the sickness infecting them. The Ouroboros goes up in smoke as Syl purges it from them. As one the Guard fall forward, unconscious but purified.

Circuit Fae no more.

"Heh." Without ceremony, I launch across the chamber. My fist smacks Fiann square in the face, knocking her down. Shock lights her green eyes.

"You," I say, standing over her while she wipes blood from her mouth, "can call me Your Majesty."

She snarls, "You'll regret that."

"Make me."

Quick as a whip, she's on her feet. Tendrils of Ouroboros rips from her sides like foul black ribs, spearing in to pierce me. I smash one and dodge the others. Behind me, Syl lights up in white flame.

Fear pales Fiann's face. She backs away, thrusting up her arm. Wave after wave of Ouroboros crashes against us in the echoing chamber. Syl burns it down; she steps level with me, throwing up her white shield. The Ouroboros crashes off it, waving all around us, hitting the walls, bolstering the remaking of UnderHollow.

Fiann knows all she has to do is stall us, and the Ouroboros will do her dirty work for her. Once she controls the castle, the deep wards...

She can still kill us with ease.

But we press the attack, coming on and on and on. She had her chance, and she took it. Now we take ours.

"The master-key circuit," I send to Syl.

She nods.

Fiann thrusts a hand out, and more dark Ouroboros tendrils wing in at me. I dodge them; one rams me in the shoulder. She pins me to the ground, smiling, blood on her teeth.

"I'll still kill you, Rouen. I still have this."

I do the whole "behind you" gesture, but she just laughs.

"You think I'm stupid enough to fall for—"

That's when Syl hits her square with her white flames. "Sorry, not sorry!"

Fiann hisses like a boiling pot, and whirls around. Her arm comes up, but I grab her and hold on. Syl targets the master-key.

She hits it dead center. The heart of Fiann.

We're lit up like Christmas and the Fourth of July all rolled into one. I should be terrified—a dark Fae caught in the power of Summer—but this is Syl. Syl's power.

And we are soul-bound.

I am not harmed; I am strengthened.

I hold Fiann as my Summer girl blasts the heart of her.

Fiann screams like a burned cat, writhing. Unlike Agravaine, she doesn't get consumed by the white flame. No, instead, the white flame eats a hole right through her, boring like a drill straight to the master-key and burning it, hollowing her out.

Heh. I guess it's fitting considering what she had planned for us.

Finally, the master-key circuit is smoking and dead.

"No!" Fiann gasps, reeling back to a place suitable for dying.

Ooh, that's lyric worthy. I almost wish I had my notebook.

The Ouroboros inside her sparks, then zaps and pops. At first I think it's short-circuiting, but then I remember: it's devouring her.

"Good luck with that, Fiann." I flip her a jaunty salute.

She racks and racks. She reels against the hearthstone font.

I go to Syl and hold her. Her face is pale as she takes in what's happening to Fiann, the girl who was once her best friend.

"I'm sorry," I whisper into her hair.

"You will be," Fiann chokes out. An evil grin lighting her eyes, she grabs up the hearthstone. "You think you're so smart. I will be queen. No matter what."

She holds the sickly, infected hearthstone high in one clawed hand.

And then she shoves it into her chest.

CHAPTER THIRTY-NINE
SYL

A faerie scorned
Is a dangerous thing indeed
- Glamma's Grimm

Fiann's hand shakes as she shoves the hearthstone deeper into her chest with a sickening *sclorch!* Ugh, so gross!

Not to mention, totally bad news for me and Rouen.

I shoot my Winter girl a horrified glance. *"How can she even survive?"*

"She's Ouroboros now, through and through." Rouen never takes her gaze from Fiann, from the hearthstone.

All around us, the castle is shuddering, shifting, the green glow of the Ouroboros bleeding over everything, blotting out adamantine and wintersteel, marble and adamant. Below us, the Winter Chamber shivers, the dark Fae wakening one by one into their new Circuit Fae existence.

Only Rouen and I can stop it.

But Fiann's totally gone all murder-death-kill on us. The hearth-stone nestles in her chest, an icky, dripping dragon's egg glowing, lighting her face up like a ghoul's.

She takes a step toward us. "The deep wards, the castle, Under-Hollow, Winter—it's all mine." With a gesture, she calls the brutal cold down upon us.

The wind howls and blows, it cuts through me like knives, and a sudden squall of sleet and wet snow kicks up. The walls, the vaults come alive, writhing with Ouroboros circuitry. Stone breaks, and black tentacles slam out from the walls.

Rouen and I lash at them. I blast them back with white fire. She, with violet lightning. Everything is white and blowing and stinging.

Fiann's laughter goes from evil chuckling to full-on super-villain muwahahahaha-ing. "I am queen, and you will bow to me."

I don't even have to look Rouen's way.

Neither of us is ready to kiss the ring.

But will we have a choice?

My Summer powers are taxed to their limits. We're both wounded, both bleeding. Our blood makes red roses in the snow.

It will take both of us to defeat Fiann once and for all.

"You're no queen," I tell her. "You're just a spoiled little girl!"

Fiann snarls and rears back.

"Ooh, that hit a nerve."

Joke's on me, though. Because, with her next move, she lashes out, black tentacles of Ouroboros slamming into the glassy floor.

Cracks spider web outward.

Ruh-roh.

I grab Rouen's hand, but before she or I can windwarp, the floor shatters, and we plummet straight down, down, down, into the Winter Chamber.

Thud! Whud! We land unceremoniously, spilling out in a sprawl of legs and arms.

"Ugh," Rouen groans.

"Yeah, I feel you."

Together, we get to our feet. We're surrounded.

On all sides, dark sarcophagi rise up, their fronts sheer, see-through ice. Inside each, a dark Fae lies, green and black circuitry splicing their body. They shudder and shake, their mouths open in silent screams.

I'm squeezing Rouen's hand so hard I'm sure I'll break her fingers.

I try not to be creeped out that we're standing amidst a bunch of dark Fae who'll want to kill me the second they wake up.

Ha-ha…nothing to see here, folks! Just your friendly neighborhood sleeper-princess!

"It's all right," Rouen tells me, looking around for Fiann. Where is she anyway?

I nod, swallowing back my fear. "Yeah, I mean, it's not like they're awake, right?"

It's like Murphy's Law that the nearest coffin to me tilts and sways, cracks running over the front of it in a silent spiderweb.

Crappity, crap, crap, crap.

Crack! Crack! Crack, crack!

All around us, the sarcophagi are cracking open, the dark Fae—no, the dark Circuit Fae—waking up from Winter's Sleep. Frost plumes like smoke from the coffins, cracks widening, chunks of ice falling to the snow-crusted floor.

The first of the dark Circuit Fae pull free, faces blank, their eyes lit with that green Ouroboros glow.

Fiann's laughter rises above the howl of the storm. "You think you can stop them from waking, becoming Circuit Fae? Well, you can't!"

"Yeah, thanks, Captain Obvious," I mutter.

More and more Circuit Fae wake, bursting from their sarcophagi like ice zombies, and just like that, we're in the middle of a *Game of Thrones* episode.

Wheeeee!

Fiann lands like a bloody angel among her subjects, drawing her ragged wings around her. "Kill them! Kill them both!"

She doesn't have the master-key, there's a huge burned-out hole in her chest, and the Ouroboros eats across her, turning her into hollow Moribund machinery, but…

I flick a glance at Rouen. "Gotta give her an A for effort."

"Um, Syl…"

As one, the Circuit Fae lurch toward us, those same scales over their eyes.

Were we too late in destroying the master-key?

"You're gonna need a whole lot more blood," I joke unhappily to Rouen as we back up, dodging between sarcophagi as the world lights up in Circuit Fae lightning all around us.

She smiles that dangerous, grim smile. "We've been in worse scrapes than this, princess."

"Seriously?" I look aside at her.

"At least I'm not tied to an ice castle."

For a brief sec, I wonder if she got hit in the head with a glaive. Because being trapped in eternal Winter while everyone around us gets turned into Fiann's little puppets… I can't imagine what could be worse than that.

And then we're under serious fire—er, lightning. Every color of the rainbow lights up the Winter Chamber, bolts zigging and zagging, slashing through the air. The stench of ozone stings my nostrils. I wipe sleet and snow from my eyes as we use the sarcophagi as shields.

Wham! Crack!

Lightning bolts blast them to smithereens, the sounds of stone shattering super-loud. The sharp stings of jagged marble hitting me barely register.

I'm super-jazzed up on adrenaline.

I mean, I'm a fair Fae in the Winter Court, and Winter seriously just got an upgrade. A Circuit Fae upgrade.

TL;DR: I'm freaking out.

I could purify them one by one, but where to start?

Bit by bit, Fiann's army of Circuit Fae blasts away at our coffin shields until almost nothing is left. Besides, I need to concentrate to push that much power. I could purify one, but the other gajillion would murder me. We're super-exposed in the center of the Winter Chamber, surrounded by Rouen's people turned against us.

And if that wasn't bad…

The deep wards rutter and activate, flashing green across the wall. Ouroboros tendrils and tentacles tear outward, collapsing one of the smaller vaults. Chunks of stone wham down into the floor. One smacks me in the chest, all Hulk smash.

Whoosh! My breath goes out. I slam into a bank of ruined sarcophagi, and spill onto the floor. The Circuit Fae nearest me raise their hands, lashing tendrils of lightning.

Oh, crap.

They blast me.

A thousand colors light up the gloom, electricity from a zillion different sources blazing in at me.

Desperate, I throw up my white shield. Bolt after bolt after bolt cracks and zings off it, the thing vibrating on my arm. *Please hold…please hold…*

Rouen windwarps to my side. She puts up a lightning shield and meets my gaze.

Our situation's pretty grim.

We can only defend against her people, and our power is failing.

Fiann steps forward, ghoul queen, her fake hearthstone heart pulsing sickly.

Rouen and I lunge, firing at her, but black tentacles snap up in the way, burning apart under our onslaught, leaving Fiann unharmed.

"Nice try!" Her eyes flash gross green, and an anvil of Ouroboros circuits slams into us, knocking us back. Lightning follows.

We dart back beneath our shields.

"We need to purify them all." Rouen grits her teeth, pouring more power into her shield. Winter plumes frostily off her.

I look at the vast number of her people. Hundreds, thousands. I could never purify them all.

And Fiann knows it.

Fiann comes forward, the army of wakened dark Circuit Fae behind her.

"You were saying about worse scrapes?" I joke unhappily, but I send, *"We need a plan."*

Lightning crackles all around us.

Fiann laughs and eggs them on. "Yes, that's it! Attack them for your queen. Burn them down!"

Another two dozen Circuit Fae push free from their wintry coffins and join the others.

Rouen and I are pressed into a corner, the last of the coffins swaying around us. Everything is smoke and bitter ozone and lightning.

I pour more energy into my shield, Summer's heat flaring as bolt after bolt crashes into it. I can't keep this up for much longer. We might be able to windwarp, but—

The wind. A *solar* wind. That's it!

All my nerdery is about to pay off big-time, because that paper I wrote on solar winds for Miss Mack's Astronomy class comes back to me, "*Solar wind can accelerate particles in the atmosphere, making lightning strikes more severe.*"

More severe. A grin slips across my lips. "I have a plan."

"Eleven percent of a plan?" Rouen asks.

"Yup."

Lightning…solar wind. This is the craziest, most reckless plan ever. I meet her gaze, *sending* my need for her to trust me. "*When I give you the signal, fire your lightning.*"

"*At what?*" She looks at our gajillion attackers.

"*Don't worry, I'll do the steering. Trust me.*"

She does. I feel it deep in my soul.

Another volley blasts us. Rouen's shield fizzles, but she shakes it back to life. We can't take much more.

I stand up from behind the shield and summon my fairy wind, pouring as much sunfire and heat into it as I can, ramping it up into a solar wind.

Jagged bolts of lightning arc in toward me, too many to count.

"*Syl!*"

"*Now!*"

Rouen's lightning hits my solar wind, *igniting*, blasting from a forked lick to a wide beam. It's so wide, it encompasses the room from side to side, a massive sheet of violet careening toward the dozens of smaller lightning strikes coming in at us.

It hits the others, and with a monumental *crack!* tears, a hot knife through butter. I pour my flame on, letting her lightning ride the wind.

Ride the wind, be the wind.

A wild smile curves my lips. *Look, Ma. No hands!*

My fairy wind kicks up around me, flaring hit in a column of sunfire and heat and everything Summer Court.

Fiann jerks back from the light.

The lightning splits, and my fire rides it to the source to each Circuit Fae, striking each of them, racing along their Ouroboros circuits, purifying them in ginormous billows of black smoke.

"No!" Fiann shrieks.

Boy, she's going to be shouting that a lot more before this is over.

As one, the dark Fae fall, unconscious, taxed to the limits from being corrupted then purified.

Circuit Fae no more.

My hands still smoking, I turn to Fiann.

She clutches the hearthstone in one clawed hand. "I'll use the deep wards! I am queen!"

"Shut up already." I blast her in the chest again, this time targeting the hearthstone, purifying it. Rouen stands up, and adds her lightning to it, searing away Fiann's Ouroboros armor as it tries to protect its dark mistress.

And we attack that way, Summer and Winter together. Our powers aren't so much combined as they bolster each other, giving and taking as need be. When Summer is needed, Summer takes the lead. When Winter is needed, Summer gives way.

Rouen and I let our powers surge and ebb.

Together.

This, this is the place where we can exist together.

Fiann jerks and spasms, screaming.

"Head's up, Fiann. You're about to lose. Big-time." I focus on the hearthstone, burning away the Ouroboros. The hearthstone glows from green to white, its surface beginning to heal, white flame and violet lightning flaring over it.

Rouen and I remake it. Together. Darkness healed by light.

The Ouroboros armor chitters and shrieks and pulls back from that glowing orb in Fiann's chest. She goes to tear it from her, but it burns her. Hissing, she draws back, her hand scalded.

"Let me help you." Rouen windwarps in and tears the healing hearthstone from Fiann's chest.

Fiann falls to the ground in a bloody heap. "I…am qu…" And then the Ouroboros has its way with her, devouring her faster than even my white flame can.

I pour it on. I try to give her a painless end, but I'm not sure if I succeed.

She's gone in an instant, leaving me and Rouen standing among all Rouen's people. Slowly, they rise to their feet and then seeing Rouen before them, bloody and magnificent, they go to a knee.

She stands before them like a queen, and they bow to her.

Tears sting my eyes as I step back, let her have this moment.

She is their queen. *"You saved them."*

She gazes at me, tears in her eyes. *"We,"* she stresses, and I feel her love in her sending. *"We saved them."*

A dark figure comes forward. His long raven-black hair is kept back from his face with a circlet of ice, and his dark eyes see everything. He's tall and powerfully built, though he's older.

"Rouen," he says, his voice a deep rumble. "My daughter."

"I just love family reunions," I say, super-dork that I am.

And then, because I am a super-duper dork, the blood loss catches up to me, and I faint dead away.

EPILOGUE
SYL & ROUEN

I swear, I'm only out for a minute, but when I wake, I'm in my own bed in my own room. Ohhhh… I let that sink in for a moment. No more being trapped at the school, no more torc or Aldebaran or Fiann. Or Ouroboros.

Only me and—

I sit bolt-upright. "Rouen?"

"I'm here." Her sending, the gentle brush of her thoughts and emotions in my mind immediately soothes my brainmeats. A sec later, she climbs in through my open window.

I watch her unfold long legs and stand, brushing her black hair from her beautiful face. Her bronze skin is radiant with an inner glow, and when she turns those sapphire-blue eyes my way, my heartbeat launches into the stratosphere.

My Winter girl. So strong and beautiful.

"How are you feeling?" she asks, and I feel her concern through our soul-bond, all warm and gooey, like fresh-baked chocolate chip cookies. Only better.

"I'm okay. Are you?"

"Yes." Rouen—it's weird that I can't really think of her as Euphoria anymore, not now that I've touched the deepest parts of her soul—leans against the wall. "Your mom was worried. You pushed a lot of power in Dark Faerie, princess."

I blow out a breath. "Yeah. I got lucky. I could've ended up like Aldebaran." I meet her eyes. "Was he...? I mean, did the deep wards...?"

Rouen wrinkles her nose. "He escaped, but given the amount of blood he left behind, he won't bother us for a good long while."

"Good. Fiann?"

Slowly, she shakes her head. I sink back into my bed. Fiann's dead. Gone. A pang of pity hooks my chest.

I know Rouen feels it. We feel everything now, with the soul-bond.

She comes to sit at my side. "She didn't give us a choice, Syl."

"No. She didn't."

She searches my eyes, and I see the uncertainty there, all the things she doesn't say—about the soul-bond, her people waking, her father. I shift in the bed to buy some time to answer. Pins and needles shoot through my left hand, and through the tingles, I realize I'm clenching it tight.

Slowly, I open it.

Glamma's ring. I've been holding it this entire time.

I look up, meet Rouen's gaze, everything else forgotten. "I..." Butterflies are doing the cha-cha in my stomach. I swallow hard and try again. "I'd like to give this to you. If you want to wear it."

Her smile is instant and radiant. "I do." Her voice is husky, filled with emotion, and her eyes are suspiciously damp, but I don't mention it.

Across our soul-bond, I feel all her emotions: hope, love, anticipation, desire. It's so much it almost overwhelms me.

She holds her hand out.

I slide the ring on her finger, and my vision blurs. "Oh, my God. I'm not crying. You're crying."

I look up and see that she is. And then I sense the one emotion she's trying to hide. Fear. Fear that I won't want her as much as she

wants me, fear that after everything that went down with Aldebaran, I won't want to wear her ring.

I raise her hand and kiss it. "I adore you," I whisper. "I belong
to you."

I hold my hand out and meet her gaze meaningfully. "Will you
do the honors?"

"Will you do the honors?" Syl's words, her sincerity, the love I
feel across our soul-bond—all of it threatens to make me cry even
harder.

Dark Fae aren't supposed to show emotion.

I duck my head, lifting my hand to wipe at my wet, stinging
eyes—

No. Forget that. I'm not ashamed. Not of crying. Not of anything
that has to do with me and Syl. Instead, I raise my chin and look
into her summer-storm-grey eyes.

Tears stream down my face, hot and wild. I don't wipe them
away.

I want her to see them, to see me. The real me, with no barriers
or Glamouries. No hiding.

She cups my cheek and leans in. Carefully, she kisses away my
tears and then brushes her lips across mine. Her kiss is sweet and
sultry all at once, and for a long moment, I lose myself in it.

In her.

Here, in her arms, in her kiss, I am home. Where I belong.

And then I pull back gently. I take her hand and lift it to my lips,
kissing it as she did mine.

Mother's ring, the winter topaz that, for months, has lain heavy
in my pocket now feels lighter than air, no more than a wisp of
wintersteel.

Syl holds her hand out, her grey eyes steady on mine.

Trembling, I slide the ring on her finger.

"I belong to you, Rouen Rivoche."

"And I to you, Syl Skye."

We link our hands, the rings gleaming, a symbol of our promise, our soul-bond, our love.

Aldebaran might still be out there. My father might still be angry. My people still wary of me and my trust in a certain fair Fae princess, but whatever happens next, Syl and I will face it.

Together.

The End

Read on for a sample of INIMICAL, Book 3 of the Circuit Fae
The Adventure begins in... *MORIBUND*
Book One of *the Circuit Fae*

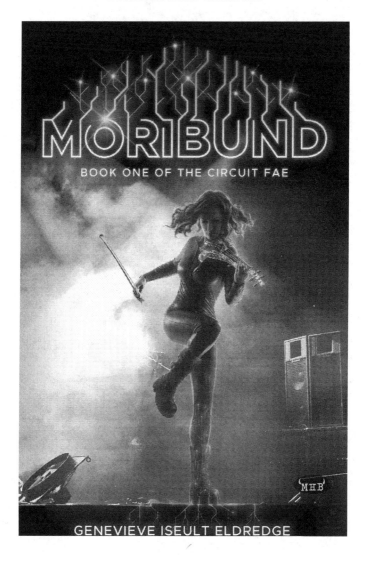

MORIBUND

BOOK ONE OF THE CIRCUIT FAE

GENEVIEVE ISEULT ELDREDGE

Also from Monster House Books
The shifter fairy tale, *Wolves & Roses*
Buy Now

Also from Monster House Books:
The snarky dystopian novel, *Dimension Drift*
Buy Now

BOOK THREE OF THE CIRCUIT FAE

GENEVIEVE ISEULT ELDREDGE

CHAPTER ONE

SYL

Sleeper-princess,
Half-human, half-Fae
Part of both worlds
Belonging fully to neither
- Glamma's Grimm

Being a Faerie sleeper-princess isn't all it's cracked up to be. Some days, it can be darn inconvenient. I mean, you'd think being Fae royalty, I'd be automatically excused from certain things: doing chores, working afterschool, detention, eating Brussels sprouts.

Summer school.

But no.

"Miss Skye, I'm waiting…" Miss Mack taps her shiny black pointer against the equation on the board as all the other kids in class snicker. "Solve for X, please."

Easy for you to say. You weren't up half the night.

I look up at the board, at the algebraic equation. It's simple enough, but my vision blurs, and all the numbers and symbols run together like gibberish. Quadratic equations. I should be able to do these in my sleep.

But sleep's been the problem lately. The same nightmare playing on a constant loop the second I close my eyes.

"Miss Skye?"

The snickering gets louder, and my face gets exponentially hotter and redder. *Exponentially. See?* I think desperately, *I can do math!* I tap my pencil against my bottom lip. *You can do this, Syl.* But nothing comes to me. Next to me, Rouen shifts in her seat, her concern for me shooting down our soul-bond.

Did I mention I'm dating the princess of the dark Fae, my mortal enemy? Our people have been at war for a million years. That's way more complicated than this summer school deal, let me tell you.

One day, I promise myself. One day I'll be queen of the Fair Faerie realm, and then we'll see who has to go to summer school.

But that doesn't help me right now.

"Maybe if *someone* hadn't skipped school for six months"—Miss Mack looks pointedly at me over her crescent-moon spectacles—"she'd know about quadratic equations, hm?"

"Yes, Miss Mack," I mumble, shrinking in my seat.

The summer school teacher *tap, tap, taps* her pointer on the board. Miss Mack is one of the youngest teachers at Richmond E, even if she doesn't look like it with those witchy white streaks in her black hair. She stares me down for another long moment before moving on to her next victim. I slouch deeper.

The real truth is: I didn't skip school, and neither did Roue.

We got trapped in the Dark Faerie realm, trying to secure her throne. By the time we escaped, we'd missed half our junior year.

And the worst part?

It's not summer school. It's the fact that we didn't even succeed. Roue's been dethroned. By her own dad, to boot.

"Are you all right?" Roue's voice, deep and smoky-sexy, gently prods my mind. Months ago, we committed to each other (with rings and everything), we became soul-bound (which is just like it sounds), and now I can hear her thoughts and feel what she feels.

There are some things about being a Fae princess that are pretty darn awesome.

"I'm okay." It's hard to keep my anxiety from my *sending*. I'm still learning how to control the bond so I don't send everything, even the embarrassing stuff, right down it 24/7. *"I'd be better if we didn't have to be at summer school."*

Roue's nonverbal agreement flashes down the bond. Ever since we first met, she's been masquerading as a normal high school student, but really, she's supposed to be the queen of Dark Faerie.

Tell that to her dad. The jerk.

I shift in my seat. *"Maybe you have some ideas to get us out of this?"* My beautiful girl's broody, cunning snark wrapped up in sexy black leather, her powers all things Winter: thundersnow, lightning, storms and snow squalls.

As a fair Fae princess, that should scare the pants off me, but really what I'm thinking is: *Maybe a freak snow squall in May would get us off the hook.* It'd only take two inches, and every school in Richmond would be closed for a week.

Roue's laughter rumbles in my mind, turning my insides electric-gooey and warm. She twiddles her fingers, and a teeny snow tornado the size of a mini soda can swirls on her desk, all white and wintry. I jerk upright in my seat, but then notice the shimmery glimmer blanketing my girl's actions.

A Glamoury. It's how we Fae hide from mortals—at least those who aren't Wakeful and able to see through our magic.

In my mind, Roue's chuckle turns to a laugh. She waves a hand, dispelling the snow tornado into tiny crystals. They melt on her desk in Richmond's seventy-degree spring day.

Spring. May 1st. We missed five and a half months of school.

The second we got back from Dark Faerie, we got pulled out of regular classes and put into summer sessions in the old section of Richmond Elite High. It's me, Roue and a handful of other kids in the library. A few students from the principal's elite Academic Achievement Program hang at the tables in the back, overachieving for college courses.

Me? I'd do anything to be out in the late spring/early summer afternoon, sun on my face, the breeze in my hair. As a fair Fae, my powers are all things Summer: heat, sunfire, and balmy breezes.

I'm naturally restless at this time of year. May 1st is also the time of year when power shifts from Dark Faerie back to Fair Faerie.

Maybe that's why the nightmare's getting worse?

"Still having bad dreams?" Roue asks gently.

Ugh, did I really send that?

"Yes, you did."

Darn it! I scribble on my *Star Wars* notebook, looking down, stalling. I mean, how do you tell your girlfriend that you keep having nightmares of stabbing her in the heart?

Just the thought of it sends my own heart into a near-frenzy.

Roue reaches across the aisle and puts her hand on mine. Her skin is the perfect combination of cool and silky-soft. Electric zings shoot through me, and suddenly, I'm not thinking of that nightmare at all. Nope. I turn to look at her.

I'm thinking of my dream girl.

"Whatever's happening..." Roue meets my gaze, her eyes so deep blue I could get lost in them. "We'll tackle it together."

Whoa. My breath catches in my throat. Okay, can I just say that no matter how many times she says things like this, it always,

always gives me shivers? The good kind. I lean in, drawn by her magnetism, her beauty, her strength—all the things that made me, a fair Fae, fall for a dark Fae.

Lately, we've been thinking of taking the next step in our relationship. It's scary, but a good kind of scary. Truth be told, I want to do more than kiss her, but for right now, I'll settle.

Roue's sexy smirk makes my insides leap. Her lips barely brush mine—

"Miss Rivoche! Miss Skye!" Miss Mack's voice rings out like the Horn of Gondor, killing the moment. Roue and I jump apart, jerking back into our seats like we weren't just caught nearly kissing in the middle of Advanced Algebra 2.

Sorry. Not sorry.

"Do I need to separate you two?" Miss Mack has to almost shout to be heard over all the snickering, jeers, and whispers that erupt around us.

"No, Miss Mack," Roue and I chorus dutifully.

But my girl's smirking her face off. We've faced down hellhounds and Hunters, Circuit fiends and Circuit Fae, Ouroboros, even the deep wards that protect Dark Faerie.

Mortal teachers don't really scare us. Well, except Miss Jardin.

Then again, she's not mortal.

Still, my mom will officially kill me if I get into any more trouble. She was not keen on me having to go to summer school. Roue, either, considering she lives with us and Mom's her guardian.

As much as a dark Fae princess can have a mortal guardian.

To be fair, Mom's not 100% mortal, either. She was a sleeper-princess before I was. Long story.

"Maybe we should..." I glance at Roue and gesture at my laptop.

"Right." She pulls hers out, too, and we settle into actually paying attention to class.

Only...I'm super not good at that right now because I've had about two hours' sleep and a whole lot of worrying. I'm exhausted. No sooner do I start following along with the lesson than I also start nodding off.

My head's heavy, my eyelids weighing a million pounds. The sun's slanting in the windows now, warming my feet, then my legs. I slump down into the sunbeams, letting my mind drift. No worries. I'll tackle quadratic equations later, maybe get my bestie Lennon to help me. She's a fellow mathlete, but she's good at everything.

Miss Mack drones on and on about values and sums and equations. I prop my laptop up. Maybe I can take a quick catnap behind it.

My eyes close halfway, my head gets heavier and heavier...

Yoink! A small tug jerks inside me, a snag in my stomach, like tiny hooks digging in. *Not again.* Along with my Roue-killing nightmare, I've been feeling this...*pull* toward the Fair Faerie realm.

It's not something hiding behind my laptop can fix.

Because the realm of Fair Faerie, the half of Faerie that governs all things sun and Summer, has been calling me nonstop. Like an ex that won't stay broken up with. Except me and Fair Faerie?

We never officially went out.

I groan, trying to fight off the weird *pull.* It's like Fair Faerie's grabbed hold of my insides and won't let go. I poke at my stomach. *Quit it, you.*

We're kind of not even on speaking terms, me and Fair Faerie.

I might be new to this fair Fae princess gig, but even I know that the princess of the Summer Court should not be dating the princess of the Winter Court. In fact, I should be dating Aldebaran, Prince of Fair Faerie. According to him, Fair Faerie will die this year on Midsummer Day if we don't become king and queen together.

Now for a few things about me: I'm into Roue. I'm not into guys. And I'm definitely not into being forced to date anyone—or go back to Fair Faerie, for that matter.

Because according to my nightmare, if I go back to Fair Faerie and take my crown, I'm as good as dead.

And so is Roue.

CHAPTER TWO
ROUEN

Rebel, Rebel,
I'm a rebel for you
I'm anything for you
You're everything to me
"For You to Me," Euphoria

I've always been a rebel. Even among my own people. But the dark Fae, rules-bound and tied to tradition, have never appreciated my rebellious side.

I have the scars to prove it.

But if there's one thing Syl taught me, it's to live a little, let go and have fun. Besides, it's true what they say: some rules were meant to be broken. Not to mention, my sweet Summer girl's been under a lot of stress lately, what with our two opposite halves of Faerie trying to tear us apart.

If there's something I can do to ease that stress, I'm in.

So when she mentions a random snow squall in May, I don't hesitate.

I'm the princess of the dark Fae—royal, regal, *powerful*. A little push from the Winter in my blood is all it'll take.

"Come on." I tug Syl from class as soon as the bell rings. Summer school's held in Maura Hall, the old section of Richmond Elite High. The halls here are longer and the crowds thinner. Once no one's looking, I throw up a don't-see-us Glamoury.

A shimmery shiver runs the length of my spine as it settles into place.

Students, teachers, even witchy Miss Mack pass us by, completely unaware.

"What are we doing?" Syl's voice is a hushed whisper, her excitement rushing down the bond, making me feel warm when all I should feel as a dark Fae is cold. I love it. I love her.

I've already broken every rule of Dark Faerie by being with her.

What's one more?

Besides, I'd do anything to erase the worry from my girl's eyes.

"You'll see." With my Glamoury protecting us, I lead her down the hall, her small hand warm in my chill fingers. I can't help but look back and take her in: red curls that fall to her shoulders, summer-storm grey eyes full of mischief and life; she's adorable even in the school uniform. And those freckles.

I could spend a lifetime counting them. I fully intend to, Dark Faerie *and* Fair Faerie be damned.

We come to the exit door leading out to the quad, and I hit it without slowing. My Glamoury can cloak small physical changes— a door opening, us walking down the hall—making it so onlookers either don't notice or don't think to ask questions.

Being a dark Fae princess, even a dark Fae princess in exile, has its perks.

The door opens in a burst of balmy spring air and the oversweet scent of Miss Jardin's rose garden. Syl and I step outside into the quad. The day is crisp and sharp. The spring sun shines bright, and I squint against it, moving immediately to the closest umbrella-covered picnic table.

Syl, though, she basks in it. My beautiful Summer girl.

359

The sun on her red curls turns them to fire, turns her grey eyes to gold. Everything about her brilliant and bright. So bright she could burn me.

Like in my nightmare.

Even now, I feel it encroaching on the corners of my mind—the images of Syl stabbing me with a sunfire blade, of me stabbing her, my dagger a wicked thing of jagged ice.

It's just a nightmare, but it feels real enough, me waking up in a cold sweat in the wee, dark hours, clutching my heart, tiny snow squalls eddying around my cot.

And the *pull* from Dark Faerie...

Ever since we got back, it's been *pulling* at me, urging me to come back to fight my father the king, to claim my throne in battle and bloodshed.

I might be tempted. I *am* dark Fae royalty, after all. Conquering, possessing, *ruling* is in my blood. Plus, more than half my people want me as queen. They want change, for my father to step down. Because the hearthstone, the source of power for my entire realm, is dying again.

And he's not doing anything about it.

But the nightmares are clear.

If I go back, if I claim my crown, it'll mean Syl's death. Mine, too.

It's the one downside to being soul-bound.

"Roue?" Syl's gentle prod brings me out of my brooding. She's smiling at me, and I can't help grinning right back. Most times, I feel like a complete goof smiling around my fangs the way no dark Fae—especially a dark Fae princess—ever should. I'm supposed to be reserved and cold, a calculating killer.

But with Syl, I can be just me. Even if that means being a goof sometimes.

"Ready?" I ask, lifting my hands, stretching my fingers, readying my personal magic, my gramarye. This will be tougher without my violin to act as a magical focus, but it's nothing I can't handle.

"For what?" she asks, her summer storm-grey eyes glinting. She senses my mischief down the bond, and excitement flushes through her body.

Feeling what she feels makes me giddy. I'm suddenly warm in all the right places. "For this." I call upon the Winter in my blood, my fingers weaving in the air.

I exhale, my breath frosty.

Immediately, the temperature drops. Above, the clouds swirl, growing a thicker silvery-grey. The crisp spring morning turns crisper, sharper. Tiny snowflakes crystallize in the air, and a few spring puddles glaze over with ice. In the falling cold, the sky opens up, spilling out heavy, wet snow. It spirals down around us, cloaking us, muffling the world.

"Ooooh...." Syl's smile breaks wider across her face as the world turns white and wintry. "Oh, *Roue.*"

Already inside, I can hear people scrambling—students, teachers, administrators—everyone rushing to the windows to check out the freak May snowstorm. My Fae hearing picks up shouts of glee and whoops of joy, calls placed to the principal's office. I hear the decision as it comes down.

The rest of the school day's canceled.

I fold my arms across my chest, smirking at a job well done. "How does an early dismissal sound?"

"Yes!" Syl hurtles into my arms, exuberant and warm, her body pressing against mine in just the right way. Instantly, I'm hot where I was cold, and captured by her grey eyes.

I can barely breathe, can't speak at all.

"There are better things we could be doing with our mouths," Syl sends, blushing furiously. She leans in, gently brushing her nose against mine.

That simple touch is everything to me. Usually, I take the lead in our makeout sessions, but Syl's hands tangle into my hair, lips brushing mine, her breath warm on my face, sending shivers through every inch of my body...

Yes, please.

I pull her closer. "Happy snow day, princess."

Syl kisses me, her lips soft and sweet against mine. I melt into our embrace, my chill body basking in her warmth, drawn in by her intoxicating scent, vanilla and musk. I nip her bottom lip, and she gives a breathy little sigh that nearly brings me to my knees.

I would do anything for this girl.

I love her dearly, and I put all that love into my kiss.

The snow swirls around us, eddying in little dervishes like we're in our own perfect snow globe. Our own perfect world where not even Fair Faerie or Dark Faerie—and certainly not any nightmare—can touch us.

It's not until much later—after we get home to the tenement Syl, me, and her mom share in Jackson Ward, after dinner, homework, and a little late-night pizza, after Syl and I say our good-nights and she heads to her bedroom and I head to my little alcove off the tiny living room—that I feel the consequences of causing a snow day in the middle of May.

I'm lying on my cot, scribbling in my lyric notebook, when the Winter in my blood surges up, that *pull* toward Dark Faerie wrapping around my guts and yanking hard. *Gah!* I nearly fall of my cot, managing to stifle my scream and not tear my notebook in half.

Go, me.

I fight the *pull*, gritting my fangs, jerking back with every ounce of my willpower. Normally, it takes complete concentration and an act of will to get to Dark Faerie. You have to tap into the Winter in your blood, align it with the moon's natural power, the ley lines, and then you can snickle-step from the mortal realm into Dark Faerie.

I've never heard of someone being forced.

Yank! Of course, there's a first time for everything.

I grab hold of my cot as Dark Faerie calls to the Winter in my blood. *Nope. No way, Dark Faerie.* Out the window, I see the moon rising, crescent and bright, knifing through the sky.

The way I knife Syl in my nightmare.

The way she knifes me.

And that's when I feel it—Syl's panic. It rockets down the bond, slamming into me, stealing my breath. I jerk off the cot, the blankets catching my feet. Bam! I land hard on the floor, biting my tongue. Blood flows into my mouth.

"Roue!" Syl's scream tears through my mind, my soul.

She's being pulled in, too, but to Fair Faerie.

There's only one reason this would be happening: the opposing Faerie Courts want to force us to take our Thrones, to rekindle the age-old war between our peoples.

"Syl! Hold on!" I spring to my feet, grabbing up my violin and bow. Having the focus for my magic in my hot little hands gives me strength. Instantly, my power thrums in response. *It's on, Fair Faerie. You want a fight with the dark Fae princess, you got it!*

But Dark Faerie's got other ideas.

Before my eyes, the moonlight slanting in through the window shimmers into dozens of glowing-blue, crisscrossing ley lines. *Blast and bloody bones!*

Yank! Yank! Yank!

Dark Faerie *pulls* harder on the Winter in my veins. The temperature in the room drops ten degrees, the air shivers, and snow swirls in the living room. Behind the wall of white, a convoluted dark shape rises, a massive grate of adamant tipped with icy wintersteel.

The Gates of UnderHollow.

My blood is a beacon calling the Gates into the mortal realm, Dark Faerie forcing me to *manifest*.

Still, I hold on. For Syl. For me. For us. "Hang on! I'm coming!"

But I'm not. The Gates to UnderHollow slam open and suck me in.

The only place I'm going is straight to Dark Faerie.

The place that wants me and Syl to murder each other for our crowns.

End of Sample
Order the full copy of Book 3 of The Circuit Fae, INIMICAL now

INIMICAL

BOOK THREE OF THE CIRCUIT FAE

GENEVIEVE ISEULT ELDREDGE

Genevieve Iseult Eldredge

Raised by witches and dragons in the northern wilds, GIE writes angsty urban fantasy YA romance—where girls who are mortal enemies kick butt, take names, and fall in love against all odds.

She enjoys long hikes in the woods (where better to find the fair folk?), believing in fairies (in fact, she's clapping right now), dancing with dark elves (always wear your best shoes), being a self-rescuing princess (hello, black belt!), and writing diverse books about teenage girls finding love, romance, and their own inner power.

She might be planning high tea at the Fae Court right now.

GIE is multi-published, and in her role as an editor has helped hundreds of authors make their dream of being published a reality.

Don't miss out on the latest discounts, news and release updates from Genevieve Iseult Eldredge and Monster House Books!

http://tinyurl.com/iwantMHB